Journey of the Pearl

Journey of the Pearl

A. E. SMITH

For my sweet friend, Crystal. I hope you enjoy the story Sept. 2022

A. E. Smith

RESOURCE *Publications* · Eugene, Oregon

JOURNEY OF THE PEARL

Resource Publications
An Imprint of Wipf and Stock Publishers
199 W. 8th Ave., Suite 3
Eugene, OR 97401

www.wipfandstock.com

PAPERBACK ISBN: 978-1-5326-6557-8
HARDCOVER ISBN: 978-1-5326-6558-5
EBOOK ISBN: 978-1-5326-6559-2

Manufactured in the U.S.A.   11/09/18

For Betty, Louie, and Ken.
They always put the needs of our family first.

My heartfelt gratitude goes to my editor, Sandra Woolsey,
who has the patience of Job and the wisdom of Solomon.

Preface

Longinus (Lown-GEE-nus) is the reported name of the centurion who executed Jesus. When he announced, "This man must have been the Son of God!" he sealed his place in history. The rich young ruler asked Jesus how he could have eternal life. The answer was not well received, but perhaps later events helped him to embrace it. Zacchaeus, a once dishonest tax collector, made amends. Jesus was nearly arrested by Malchus, but Simon Peter cut off his ear. Then Jesus healed him. Did Malchus become a believer? Cornelius and his household were the first Gentiles baptized into the faith. How did that dedication change their lives? A Roman centurion asked Jesus to heal his dying servant. How were their lives changed? Jesus forgave a woman caught in adultery. Did she squander her second chance or did she become a better person? Demas, one of the thieves crucified with Jesus became a believer while he was dying. Perhaps it was not the first time Demas and Jesus had met. Theophilus, for whom Luke wrote The Gospel of Luke and The Acts of the Apostles, was a high-ranking Roman. Did it change his life? Herod Agrippa, grandson of Herod the Great, sentenced sixteen soldiers (four squads) to death for "allowing" Simon Peter to escape. Could there be other reasons these men were put to death? The time Christ spent in this world leaves us with many unknown accounts. What happened to the people who encountered Jesus, and either accepted him as The Christ, or rejected him? Where history leaves off, the storyteller may carry on.

Pearls in ancient times were valued as highly as diamonds are today. A perfectly spherical pearl with an unusual color would have the same value as the fifty-nine carat Pink Star Diamond which was sold in 2017 for $71,000,000.

Words of emphasis, Latin, Hebrew, and direct Biblical quotes are in italics.

Chapter 1

⎯⎯⎯⎯⎯ ✿✿ ⎯⎯⎯⎯⎯

God stretched out his hand and took hold of the sun. He shrouded the blazing star with an impossible darkness. The beauty of the world faded. The colors of nature withdrew into shades of gray. Death kept watch, waiting to hear the words, "*It is finished.*"

A young man named Jamin was awake all night, dreading the coming day, but he finally fell asleep just before sunrise. His mind was blank when he first awoke, but with gut-wrenching agony he remembered his younger brother was to be crucified along with Yeshua, the Nazarene. Jamin's lean face was lined with grief and regret.

The young Hebrew looked from the rooftop of his employer's house in Jerusalem where he slept. He thought Cleopas and his wife, Mary, must be gone since no one had awakened him. Out of habit, he shielded his eyes to determine the position of the sun. It was overhead, noonday, but something was terribly wrong. The sun was darkened like a black cloth draped over a lantern. Sick with anxiety, he lowered the ladder and hurried down.

Jamin entered the house and grabbed his knapsack, a wineskin, and a stick. He left the house and tried to hurry through the twisting dirt roads crowded with visitors, donkey carts, street merchants, and beggars. His progress was slow. About a million people were in Jerusalem for Passover, even though the city was home to only twenty-five thousand. He pushed his hair back and peered at the sky. He didn't bother to shield his eyes. Jamin knew the darkness could not be an eclipse. From boyhood lessons, he knew a solar eclipse could only occur with a new moon and it never lasted more than a few minutes. Passover was celebrated during a full moon.

He bought a loaf of bread in case the soldiers let him give some to his brother. "Sir, how long has the sun been black?" he asked the street vendor.

"For hours!" The merchant gestured at the sky. "It started at the 6th hour and now it is past the 8th hour. This was foretold in The Book of Psalms. It is the end of the world!"

1

Jamin thrust the bread into his knapsack as he scurried across another intersection. The absence of a breeze gave the air an oppressive weight. He choked on dust and tripped over a street beggar. The man cursed, but Jamin didn't bother to respond. Blocked by a throng of people staring at the sun, he shoved his way forward. Expressions of fear rippled from person to person.

Jamin fingered his robe. No matter how closely he held the cloth to his eye, the red and yellow stripes appeared to be dark and light gray. He scanned the sky in all directions. The intense blue of the Jerusalem sky was the color of ash. He caught a blur of motion just in time to avoid a Roman soldier struggling to control his frothing horse. Jamin wished he could steal the man's horse, but stealing was why his brother, Demas, had been sentenced to death.

The circumstances surrounding the execution of his brother were highly unusual. Jamin was horrified when Demas told him of his plan to surrender and confess his crimes. Jamin tried to talk him out of it. When Demas explained how Yeshua convinced him to confess, Jamin was furious. Demas explained that it was the right thing to do, but Jamin could not understand why he would willingly forfeit his life. The rest of his family was dead. Jamin would be alone.

Many people believed Yeshua was the promised Messiah, but now that he was being executed, they knew it was false hope. Surely, the real Messiah would free his people from the Romans, and reinstate the Kingdom of David, not die like a lowly criminal. This overthrow of the Romans seemed imminent only a few days before when Yeshua arrived in Jerusalem. The people shouted praises to him and placed palm fronds before him.

Yeshua said, "*He who hears My word and believes in Him who sent Me has everlasting life, and shall not come into judgment, but has passed from death into life.*" But the same man who promised eternal life was about to die. Jamin hated himself for believing the outrageous statement. He thought when Yeshua established his kingdom, he and Demas would have places of honor. Jamin wondered how he could be so naive.

Jamin recalled the words of the prophet Isaiah: "*The rising sun will be darkened and the moon will not give its light. Therefore I will make the heavens tremble; and the earth will shake from its place at the wrath of the Lord Almighty, in the day of His burning anger.*"

When his father made him memorize this passage, Jamin thought it was merely symbolic. Could it be possible the centuries-old prophecy had a literal meaning? Jamin reached a shortcut and slipped out of the crowds. He prayed he would get to his brother in time to drive away the carrion birds. He would need to collect rocks to throw. The limestone blocks of the city wall behind the crosses were chipped by thousands of rocks thrown for this purpose.

Jamin passed through the east gate of the main city wall. He could see the low hill of Golgotha pockmarked with *stipes*, the wooden beams permanently installed to form crucifixion crosses as near to the main road as Jewish law allowed. If the

Romans had their way, the entire road would be lined with *stipes*. Leaving the beams was not only for convenience, but to be a constant reminder of Roman authority. Anyone standing in nearly any part of the city would be able to see Golgotha. Since the crucified criminals were left to rot on the crosses leaving skulls and bones scattered on the ground, it was known as Golgotha, The Place of the Skull.

Jamin turned north to the sloping path of Golgotha. The air held the acrid smell of hot sand, animal dung, and cooking fires. The bitter taste of dust stung his tongue. Jamin coughed and tried to clear his throat. He started to drink from the wineskin, but stopped, remembering that he needed to save the wine for his brother.

As he hurried further up the path, the full line of upright *stipes* came into view. It was the crossbeam or *patibulum,* that the prisoner was forced to carry from the Antonia to Golgotha. Jamin saw the men hanging from three crosses. People were shouting insults at the dying men. Anger seared his heart as spectators entertained themselves at his brother's misery. How could they not understand the courage it took for Demas to confess his crimes, knowing he would be sentenced to death? Jamin picked up a rock to throw at a particularly vocal offender, but then he realized the scoffers were baiting only the man on the center cross.

Jamin dropped the rock. He had been so intent on the crowd of hecklers, he had failed to acknowledge his brother. Demas was on the cross to the right of the center one. Jamin cringed in despair when he saw his little brother watching him. His heart burned with shame as he stared up into his brother's face, shadowed with pain and exhaustion.

Jamin croaked, "I am here, Demas. I am here." But Demas couldn't hear him.

Jamin sat in the sand, cross-legged, holding his knapsack in his lap. He was relieved the birds were keeping their distance. Still, he began collecting small stones. It wasn't until then he realized the man on the center cross was Yeshua.

A few hecklers challenged him. "*He saved others; Himself He cannot save. Let the Christ, the King of Israel, descend now from the cross, that we may see and believe,*" said one after another, each thinking his insult was unique and clever.

Jamin was going to shout his own insults when he saw Yeshua's followers nearby, including Mary, the mother of Yeshua. He remained silent out of respect for Mary. He was losing his brother, but she, already a widow, was losing her beloved first-born child.

When Demas and Jamin were teenagers, they lost their entire family. Eventually, the brothers made their way to Jerusalem and found work with a metal engraver named Cleopas. He and his wife, Mary, took pity on the brothers and invited them to live at their house. While staying in Jerusalem, they heard about a man called John the Baptist and his message of hope. Jamin wanted to hear John, but Demas was reluctant.

Demas declared, "This John the Baptist is another crazy man claiming to be the Messiah. You know the Messiah will never come, not the real one. Why do you believe the ranting of some long-dead men who called themselves prophets?"

"Don't say that, Demas! God can hear you."

"God can hear you," mimicked the younger brother with a sneer. "If God is so great why did he let the Romans kill our parents and sisters? You feel the same; you just won't admit it. The God who let our family die was the same God who claims to love us. How does that work?"

"God isn't mistreating us, Demas. It is the way of the world. Don't you listen when they read the scrolls in temple? Ever since God brought us out of Egypt, we have trusted other nations instead of him. They have always betrayed us."

"I don't want to hear it. We trusted in God and look what it got us. The soldiers sold us into slavery. We were getting shipped off to who knows where. Have you forgotten? We're just lucky we escaped."

"There's no such thing as luck," grumbled Jamin under his breath.

They joined the crowd listening to John. He sat on a rock and spoke to the people as they gathered along the river bank. He began baptizing new believers in the river.

His words rang out. "The living Word of God will baptize you with the Holy Spirit. He will gather his wheat into the barn and burn up the chaff with unquenchable fire. His judgment will be true and final."

"This is ridiculous, Jamin! He's talking about harvesting wheat. Can we go now?"

Jamin didn't take his eyes off John. "Little Brother, he *is* talking about harvesting wheat and burning the chaff. I do not wish to be the chaff, do you? And he's not the Messiah, but he's talking about the Messiah. Listen!"

Listeners began questioning John, wanting to know how to avoid condemnation. Even a Roman soldier with his squad spoke up. He had short-cropped, blonde hair and pale gray eyes. His face was marked with a scar from the right temple down to the jaw. He was an unusually tall and powerfully built man.

The Roman gestured at himself and his men. "And what shall we do?"

John answered, "Do not intimidate anyone or accuse anyone falsely. Be content with your wages. Enforce your laws justly." The Roman did not reply, but spoke harshly with his fellow soldiers. He started to leave until he noticed the other soldiers were not following him. One of the soldiers started to walk toward the river, but the man with the scar called to them angrily, and they left.

A man brushed past Jamin and Demas. He was average height, wearing simple clothing, but that could not hide his aura of authority. The man stepped into the river and approached John. No one could hear what he said, but John's shocked reaction was unmistakable.

John put his hand on the man's shoulder and they both bowed their heads. The man knelt down until the water covered him. At the exact moment he came out of the water, Jamin saw a small bright light fall from the sky and settle on the man's shoulder. He couldn't believe what he was seeing. Then he heard the voice. It was a powerful, resonating voice that came from everywhere at once. He glanced at his brother to see if he heard it, too. Demas was staring with wide eyes; his mouth hung slack.

The mysterious voice declared, "*This is my Son, whom I love; with Him I am well pleased.*" Everyone gasped and looked around, trying to locate the speaker.

"Did you see it?" exclaimed Jamin. "Did you see the beautiful light settle on him? It was as beautiful as a snow white dove. And the voice, did you hear it?"

"The light was brilliant, yet it didn't hurt my eyes. I heard the voice, too,"

A stranger grumbled at the brothers. "Are you drunk? It was just thunder."

"Then where are the storm clouds?" Demas demanded.

The baptized man walked out of the river. A hush fell over the crowd as they made room for him. Jamin turned to his brother. "Come on. I want to find out who he is."

"I don't see him anymore," said Demas, scanning the crowd.

Jamin pointed at John. "Then let's talk to him instead." Jamin only intended to find someone who would convince his brother to stop stealing. He never thought this first conversation with John the Baptist would lead Demas to his execution.

An intruder interrupted Jamin's thoughts. A man wearing a fine linen tunic and an elegant gold-accented silk toga separated himself from the crowd of hecklers. His pallid skin was tightly stretched over his dominant cheekbones and forehead giving his face a skull-like appearance. His clothes hung loosely as if draped over bare bones. His sunken, pale eyes were surrounded by dark shadowing, which emphasized his penetrating gaze. The stranger approached a Roman soldier who wore the belt, *caligae*, and *lorica musculata* of a centurion. Only centurions wore the metal, muscle-contoured armor. The *caligae*, sandal boots, were a distinct mark of a Roman soldier. The centurion's *gladius* and *pugio* were weapons of the highest craftsmanship, which only a privileged officer could afford. When the richly attired man drew near, the soldier turned his back.

"*Centurio!*" said the stranger in a whispery voice. "May I speak with you?" Fingering his many gold necklaces, the stranger said, "Excuse me for interrupting your grand *actionis militaris*. I am a merchant of purple silk from Rome. The inscriptions say the men on the right and left crosses are thieves. The inscription over the center cross is not a crime if it's true. What proof is there that he is *not* the Son of God?"

Centurion Adas Clovius Longinus answered curtly, "I wasn't present at the trial. I only know his conviction was demanded by the people."

"That is not a legal conviction. Apparently, no crime was committed, or proof would have been offered, instead of the ranting of a mob. You are executing an innocent man, which makes you are a murderer, Centurion."

Adas was shocked at the accusation. "I do not question my orders, Sir! Who are you to accuse me? Accuse those who sentenced him."

"Oh, I will, in due time. I find fault with everyone. However, *you* are the one carrying out a false conviction. I see the banner." He pointed to the sign nailed at the top of the beam. "It plainly states 'Yeshua of Nazareth, King of the Jews.' Yet, you use crucifixion, which is reserved for the lowest criminal. Likewise, I've never seen a man so severely scourged. Is this how *you* treat a king?"

"I obey my orders! Leave or be arrested." Adas, again, turned his back and walked away.

The other three soldiers stepped closer as the stranger approached them. He spoke softly as he gestured toward the centurion who was out of earshot. The soldiers leaned in, eager to hear the peculiar man's criticism. His voice was hypnotic.

When Adas saw the intruder talking to his men, he confronted the merchant. "As I said, you need to leave. Now! You have no business here!"

The merchant chuckled softly. "Not true. I have business everywhere, but my work here is done." He threw a sidelong glance up at Yeshua, but dropped his gaze quickly when the Nazarene locked eyes with him. Yeshua and the raspy-voiced intruder had previously met. It had been a very long meeting. The silk merchant started to confront the centurion again when he saw an approaching mounted patrol. He spotted a group of Pharisees heckling the Nazarene and joined the group. He introduced himself. They gathered closer to listen.

The patrol halted near the Pharisees. Adas approached the lead decurion, a cavalry officer. "Longinus, you only have one squad? You should have more men."

"Not the usual protocol, is it?"

"No, especially with the Nazarene. I can't believe there isn't a full scale riot, as popular as he is—was. Want us to stay? We're coming off shift, but we can spare you an hour."

"We were also about to go off duty when Valentius snagged us. We're tired, but we've got it covered. *Gratias.*" The patrol lingered a short time, and then left.

Jamin kept a wary eye on the three legionaries as the centurion talked with a decurion. One of the legionaries pulled out a pair of wooden dice from his belt pouch. It was a common practice to gamble for executed prisoners' garments. The clothes of the three prisoners were piled on the ground before them.

"Centurion," called one of the soldiers, "the Nazarene's tunic is high quality, no seams. Do you want a turn with the lots?" Adas shook his head.

One of the legionaries, named Falto, threw the dice, laughed and snatched up a sandal. He shook it in the face of the legionary who won the first sandal. Falto was no one's friend, but everyone's fool. He was a large man with a small mind, a dangerous combination. The men called him *Mustela*, Weasel. Some had even forgotten his real name.

Falto grinned at the winner of the first sandal. "So Lucius, how far will you get with only one sandal?" He dangled it in front of the others and reached for his wineskin.

Lucius Equitius Octavean slapped the wineskin out of Falto's hand. "Far enough to take that one away from you! I saw you cheat. You couldn't trick a gaggle of old women."

Few men would have insulted a fellow soldier so blatantly, but Lucius's heavily muscled physique enabled his volatile temper. He was known as the Lion, and not only because his initials were LEO. He was only thirty-four years old, but had belonged to the Roman Imperial Army for twenty-six years. Women considered him handsome, but the abuse of wrath and warfare was taking its toll. His blonde hair was already peppered with gray, matching his pale eyes. A graphic scar ran down the side of his face. Jamin thought he looked familiar.

Falto was too drunk to be offended. He jutted his chin forward and offered to give up the second sandal in exchange for Lucius's wineskin.

"How 'bout I just beat it out of you?" Lucius snarled.

Even drunk, Falto knew he had pushed too far and turned his attention on Yeshua. "*Ohe*, you there! King of the Jews! They say you healed people. Prove it! Take that ugly scar from Octavean's sour face!" Falto snickered, missing the annoyed flash in Lucius's eyes.

The third soldier, a brown-haired, brown-eyed Greek named Hektor, interrupted the brewing fight with a suggestion. "Why don't you throw the lots again? Winner gets the pair."

He knew Falto had cheated, but saw no reason to side with Lucius. As was his habit whenever he was assigned to a crucifixion detail, Hektor took bets on how long the criminals would survive. Yeshua was famous, and the more famous the criminal, the higher the betting. Hektor expected to make a great deal of money.

Lucius stood with his feet wide apart and his hands on his hips, giving Jamin a better look at his features. It was the soldier who had been at the river when John baptized Yeshua over three years ago.

Taking up with the hecklers, Lucius vented his bad humor. "*If You are the King of the Jews, save Yourself!*" His words were slurred from drunkenness.

Centurion Longinus stood apart from the legionaries. He ran his fingers through his raven-black hair. His square jaw and high cheekbones gave him an aristocratic appearance, but his expression lacked arrogance. He was average in height, but had a well-defined build. Adas was awarded the centurion title two years previously, and transferred to Jerusalem. He was at the lowest status and the youngest centurion in the entire 10th *Legio*.

A minimum of sixteen years of military service was a basic requirement before earning the title of centurion. Adas had only served nine years. A boy could begin army training at eight, but would not become a legionary until the age of seventeen, making the youngest centurion thirty-three years old. Only highly experienced, battle-tested soldiers from high-ranking families were awarded the title, a mark of status, not rank. Even though Adas had the makings of a centurion by his own rights, his father, *Consul* Aquila Clovius Longinus, was offered the title for his son by Emperor Tiberius. Without even discussing the offer with Adas, Aquila accepted. Unfortunately, Aquila had no idea he had put his son in danger, not only from enemy combatants, but also from the legionaries of his own cohort and the other centurions.

A Roman legion was divided into units called a *cohors*. Each *cohors* was divided into six *centuriae*. Each *centuria* usually consisted of a hundred legionaries. The *primus pilus* centurion commanded the 1st *cohors,* 1st *centuria* and was the highest ranking centurion in the legion. The other nine *cohors* were commanded by *pilus prior* or cohort centurions. All of the remaining fifty centurions had no other title. As the lowest ranking centurion, Longinus commanded the 10th *cohors*, 6th *centuria*.

Adas shouted, "Octavean, shut your mouth! You may be drunk, but don't defile any honor you might have by taunting a defenseless man. I know you are not a coward. Don't pretend to be one."

"Yes, Sir!" Lucius's mouth tightened as his gray eyes narrowed with resentment. He rejoined the other soldiers. Falto and Hektor exchanged glances, but didn't dare make a comment. Jamin could see that the centurion was genuinely angry at the legionary's disrespect. Unlike the other soldiers, the centurion was not drunk, not gambling, and not ridiculing the criminals.

Curious, Jamin watched him. The centurion stepped a few feet away from his men. Guardedly, Jamin looked at the soldier. The centurion's eyes had an unsettling appearance, deep-set with a piercing stare, not dark, but not pale. Jamin lowered his gaze.

Adas fingered the handle of his dagger. Even though he hated this part of his job, he accepted it. His usual tactic was to focus on the crime of the condemned, rather than the person. Today, none of his coping skills were working. His growing anxiety made him irritable. Looking for a distraction, he glanced at Jamin.

Adas looked from Jamin to the thief on the right and saw the same features. All the soldiers knew that Demas had confessed. They could not believe anyone would willingly surrender himself for crucifixion. They joked about the young Hebrew who had lost his mind. A few were skeptical enough to suspect it was a trick to get inside the garrison. The others retorted that if it was a trick, it was a very stupid trick.

"Is he your relative?" Adas asked. Jamin was amazed he spoke to him in Hebrew, and nodded in answer. "Do you wish to give him something to drink?"

Jamin thanked him, took a sponge from his knapsack and secured it to his stick. He poured wine into the sponge. "He's my little brother."

Lucius looked up from his gambling and frowned at Adas. "Is there something you want to say, Octavean?"

Lucius came to his feet at attention. "No, Centurion. I have nothing to say."

"Then get that sneer off your face."

"Yes, Sir." Lucius sat down. He clenched his fists, but his expression turned stoic.

Hektor wondered why Lucius went out of his way to antagonize Longinus. It was foolish at best, dangerous at worst. Yet, Hektor knew Lucius was no fool. Something odd was going on. He wondered if a profit could be made. Taking bets on a fight to the death between Longinus and Octavean would garner a great deal of money. The risk of such a scheme would be substantial, but Hektor was a gambling man. He never could resist a good wager.

Chapter 2

⸻⸺⸻

Lucius tossed his wineskin down. Since it was nearly empty, he didn't bother to reseal it. "By the gods, I will teach that fraud of a centurion a lesson someday. I hate sitting here with flies and heat waiting for these convicts to die, especially under his command. Valentius pulls Longinus out of rotation for the worst assignments, and us along with him. As long as we're in his *centuria* we're going to suffer." The other two soldiers nodded in agreement.

As Jamin tended to Demas, Adas walked a short distance away, giving the brothers some privacy. Adas didn't hear what Lucius said to the other two soldiers, but Jamin did. It surprised him to hear dissention in the ranks. He thought Romans were always brutally well organized.

When Demas could take no more wine, he turned his head away. Jamin lowered the stick and retreated to his place on the sand. Lucius watched, disgusted that the thief was allowed to receive aid. He could be punished for insubordination, but in his drunkenness, he didn't care.

"Centurion Longinus, *Sir*! Do you wish us to give comfort to the other two as well? If we ignore them it might stir up a riot." If he had been sober, Lucius would never have called the centurion's judgment or courage into question.

Adas bristled with anger. "Are you mocking me, Octavean? Are you too stupid to know it makes no difference what you think of me? I can order your execution, and it will be done."

Lucius leapt to his feet. He wanted to say, "Are you sure about that?" Instead, he caged his temper and apologized. "I meant no harm, Centurion. Pilate has made it clear he does not want another riot. The criminal in the center is popular with the people. They may rally against us, and there are only four of us."

"Your feigned concern doesn't fool me! Offer the wine to the other two men."

While Lucius obeyed, Hektor whispered to Falto, "Want to wager on a fight to the death? Octavean or Longinus?"

Falto nodded. "Put me down for ten *denarii* on the Lion."

Lucius often got into fights, but always with people of lesser status to avoid severe punishment. But with this young centurion, he seemed to be purposely baiting him. The two legionaries were unaware of what motivated him to play this dangerous game, but they figured the end result would be entertaining.

Adas again fingered the handle of his dagger and glared at Lucius. He was tired of the legionary's questionable attitude. Adas tried to focus on anyone other than Lucius and his eyes fell on Yeshua. The man watched him with the most unexpected expression—sympathy. Yeshua had been silent for some time, but now he spoke with clarity. The centurion stared in shock. The other three soldiers stopped what they were doing and frowned at Adas.

"Centurion, what did he say?" asked Hektor, surprised at the astonishment on his commanding officer's face. Adas did not respond at first, but then he translated.

Lucius shrugged his shoulders. "Forgive us? For what? We're following orders. He tells his father to forgive us. Who is his father? Where is he?" He scanned the crowd of spectators. "I don't see anyone who could be his father."

Adas tugged on his armor as if the metal chest-plate was uncomfortable. The legionaries returned to their game, but Lucius shouted no more insults at the Nazarene. Adas studied Yeshua as shame pierced his heart. The heat was making him slightly sick, or at least, that is what he told himself as he sat down on the sand. However, his persistent nauseous feeling was getting worse. He tried to imagine he was somewhere else, anywhere but here. Nothing on this day was as it should be. His fellow soldier was his enemy, and the Nazarene, who should have cursed him, had instead forgiven him. The eerie darkness which started as soon as Yeshua was on the cross only increased the dread he felt as soon as Valentius assigned him the executions.

A childish voice interrupted the centurion's thoughts. "Soldier, why are you sitting there with your eyes closed? Don't you like to watch criminals die?" A Roman boy of nine years old stood next to Adas with his small hands on his hips. Annoyed with the intrusion, Adas snapped his eyes open and glared at the child. Startled, the boy stepped back.

A man yanked him away. "What did I tell you about wandering off? It's not safe, especially *here*." The boy's father spun away, dragging his son after him.

Adas watched them disappear into the crowd. A particularly unpleasant childhood memory surfaced. His father had reprimanded him for the same reason, but with a different result. He signaled for Lucius to approach. "Octavean, your behavior is inexcusable. I will report it to Centurion Valentius." Adas curtly dismissed him.

The legionary turned away quickly to hide his calculating expression. Involving Valentius was what Lucius wanted. As a legionary, he was not allowed to initiate direct contact with any cohort centurion, but Lucius had an understanding with Valentius. Pretending to be concerned by the reprimand, he rejoined the other two legionaries. He inspected the last item of clothing and picked up the dice.

"*Ohe!* I want this tunic with no seams. Let's cast the lots and see who gets the highest number." The other two nodded agreement, relieved that Lucius's temper had cooled.

Lucius had never been promoted above the rank of legionary, in spite of his intelligence, battlefield prowess, and regal stature. A daunting curse seemed to hang over his head. His father gave him to the army when he was eight years old, hoping his son would acquire the best benefits the Roman army offered. His hope was more than possible since Lucius excelled at his training. His superior strength, quick reflexes, and fast thinking made him the most feared sparring partner among the boys in training.

Junio, the chief training officer, set Lucius on a special program since he showed the most promise. Lucius was eager to please his training officers, but mostly, he wanted to please his father. Lucius understood that his parents let him go so he might have a better life. But the dream was shattered when he, at the age of eleven, killed a man. That man was Rufino Equitius Octavean, his own father.

It was a double tragedy. Not only did Lucius lose the father he dearly loved, he never saw his mother, Sevina, again. She never remarried, but lived in Rome, sharing her time between the homes of two daughters. Lucius sent a portion of his pay to her every month, and she accepted it. He made no attempt to see her, neither did she ask to see him, nor did she acknowledge his financial support. Worried the pay claims weren't getting to her, he sent letters to his sisters. They confirmed their mother received them every month. However, guilt for his father's death made his heart grow as cold and unforgiving as the blade of a sword. His only goal was to stay alive longer than the next man.

Adas Clovius Longinus was on the opposite end of life in the Roman world. His father, Aquila, was a wealthy land owner and architect who bore the title of *Consul*, the highest elected magistrate in the Roman Empire. However, Adas was not allowed to take advantage of his family's position. As a child, his parents taught him humility, but not just toward them. Adas was expected to treat the servants the same way, which was unusual for a wealthy Roman family.

Fascinated by horses, Adas spent most of his time with the horse masters at the garrison in Rome. They mentored the teenager in battle skills and horse care. By the time Adas turned sixteen, he could go the distance with some of the legionaries in sparring competitions. Adas idolized the *veterinarim*, and wanted to be a *primus veterinarius*. To do that, he could join the army when he turned seventeen.

His father did not approve of his son's career choice. Likewise, Adas resented his father's intolerance of the "unsophisticated" soldiers at the garrison. As Aquila attempted to control his son, Adas grew increasingly rebellious. Adas's mother, Marsetina, hoped father and son would eventually bond, but as her son matured that hope faded. When Adas enlisted in the army without consulting his father, Aquila was furious. He wanted his son to become an architectural engineer like himself and take over the management of their extensive vineyards. After Adas enlisted as an apprentice *medicus veterinarius*, he was stationed in Caesarea Maritima in Judea. Communication with his father was only through letters Adas wrote to his mother. Since Judea was a long way from Rome, Adas rarely came home on leave. The two men became virtual strangers.

When Adas was given centurion status, he was also forced to transfer to Jerusalem. These were changes he did not want. Aquila's status among the voters was enhanced by having a centurion for a son, but Marsetina was heartbroken. In Caesarea, Adas had served primarily as a *veterinarius* and secondarily as a reserve battlefield soldier. Now, he would be a frontline warrior. Adas hated not earning the centurion title honorably. However, to refuse the title would spell disaster for his father. Emperor Tiberius could be vindictive if his "offers" were rejected.

Initially, the title of centurion bestowed on such an inexperienced youth fueled the hostility of the other centurions and legionaries, alike. To make matters worse, the young centurion was easily recognized, so keeping a low profile was impossible. The Antonia Fortress housed a full legion of ten *cohortis* comprised of about five thousand soldiers. Gossip spread quickly, especially in the legionaries' barracks where row after row of bunks provided easy access to the conversations of others. Adas was a favorite subject.

Keenly aware of the penalty for showing disrespect to an officer, the legionaries were careful with their judgments, but Adas knew how they felt. In fact, he didn't blame them. To go from a *veterinarius medicus* to a centurion in seven years was an insult to every ranking officer, but Adas was determined to earn their respect.

As Adas put himself in harm's way before his men and treated them well, their attitudes changed. Many soldiers were foreigners who joined to acquire Roman citizenship. Adas could usually speak with them in their native languages, being fluent in Greek, Egyptian, and Hebrew, which cultivated their favor. On occasions, Adas had to treat an injured soldier himself. Wounded soldiers claimed the centurion's calming voice distracted them from their pain. Adas used the same technique with injured horses to reduce their fear. It usually worked.

Even though Adas was building a solid relationship with his men, he still resented his father's interference. He suspected Aquila, having never served in the military, had no idea of the difficult position he had forced upon his son. However, the worst result of the transfer to Jerusalem was that it broke his heart.

During his years in Caesarea, Adas developed a close tie to the family of his commanding officer, Centurion Marcus Claudius Cornelius, the cohort centurion of the 2nd *Cohors* of the 10th *Legio* in Caesarea. Adas suspected his father heard of his loyalty to Cornelius and was jealous. Aquila Longinus instigated an investigation of Cornelius when he was forced to kill a man who was threatening his own family. Instead of a reprimand, Cornelius was promoted to *Primus Pilus Centurion*, of the *1st Cohors*. Adas was greatly pleased at this outcome, especially since it seemed to undermine his father's intentions.

Not long after Cornelius was promoted, he invited Adas to dinner at his villa. It was the first time he met Dulcibella, the second daughter of four children of Marcus and Iovita Cornelius. She was nine years old; he was seventeen. Whenever he was invited to Cornelius's home, Adas answered the inquisitive child's questions and listened to her observations. He was amused at her attempts to garner his attention. He granted her requests for lessons in Greek, archery, and horseback riding. Unlike the children in Rome, and some of the adults, she showed no fear of him, despite the disconcerting look of his eyes.

In return, Dulcibella found Adas to be a friend who did not patronize her need to learn and explore the curiosities of life. As time passed, Dulcibella matured into a lovely, intelligent, young woman, and Adas looked forward to their time together. When she reached fifteen, Adas recognized his relationship with Dulcibella was changing. He no longer thought of his future without her. In fact, if he had been given the title of centurion, with no transfer, he would have asked for Dulcibella's hand in marriage, since only centurions were allowed to wed. But the transfer to Jerusalem postponed this possibility. Even though Adas hated to leave her, and she was willing to go, he felt it would be unsafe to take her to Jerusalem.

On his last day in Caesarea, he gave a pair of miniature greyhound puppies to Dulcibella. Hugging the squirming little pups, she smiled at him with her turquoise eyes as the sea breeze swept through her glossy brunette hair.

"They will keep my heart warm while you're away," she informed Adas, laughing as the puppies licked her hands. "I shall name them Alpha and Omega because I think of you first every morning and last every night."

Adas was delighted to see her gentle smile. Her upturned, pixie eyes enchanted him; he marveled at their ability to change from sea-blue to pale green, depending on what colors she wore. A cobalt-blue ring around the irises added a stunning last touch.

In return, she presented him with an eilat stone, or Solomon's Stone, comprised of green and blue minerals found in the areas high in copper in Judea. "Every time you look at this stone I am thinking of you. Even when you put it away, I will still think of you."

Marcus Cornelius presented Adas with an Arabian horse since he never accepted pay for Dulcibella's lessons. Dulcibella selected the horse, herself, making Adas treasure the mare even more. It grieved him to lose the guidance and support of Marcus and Iovita, but separation from the captivating company of Dulcibella crushed his soul. After a minimum of two years, he could request a transfer back to Caesarea. Dulcibella would be eighteen by then, a few years past the usual age of marriage, but she assured him she would wait for him. And he would wait for her.

Chapter 3

⸻❊⸻

Adas wondered how his legionaries could be so oblivious to the veiled sun and the bitter taste in the air. It made him yearn for Caesarea, where the breeze wafted off the Mediterranean Sea and the sparkling water matched the color of Dulcibella's eyes.

Lucius threw the lots to the ground. "*Ohe!* There's the winning number. I get the tunic." He started to stuff it in his knapsack, but a bout of coughing made him pause.

"You better sell it for a good price, Lucius," Hektor said. "That's the only reward you'll ever get in this army, along with that cough of yours."

Lucius wiped his mouth. "Not true. Centurion Valentius has promised me a promotion to the Special Forces unit, specifically as a *beneficiarius*, if I continue to succeed at my assignments. My pay will double and that will be the end of menial labor for me."

Falto snorted doubtfully. "Valentius offered you *beneficiarius* status? When? Years ago? He has made the same promise to others without ever making good. You know Valentius cannot promote anyone above a non-commissioned *principales* without the tribune's approval. What assignments did he give you? Find the best brothels?" Falto laughed, but saw the centurion frowning at him and shut his mouth. Falto winked at Hektor, thinking the gesture made them allies against Lucius's bragging.

"You love to hear yourself talk, don't you, Weasel? I don't work for free. Compensation can be in many forms. Valentius trusts me with. . .well, he trusts me. He sent me to spy on that so-called prophet camped out by the Jordan River, the one Herod beheaded. Just to see what he would say, I asked what we should do to follow his teachings. You know what he said?" The other two shook their heads. "He said, 'Carry out Roman laws justly.' As if the law ever did justice for me! I spit on Roman law!"

"Watch what you say!" Hektor warned. "You're close to treason. And even a Roman citizen is crucified for treason."

Falto slapped Hektor across the shoulder. "That's only for high treason and Lucius doesn't do anything worse than a fist fight. Besides, we're the only ones who heard what he said. A cut from the wages of a *beneficiarius* would insure our silence, don't you thi. . ."

Lucius leapt to his feet so fast Falto didn't have a chance to move. The enraged Roman grasped him by the straps of his leather armor and yanked the foolish man to his feet. His fist crashed into Falto's face, knocking him to the ground. Fortunately for Falto, Lucius was still recovering from a previously broken arm and dislocated shoulder. If he had used his uninjured arm, Falto's jaw would have been broken.

"Don't you ever threaten to blackmail me again or I'll kill you!" His pale eyes gleamed with malice as his lips curled back from his teeth.

Adas spun around and saw Falto sprawled on the ground. "What do you think you're doing?" Lucius faced the centurion but said nothing. "You two are disgraceful!" He tossed Falto's wineskin at him. "Wash the blood off your face."

"There's a waste of good wine," Lucius muttered.

"Did you say something, Octavean?"

"No, Sir!" Lucius lowered his eyes.

Adas stalked away and sat down. He dropped his head to his fingertips and massaged his temples. He looked up at the tortured men on the crosses and his annoyance ebbed in the face of their agony. Shaking his head, Adas wondered why the Nazarene had been condemned to this misery since Pilate found him innocent of any crimes. Perhaps, the silk merchant was right to call it murder. Adas looked at the followers of Yeshua. The thought of Dulcibella or his own mother being forced to witness such a thing sickened him. He scrutinized the mysteriously darkened sun and wondered if the man on the center cross could be divine after all, but he immediately dismissed the idea. Adas knew about the Hebrew God, but how could *Elohim* allow a part of himself to be treated like the worst of the lowest criminals.

When Adas was a child, his nanny, Misha, told him stories about God, the Father of all creation. Misha said, "God loves humanity, but demands obedience and he will punish those who refuse to obey him. You can ask for forgiveness from God, but an animal which is innocent of all sin, must be sacrificed. There can be no forgiveness without the shedding of innocent blood."

"That's terrible!" six-year-old Adas cried. "They've done nothing wrong?"

"It is for that very reason," Misha answered. "Anyone can take the punishment for a convicted criminal, if he is innocent of the crime. That is the law. But only someone who is pure and innocent can stand in for all sin. However, only animals are sacrificed, never children, no matter how innocent they are, for God strictly forbids passing any child through the fire. The pagans practice foundation sacrifices—killing their own children to bury them in the foundation of a new home or a city wall. *That* is terrible."

Young Adas then asked his mother about the Roman gods. Marsetina answered, "The Romans and Greeks worship gods and goddesses who take pleasure in making humanity suffer. Their religion gives those 'worshipers' an excuse to do the same thing—for pleasure or greed. If you want to know the mind and heart of a people, look at what or who they worship. There are people who form a lump of clay into a figure, call it by a name, and bow down to it. They are mindless fools. They plead with hunks of marble or casts of bronze and expect miracles. They are too stupid to see the futility of praying to their own designs."

"So if there are no gods," Adas asked, "what made the world and everything in it?"

Marsetina shrugged. "If the gods exist, who made them?"

"Misha says there is only one God. Don't you believe her?"

"Misha has great wisdom, but I do not share her belief. She worships a God who cannot be seen. Her faith exceeds her logic."

"What is faith and logic?"

"Faith is when you believe something *before* it happens. Logic is when you believe something because it has *already* happened."

"Then, I have both logic and faith," said Adas, pleased with himself, "because I believe you and Father will love me tomorrow as much as you loved me yesterday."

Marsetina kissed her child's forehead and smiled, but there was sadness in her eyes. "You are right, *we* will always love you. But a parent's love can die."

"How can love die? Your mother and father always loved you, didn't they?" She left the room without answering. Adas was sorry for asking the question.

Young Adas asked his father about the gods. "Son, you have to make your own way and take responsibility. Divine intervention is not going to save or ruin you. You must be the master of your own life. Let experience be your guide, not the mutterings of soothsayers for hire."

Forcing himself back to the present, Adas retrieved his wineskin and some bread from his knapsack. As he ate, he could hear Demas struggling to talk to the Nazarene. At first the robbers baited Yeshua challenging him to prove himself. But now Demas was listening to Yeshua and his anger dissolved. The two talked as best they could as Adas listened, increasingly fascinated. He wondered how the Nazarene had the strength to talk so calmly and at such length.

He heard the thief say, "Then you are the final blood sacrifice, Yeshua. Why didn't I understand this before?"

The other criminal was listening, too. He spit words from his mouth as if they were sawdust, "*If you are the Christ, save yourself and us!*"

Demas called out, "*Do you not even fear God, seeing you are under the same condemnation? And we indeed justly, for we receive the due reward of our deeds; but this Man has done nothing wrong. Lord, remember me when You come into Your kingdom.*"

Yeshua answered, "*Today you will be with Me in paradise.*"

Adas was astonished at the audacity of the Nazarene's statement. He studied the sign posted above his head: *Jesus of Nazareth—the King of the Jews.* There was no chance he could misunderstand the message since it was written in Hebrew, Latin and Greek. He thought of the stories of this man healing sick and crippled people, and bringing the dead back to life. At the time, he thought it was exaggeration. But what if it were true? What if the Nazarene was divine? But if so, how could he allow himself to be crucified, the most degrading form of execution?

Yeshua spoke to one of the women and to the only man in the group of grieving followers. She turned to the man and cried, her head sagging against his shoulder, her hands covering her face.

Suddenly Yeshua lifted his head and cried out, *"Eloi, Eloi, lama sabachthani?"*

Jamin knew he was quoting from the Book of Psalms. He often recited these same verses after his family was murdered. *"My God, My God, why have You forsaken Me? Why are You so far from saving Me, so far from the words of My groaning? I am poured out like water, and all My bones are out of joint. My heart has turned to wax; it has melted away within Me. . . .a band of evil men has encircled Me, they have pierced My hands and My feet.. . .people stare and gloat over Me. They divide My garments among them and cast lots for My clothing."* Jamin realized everything in this Psalm, written hundreds of years ago, was happening to Yeshua.

Yeshua cried out, *"I thirst!"* Adas dipped the sponge into a jar of wine vinegar. When he raised the sponge on a stick, Yeshua looked him directly in the eye. The centurion blinked in surprise at the intensity of the man's expression.

A few observers cried out, *"Let Him alone; let us see if Elijah will come to save Him."* Adas ignored them and concentrated on holding the stick as steadily as he could.

When Yeshua received the drink, he announced in a loud, clear voice, *"Father, into Your hands I commit My spirit. It is finished!"*

Immediately, there was a low rumble, and the earth began to shake so violently boulders split apart. The crowds of people were knocked off their feet. Splintered rocks crashed down from hilltops scattering screaming people in all directions. Jamin jumped to his feet, but immediately fell on his back and elbows. He choked on clouds of dust that filled the air. He struggled to his feet again, to get above the dust, but the quake knocked him back down. Everyone was sprawled on the ground, including the Roman soldiers.

The shaking intensified. The soldiers threw their hands out to steady themselves. They looked around with mild surprise which escalated into panic. The crosses swayed and both criminals struggled to get a footing. Yeshua hung lifeless. His drooping head swayed as the cross moved with the convulsing ground. The Nazarene's followers cried aloud, clutching at each other as they fought to get to their feet. Then the oppressive darkness began to wane, but the air seemed to thicken. It pressed into the people with an inexplicable weight, making it difficult to breathe. The earthquake continued unabated.

Adas gave up trying to get to his feet. It seemed as if the shaking would never end. After what felt like an eternity, the tremors finally subsided. The sun returned to its natural state, restoring color to the world. There was complete silence, as if the earth had gone mute. Adas stared at the dead man above him. He was overcome by the timing of Yeshua's crucifixion and death with the darkness and the earthquake.

Thinking of everything he had ever heard about Yeshua, Adas exclaimed, *"Certainly this was a righteous man!"*

Demas gasped for air. He could barely speak above a whisper, but Adas could hear him. "A mortal can be righteous. This man is not mortal. He is the Son of God. Tell my brother that because I willingly took up this cross, I go to be with God. I will wait for Jamin there." Demas fell silent.

Adas turned and scanned the crowd. A flood of memories from Misha's teaching raced through his mind. In one defining moment, he knew the greatest truth of all. For the first time in his life, he acted on pure faith. Centurion Longinus cried out, *"Surely this was the Son of God!"*

Lucius scrambled to his feet. "Sir! You can't really think any god would let his son die like a slave. It got dark and the earth shook. So what? He was just like any other man."

"Would an ordinary man forgive us while we tortured him to death? I have never even heard rumors of such a thing. Have you?"

Lucius started to speak, but could think of no reply. He shielded his eyes from the sun's glare and grumbled to no one in particular, "I hate crucifixions. They always take so long to die."

Hektor glanced at his wager tally and gloated, "Nazarene, you have made me a rich man."

Lucius ground his teeth in anger. Not only had he lost his wager money, but Centurion Valentius had borrowed money from him to place a bet. He knew Valentius would never pay him back. Lucius looked around for his wineskin and snatched it up, but he had not resealed it. What little wine was left had run out during the earthquake. The *blood of the grape* joined with the blood of Yeshua as it soaked into the ground.

Yeshua was dead. The crowd began to disperse. Yet his followers remained. Their grief was only too evident, still they lingered. The other two crucified men would last much longer, perhaps days.

Adas spoke to Jamin in Hebrew. "I have wine if you've run out. For your brother."

Jamin nodded gratefully. He again attached the sponge to the stick. Adas retrieved his wineskin when Jamin stopped him. "Why are you giving them aid?"

"It is a matter of decency. If I were up there, I would want someone to give me aid. They know Yeshua is dead. Why don't they leave?"

"They stay for the same reason I stay for Demas," said Jamin. "They just want to be with him a little longer, especially his mother, the woman that man is trying to comfort. The man's name is John. He was one of Yeshua's disciples."

"Didn't he have other disciples?"

Jamin nodded, but offered no excuse for their absence. He held the stick carefully so Adas could pour the wine onto the sponge. Jamin lifted the sponge to his brother's lips. Demas took as much as he could. Jamin turned to Adas to thank him. Now that the sun shone brightly and color had returned, Jamin was startled to see the eyes of a wolf looking back at him. The centurion's eyes were the color of opaque amber. The grayish-brown rings circling the irises gave the finishing touch. Jamin looked away to hide his distress.

Hours passed. The crowds were gone. Everything was strangely silent and still. It had only been a matter of hours, but Adas felt like he had been at Golgotha for days. He lay on the ground, his knapsack under his head, and his arm thrown over his eyes. He heard galloping hooves and sat up.

A horseman appeared on the path to Golgotha. Adas recognized the big, mahogany bay as Draco, the war horse of Decurion Cassius Sabinus Quintus. Cassius was tall for a Roman, with short dark hair and dark brown eyes. He sat a horse well with his straight back and broad shoulders, but walked with a right-legged limp, a reminder of a Scythian's arrow.

Cassius reined in his horse. "Centurion Longinus, Governor Pilate sends orders! You're to break their legs before the sun sets. They must be off the crosses before the Jewish Sabbath begins. Looks like the one in the middle is already dead. That was quick. And there still might be a riot. Some curtain in the temple was destroyed. I don't know what it means, but they're in an uproar, as if some old curtain could be the end of the world. Unfortunately, I have more bad news. Centurion Valentius says Governor Pilate wants the four of you to guard the Nazarene's burial site until sunset on Sunday. There are rumors the Nazarene will come back to life. Some fear the zealots will steal the body. If you catch anyone, Valentius says to take them to the Sanhedrin, the Jewish court of law. Governor Pilate does not wish to be involved."

"He wants *us* to guard the tomb?" Adas demanded.

Cassius nodded, but signaled for Adas to approach. He leaned down. "Adas, everyone knows how popular the Nazarene is—*was* with these people. I'd feel better if you had a few more squads."

"I don't understand why Valentius wants us to pull more duty, especially since we were at the end of our shift of night patrol."

Cassius shrugged. "Those are his orders."

Adas groaned in frustration. "If the crucifixions had been delayed just a little longer, a squad from day shift would have been in charge, and now we've got two more days."

"Just be careful." Cassius glanced at the other soldiers. "And what's with those three? They are the most unreliable legionaries in your whole *centuria*. Why did you pick them?"

"I didn't. Valentius assigned them, which is odd." Adas stroked Draco's neck. The spirited horse snorted and pawed the ground. "Today has been nothing but strange."

Cassius lowered his voice. "I need to talk to you about Demitre, Valentius's slave. I'll tell you later when we can talk safely."

"Until then, Cassius." Adas rubbed the horse's neck. The stallion stopped fidgeting. "Draco seems to be recovering well."

"Yes, he is. I believe you saved his life, my friend. I don't know what I'd do without this brave-hearted beast. He is fearless in battle. I owe you, Adas."

"I may need to collect on that someday."

"In the meantime, could you take a look at Tigula? He's not eating well." Decurion Quintus loved his dog. He slept soundly every night knowing the mastiff slept against the door. "I would take him to a *veterinarius*, but you know how Tig snarls at everyone except you."

Adas turned his back to the crosses. It was hard to talk about common things with death so close. "I'll take a look at the grouchy old beast as soon as I get back. By the way, the bolt on my door keeps jamming. Do you mind if I borrow your tools? I think I can fix it myself."

"Sure. You can pick them up when you check on Tigula. *Gratias*, Adas." Cassius started to leave, but a runner approached the men.

"Centurion, Governor Pilate summons you."

Cassius slid from the saddle. "Here, take Draco. I'll keep an eye on your men."

Adas leaped into the saddle and urged the horse into a gallop. Jamin watched as the centurion rode away. He glanced at Lucius anxiously, but relaxed when the decurion spoke harshly to the legionaries. It wasn't long before the centurion returned. Jamin sighed with relief when he dismounted. The centurion talked briefly with the decurion, thanking him for the use of his horse. The decurion ordered Falto to "present" his back so he could climb into the saddle. Adas frowned to see Falto on his hands and knees, knowing that normally only a slave would be expected to "back" a man into the saddle. Without a word, Cassius spun his horse around. Draco's pounding hooves kicked bits of gravel at the legionaries as he sped away. The soldiers hurriedly turned their faces and waved off the cloud of dust.

Jamin had overheard the decurion and knew his brother's suffering would soon end, but it would get much worse before it would be over. Falto picked up the hammer. Jamin couldn't bear to watch Demas suffocate when he would no longer be able to push himself up to exhale. Instead, Jamin concentrated on the order to remove the bodies from the crosses as a blessing. Letting the corpse slowly disintegrate in public view was the epitome of scorn. A new thought occurred to him. If Demas had not surrendered himself when Yeshua said he needed to face the consequences of his crimes, he would have missed the high Sabbath. His body would have been left on the cross until it rotted away.

Lucius snatched the hammer from Falto and faced Adas. "Shall I finish the job for you, Centurion?" Lucius waited as he cradled the hammer in his hands.

Adas fixed a cold stare at Lucius. "Do you think I have never killed a man? I assure you, I have. What of it? It's easy to take a life. The other thing is much more difficult."

"What other thing?"

"To put life back into the dead."

"Those tales are just superstitious rumors."

"Perhaps, but what if on the third day, Yeshua does come back to life? Such a thing would change the world."

Lucius curled his lip in disgust. "I don't pay attention to the ranting of idiots and zealots. Anyone can say anything. It means nothing."

Adas turned his attention back to the two thieves. "I find it disgraceful to kill a man who can't defend himself. Since you're holding the hammer, apparently you don't mind, Legionary." He was surprised to see Lucius's face turn pale. Adas had unintentionally struck a nerve. He pressed the advantage as he eyed the scar on the legionary's face. "So tell me, why did someone leave his signature on your face."

Without warning, the memory of killing his own father possessed Lucius. He could still feel the gut-wrenching dread when they dragged Rufino Octavean into the arena, tied him to a post, and claimed he was caught stealing. Training Officer Junio thrust a spear in Lucius's hands and ordered the eleven-year-old to execute the thief on the spot. Lucius begged his father to explain, but he remained silent. Rufino stood very still, watching Lucius with an expression the boy could not understand. The look on his father's face would haunt Lucius for the rest of his life. When Lucius hesitated, the training officer shouted, "Octavean, I have given you a direct order! If you can't obey then you are no use to me!" Lucius saw a blur of motion and a savage pain ran down the side of his face. He flinched, but held on to the spear. Again, Junio raised his dagger. "Obey me! Kill the thief or I'll kill *both of you!*"

Just as quickly as the image had risen in his mind, it was gone. "Yes, I did a very brave thing when I earned this scar. I killed a thief. I obeyed my orders, as I will now." Lucius stepped up to the central cross and hefted the hammer to his shoulder.

"Stop," ordered Adas. "Not him. He's already dead. He has been for hours." Lucius lowered the hammer and peered into Yeshua's still face.

Demas called out, *"He guards all His bones; not one of them is broken."*

Jamin heard his brother, again, quote from Psalms. He whispered, "Like the lamb of Passover, the bones must never be broken."

"I don't care if he is dead," said Lucius as he grabbed a spear. "Our orders were to make sure he's dead so no one can question it later." He faced the central cross and stepped forward. Suddenly, his face drained of color. He stumbled backwards and dropped the spear as if it were on fire. Lucius stared at something no one else could see. Someone was standing between him and the Nazarene's cross. What he saw was impossible in so many ways.

"Octavean, what is the matter with you?" demanded Adas.

Hektor and Falto watched in bewilderment. The two men exchanged glances, silently confirming each was witnessing the same thing. Adas looked at the center cross, but nothing had changed. Thinking Lucius was in a fugue, Adas slapped him across the face.

"What is wrong with you?" Adas demanded again. Lucius didn't answer. With no patience left, Adas hit him with a fist. Lucius staggered back and shook himself as if from a trance.

Adas picked up the spear, spun around, and thrust it deep into the Nazarene's side. *Immediately blood and water came out* from the wound. There was no reaction from the lifeless body. Adas threw the spear to the ground and wheeled on the men. "Do you see this? You've seen it hundreds of times. That's how we know a prisoner has died during the night. They always bleed water and blood from the heart when they've been dead for hours. He died right before the earthquake."

Hektor muttered, "So, our fearsome lion cringes at stabbing a dead man."

Overhearing the comment and desperate to save face, Lucius turned on him. The glazed look was gone. A silver fire had rekindled in the man's eyes. "Watch yourself, Hektor. I have killed others for much less."

Adas pulled a second wineskin from his knapsack filled with strong wine and herbs. He gestured at the older thief. "Octavean, give him some wine." Then Adas addressed Jamin in Hebrew, "When he's done, give your brother as much as he wants. It is potent wine. We will wait for it to take effect before we break their legs."

Jamin didn't try to hide his surprise. "You brought this wine for them, not yourself. Is it because Demas confessed?"

"No, they have already suffered enough."

The three legionaries were barely able to hide their scorn. They kept their expressions neutral only because of the possibility of punishment, but they saw the centurion's compassion as weakness. Lucius was beginning to understand the hatred Valentius had for Longinus.

Adas looked beyond his men and saw the agony of the women who stood clutching each other. They made him think again of his own mother. His last two letters to her had gone unanswered, yet nothing came from his father warning him of accident or illness. It was possible her letters were lost en route. He needed to be patient. Despite his self-assurances, his stomach twisted with a sudden knowledge that he would never see her again. All the ways he could be killed paraded through his mind. Lucius's belligerent behavior could be based on orders from someone else, which meant he had a more powerful enemy. Life was unpredictable. His own men could turn on him and it wouldn't matter if they were executed. He would be dead.

Chapter 4

———— ✺ ————

Adas reached for the cord he always wore around his neck under his tunic. The cord was attached to a pouch that carried a treasure virtually beyond price. It was a pearl, the most costly gemstone in the world. Adas believed the pearl was a miracle in itself. After attending to an official errand in Jericho, Adas came upon several men beating an old Hebrew man on the outskirts of town. He ran his horse into the melee, forcing the attackers to flee in different directions. The old man, beaten about the head and chest, was seriously wounded, but conscious. Adas put him on his horse and took the man to his home. Despite being against Jewish law, the old man invited Adas, a Gentile, into his home. The servants attended to the man's wounds, propped him up in bed, and brought wine to both men.

The room was furnished in a comfortable but simple manner. There were several wood and reed chairs set against a wall. The bed was a plain wooden frame with the usual leather straps to support the wool-stuffed linen mattress. The walls were white-washed adobe with no tapestries or decorations. The ceramic tiled floor, however, was extravagant with bright colors and geometric shapes inlayed in a complicated pattern. The old man gestured to a chair and invited Adas to sit.

"Thank you for staying. You must rest after your walk. I never thought I'd see a Roman give up his horse for a Jew. I'm surprised you are alone. Where are your squads?"

"My commander did not deem a squad necessary even though it is protocol."

"He must have great confidence in your survival skills."

"I doubt that was the reason. If I had a squad, we could have caught those men."

"I leave them to God. No unconfessed sin goes unpunished. I wanted you to stay so I could tell you a story, but first, please tell me your name."

"My name is Centurion Clovius Longinus. I use Adas as my *praenomen*."

"Interesting. Your *praenomen* is a Hebrew name, and your Hebrew is excellent. That is most unusual for a Roman, as is the color of your eyes."

"I've heard."

"May I ask if your mother is Hebrew?"

"No, she isn't. My nanny taught me Hebrew."

"Ah, you're an interesting enigma. Now, let me tell you my story. Once, a great rabbi came to Jericho. I wanted more than anything to see him. Being a tax collector, I did not fool myself into thinking this great man would want to speak with me. So I planned to catch a glimpse of him as he passed by. I climbed a sycamore tree and waited. When I saw him approaching, I was surprised. He was plainly dressed and looked quite average. Perhaps, I expected a king wearing purple and gold. He was about to pass by, but stopped, looked up into the tree, and called my name. He said, *'Hurry and come down, for today I must remain at your house.'* I was so happy, I did make haste, and I nearly fell out of the tree. We talked for many hours. This great rabbi spoke of things I had never imagined. He began to tell me about the kingdom of heaven, how it is more precious than anything. Wanting to impress him, I showed him a precious treasure of mine." The old man coughed. When he lowered his hand, there were spots of blood on his palm.

"Sir, the thieves have broken your ribs. You should rest. Maybe I should be on my way."

"No! You must stay." He pointed to a chair by the wall. "Please, bring me my robe. Yes, the one I was wearing when the robbers attacked me." Adas retrieved the dusty garment and handed it to him. He ran his hand along the hem. "Please, cut the cloth here."

Adas felt a lump inside the hem. When he cut the cloth open, he gasped at the object that rolled out into his hand. It was a pearl of such unique beauty that Adas thought he must be dreaming. It was large, the size of his thumbnail, and a perfect sphere, the rarest shape for a pearl. The color of the gem was a radiant soft blue. He held it up and slowly turned it between his fingers. The opalescent glow of the gem danced in the light. It seemed to be a magical thing. For a moment, Adas wanted to squeeze his hand shut, and never let go. He reluctantly handed the pearl to its owner.

"It is told," said the old man, "that Cleopatra made a bet with Marc Antony that she could serve him a ten million *sesterces* dinner. She won the bet when she dropped a pearl earring in a glass of wine and drank it. This pearl is exceedingly beautiful and the rarest color. It is worth much, much more than Cleopatra's earring. I told the rabbi I sold my entire fleet of ships and cargo, everything I owned, just to buy this pearl. That is how desperately I wanted it. Of course, I no longer had a means of support so I took the job of collecting the taxes here in Jericho. Collecting taxes is a miserable job, but I made a grand profit of it. I had again become a rich man. I thought my wealth would impress the rabbi." He coughed and his face paled. Adas rose to get one of the servants.

"No. I am fine. Please stay." He was obviously not fine, but Adas sat down. "When I showed the great rabbi the pearl, he barely glanced at it, a gem worth more than my own life. Instead, he said 'The kingdom of heaven is like a merchant seeking pearls, who, when he had found one pearl of great price, sold everything he owned and bought it. The pearl is the kingdom of heaven.' After talking with the rabbi, I promised to return four times over what I had overtaxed the people. I asked if I could travel with him."

The old man took a sip of wine. "The rabbi said the job of collecting taxes is necessary and not evil, if done honestly. He said if I did the job with honor, then he would stay with me in my heart. I offered to sell the pearl and give the entire fortune to the poor. I was very surprised when he said to keep it, and that one day I would know what to do with it. He was right."

The poor man's face was growing pale. There was a bluish tint to his lips. His injuries were slowly killing him. He held out the pearl. "Here, take it. I want you to have it. The rabbi told me I would know what to do. This is it. You must take it."

Too surprised to argue, Adas held out his hand. The old tax collector carefully placed the pearl in his palm. "Why would you give me this priceless treasure? You don't know me. You haven't even told me your name."

"Zacchaeus. My name is Zacchaeus. You saved me from the robbers which is the last thing they expected you to do. The looks on their faces was almost worth the beating." He tried to chuckle, but it only made him sputter. Adas knew the man was dying and decided to stay with Zacchaeus until he passed away.

"You are seriously injured, Zacchaeus. I think a broken rib has pierced your lung. I did not come to your aid in time."

"Yes, you did. You have proved yourself worthy of this gift. It is because of you I will die in the comfort of my own home—not where the birds would pick my bones. I have had a long life. I do not fear death. The pearl is yours. Remember my story." He closed his eyes. "I will rest now."

Adas wondered if he should refuse the gift since he felt he had done nothing to deserve it. Then it occurred to him that no one truly *deserved* such a treasure, but could only accept it. "I don't know what to say. I thank you, Zacchaeus, but mere words are so inadequate. I will always remember your story." He held the pearl up to the light again, marveling at its shimmering loveliness. "The rabbi you spoke of—what was his name?"

"Yeshua. He fulfills the great prophesy foretold to us. He is the Messiah."

The memory of that one sentence staggered Adas as if he'd been struck. Why had he not realized the great man who inspired Zacchaeus to embrace an honest life was this same man on the center cross? Adas peered into Yeshua's face. "What have I done?" Again, he felt for the pouch around his neck. Zacchaeus gave him a priceless gem in remembrance of Yeshua, the man he had just executed.

Lucius saw the look of misery cross the centurion's face and grinned with pleasure. With renewed confidence, he asked casually, "Do you still want me to break their legs for you, Centurion Longinus?" He again picked up the hammer.

Demas saw the soldier eyeing him. Terrible dread rose in his heart. He squeezed his eyes shut and held his breath, hoping he would black out before the crushing blow hit him. A soft puff of wind touched his body. He opened his eyes and sensed a fragrance he couldn't identify. Demas remembered what Yeshua said to him just a few days ago.

"Demas, you have repented of your sins and God has forgiven you, but you must face the consequences of the law you broke and submit to the authorities."

Demas was horrified. He thought confession alone would release him from his responsibilities. "Lord, they will crucify me. I will not be able to work in your ministry. Since John the Baptist is dead, shouldn't I help spread your message?"

"They will crucify you. You will suffer for a short time, but then you will live forever with God. Do not worry. Others will spread my message. Your belief in me will be part of the message. I tell you this truthfully, when the worst comes, you will feel no pain. I will be with you. Do you believe this?"

"Yes, Lord, you will save me from the cross."

"No, Demas, you will be crucified if you surrender yourself. King David committed adultery and murder. He repented and was forgiven by God, but the consequences of his sin remained. His first child with Bathsheba died. You have broken God's commandment, 'You shall not steal.' You have, like David, repented and been forgiven, but the consequences of your deeds in this world still remain as they did for David. When you stole, you knew what the penalty would be. If you turn yourself in, when you face The Judgment, your penalty will already be paid and your sins forgiven. The choice is yours."

As this memory played through Demas's mind, the pain faded. There were two brief moments of vague pressure against his legs. His body slumped down the center beam of the cross, but he felt no discomfort. He heard the ropes around his wrists creak as they stretched under his full weight. He was aware of the nails driven through his hands, yet he felt no pain. There was only a sense of weightlessness. Demas looked about with an expression of joy and called out in Hebrew. Adas frowned in confusion at the statement, but it was sealed in his memory. Adas and his men stared in astonishment at how peacefully Demas accepted death.

Jamin cried out when he saw his brother was dead. An unbearable loneliness pressed upon him like a great weight. He dropped to his knees and buried his face in his hands. Overcome with grief, Jamin failed to notice how calmly Demas died. He only knew his brother was dead. John the Baptist was dead. Yeshua of Nazareth was dead. Jamin couldn't understand how their lives could end so disastrously, leaving him alone in a world of unending misery.

Chapter 5

Pontius Pilate, the fifth Roman prefect appointed to the Judean province, scanned the city from a window in Herod's Palace. He watched with relief as the activity of life, once again, was ordinary. The sun, which had regained its familiar brilliance, was edging toward the west. The Roman sighed with sorrow and satisfaction. He regretted sending Yeshua to his death, but he had satisfied the Jewish Sanhedrin.

Pontius despised the complicated Jewish religion. He had caused riots by displaying the Roman standards overlooking Solomon's Temple, and inside Herod's Palace. Pilate had raided the Temple treasury to pay for improvements to the aqueduct system that brought water to Herod's Palace, which brought the province to the brink of revolt. The governor turned his Roman soldiers loose on the protesters who were massacred. Every offensive act stirred up protests, costing Emperor Tiberius resources and manpower. Finally, Tiberius issued an ultimatum—one more riot and Pilate would be exiled.

Pontius was pleased with the frustration his last order caused the Sanhedrin. The crimes were posted over the heads of every crucified criminal as a lesson to would-be offenders. Instead of posting blasphemy as the crime, Pontius ordered an inscription proclaiming Yeshua "King of the Jews." Yet, it wasn't only to exert his authority; it was because of Yeshua's response when the governor asked him, "What is truth?"

Yeshua answered, *"I am the Truth."* For a moment, Pontius believed him.

Every Passover, a convicted criminal would be released to the people. Pontius offered Yeshua, but the crowd wanted Barabbas, a depraved man, who had instigated a revolt causing many deaths. Pontius chaffed at releasing Barabbas. The riot he had led was the "final straw" for Emperor Tiberius. However, Pontius gave into the demands of the crowd, freed Barabbas, and sentenced Yeshua to death by crucifixion. The crowd quickly dispersed. Pontius was left alone with regret, which gave over to gnawing anxiety when the impossible darkness lasted for hours. During the earthquake,

Pontius feared he had made a terrible mistake. When the shaking stopped, and the sun shone once again, he dismissed his panic as momentary hysteria.

A voice pulled him back to the present. "Your Excellency," said his personal attendant, "there is a council member from the Sanhedrin who wishes to speak with you."

Pontius waved a hand of dismissal, but changed his mind. "Take him into my library."

The man's name was Joseph, from the town of Arimathea. Pilate gestured at a chair. "Please, sit down. Joseph of Arimathea, one of the richest men in Judea. I've heard you own every tin mine in the province. What can I do for you?"

"Governor Pilate, I ask for the body of the man named Yeshua who has been crucified. I wish to bury him according to our customs."

"If you are willing to bury him, why didn't you defend him?"

Joseph did not care to satisfy Pilate's curiosity. "My actions are irrelevant to my request. Will you release his body to me for burial?"

"Perhaps you should wait until he is dead."

"He is already dead."

"So quickly?" Pontius curled a lip. "I doubt that." He called for his servant. "Bring the centurion in charge of the Nazarene's crucifixion." Pilate studied Joseph. "Why do you pay him this honor? Your own people demanded his execution."

"I did not side with my brethren on this matter. I saw the miracles Yeshua did. No one could do these things unless he was from God."

"If so, why would God let him die like a slave?"

"I don't have all the answers. Yet that does not stop him from being God's servant. It is not for us to question the actions of God."

"I have heard some say that this Yeshua was your long foretold Messiah. Haven't you had countless men claim the same thing?"

Joseph explained how the age-old prophesies concerning the Messiah had occurred this day. Many of these events were out of human control, especially for Yeshua. There were many more prophecies Joseph described in detail, thinking Pilate's lack of interruption was a sign of interest. In reality, Pilate was thinking how he might discuss these issues with Herod, hoping to bond with the ruler. One always needed allies, especially when in disfavor with the emperor.

When Adas appeared in the doorway, the governor shook his head impatiently. "Whoever he was, it is done and I washed my hands of it. Centurion, tell me the condition of the crucified Nazarene."

"Your Excellency, the man called out, '*It is finished,*' and immediately died. Then the earth shook. He has been dead for some time."

"How would you know what the Nazarene said? Surely, he spoke in Hebrew."

"I am fluent in Hebrew, Your Excellency."

"Leave us." Pilate gestured impatiently. "Return to your post."

"Your Excellency," said Joseph, "When Yeshua died, the earth shook. I am told that when the earth shook, the veil which separates the people from the Most Holy Place in the Temple ripped apart from the top, where no man can reach."

"Isn't the veil as thick as a man's fist? How did it rip?"

"By the hand of God."

Pontius gave Joseph a surly glare. "Take the body. Do with it as you please."

Joseph expressed his gratitude and left. Hurrying out of the palace, he found Nicodemus, his fellow councilman. Together, laden with oils and spices, they went to Golgotha. They greeted John and the women who had been huddled on the ground.

"Come on," Adas said to his men. "We'll wait over there," he tilted his head over his shoulder, "and let them take care of their dead."

The soldiers moved off, but kept watch. John spoke to Joseph and Nicodemus as he glanced at Adas. Joseph looked at Adas and nodded. Adas acknowledged the gesture.

Joseph turned his attention to the mother of Yeshua. "My dear woman, with your permission, I will prepare your Son for burial. I own an unused tomb in the garden. May I bury him there?" Mary thanked him.

John and the two councilmen took Yeshua down, wrapped his body in strips of linen, and spices, and carried him to the garden nearby. It required all three of them to roll the stone to seal the tomb. Mary Magdalene followed behind to see the tomb's location. She and the other women planned to anoint the body with oils after the Sabbath. Moving the heavy stone would be a problem, but they prayed that God would provide help.

Mary Magdalene thanked Nicodemus and Joseph, and returned to Yeshua's mother. Mary helped the grieving woman to her feet. She moved slowly for every joint of her body ached with sorrow. Nicodemus and Joseph offered to escort the women to their homes.

Jamin didn't have enough money to buy spices, but he had linen for his brother's burial. He asked John if he would help take Demas down. Jamin was glad he had not vented his anger against Yeshua, since he needed John's help. They removed the body from the cross.

"Jamin, I will help you carry him to the field," John offered.

Before they left, Jamin saw there was no one to remove the other thief. He glanced at the centurion and back at the man hanging from his cross. Jamin asked John to wait and approached the soldiers as they gathered their gear.

"Sir, there is no one for the other man. After I bury my brother, I will come back. Is there anyone to help?"

"No need," answered Adas, "I will see to the other man." Jamin thanked him.

"Octavean, you and Falto take that man down. Hektor, go tell two guards in the south tower to report to me." The three legionaries obeyed. Since Golgotha could be seen from the watch towers of the Antonia, Hektor didn't have far to go. Within minutes the guards appeared.

"Take the body to the potter's field." Adas gave one of the soldiers a copper *dupondius*. "Make sure the attendant buries him properly." Lucius and Falto helped the two soldiers remove the body. The two soldiers left, carrying the dead man between them.

"Sir, who will pay for his burial?" asked Jamin.

"It has been provided," Adas said. "No one will see his decay." He turned away as the three legionaries joined him. Together they walked the short distance to the garden.

Jamin and John carried the body of Demas to the burial field. Jamin watched as Demas was properly buried. Jamin turned to John. "Demas said something just before he died, but I could not hear him. Could you?"

"No, but the big legionary and the centurion were close enough to hear. Of course, Demas spoke in Hebrew, so you'll probably never know."

"The centurion speaks Hebrew."

"Then he would have heard every word, even what Yeshua said."

"I wish I could talk to him without the other soldiers around."

John gazed off into the distance. "You know when my Lord died, I couldn't. . .I couldn't believe he was really gone. I was so sure he was the Messiah. Did you hear what the centurion said? I thought my ears were playing tricks on me."

"Yes, I heard him, too. He said Yeshua must be the Son of God. Why would a Roman say that about someone he had just executed? But he is not a typical Roman. He was respectful."

"I noticed that as well. I told Joseph and Nicodemus."

Back inside the city they parted ways. Jamin returned to Cleopas's house. He climbed onto the roof and sat on his mat. He curled his knees up to his chin, folded his arms around his shins, and sobbed. Jamin cried aloud, "God, why do you hate me? Why do you turn your face from me? You let the Romans kill my whole family. You let me believe in. . .in a dead man. Why don't you kill me, too?" There was only silence.

Beyond grief, Jamin contemplated a yellow glow in the darkening sky. The rising moon was huge against the background of squat houses terracing the hillsides. Slowly, it rose higher, shrinking as it changed to a brilliant white. Jamin shivered in spite of the warm evening. His family was dead. His faith was dead. His hope was dead. Jamin wanted to be just as dead.

Across the city, the chief priests entered Herod's Palace to beg Pilate for a favor.

"Governor, the Nazarene claimed he would live again on the third day. We request that you order a guard for the tomb so his disciples cannot steal the body."

Pilate grunted with disdain. "You have your own security guards. Superstition is not a concern of the Roman Empire. What do we care if your gullible people believe a dead man lives? *You have a guard; go your way, make it as secure as you know how.*"

They left, grumbling among themselves. A chief priest said, "It may be too late already. They could have carried the body off without burying it."

"Yes, that is possible," agreed Joseph Caiaphas. "Perhaps we should see the tomb for ourselves. We know where they took the body. If his followers have already hidden it, then we will accuse Pilate for allowing this deception."

Caiaphas and the others took the road to the old quarry, now converted into a burial garden. At the gate, they were surprised to find a squad of Roman soldiers standing guard. They glanced at each other, puzzled, but decided to ask no questions. Perhaps someone at the Antonia assigned the soldiers to guard the tomb, even though Pilate refused. The chief priests didn't care why the soldiers were there. They smiled with relief and turned away.

Chapter 6

⎯⎯⎯⎯⎯ ∞ ⎯⎯⎯⎯⎯

It was the morning after the High Sabbath. Jamin was startled awake by the crash of a wooden keg onto stone pavement, followed by the loud cursing of several voices. Jamin lay on his mat, staring at the sky. On Cleopas' roof, he felt safe during the night, where no wild animals could attack or thieves plunder. But it was awkward being around Cleopas and his wife, considering they believed in Yeshua, even to the end. He was grateful Cleopas employed him, but he couldn't bear another day in Jerusalem. In fact, he couldn't bear another day of life.

He rolled up his pallet and stuffed it in his knapsack. It would be a nice donation to a street beggar. The sky was just beginning to lighten as the sun embraced the horizon. Jamin could see a few wind-teased clouds in the east. There was a gentle breeze, free of dust and the smoke of cookfires. This was once Jamin's favorite time of day. Not a time of darkness with its many dangers, nor midday with the bustle of people, but a time in between when dreams were recalled and plans were a possibility.

Jamin lowered the ladder and crept down. He paused in front of the house to adjust his knapsack when he heard someone walking from around the street corner. It was Cleopas.

"Jamin!" Cleopas called out, seeing the knapsack. "This is how you repay my hospitality? Leaving without a farewell? How can you do this to Mary, especially now? She has witnessed the death of Yeshua and your brother. She would be so hurt if you left without saying good-bye. Please, come inside. We need to discuss something with you."

Cleopas' hurt expression made Jamin pause. "I'm sorry. I didn't want to disturb anyone and you and Mary have already done so much for me, but I must be going."

"Why? Mary and I wish you would stay here permanently. I will promote you to apprentice and full pay." He glanced at the knapsack. "So where are you going?"

"Somewhere—away from here. But thank you for the offer. It is most generous."

"Why don't you stay for breakfast, then perhaps I can help you get out of Jerusalem for a few days? I must go to Emmaus and I need a traveling companion. Mary wants me to invite her cousin's family to visit since they could not come for Passover. Besides, I have some interesting news I'd like to share with you when you're ready to hear it. Will you go with me?" Jamin could not refuse. Cleopas and Mary had treated him and Demas like sons.

In another part of the city, a small group of women carrying spices and oils were walking to the tomb of Yeshua. Even though it was a beautiful morning with a soft breeze and the trill of songbirds among the terebinth trees, the women were unaware of the beauty. They could only concentrate on the task at hand. To the east, the budding sunrise was majestic as rays of light radiated through air-brushed clouds. The colors of the clouds changed from ruby red to vermilion pink edged with citrine. But the women kept their eyes on the ground. They discussed what to do if they could not move the stone sealing the tomb. Grief clutched at their hearts, but they were determined to finish this last task. They walked past Golgotha with bowed heads.

As they approached the garden, they could see the tamarisk and terebinth trees that bordered the garden walls on three sides. The abandoned hillside quarry made up the fourth side and held the numerous caves which had been sold as tombs. A stone arch served as the gateway into the garden. The tombs and the arch faced the east. When they entered the garden, they saw four Roman soldiers guarding the tomb. Adas saw them approaching and was about to hail them when the earth gave a violent jolt and began to shake.

Alarmed, the women cried out. They tried to keep their balance without dropping their precious burial spices and perfumes. A man clothed in brilliant white with a radiant appearance suddenly stood before the tomb. Without a word, he looked at the soldiers, and they collapsed to the ground.

Mary Magdalene dropped to her knees in fear. "It is the angel of the Lord!" she cried. "Cover your eyes!"

The angel grasped the heavy stone with both hands. With no effort, he broke the stone away from the concrete seal, and rolled it away. With a gentle voice, the angel said to the women, *"Do not be afraid, for I know you seek Jesus, who was crucified. He is not here; He has risen, just as He said. Come and see the place where He lay. Then go quickly and tell His disciples this message, 'He has risen from the dead and is going ahead of you into Galilee. There you will see Him.'"* The angel bent down and stepped inside the tomb. The women followed. He sat down where Yeshua's body had been and gestured with his hand. *"He has risen! He is not here."*

Trembling and bewildered, the women hurried out of the tomb. They ran through the garden without a backward glance. Out of breath and shaking, the elder Mary called to the others to stop. "What does this mean?" she cried.

"We must tell the others," said Mary Magdalene. "But I know they won't believe us."

"My sons are with Peter at John Mark's house," Salome declared. "They must be told."

They hurried to the house. When John opened the door, Mary blurted, "They have taken the Lord out of the tomb, and we don't know where they have put him!"

Peter and John questioned the women for details, but everyone was talking at once. "John, let us see for ourselves!" said Peter. They ran from the house.

The women followed, but could not keep pace. John had outdistanced Peter when he passed through the east gate. When the women caught up, John and Peter were standing outside of the tomb, talking and gesturing. No one else was there, not even the soldiers. Fearfully, the women approached the open tomb and Joanna stepped inside. Mary Magdalene followed her and set her knapsack down near the burial linen. For the second time, Mary saw no one was there. The strips of burial linen were lying on the ledge outcrop and the burial face cloth was neatly folded nearby. The two women stepped outside and joined the others.

Peter said, "Come, we must tell the others." John and Peter left the garden.

Salome spoke first, "Where did they take him? Why would the soldiers do this?"

"They didn't," said Mary Magdalene. "Remember how they fell as if dead when the angel appeared? They were still there when we left. They didn't take our Lord's body because the tomb was still sealed and they did not seal an empty tomb! I saw with my own eyes." Not knowing what else to do, the women turned to leave once more. At the top of the rise, Mary Magdalene remembered she left her knapsack in the tomb.

Alone, Mary approached the tomb for the third time. Overcome with grief, she buried her face in her hands and sobbed. Her slender shoulders shook with the wrenching grief for the man who had cured her and taught her the compassion of God. Still weeping, she stepped into the tomb to retrieve her knapsack. Two angels dressed in white were seated where Yeshua's body had been.

"Woman, why are you crying?" they asked her.

Too absorbed in her grief, Mary dismissed their startling appearance and didn't question their presence in the tomb. "They have taken my Lord away. I don't know where they have put him." She closed her eyes and wiped away her tears. When she opened her eyes, the angels were gone, but no one had pushed past her in the narrow entrance of the tomb. Mystified, she stepped outside, scanned the garden, but didn't see them. She saw a man walking down the garden path, but he was not one of the men who had spoken to her.

"*Woman,*" he said, "*why are you weeping? Whom are you seeking?*"

Thinking he was the man hired to tend the garden, Mary said, "*Sir, if You have carried Him away, tell me where you have laid Him, and I will take Him away.*" The man didn't answer. Mary thought he must not have heard her, when she noticed the outline of his face, the kindness in his voice, and the depth of compassionate in his eyes. Desperately afraid to believe what her senses were telling her, she turned to run.

"*Mary!*" The man called to her.

Impossibly, the man standing before her was Yeshua, alive and healed. *"Rabboni!"* she cried out, and fell to the ground sobbing, but this time with pure, awestruck joy. She struggled to her feet and reached for him. He raised a cautioning hand and stepped back.

"Do not cling to Me, for I have not yet ascended to My Father; but go to My brethren and say to them, 'I am ascending to My Father and your Father, and to My God and your God." Overcome with joy, Mary hurried from the garden to carry the message.

She ran to the top of the rise and called out to the others. "Come back! Come back! Yeshua is here! He is standing right there!" she pointed back toward the tomb. They ran back, but no one was there.

"Mary, you have been deceived by grief," said Joanna, not even bothering to look around. "No one is here. You saw him die the same as the rest of us,"

From behind them, a voice called out, "I am here." They whirled around, and overcome with awe, they fell at Yeshua's feet. They cried with praise to God for returning him to them.

After her friends ran to tell the others, Mary Magdalene withdrew one of the perfume bottles from her knapsack. She smiled at Yeshua. "You are alive just as you told us." She looked down at the bottle. "What shall I do with these?" When she raised her head, he was gone. With the sweetest joy she had ever known, she closed her eyes and savored the moment. Then she hurried to join the others.

Chapter 7

Early Sunday morning, Adas and his men were eating a light breakfast as they stood guard. The brilliance of the sun burst through crystalline clouds stretching from the horizon to the zenith. Adas thought the rays of sun light looked like the tines on a tiara. He took in a deep lungful of the clean air. If only the whole day could be this peaceful. Lucius pulled some figs, a half loaf of bread, and a short stick from his knapsack. He stuck the stick in the ground, and drew a line in the sand along the shadow to mark the present time.

"I swear, if this wasn't our last day on this accursed assignment, I think I would desert this army," Lucius groused.

"Where would you go?" Hektor mumbled, not really caring if he got an answer.

Lucius started to speak, but saw Adas was close enough to hear. "Honestly, I would never desert. They crucify you if you get caught. But when I retire, I will go to the mountains of *Gaul*, to the land of my ancestors, far from war and killing. I will find a wife and build a house on the land I will take for my pension. I will build a cottage for my mother nearby and she would want for nothing. They even say it snows there in the mountains. They say lakes turn into ice in the winter. It becomes so solid you can run a horse across it. They say the ice is like rock. I've never seen water turn into rock."

Hektor was surprised at Lucius's uncharacteristic candor, but he thought it to be nonsense. "I don't believe such a thing can happen. I've never seen water turn into rock. Some people will believe anything."

Falto snorted with self-assurance. "It's just a myth. Any fool knows water cannot change. I've heard of snow and ice, but it doesn't come from water."

"What do you think snow and ice comes from, Weasel?" Lucius was annoyed that they would question his knowledge.

"Snow, if it exists, must be pieces of the clouds and ice is. . .I don't know what ice is. I've never seen it. It's just a word," declared Falto, absentmindedly picking his teeth.

"And why do you think there is such a word, *Weasel?*" He spat the nickname with contempt. "Many things exist we haven't seen. I've never seen Emperor Tiberius, but he certainly exists. I've never seen an *elephantus*. Who would believe a huge animal with a 'snake' for a nose could be real? But they are! Can you see the air? No? Then how do you know it exists? Is your skull empty? I see no evidence of a brain."

"Insult me all you want. I still say water cannot change."

"If water cannot change then what do you think steam, is?" Lucius shot back.

"Everyone knows steam is smoke. Don't be stupid."

Lucius started to get up, but Adas intervened. "How can *you* be so stupid, Falto? Of course ice and steam comes from water. Cold water turns to ice; hot water turns to steam. I can't believe you're even arguing about this. Now both of you—shut your mouths!"

Adas strode up the garden path to put some distance between himself and his men. It had been a long three days and he was desperate for some privacy. However, Lucius's break from his usual reticence was informative. Adas had been unaware Lucius's ancestors originated in Gaul, which explained his height, pale eyes, and aggressive temperament. The warriors of Gaul were feared for good reason.

Lucius eyed Weasel with contempt. He stood up and trod around Falto, "accidently" kicking his foot. Falto started to protest, but instead blinked into the man's menacing expression and shut his mouth. Falto could occasionally exhibit some good sense when it came to self-preservation.

A hush settled over the men, enabling Adas to think about the last few days. Fortunately, none of the expected riots had occurred. Adas made sure the tomb was well sealed. Volcanic ash and water made good cement. For two nights, nothing happened. No one came. The cement hardened. No one could possibly tamper with the tomb. Adas looked around at the sound of female voices. A group of Hebrew women carrying knapsacks were approaching. Adas stepped forward to confront them.

Abruptly, the earth shifted. Everyone tensed, trying to steady themselves. A man appeared before them dressed in brilliant white. His face glowed as if lit by an internal light. The four soldiers stared, mouths gaping open, eyes wide with terror. The man looked directly at Adas. In that instant, he knew the man was not of this world. Then there was nothing. Adas and the other three soldiers lay unconscious on the ground.

Adas opened his eyes and sat up. He had no idea how much time had elapsed, but he knew something phenomenal had happened. His men were lying on the ground. The women were gone. Seeing the tomb was open, he hurried inside. It was empty. There was a short track in the sand where the stone had been rolled. Next to the track were footprints of a single individual. The mysterious man had pulled the boulder from the seal, even though it weighed as much as ten men. Adas was numb with shock.

Lucius and the other two sat up, and tried to shake off their bewilderment. "Who was that man?" Lucius demanded. When he saw the tomb was open, he stumbled over to it. "By the gods, Valentius will have us executed for this! How can it be empty? The body was there when we sealed the tomb!"

Hektor and Falto looked inside. Hektor exclaimed, "How did this happen?"

"I don't know," said Adas. "None of this is possible, yet, it happened."

"It seems obvious to me," declared Lucius. "They stole the body!"

"Did you look in the tomb?" asked Adas. "The burial linens are there. They wouldn't take the wrappings off the body first, and then steal it."

"Maybe they did," Lucius said defiantly, "who can understand these people?"

Falto looked at the sun-dial stick. "*Ohe!* The shadow has barely moved!"

"That doesn't mean anything," said Lucius.

"Yes it does," said Adas. "We were unconscious only a few minutes. But go look at the burial linen. The wrappings are still in the shape of a body. The linen wasn't unwrapped; it was—*vacated*. All of this is *impossibilis!*"

"What have we done?" exclaimed Hektor. "Did we really kill a son of the gods? Perhaps the glowing man was Zeus, himself. He will come back and take revenge on us."

"No, I think the man was an angel of God," said Adas.

"This talk is useless," Lucius grumbled. "Pilate won't care about an angel or an earthquake! In fact, we don't need to tell Pilate anything. It's the Sanhedrin we need to inform. They were afraid the Nazarene's followers would steal the body. I say we turn this to our advantage."

"Are you forgetting who is in command here?" Adas demanded. "You don't make suggestions unless I ask for them."

"My mistake, Centurion, but Decurion Quintus told us Pilate does not want to be bothered with this matter any further. He said we are to go to the Sanhedrin if there is trouble. So what are your orders?"

"I agree Pilate won't care about an explanation. All he will care about is our failure. He will care very much about that."

Hektor pursed his lips. "Sir, why do we need to report anything to anyone? Why don't we just reseal the tomb? As far as we know, the women ran off and don't even know the body is gone. If we reseal the tomb, no one will know besides the four of us."

"I suppose we could," Adas admitted. "However, something extraordinary happened and our lies won't change that. I think if we cover this up, it will haunt. . ."

"*Ohe!*" cried Falto. He pointed toward the city gate. "Two men are coming! It's too late to re-seal the tomb! What do we do now?"

Lucius grabbed his gear. "I'm going to the Sanhedrin. If they want me to lie they're going to pay me."

Adas rounded on him. "Legionary Octavean, stand down! I'm going to report to Valentius and the three of you are going with me." At the centurion's order, Hektor and Falto picked up their gear and prepared to go.

"Do you want to risk punishment—*or worse?*" demanded Lucius. "Valentius could have us executed! He will start with you, Centurion!"

"You dare to challenge a direct order?" Adas's hand went to his dagger.

The legionary took hold of his sword, meeting Adas's anger with defiance. "Would I disobey a direct order from you? Maybe. However, I do not disobey orders from *Cohort* Centurion Valentius. He outranks you, Centurion. *All* the centurions at the Antonia outrank you."

Lucius turned and ran. Hektor and Falto glanced at each other, and then ran after Lucius. Adas would have shouted for them to stop, but he didn't want to alert the approaching strangers.

Two Hebrew men were almost to the garden entrance, and there could be more. There was nothing he could do about his men, and he was out of time. He grabbed his gear and dove behind a ground-sweeping tamarisk tree in a corner of the garden. He was well hidden behind its dense grey-green foliage, but he could still see the tomb.

Lucius and the other two ran from the garden and circled around behind. Safely out of sight, Hektor caught Lucius by the arm. "Octavean, you had better know what you're doing because we just signed our death warrants if Valentius betrays you."

Lucius shook the man's hand off. "I know what I'm doing. Valentius is desperate for revenge against the Longinus family. Believe me; he will cover for us against the centurion's accusations. For now, we need to tell our story to the Sanhedrin. They'll pay to cover this up. Falto are you with us?" Falto nodded. Lucius headed for the city gate. "Then let's go."

Hektor stopped Lucius again. "And tell them what, exactly?"

"The truth, of course! I can't think of a better story than what really happened. Can you?"

"Will they believe us?"

"They better not! If they do, there will be no need to bribe us. Do you really think they would admit they had their Messiah killed?"

"What if Pilate finds out?" asked Hektor, still not convinced.

"The Sanhedrin will cover for us because an investigation would spread the news faster than a rabble of gossips. The last thing the Sanhedrin wants is for Gentiles to claim this Nazarene is alive."

"What does being Gentile have to do with it?" Falto asked.

Lucius groaned in frustration. "Gentiles don't care who the Nazarene claimed to be. It doesn't matter to us. The people of Jerusalem will see us as impartial observers."

"*Ohe!* We don't have time for this, Weasel!" exclaimed Hektor, losing patience.

"No, we don't! Let's go!" ordered Lucius.

The men made their way to an area of the temple where Gentiles were permitted. They sent a boy to find Malchus, the chief servant of Joseph Caiaphas. Malchus was also a temple guard and known to some of the soldiers at the Antonia, including Lucius. When he came out to them, they demanded to see the high priest. Lucius was growing impatient when Malchus returned with Caiaphas. Lucius explained why they were there.

"Listen, it's quite simple. The body of your Messiah is gone. The tomb is open and empty and people have seen it. No telling how many more have seen it by now. We can help you for a decent price. You tell us what you want us to say, or we tell all of Jerusalem what I just told you. Decide quickly. Every hour that goes by, more people will know."

Caiaphas eyed Lucius with distaste. "Wait here. I must meet with the chief priests and elders." The two men walked away. The soldiers sat under an acacia tree to discuss what they would do with their new found wealth. Lucius set his "sun-dial" stick in the ground. "I give him an hour. If he's not back by then, we go to Valentius."

"If a squad doesn't arrest us first," muttered Hektor.

Inside the temple, a small group gathered to discuss the situation. Annas, father-in-law to the high priest said, "Those soldiers buried the body somewhere else to blackmail us."

"It doesn't matter. The body is missing," said Gamaliel, one of the high priests. "However, will they dare to tell this story knowing Governor Pilate will not be pleased? I think they're bluffing."

"What if they're not?" Caiaphas gestured impatiently. "We're in a dangerous position. The people will believe their story. I propose we pay them, but only once. Let's make sure they don't come back for more. We'll pay the soldiers to say the disciples stole the body. We tell them that if Pilate hears of it *and* they never ask for more money, we'll cover for them."

"I thought once Yeshua was dead, it would be over," said Annas. "Yet the blasphemer reaches out from the grave and torments us."

"You're being overly dramatic," chided Caiaphas. "Believe me, in a few weeks no one will even remember his name. You'll see."

They determined the amount of the bribe. Caiaphas took the money from the treasury and put it in a leather money belt. He gave it to Malchus along with instructions. Malchus slung the belt over his shoulder. It was heavy. The chief priests and elders were taking no chances. As he walked along the corridors of the temple, he touched his right ear. He slowed his steps, stopped, lowered his head, and cradled his right ear with the palm of his hand.

Only a few days before, Caiaphas sent Malchus with Judas Iscariot to arrest Yeshua. Because of Yeshua's popularity, they planned to arrest him at night. As the group of temple guards and officials came within sight of the Mount of Olives, Judas said, "The one I greet with a kiss is the man you want."

Malchus gave Judas a sidelong look. "Why are you doing this?"

"How can you ask such a question? He says he is the Son of God. He makes a mockery of the law when he heals on the Sabbath. It is God's will for this man to die. The prophets say the Messiah will be a priest forever in the order of Melchizedek. Yet we know Yeshua was born of Joseph and his wife Mary. Can a man be born of a woman, yet have existed forever?"

"The prophets also say the Christ comes from the seed of David and from the town of Bethlehem. So the Messiah must be born of a woman as God in human form. The Messiah will conquer the Romans and re-establish the kingdom of David. The prophet wrote, *'The government shall be upon his shoulder.'* Of course, we know Yeshua is from Nazareth."

"He is dangerous," Judas exclaimed. "He knows what you are thinking. *What!* Why do you look at me with condemnation?"

"Why do you look guilty? Are the rumors true? Did you steal money from the disciples?"

"You hypocrite!" Judas fired back. "What is the high priest paying you to do tonight?"

"He instructed me to arrest Yeshua for questioning. We do this at night only to protect the people from the Romans in case there is a riot."

"Can you be that foolish? Do you really not know of the three secret meetings when the death penalty for Yeshua and excommunication for his disciples was decided?"

"Impossible! No one can be sentenced without the accused being present before a quorum of the Sanhedrin."

"Your allegiance is commendable, but you are naive. I was in the meeting, just days ago. They have instructed witnesses to present against him. The Sanhedrin hopes to trap Yeshua into declaring himself the Messiah. It will be their proof he is a false prophet."

"Now I know you are lying. The Book of Moses states that no man can be condemned by his own confession, neither can the high priest pose as *both* accuser *and* judge to pass sentence. They only want to question him. Besides, only the Romans can execute a man. The Romans are not involved in this arrest."

"Then what are they doing here?" Judas pointed at four Roman legionnaires walking closely with a man they addressed as Tribune. The tribune looked as if he had been ill and malnourished. His face was thin with a waxy paleness, but his gaze was intense, almost feverish. Judas moved closer to listen, but the tribune's voice unnerved Malchus. The man kept touching the soldiers on an arm or shoulder, withdrawing his gnarled fingers too slowly.

The guards and officials reached the end of the path and entered the Mount of Olives. Judas walked up to the only one who was awake and greeted him with a kiss. Not waiting for the others, Malchus pushed Judas aside and reached for the Nazarene. Awakened by their approach, Simon Peter moved in front of Yeshua, brandishing a sword. Malchus didn't see the sword until it was too late. His ear was gone and he cried out in pain. He slapped his hand over the gaping wound. Staggering backward, he held the side of his head, trying to staunch the bleeding.

Yeshua stepped in front of Peter and said, *"Put your sword into the sheath. Shall I not drink the cup which My Father has given Me?"* Then Yeshua said to Malchus,

"Permit even this." Yeshua pulled Malchus' hand away from the wound and touched the side of his head. Instantly, the pain was gone. Astonished, Malchus felt for the wound, but there was none. There was an ear. He wiped at his face with his sleeve and felt for his ear again. It was as if it had never been severed.

Pushing aside the memory of the dramatic healing, Malchus thought about the bribe money he was about to hand over to Lucius and the others. For a moment, Malchus considered keeping the money and fleeing Jerusalem for good. He had no wife, since she had died giving birth to their first stillborn child. But Malchus knew he could not leave. Resigned to his fate, he followed his master's instructions. He always did.

Lucius watched Malchus approach. "What took so long? It's been an hour."

Malchus said nothing and handed the money over to them. All three of the men reached for it, but Lucius snatched it away. Malchus related the high priest's instructions. Lucius grinned at the threat of reprisal the Sanhedrin had tacked on to their deal. They started to leave.

"Wait! Why are there only three of you?" Malchus demanded. "Where is your centurion? Will he tell a different story?"

"Let him talk of angels and earthquakes. Let him tell the people an angel ripped the stone from its seal, and a dead man vanished from inside his burial linens? Doesn't that sound insane to you?"

Malchus watched them leave. For the first time, he wondered if their report was actually true. Octavean already had the bribe money. Why would he continue to describe such unbelievable detail? Why did he say that the centurion might report miraculous events, but have no interest in bribery? Malchus decided he had to find this centurion. He followed the three soldiers, hoping they would lead him to their commander. Malchus knew he was taking a huge risk, but his need to learn the truth was stronger than his fear.

Chapter 8

———— ⊙⊙⊙⊙ ————

Adas watched from behind the ground-sweeping tamarisk tree as the drama unfolded. The Hebrew men came and went. The women also came and went, but not before a man appeared who caused them to fall to the ground in shock, and then incredible joy. Adas wondered who the man could be. Then everyone was gone.

Adas waited, listening intently, but all was still. He sat down and ran the day's events through his mind, trying to make sense of it. He tried to remember everything his nanny had taught him about the Hebrews. He heard something and peered through the tree leaves. A man stepped in front of the tomb. He turned and looked directly at Adas. Seeing the intensity of the man's dark eyes, Adas instinctively moved his head back. He thought he was obscured by the dense foliage of the tree, but the stranger nodded once in greeting. A subtle upward curve to the corners of his mouth appeared. Adas saw welcome recognition in the stranger's eyes. The centurion stared, mesmerized by the depth of kindness in his expression.

The man was not one of the two Galileans who had inspected the tomb. This man was clothed in a white tunic and robe which draped from his broad shoulders to his sandaled feet. His dark hair flowed back from his rugged features, revealing a close cropped beard. He appeared to be in his mid-thirties. Adas thought he looked familiar, but something was different. It was like meeting a sick man, then seeing him the next day, completely cured. Yet Adas had no doubt the mysterious man knew him. The recognition in his eyes was undeniable. This was the same man whose presence shocked the women so dramatically. Why he had returned?

Without taking his gaze from Adas's face, the man nodded once more. Adas blinked and he was gone. Adas ran to the garden entrance and scanned the area, but no one was there. Hopefully, the man would return.

Adas went back in the garden and peeked into the tomb. It was still empty. He sat next to the rock that once sealed it and reviewed his options. Eventually, his thoughts circled back to Lucius's cryptic words concerning their commanding officer.

The legionary implied that their *cohors* commander, Centurion Valentius, had given orders that undermined Adas's authority. Octavean was insubordinate. Roman law required severe punishment or execution for insubordination. However, the law is only as good as the willingness to enforce it.

Deeply troubled, Adas wished he could discuss these matters with his former commander, Centurion Cornelius. He pulled a letter from his knapsack which he received only a few days ago.

Cornelius wrote,

"I have to tell you about Claudius Flavius Januarius, the centurion I introduced you to in Capernaum. He sent his servant, Andreas, to tell me Claudius was ill and not expected to live. I went to bid him farewell. He told me the most amazing story about this same servant. Andreas's entire family died during a plague and the boy had no one. Claudius hired him as a stable hand. He excelled and became Claudius' personal aide. He depended on the young man more and more as the years went by. Then Andreas became deathly ill, even paralyzed. The doctors tried everything, but nothing worked. Then a great Hebrew prophet and healer came to Capernaum and Claudius heard of it. Claudius heard many stories of how this man, sent by God, could cure all illnesses. So Claudius sent his Jewish friends to ask if the healer would cure Andreas. Then he reconsidered since it is improper for a Jew to enter the home of a Gentile, so Claudius went to the healer and said, "I am not worthy for you to enter my home. Say the word, and my servant will be healed." The Hebrew man praised my friend for his faith and said, "It is as you ask." Claudius hurried home and Andreas was completely healed that same hour.

We talked as much as Claudius was able and he told me many stories about the healer, Yeshua. I stayed with Claudius until he died and asked Andreas if he wanted to work for me in Caesarea and he accepted. Since then, I have tried to learn as much as I can about the Hebrew God. They say Yeshua is his son, in human form. Before Claudius died, I begged him to let me find Yeshua. Claudius refused, saying it was his time to die and was not afraid. His peaceful acceptance of death is what caused me to be even more curious.

When you come to Caesarea again, we can discuss this in more detail. Andreas is doing quite well now. He is my chief horse trainer at the garrison, since I have no one to take your place. Actually, no one will ever take your place in my heart since you are a son to me. Dulcibella sends her love. She has no eyes for any other man except you. One of my officers, a man named Gnaeus Flavius Ovidis, presented himself recently without an invitation. I was prepared to expel him from the premises, but my spirited daughter sent him on his way. I don't know what she told him, but he left hastily. He has since resigned his commission after the death of his father, and returned to Rome.

Dulcibella has kept busy since you left. She has me supervise her archery lessons. She studies her language lessons every day. She also studies with us when Philip, the evangelist, meets with us. She has learned as much as her mother could teach her about cooking and gardening. And most amazing to us, she has developed an acceptable skill with a sword. When she requested boxing lessons, we jokingly asked if she planned to enlist in my cohors as a bellatrix to fight along with my legionaries. She only gave us her sweet smile for an answer. Her little brothers enjoy being her sparring partners, and they have made a fun game of their "competitions." I look forward to seeing you again, Adas, as does the whole family.

Yeshua had miraculously cured the servant of a Gentile and asked nothing in return. This was the same man who inspired Zacchaeus to change his life after one afternoon's visit and motivated Demas to confess and turn himself in for execution. Adas realized why anxiety gripped his heart the day of the crucifixions. He had buried his knowledge of Yeshua in a pit of excuses. He told himself Yeshua was a common name, and the man to be crucified could not possibly be the same Yeshua who worked miracle after miracle. But a sickening surge of guilt swept over him. His participation in the crucifixion could never be rationalized.

Trying to relieve his guilt, Adas spoke Yeshua's words aloud. *"Father, forgive them."* It didn't help. The terrible deed was done and could not be undone. If only he could step back in time, he thought, but he knew thinking this way was useless. Adas dropped a hand to his dagger.

"I knew you were innocent," he thought to himself. "I killed you, anyway."

A voice within his head answered, "I still forgive you."

But it wasn't enough. He wanted to share the physical pain Yeshua suffered even if it was only a semblance of his agony. Adas wanted a permanent reminder to never again execute an innocent man. He grasped his dagger with his left hand and studied the blade. He tilted the dagger back and forth and watched the sunlight glint off the polished metal. He held his breath, clenched his teeth, and held up his right palm. Quickly before he lost his resolve, he cut a cross from fingers to wrist. Adas dropped the dagger and grasped his wrist. Emotional relief flooded over him as blood ran from his hand.

Adas thought of the nails in Yeshua's hands and feet driven by his orders. Adas had marveled at the strength of the man and his lack of fear. Even the other three soldiers exchanged astonished glances. Adas hoped if they had remained sober, they would never have mocked Yeshua as they did, especially Lucius. However, his own behavior tore at his heart the most.

Adas cut a long strip of linen from the hem of his tunic. He wrapped the linen tightly around his hand. He remembered being injured as a child and the gentle way his mother would bandage his wounds. Thinking of her made him think of the pearl. Adas pulled the pearl's pouch from under his tunic. Satisfied it was securely sealed, he prayed. "God of the Hebrews, you know why I have this pearl. I am not worthy to own it; therefore, I give it to you. I have heard you are the *Creator Spiritus* of all things. Since the earth belongs to you, I will put this pearl in the earth. If it is your will, I will take it up to pass it on as it was passed to me. For now, I am ashamed to even hold it in my hand."

Adas made sure he was still alone and slipped into the empty tomb. He dug a hole in the floor of the cave and put the pouch in it. Just for a second, he was tempted to take it back, but instead, he brushed dirt into the hole and pressed it in.

The sun was low in the west when Lucius and the other two reached the gate to the garden. They seemed very pleased with themselves and very drunk. They had been celebrating their new-found wealth over expensive wine in the company of women who sold their favors. Lucius paused at the entrance to the garden and fumbled in his knapsack. He found a vial, pulled the cork out with his teeth, and swallowed the contents. He steadied himself against the garden archway and threw the vial as far as he could. The ceramic container shattered against the rock.

"Lucius," implored Hektor, "do you still need the opium?"

"What does it matter to you?"

Hektor knew Lucius was even more dangerous if he had become an *opio addicta*. A man had tried to kill Hektor once over a vial of curative *gentiane*, thinking it was opium. They entered the garden and found Adas sleeping in the shade of the tamarisk tree.

"Well," snickered Falto, "The boy is curled up in his cloak like a bug in a cocoon. Why is he still here?" The drunken man laughed uncontrollably.

Lucius swatted him across the back of the head. Falto lurched forward, nearly falling. "Shut up, you imbecile!" Lucius hissed. "Let him sleep. I only came here to make sure the tomb is still open. We need to get back to the Antonia before he does." He tried to drink from a wine bottle, but tripped and fell over. The other two soldiers doubled over in raucous laughter.

The noise woke Adas. His hand automatically reached for the handle of his dagger when he saw the men. He scrambled to his feet and faced them. "You dare to return here. Do I need to remind you of the punishment for disobeying a direct order?"

Unknown to the soldiers, two men had taken a position among the rocky outcrops above the garden. Unseen, a third man approached from the lower slopes.

One of the two men spoke to his companion, "Are you sure you want to stay, Cleopas? You could have gone with the others to Bethany," Jamin whispered.

"No, Jamin, I know how important this is to you. I only wish we had approached the centurion before the soldiers showed up. Besides, you and I were blessed with Yeshua's presence twice today."

They watched as the centurion confronted the three inebriated soldiers. "You recognize them, don't you?" asked Cleopas. "They're the same ones who crucified Yeshua?"

47

"Yes, and it looks like the big legionary is still trying to pick a fight with the centurion. That legionary is going to get himself executed."

"Jamin, this is not good for your friend. He is outnumbered and he's already injured."

Lucius swayed on his feet as he shouted, "Punishment? I think not! After I tell Valentius how you helped the Nazarene's followers steal his body. You will suffer punishment, not us!"

Adas had underestimated the legionary's confidence in Valentius's protection. "You think your lies will succeed, Octavean?"

A cold smile crossed Lucius's face. "No, I don't *think* they will. I *know* they will. Your counterfeit status will not help you." Lucius threw down his knapsack and the wine bottle. He stared at the bandage on Adas's right hand. "Besides you're a bit— handicapped! Perhaps I should demonstrate how a fraudulent centurion does not equal three legionaries."

Lucius drew his sword. Alarmed at the challenge, Hektor stepped back. Lucius tried to circle Adas, but he stumbled. The wine had affected his judgment and his coordination.

Adas shifted his dagger to his right hand and held it as best he could. He drew his sword with his left hand, and waited for Lucius to attack first. Lucius knew he was in no shape to take on Adas in a swordfight. Even sober, his success would not be assured. The centurion was deadly quick. Hektor and Falto exchanged glances as they tried to decide what to do. Falto feared Lucius more than he feared the centurion. He pulled his dagger and held it behind his back. Hektor hesitated. Watching was quite another thing from participating. Then he thought of the money in his knapsack and what would happen to it if he sided with the centurion. But if he sided with Lucius, there would be no going back. Longinus would have to die, here and now.

Hektor made his decision and signaled to Falto to circle behind Adas. Even Falto understood the moment they should have sided with their commanding officer was long past. Valentius's protection would only go so far since he answered to Tribune Salvitto who protected no one from Roman justice. If Longinus got to Salvitto, they would be dead men. Reluctant to draw a weapon against a superior officer, Hektor picked up a rock.

From their hiding place, Jamin and Cleopas saw what was happening. The third observer had an even better view.

Hektor darted behind Adas just when Lucius lunged with his sword. Adas deflected Lucius's attack, but could not avoid the other two. He looked over his shoulder in time to dodge Falto's dagger, but from his safer distance, Hektor threw the rock. It hit Adas across the left temple. Dazed, but still on his feet, Adas shook his head, trying to clear bright popping lights from his vision. Adas turned in Falto's direction and brought the flat side of his sword down on his hand. Falto yelped with pain as he dropped his dagger. Trying to step back in retreat, Falto tripped and landed on his back. He crawled behind Lucius on all fours.

As Adas tried to keep all three men in sight, Hektor dodged to the side and snatched up another rock. Adas saw the motion of his arm and managed to duck in time, but the distraction gave Lucius a chance to knock Adas's sword out of the way with his own sword. Adas retaliated, bringing his sword crashing down on Lucius's sword. The legionary howled as pain shot down his arm from his previously dislocated shoulder forcing him to drop the weapon. Lucius was defenseless, but Adas shifted his grip and brought the flat of the blade down on Lucius's arm. Confused, Lucius realized the centurion was not using deadly force. Adas could have thrust the sword under Lucius's leather chest armor, killing him instantly.

Then Hektor grabbed Adas's left arm and forced it behind his back. Lucius hit Adas with his fist as hard as he could. Adas collapsed, hitting his head on a rock outcrop behind him. The double impact knocked him unconscious. His weapons dropped from his hands. Still on his hands and knees, Falto scrambled for his dagger. He raised the weapon, but Lucius grabbed Falto by the back of the neck and threw him on his back.

"What did you do that for?" Falto shouted.

"No, not with a dagger." Lucius panted. "I have a better idea."

As he stood staring down at the unconscious centurion, euphoria from the opium overcame him. Gratification crossed his face as he rubbed his fist. "How did that feel—boy!" Lucius gingerly touched his jaw, bruised by Adas's fist the day of the crucifixions. The permanently etched lines of anger in his face eased. "Looks like we won't need to cower behind Valentius's shield, after all." Lucius retrieved his sword.

Watching from the rocky outcrops, Jamin and Cleopas both gasped in horror. "We've got to do something," Jamin whispered. "If they kill him, I'll never know what Demas said." He started to move, but Cleopas pulled him back.

"No. Wait. Look! There's someone else hiding above the tombs, and he has a sword. He's moving."

Hektor watched Lucius snatch up his knapsack and start for the garden gate. "Lucius, have you lost your mind? You can't leave now! You have to finish him off, or have you lost your nerve like you did when the Nazarene died? You couldn't even spear a dead man." Falto clumsily got to his feet and backed away, not sure who would take control.

Lucius rounded on Hektor. "What are you talking about? The only one who lost his nerve is this pathetic boy. He could have killed both of us just now! But we can't kill him with our weapons! We have to make this look like zealots attacked him."

Hektor doubtfully eyed Lucius. "Tell me. What happened at the crucifixions when you had the spear in your hands?"

"Longinus hit me for defying him."

"You weren't defiant. You were afraid, my friend."

Lucius's eyes closed to slits of icy silver. "Really? What do you think I was afraid of?" He grasped his dagger. "And I'm not your friend."

Hektor backed away. "What do I care, anyway?"

Lucius released his dagger. "Good answer, Hektor. You might live another day."

Hektor pointed at the unconscious centurion. "Well, we can't let *him* live another day."

"Don't worry. We won't. Hitting him with the rock gave me an idea. We stone him to death. We say Longinus sent us to buy food and when we returned, we found him dead, surrounded by rocks. It'll look like zealots killed our noble centurion so they could steal the Nazarene's body."

"You're smarter than you look, Lucius. I guess we'll need more rocks." He picked up the rock stained with Adas's blood and put it in his knapsack. "There's one," he laughed. "I'll show it to Valentius when we make our report. Come on, Weasel. Grab your knapsack."

"I'll stay here. Hurry! It'll get dark soon," called Lucius. The two soldiers left the garden. They headed north on the road, searching for fist-sized stones. Jamin and Cleopas saw the other observer moving among the outcrops. They decided to even the odds and follow the rock-hunting soldiers.

Lucius smirked as he knelt down. "So, Centurion Longinus, what do you have that I want?" He dismissed the fine metal armor. It would be too dangerous to have it in his possession. The sword and dagger were elegantly crafted and obviously expensive. He picked up Adas's dagger and admired the sharpness of the blade and the ornate handle. The dagger was adorned with the head of a wolf at the top of the handle, fashioned in brass. The eyes consisted of opaque golden amber. Heavily arched brows hooded the eyes and a downward tilted head gave the wolf an aggressive stare. The jaws were slightly apart and the lips were curled in a permanent snarl. The ears were turned to either side giving them a horn-like appearance. The handle was covered with leather to increase its comfort and efficiency. The blade was wide at the hilt, tapering down to a deadly point.

Lucius set the dagger down and disconnected the sheath from Adas's belt. The sheath was made of leather-covered wood decorated with an amber-eyed wolf head etched in a brass plate. There was an inscription etched in the plate under the wolf which read: "Son of the Father, Longinus." He slid the dagger into the sheath. Lucius knew his entire salary for several years would barely be enough to buy a weapon like this one.

Lucius picked up Adas's sword. The handle of the sword also boasted a wolf head. The amber eyes were larger, but gleamed with the same luster of sunlight-yellow flames, with one difference. At the center of each eye was an irregularly shaped black object. The shapes were each half of a small black beetle petrified in the amber. The pair of eyes came from the same piece of amber, cut in half. The distorted black pupils gave the golden eyes a malevolent appearance. The blade was highly polished, very sharp, and looked as if it had rarely clashed with another weapon or shield. Lucius reasoned that Adas must have little battlefield experience. He placed the sword on the palm of his hand. It was perfectly balanced. Rotating his wrist, he twirled the sword in figure eights. The blade sang with an undulating hum. Stabbing and slashing, Lucius reconsidered his initial assessment of Adas's battle experience. With a weapon like this, the enemy might not live long enough to defend himself.

Lucius set the sword down and unfastened the leather-covered scabbard from the centurion's belt. There was another inscription. It read: "Loyalty Above All. Son of the Father, Longinus."

Lucius thought of his own father and grimaced. Loyalty was a virtue he had never understood. It seemed others demanded it of him, but used it against him in the end. Everyone Lucius had ever trusted betrayed him, especially his own father. The legionary wondered what it was like, growing up in Rome as a pampered son of a high-ranking man of authority. Assuming *Consul* Longinus gave these extravagant weapons to his son, were they given to reward loyalty or to demand it?

The legionary returned the sword to the scabbard. He put both weapons in Adas's knapsack, and put it into his own knapsack. He pulled his own dagger from his belt and scrutinized it. The handle bore no ornamentation and the blade was dented and dull from long use. The simple wooden sheath was cracked down the front. His sword was in worse shape than the dagger. The sword had many previous owners before Lucius took it off a dead combatant.

Lucius felt as battered and cheap as his few possessions. All his life he worked to acquire just a morsel of security, but never succeeded. Then there were men like Longinus who were given all these things, with no effort. He looked down at Adas. The gash on his forehead had dried, but his hair was matted and the side of his face and neck was stained with blood.

Lucius remembered what the silk merchant whispered in his ear the day of the crucifixions. The stranger pointed out how the privileged centurion was given so much while the legionaries did the work for little pay and no respect. The man's words spurred an intense jealousy that coursed through Lucius's heart like venom. His heart rate increased. Sweat broke out on his forehead. The opium was fully digested now, enhancing his confidence. Lucius made a low growl as he grasped his dagger in his fist. He pressed the blade against the side of Adas's throat. A narrow cut, just under the jaw, from ear to chin, appeared beneath the blade. Lucius could hear his own breath coming faster. His mouth went dry. His hand grew sweaty, and stinging sweat dripped in his eyes. Temptation crept into his heart as if it were a living thing. Clenching his teeth, Lucius tried to press the dagger deeper but his mind and heart were locked in a stalemate of indecision. His heart sought the gratification of a death believed to be justified, but his mind resisted, fearing the consequences of punishment.

Lucius remembered what Adas said the day of the crucifixions. "*I know you are not a coward. Don't pretend to be one.*" His hand shook as he tightened his grip on the dagger. His fingernails bite into the palm of his hand. Valentius's instructions sprang into his mind. "Watch him, but do not take action. I want Longinus for myself."

Lucius plunged the dagger into the ground inches from the centurion's head. He cursed himself for his lack of resolve. He snatched his dagger from the ground and returned it to the sheath. He tried to tell himself a slashed throat would not be consistent with death by stoning. Valentius would know what he had done and have him executed.

Lucius sat cross-legged and stared at the unconscious man. If he could not take the centurion's life, at least he would take everything else. Lucius knew most centurions wore an amulet of precious stone around their necks with the engraved name of their favorite god or goddess. Engraved crystals of sapphire, garnet, or ruby were highly prized. Lucius pulled on the front of Adas's body armor and tunic, searching for a leather cord. There was none. Frustrated, he cursed aloud. Lucius looked at Adas's seal ring on his bandaged right hand. The carved crest of the ring was an amber wolf's head with the letters ACL above the head. Since the seal ring was used to stamp authorization on documents, the wolf's head was the centurion's official "signature." Again, this item would be impossible to sell without being traced back to the centurion. Lucius detached the coin pouch all soldiers carried on their belts. He shook its contents into his hand. There were a few copper *dupondii* and a smooth green and blue nugget of eilat stone. He threw the items in the dirt. Wanting to exert some semblance of domination, Lucius got up and pulled on the front of Adas's armor, slightly raising his head. Lucius pulled his fist back.

The unmistakable sliding sound of a sword leaving its scabbard gave Lucius pause. A sharp point pressed into the base of his neck. "If you hit him, I will split your back." Lucius recognized the baritone voice immediately. The Roman lowered his fist, let go of the centurion's armor and tried to straighten up. The point of the sword bit into his skin. "I will tell you when you can move, Octavean."

"Malchus! What are you doing here? How dare you put a sword on me! You will be crucified for this." He slowly moved his right hand toward his dagger.

"Touch that dagger and I'll kill you. What happens to me will be irrelevant since you'll be dead. Now put your hands on your head and face me. *Now!*"

Instead, Lucius whirled around, grabbed his dagger, and lashed out. In his drunkenness, he fell sideways on his knee. Malchus flicked his sword under the Roman's chin, pressing just enough to break the skin. Malchus stepped around Lucius as he turned the blade, keeping it against his throat. He stood between Lucius and Adas with a view of the arched gate. Malchus pressed harder with the sword. Lucius sucked air between clenched teeth. The sharp metal stung.

"Drop the dagger." Lucius spread his fingers out. The dagger dropped to the ground. "Now, get up. Put your left hand behind your back." Malchus grasped Lucius's left wrist and pulled up. "Now walk!" Lucius stepped forward, conscious of the increasing distance between himself and his weapons. Malchus pulled his sword away from Lucius's throat but kept his left arm twisted behind him. He pushed hard as he released Lucius's wrist. The legionary sprawled on the ground, but staggered to his feet and faced the temple guard.

Lucius wiped the back of his hand under his chin, smearing his blood. His face was crimson with rage. The veins in his neck protruded. His thick shoulders heaved as he panted, barely able to restrain himself. "I will have you arrested for this!"

"Do that! Caiaphas will explain to Pilate how Yeshua's followers paid you to steal the body, and then you extorted bribes from the Sanhedrin by threatening to report that Yeshua miraculously resurrected. What a clever scheme to play both sides against the other, and double your profits. Do you think Pilate will believe Caiaphas or you?"

"Why don't you kill the other two and take their share of the money!" Lucius said, trying to see over his shoulder. He wondered what was taking Falto and Hektor so long to return. He gestured at Adas. "Leave this one to me. If he lives, his testimony will get us all in trouble."

"It is for his testimony I protect him. He is why I am here. You said, 'Let him talk about angels and earthquakes.' Why would he tell such a story if it was a lie, yet not demand a bribe? Most curious, I think. As for you, you're drunk. I am not. I am armed. You are not. Leave now!"

Lucius knew retreat was his only option, especially since Falto and Hektor were nowhere in sight. Malchus stepped back and lowered his sword. Lucius grabbed his knapsack. He eyed his sword, but Malchus shook his head.

"This isn't over! You will pay for this," Lucius retreated along the garden path. At the gateway, he turned and shouted, "You want the centurion? You can have him! But some day, I'll have you on a cross just like your precious Messiah!" Lucius stumbled out of the garden.

Malchus shook his head. "You ignorant fool. The teaching of that 'precious Messiah' is what stopped me from killing you."

The moon had risen in the east even though the sun still hovered above the western horizon. Malchus knelt beside the unconscious Roman. "You'd better have some incredible answers or I have forfeited my life for nothing." He saw the coin pouch and picked it up. He retrieved the eilat stone, and the coins, and dropped them in the pouch. He reattached the pouch to the centurion's belt. Malchus heard footsteps and whirled around, sword in hand.

Jamin shouted, "*We mean you no harm!* I am Jamin and this is Cleopas. We're here to help you with—him."

"We have to hurry. The soldiers may return soon," said Cleopas. "And when they do, they will not be happy."

"We saw you hiding on the hilltop," Jamin said. "Why are you here?"

"My name is Malchus and I came here to find this one," He jerked his head at Adas. "I want to know what happened here today. The tomb is empty, and I think he knows why."

"We want to talk with him as well," said Jamin. "So let's get him out of here."

"Agreed. They will be shutting the city gates soon. The sun is almost set." Malchus took his robe off and threw it over Adas, hiding his armor. "Be watching. The other two soldiers may come back."

"I don't think so," said Cleopas. "They were really drunk and . . ."

". . . and they're resting right now," interrupted Jamin.

Malchus looked from one to the other. "What did you do?"

"Nothing—much," muttered Jamin.

Malchus grinned. "Come on, get his arms and I'll get his legs." They lifted Adas off the ground and started down the garden path.

"Where should we go?" asked Jamin. "I hope somewhere close. He's heavier than he looks. Our friend, Peter, is staying nearby. Surely, they will allow us to bring this Gentile into the house under the circumstances."

Malchus hesitated. "Do you mean Simon Peter, the fisherman?"

"Yes. You know him?"

"We've met. Perhaps it would be best if we go to my quarters instead. It's not far, either. And there's no one at the estate tonight." They left the garden and hurried along the road.

Chapter 9

⸺◦∞◦⸺

The temple guard led them to the estate of the high priest. Malchus lived in a small house in the back corner of the grounds. Jamin, Cleopas, and Malchus carried Adas into the limestone block house. It had a tile floor and two latticed windows too high to see through, but they could convey a breeze. The sparse furnishings included a single bed butted against the wall.

"Over here," Malchus instructed. "Put him on the bed." Malchus barred the door. He lit his oil lamps with an ember. The light gently waltzed with the shadows on the limestone walls.

Malchus carried a lamp over to the bedside table. "Jamin, there's water in the jug on the cabinet and bring the towels. Cleopas, get the jug of vinegar and the olive oil from the cabinet."

Jamin brought the water jug and cloths. "Should we take his armor off and what about his *caligae*? He looks too young to be a centurion. I thought the Romans were meticulous about granting titles."

"Perhaps not always," Malchus said. "Leave his *caligae*. He's not going to be here long enough to get comfortable. But we should get the armor off."

They discussed his hand injury, but decided to treat the head and neck wounds first. They unfastened the leather straps connecting the two metal plates of armor and set them on the floor.

"Cleopas hold a lamp on the other side of the bed," said Malchus. He tilted Adas's head and inspected the wounds. "Apparently, the rock tore this gash. It's a good thing it didn't hit his eye. There will be a lot of bruising but he'll live."

Malchus washed the blood from Adas's hair, face, and neck. He patted the wounds with a fresh cloth. "Cleopas put the cloth over his eye." Carefully, Malchus poured vinegar on the injury. Adas groaned as he clamped his teeth together.

"I should have put something between his teeth. This gash must be deeper than I thought. Hold the light here, Jamin." Malchus indicated the laceration under the jaw and poured vinegar on it. Adas made a low growl.

"He even sounds like a wolf," said Jamin. Malchus and Cleopas threw him puzzled looks. "When you see his eyes, you'll understand."

Adas moaned again. "He's trying to come around. That's a good sign."

"We should look at his hand," said Jamin. "This wound must be fresh." He carefully unwound the cloth. "These cuts are deep." Holding Adas's hand away from the bed, he poured water over the wound. He removed the seal ring and cleaned it. "Look at this. His seal is a wolf. That makes perfect sense."

Malchus frowned. "Why?"

"You'll see," said Jamin. He dried the ring off and put it back on Adas's hand. Malchus picked up a lamp and held it closer to the wound.

"It's a cross," said Cleopas, peering over Malchus's shoulder. "This wasn't an accident. Do you think the big soldier did this?"

"No," said Malchus. "When I realized the legionaries were heading for the garden, I took a short cut and got there just before they did. His hand was already bandaged. If they did this to him before they left, he wouldn't have still been there when they got back. Whoever did it, I'd like to know why." He took a small towel and folded it several times. Carefully, he worked the cloth between Adas's teeth. He picked up the jug of vinegar. "This stuff should stop the bleeding. Jamin, take hold of his fingers and thumb."

Malchus poured the acid on the cuts. Frowning, Adas groaned as he bit into the towel. His jaw muscles jumped with the effort.

Jamin carefully blotted the cuts with a fresh cloth. "We should let it air a little before we re-wrap it, but the bleeding has stopped. Take the towel out of his mouth. Vinegar burns like fire, but it doesn't last long, thankfully."

Malchus examined the cut under Adas's jaw more closely. "You know, this cut is odd. Octavean must have done it. I couldn't see them when I climbed down behind the quarry. When I came up behind Octavean, he was about to hit him with his fist, but his dagger was still in his belt. He could have easily killed him then. I wonder why he didn't." Malchus inspected the red discoloration along Adas's left cheekbone. He gently pressed the area. "It's not fractured."

"That Roman has fists like Goliath," said Cleopas. "Are you sure?"

"No, I can't be sure since we cannot see through flesh." Malchus said patiently. "He doesn't even know how close he came to death. It was fortunate we happened to be there."

"No, Malchus, this Roman did not survive because of good fortune. Cleopas and I were there specifically to find him. He's the only one who can tell me what Yeshua and my brother talked about during their crucifixion. Why do you want to talk to him?" Before Malchus could answer, Adas groaned and turned his head.

"Come on, before he wakes up," said Malchus. "Cut two more strips from his tunic. Let's cover these wounds." They covered the head and hand injuries with folded squares of clean cloth treated with olive oil. They wrapped linen strips to secure the bandages.

"Your brother and Yeshua must have spoken in Hebrew," Malchus pointed out.

"This soldier speaks Hebrew and he was close enough to hear."

Adas became aware of voices, and that he was lying on a bed. He did not recognize the voices. He felt a dull pain at the back of his head. He cautiously opened his eyes. Instinctively, he slapped a hand to his belt, but his dagger wasn't there. Three men were staring at him.

"Centurion, do not be afraid," Malchus said calmly. "You're safe here."

Adas saw they had no weapons, and had not moved. He knew if they meant to harm him, they would have done so already. "Where am I?" he asked in Latin.

Malchus whispered, "I see what you mean, Jamin—he has the eyes of a wolf." He addressed Adas, "You are in my home. We brought you here for your protection. We did not know if your men would return to finish you off. My friend says you speak Hebrew. That is unusual for a Roman soldier."

Adas tried to push up on his elbows, but the room swam around him. He dropped back on the bed and brought a hand to the back of his head. He could feel a knot under the skin. Adas answered in Hebrew. "I learned it as a child." He put a hand to his chest. "Did Octavean take my armor? Are we far from the Antonia? Did he take my weapons?"

"No, to the first two questions, and probably to the third. We are in my quarters on the estate of High Priest Joseph Caiaphas. Your armor is on the floor. Neither your weapons nor a knapsack were in sight," Malchus said. "You are safe here. My name is Malchus and this is Jamin and Cleopas. What is your name?"

Adas touched the bandage across his forehead. "Could I have some water?" Jamin held the jar and Malchus helped Adas sit up. He drank deeply and collapsed back on the bed. "My name is Clovius Longinus. My *praenomen* is Adas." The three men glanced at each other, surprised that the Roman had a Jewish *praenomen*. "I'm in your debt for stopping Octavean and bringing me here. Why would you take such a risk?"

"Jamin and I have questions you can answer," said Malchus.

"You heard what Yeshua and my brother talked about. I was too far away."

Malchus described the legionaries' plot to stone Adas to death. Jamin explained that he and Cleopas intervened with Hektor and Falto's rock collecting. Adas felt along his bruised cheekbone. "I remember how this happened." He touched the underside of his jaw. "I don't remember this."

"A cut from Octavean's dagger, no doubt. I couldn't see everything that happened. But I saw the other two leave. However, Octavean's dagger was in his belt when I confronted him. We can only guess why he didn't finish the job."

"I was stupid for staying there. I should have sent a patrol to arrest them."

Malchus nodded. "Yes, that would have been smart. Why didn't you?"

"This sounds irrational, even to me, but I saw someone in the garden. I was hoping he would come back." Adas suddenly clutched at the neck of his tunic as his eyes went wide with panic. "Oh, I forgot. I gave it back."

"Gave what back?" Malchus asked.

"It doesn't matter."

"You said you saw someone in the garden?" asked Jamin.

Adas described the man as best he could. "I can't quite place where I've seen him before. Behind the tree, I could only see his face. I'd swear he looked like . . . but that's not possible."

Cleopas and Jamin exchanged glances. Jamin declared, "We know who he is." Adas and Malchus waited for an answer.

Losing patience, Malchus demanded, "Well? Who is he?"

"The man you saw *is* Yeshua, the same man you crucified."

"*What?*" exclaimed Malchus. "You know that was just wishful thinking. Besides, the prophets have been silent four hundred years, ten generations. Why now?"

"God decided it was time," said Cleopas.

"If Yeshua is the Messiah, why did God let him be killed," demanded Malchus.

"For our forgiveness," said Jamin. "Yeshua, as God's Son fulfilled eternal atonement for all humanity. Remember when he said, '*Do not think that I have come to abolish the Law or the Prophets. I have not come to abolish, but to fulfill.*' Never again will the shedding of blood be required to pay the penalty for sin. We are witnesses to a new covenant."

"Why do you think it was Yeshua in the garden?" asked Malchus.

"Because we talked with him today—*twice*," said Cleopas emphatically. "He explained about the prophecies being fulfilled when he appeared with us on the road to Emmaus and again with the others when he appeared in a locked room. He took food with us. He is alive! Yeshua *is* the Messiah. Many followers have seen him. First, the women in our group and. . ."

"What women?" asked Adas. "The ones who stood by the Nazarene when he died?"

"The Nazarene has a name!" Cleopas snapped. "You had plenty of time to learn it while you were torturing him to death."

"Cleopas, it was God's will. If this man had not carried out the death sentence, someone else would have. It had to be done. You know this. Yeshua told us himself, today. It is not this man's fault."

"It feels like it was my fault. Cleopas, I did not mean to be disrespectful." He eyed the bandage on his hand. "I did have a choice. I could have refused the assignment. Somehow, I knew Yeshua was innocent of any crime."

"Innocence is exactly the point, Adas. Only Yeshua could fulfill the law because he was without sin," explained Jamin. "It is no coincidence you were in charge of his execution. You did something I believe will be retold down through the ages. You proclaimed that Yeshua is the Son of God. You were chosen, Adas, and you fulfilled your purpose. If God had not wanted you there, he would have chosen someone else. And I suspect God has other tasks for you."

"I hope you are correct. There is something some people may dismiss, but I will never forget. When Yeshua stated, *'It is finished,'* and immediately died, I knew I was witnessing something impossible. No man can make himself die simply by saying 'It's over.' Even with suicide, a man must run on his sword, or throw himself from a cliff. When you saw Yeshua, did he have fresh injuries?"

"No, he was completely healed" said Cleopas. "But there are marks left by the crucifixion nails in his hands and feet along with the wound in his side. Jamin and I saw them. When he showed us the side wound, we also saw the marks of the whip. There were so many."

Adas looked away, sickened at the thought. Jamin glanced at Adas's bandaged hand. "You did that to yourself, didn't you?" Adas nodded, but made no comment.

"In the fifth book of Moses," Malchus said, "God tells us to bind a sign on the hand to remember His commands. Centurion, you have bound a sign on your hand. What happened to make you do this?"

"I knew I executed an innocent man. Then, when I saw him today, I knew who he was, even though I told myself it was impossible. Yeshua didn't just look *at* me; he looked *into* me. I don't think I'll ever be the same. At least, I hope not. But there's so much more I want to know."

"We all have much to learn," said Malchus. "I have much to think about. For now, we will get you back to the Antonia, but first, tell us what happened this morning?"

Jamin held a palm up. "Wait, tell me something about Friday. After you and the other soldier argued, Yeshua said something. I couldn't hear. You looked shocked."

"He said, 'Forgive them, Father, they do not know what they are doing.' I still can't believe it."

"Tell us what you saw today," said Malchus. "Was it an angel?"

Adas told them what happened over the three days. He included how the silk merchant at the crucifixions accused him of murder. "To execute an innocent man *is* murder."

"It had to be done, Adas." Jamin remembered the skeletal man and shuddered. "You were an important part of God's plan, but the question is what are you going to do about it? Are you going to ruin your life with guilt or accept Yeshua's forgiveness?"

"Jamin is right," Cleopas agreed. "I was wrong to judge you. But now you have a choice. You can stay mired in guilt, which will make you useless to God, or you can become a better man. Learn Yeshua's teachings and live by his example."

"Who would teach me? Yeshua forgave me, but will his followers?"

"Do you think *we* never asked Yeshua for forgiveness?" said Jamin. "Every one of us has failed in some way. No one is without blame."

"I spied on Yeshua for Caiaphas," Malchus admitted. "I took part in his arrest. When we got to Gethsemane, I stepped in to arrest him and one of his disciples sliced off my ear with a sword. Yeshua put his hand over the wound and the pain was gone. I reached up and felt—my ear. It felt perfectly normal. I tried to tell myself I had imagined the whole thing, but my blood-stained clothes said otherwise. To instantly heal such an injury is not possible. That's when I lost all doubt. I was there to arrest him, but he looked at me with *forgiveness*. Yeshua is the Word, the Way, and the Truth."

Adas asked, "You said you have questions, Jamin."

Malchus held up a hand. "I have been selfish, wanting my questions answered and forgetting your situation. You must get back to the garrison, but you're in no condition to walk that far, even with our help. Is there a friend you can trust?"

"Yes, Decurion Cassius Sabinus Quintus."

"Does he ride a big, dark, bay horse?" Adas nodded. "I'll go get him."

"Listen, if Cassius hesitates, tell him, I promised I would check on Tigula, his mastiff. He's not eating well. Draco is the name of his horse."

"Good to know. I will be back shortly." He patted Jamin's shoulder. "Now it's your turn." He strode out the door and was gone.

"What do you need to know, Jamin?"

"I could not hear what Yeshua and Demas talked about for so long."

"Yeshua explained why he had to die. He also talked about the completion of the prophecies. Demas didn't understand at first, but then he did." Adas told Jamin about the other thief's comments and how Demas rebuked him. "Then your brother asked Yeshua to remember him when he came into his kingdom. And Yeshua said, *'Today you will be with Me in Paradise.'* I could see Demas believed him, even though I was astonished at the statement. After the earthquake, Demas could barely speak, but he said to me, 'Tell my brother, because I took up this cross, I go to be with God. Tell Jamin I will wait for him there.' He also spoke of Yeshua. He said, 'He is more than righteous. He is the Son of God.'"

Jamin dropped his head in his hands. Adas looked at Cleopas with concern, but he gestured everything was all right. Jamin raised his head. "Thank you! You have given my life back to me. My brother is alive with God."

"There's more. Demas felt no pain before he died."

"How do you know?"

"Just before Octavean broke his legs, Demas suddenly relaxed. He said something I will never forget. He said, *'You make the clouds Your chariot, You walk on the wings of the wind.'* Was he talking about God?"

"Yes, it is from the Book of Psalms. Demas said Yeshua promised to be with him when he was crucified. We didn't know he meant that literally."

Adas asked, "Why did Yeshua say, *'Eloi, Eloi, lama sabachthani!'* as if God had abandoned him?"

"He was quoting from the 22nd Psalm. It prophesized how he would be rejected, put to death, and would live again."

"I want to read this Book of Psalms. You say Yeshua is the final sacrifice, but why did he have to die in such a brutal way?"

"Because it is the law, and Yeshua fulfilled the law and the words of the prophets. Hundreds of years ago, Isaiah precisely described Yeshua's earthly life in the 53rd section of his prophecies. Even his execution fulfilled prophesies. You refused to break his legs. It is fulfillment of prophecy for none of the Messiah's bones to be broken the same as the lamb we prepare for Passover. You fulfilled prophecy when you gave Yeshua wine vinegar when he said, '*I thirst.*' You need to meet Peter and John. They can teach you *HaDerech*, the Way."

"If I live long enough. My men were very confident when they tried to kill me."

"How will you deal with them?" Jamin asked. "Will you have them executed?"

"Of course! They also took bribes and abandoned their post. This kind of behavior cannot be permitted; otherwise, there would be complete chaos."

"You're right," Cleopas said, "There has to be order and consequences. Laws exist for the good of the people. Yet, I believe God will deal with those soldiers in his own way."

"By Roman law their execution is required. What else can I do?"

Jamin shrugged. "We don't have all the answers, Adas. But did you not provide strong wine for Demas and the other thief? Did you not provide for the burial of the thief? He was a mere stranger to you and a criminal."

"It was a matter of decency, that's all."

Cleopas frowned. "I have misjudged you, Adas. I apologize."

"No apology needed, Cleopas. You helped save my life."

"Malchus should be back by now," said Jamin as he opened the door and checked the height of the moon. "He's been gone nearly an hour."

"You have endangered yourselves for my sake long enough."

"Adas, you should not go back to the Antonia alone, especially unarmed," exclaimed Jamin. "Hopefully, we will meet Malchus coming back with your friend."

"You don't need to go with me. I don't want anyone at the garrison to know you're involved. I feel bad enough involving Malchus."

"We're going with you," declared Jamin.

"Can you stop us?" asked Cleopas.

"No wonder you two got the best of Hektor and Falto. Come on then." They helped him put his armor on. Together, they stepped out into the night.

Chapter 10

⸻◦◦◦◦◦◦⸻

Lucius circled around the garden and waited until Malchus, Jamin and Cleopas carried Adas out of sight. He went back and retrieved his weapons. He was tempted to follow them, but he was still feeling the effects of the alcohol and opium. It would be foolish to challenge the temple guard again. Instead, he would find Hektor and Falto. He walked along the road until he saw Falto stumbling across a field, rubbing the back of his head.

"Where's Hektor?" Falto stopped. Disoriented, he tried to locate the voice. Lucius waved his arms. "*Ohe!* Weasel! Over here!" Falto walked to the road and sat, nearly falling over. "What happened to you?" Lucius demanded.

Falto looked up with one eye closed and scrutinized his comrade. "I d'ah know. Some'un 'it me on the head. Was it you?"

"Yes. I wacked you with a wine jug. *No! You idiot!* I was in the garden. Where's Hektor?"

"I d'ah know. Isn't he with you?" Falto blinked at Lucius.

"Yes, he's standing right next to me. That's why I said—*where is he?*" Lucius stomped past him. "You're useless, Weasel." If he didn't find Hektor soon, he'd have to leave him, since the guards would close the city gates at sunset. A halting figure stepped from behind a tangle-branched oak tree on the far side of the field. It was Hektor, holding his knapsack in his arms.

"I keep dumping rocks here," Hektor called. "When I get back, they're gone. I think Falto was stealing my rocks."

Lucius grabbed the knapsack and up ended it.

"What are you doing? You know how long it took me to find those?"

Lucius tossed the knapsack at him. "It's too late. He's gone."

Cold fear punched Hektor in the stomach despite his drunkenness. "*What! How?*"

Lucius didn't bother to answer. He grabbed Hektor by the front of his leather armor. "I swear if you double cross me I'll serve you up to the buzzards." He shoved the man away from him. Hektor stared as the big legionary turned his back and strode across the field. He picked up a rock and calculated what his odds of success would be if he threw it.

Lucius called over his shoulder. "Come on. I have an idea."

"*Ohe,* how well did your last idea work?"

Without turning around, Lucius motioned for Hektor to follow. "Weasel's, been bashed over the head, which fits my story. Come on." They grabbed Falto and hauled him to his feet. As they hurried along the road, Lucius shared his plan. They tried to explain the plan to Falto, but he couldn't remember what he was supposed to do.

"I think we need to kill the Weasel," Hektor said.

"Probably." Lucius shrugged a shoulder. "No one would even notice."

"Why not?" Falto demanded with the blank eyes of a confused drunk. Lucius groaned with impatience. Hektor rolled his eyes.

They reached the Antonia gate just as the guards were closing it. Lucius felt his first pang of fear. The opium was wearing off. If Valentius didn't believe their story, Tribune Salvitto's unyielding code of justice would order their execution.

Knowing it was too late to try anything else, Lucius called to the legionaries in the watch tower. "Centurion Longinus is missing! Sound the alarm!" Lucius and Hektor dragged Falto between them. "And this man is injured!"

Several legionaries ran to them. "Get a *medicus!*" shouted Lucius. He and Hektor let Falto fall to the ground. Men came from the barracks at the sound of the ram's horn. Hektor saw the door to Centurion Valentius's quarters open. He gestured to Lucius to get ready.

Felix Pomponius Valentius had a slight build, but was stronger than he looked. He was shorter than most soldiers and wore *caligae* with extra thick soles to compensate. His thin lips were set in a perpetual frown. His long nose and bushy low eyebrows diminished the strength of his jaw and chin. His eyesight was failing, but squinting helped. At the age of fifty seven, he was going bald, left with only a crown of sparse graying brown hair.

Valentius was the first-line commander to Adas. He was once the cohort centurion of the 3rd *Cohors.* During an uprising in Samaria, Valentius had disobeyed orders given by Cohort Centurion Tacitus of the 4th *Cohors.* Despite Valentius's outranking him, Tacitus was in charge of the campaign, while Centurion Cornelius served at his second-in-command. Valentius ordered an unauthorized charge which resulted in the needless deaths of many soldiers. At his court-martial Valentius testified that the papyrus, explaining his orders, was damaged and illegible. The courier testified he delivered the orders intact. Neither man had collaborating witnesses who could confirm the condition of the papyrus at the time of delivery.

Centurion Cornelius contended Valentius may only have miscalculated. Centurion Tacitus countered that if the papyrus was damaged, he should have kept it for proof rather than burn it, despite protocol. Tacitus wanted Valentius sentenced to *fustuarium,* to be stoned to death by the surviving soldiers he endangered. However,

Valentius had an outstanding military record, having earned his way up to command the 3rd *Cohors*. Except for the dissenting vote of one judge, the court sentenced him to *pecunaria multa*, reduced pay, and *gradus deiectio*, reduction in rank. He was demoted to the 10th *Cohors*. Even though this was an act of mercy, it was devastating to his reputation. Rumors surfaced that Valentius led the attack in hopes of discrediting Tacitus. By rank, Valentius should have been in command of the campaign, not Tacitus.

Equally tragic, Valentius was seriously wounded, which led to opium addiction. As the years passed, bitterness hardened his heart while addiction clouded his judgment and kept him in fear of bankruptcy. He earned a significant salary despite his pay reduction, but his opium debts were accumulating at an escalating rate. Many Roman families sold their children into slavery when faced with bankruptcy, but Valentius didn't have that option. Fortunately, he had amassed a substantial retirement pension by working years past the usual age of retirement to compensate for less pay. If he could hold out until he retired, he would pay off his debts, but there would be little money left. Valentius would need more income.

"What is going on here?" demanded Valentius. He glanced at Falto and turned to the closest legionary. "Go find Demitre." The legionary headed for the slave quarters. Valentius shouted orders to reopen the fortress gates and to tell the stable slaves to saddle horses.

"Sir, we must speak to you immediately," whispered Lucius. The centurion eyed the big legionary, but ignored his request.

Valentius spotted his Greek slave, a physician, and gestured at him impatiently. He scowled at the soldiers standing by. "Get this man to the infirmary. Demitre, see what's wrong with him and report back to me." The men obeyed.

Valentius headed to his office indicating Lucius and Hektor were to follow. They stepped inside and he slammed the door shut. "What have you done, Octavean?"

Lucius stood at attention. "Sir, it had been three days, and the centurion sent us to buy food. When we came back, the centurion was unconscious and there was a bloody rock by him. I told Falto to bandage his wounds while Hektor and I hunted for the culprit, but couldn't find anyone. When we got back, the tomb was empty, Falto was unconscious, and the centurion was gone. His knapsack and weapons were still there. We again searched for the culprits who must have taken Centurion Longinus, but it was getting dark. We went back to the garden, got Falto, and came here." Lucius removed Adas's belongings from his knapsack. "Sir, the Nazarene's followers obviously stole the body, and took the centurion."

Valentius circled the two men. He stopped in front of Lucius, inches from his face and slowly tilted his head back with a finger. "And this cut under your chin. Did the centurion's sword do this, *while it was in his hand?* Longinus is mine. I told you to spy on him, not attack him. Your little story might fool Tribune Salvitto, but not me. If you have killed him, I will kill *you*. Did you?"

"No, Sir! I did not! But when he returns, he will tell a different story."

Valentius's unblinking eyes remained fixed on Lucius. "I bet he will. Which one of you hit him with the rock?"

Hektor opened his mouth, but Valentius snapped, *"Shut up!"* Valentius paced in front of them while they stood at attention. "I should behead the two of you, and sell Weasel to the *gladiatoris* for target practice."

Valentius paced a few more rounds then stopped. "But I'm not going to because you're going to tell me what really happened, every detail." He extended a hand, palm up. "You brought the rock to back up your lies, didn't you?"

Hektor swallowed hard as he pulled it out of his knapsack.

Valentius stepped in front of Lucius. "Octavean, don't ever lie to me again."

Chapter 11

M alchus stepped out into the night and paused to let his eyes adjust. He was taking a big risk going to the Antonia alone. Few people ventured out after dark, except for robbers, drunks, and the occasional mounted patrol, all of which he needed to avoid. Malchus kept close to the shadows, stopping often to listen for footsteps or the clatter of hooves. The sounds of chirping locusts mingled with distant laughter. Malchus heard a woman shouting at someone and a door slammed. He stepped around the corner of a wall at the same time a dog inside the courtyard leaped at the wall, barking furiously. Malchus jumped, unnerved at the sudden noise. He hurried down an alley. As he passed under a stand of palm trees an owl screeched, warning him away. The bird spread its wings and silently took flight.

Nearing the Antonia Fortress, he could see the torches at the iron gates. The gates were open. Mounted soldiers carrying torches exited in pairs, scattering in different directions. Malchus decided on a new plan. He would go back for Adas and help him find a patrol. Rounding a corner, he heard the clip clop of hooves. He dodged back around the corner and waited. As the horses approached, he heard the riders talking.

"Let's split up. I'll go east. I hope he made it inside before they closed the gates."

"Yes, even Tiberius couldn't get in after sunset. It worries me that three legionaries managed to misplace their injured centurion. Something doesn't add up."

"Agreed. And it's going to be difficult finding him in the dark. You should have brought your dog. He can track better than a hundred men. Anyway, I'll see you back at the Antonia."

One of the riders turned his horse, holding a torch high above his head. Malchus followed him until he was sure the other rider was gone. He called out. The horse stopped, and then came in his direction. Malchus stood with his hands raised. He could see the face of the mounted soldier in the flare of his torch.

"Sir, are you Decurion Cassius Quintus?"

"I am. Who are you and how do you know my name?"

"Centurion Longinus sent me to find you. He was attacked."

"*Who* are you?"

"I am a temple guard. I can take you to Centurion Longinus."

"Why should I trust you?" Cassius nervously scanned the area.

"Adas said, 'Tell Cassius I will check on his mastiff, Tigula.' He's not eating. And Draco is the name of your horse." The man moved the torch closer to Malchus.

He turned his horse, and gave Malchus a hand. "Get on. Where is he? How badly injured is he?" He urged the big horse into an easy trot. As they rode, Malchus told Cassius the details of the assault.

Adas, Jamin, and Cleopas heard approaching hoof beats. Adas held up a hand. "Stop. Whoever's out there, he must not see your faces."

They nodded and stepped back into the shadows. "Adas, go to the marketplace tomorrow and I will find you," said Jamin. Adas stepped out of the shadows.

"Thank the gods you are safe," exclaimed Cassius as he reined Draco to a halt. Malchus slid to the ground and helped Adas climb on the horse.

"We will see each other again," Malchus said as he stepped away.

"I hope under better circumstances," said Adas. "Thank you for saving my life."

Cassius reined Draco around and tapped the horse's flank with a heel. The big bay leaped into a canter. As soon as they passed through the gate, Cassius called for the "all clear" to be sounded. Adas slid off Draco's back and patted the horse's neck as Cassius dismounted. A young slave assigned to the stables ran forward and took the reins. He had been watching from the arena, anxiously aware of the present emergency.

Adas nodded at the young man. "Nikolaus."

The slave responded in Greek with a hushed tone, "Centurion Longinus, I am relieved you are back. Is there something I can do for you?" He briefly raised his hazel eyes as he pushed his dark, curly hair from his forehead.

Adas was a little surprised at the concern in the boy's expression. "You can tell the others I'm planning on giving a lesson Saturday morning. But if I don't make it, I want you to take charge. What would you teach them?"

The boy's expression brightened at the honor. "Sir, I could teach your hoof trimming technique, if you approve."

"I do," said Adas, managing a smile. Fatigue had set in hours ago.

Cassius stepped between them. "Make sure Draco has extra hay, water, and a good brush down." The slave acknowledged the command and led Draco to the stables. Cassius turned back to Adas. "I'll go with you to see Valentius." He tilted his head toward the stables. "You pamper them, you know? Why do you let that stable slave use Greek?"

"I like Greek," answered Adas with a matter-of-fact shrug. "And I like Nikolaus. I won't let anyone else tend to my horse. His intelligence is wasted here."

"He's a slave. He has no intelligence."

Adas was too tired to argue. They were almost to Valentius's office. "You know he probably won't let you stay, but *gratias,* all the same."

Cassius knocked on the door and it flew open. Centurion Valentius stood in the doorway. Without a word he gestured for the men to enter. Several oil lamps burned. An ornately carved desk stood in the center of the room. There was a blood spattered rock on the desk.

"Well, Centurion Longinus, nice of you to show up." Valentius sat at his desk. "Where did you find him, Decurion Quintus?"

"A short distance from the Antonia, Sir."

"Alone?"

"Yes, Sir."

"You're dismissed." Cassius left the room. Valentius got up and walked around the desk. He glanced at the bandage on Adas's hand and the cut under his jaw. One corner of his mouth curled up. Without warning, he roughly pulled the bandage away from Adas's forehead.

"Well, you did manage to smack your head a good one." Valentius yawned, ending it with an exaggerated sigh. He threw the bandage on the floor and returned to his chair. He picked up the rock and calmly eyed the centurion. "What happened?"

Adas told Valentius everything, leaving out only the names of his rescuers. When he finished, Valentius stared at him, unblinking. Then he threw his head back and bellowed with laughter. "Let me see if I understand you, Longinus. There was an earthquake. Then a dazzling figure appeared and the four of you passed out. When you came to, the tomb was empty. Your men ignored your orders and left their post. Then your own men, who have sworn allegiance to you, came back and attacked you. The followers of the man you just crucified rescued you. *They* rescued *you* from your *own* men. Do I understand you correctly?"

Adas clenched his teeth before he answered. "Yes, Sir."

Valentius crossed his arms over his chest. "Longinus, you have a head injury which has left you confused and delusional. Let me tell *you* what happened. You sent your men to buy food. While they were gone, the Nazarene's followers knocked you out, but they spied your men coming back, so they ran. Lucius and Hektor tended your wounds, and then went to find your attackers, leaving Falto behind. The zealots knocked *him* out, broke into the tomb, and stole the body. You woke up from your little nap and wandered off, disoriented. Octavean and Hektor returned, found you missing, picked up your gear, and came here. You tell me which story sounds more reasonable?"

"Yours does, Sir."

"Of course, it does."

"But it's not true, Sir."

Valentius's face went red. "I think it is true! In fact, I'm about to order ten squads to round up every Hebrew who so much as blinked at the Nazarene and give them to the *quaestionarii,* and their beloved tools of torture."

Color drained from Adas's face. "Yeshua's followers did nothing wrong."

"Perhaps they didn't," Valentius purred. "Here's another possibility—you were drunk, passed out, and hit your head while your men were getting food. The zealots took advantage of the moment and stole the Nazarene's body while you were out cold. Your men came back and *thought* you had been attacked. They separated to find your attackers. Falto caught up with them, the Nazarene's followers, by accident, no doubt, and was assaulted. You woke up and wandered off." He threw his hands up and shrugged his shoulders. "You're a clumsy drunk or I tell the *quaestionarii* to get ready to interrogate prisoners, lots of prisoners. Your choice."

Octavean told the truth; he really was under Valentius's protection. Fury glinted in Adas's eyes. Valentius dropped his hand to his dagger. Adas was keenly aware that he was unarmed. By taking the side of the legionaries against him, Valentius was denying Adas's authority and integrity, a supreme humiliation for a centurion. However, if Adas put his pride first, others would suffer far worse than humiliation.

"Centurion Valentius, you are correct. I was drunk and suffered a head injury, in fact, several head injuries. Apparently, I also cut my neck and took a blow to the face, accidently, of course. I found myself wandering the streets when Decurion Quintus found me."

Valentius snorted with triumph. "Ah, you have come to your senses. How cooperative of you. I'll even spare you the humiliation of delivering a public apology to your men. But, I do want a written apology on my desk tomorrow before the third hour. However, your false accusations don't surprise me—considering your family history."

Adas frowned in confusion. "What family history are you. . .?"

"Silence! When I want you to speak, I'll ask you a question. You should be grateful I didn't sentence you to *fustuarium* since your actions endangered your men. Now get out!"

Adas turned on his heel and left. As soon as the door shut behind him, Valentius's arrogance faded. His plan had failed. He had hoped Adas and his men would be attacked by Yeshua's followers. Likewise, Valentius yearned to force Longinus to make a public apology, but he had assigned them to guard the tomb without authorization. He removed a leather-corded amulet he always wore under his tunic. It was made of a six-sided tourmaline crystal, green on the outside with a red core. The name *Aurelius* was engraved on the crystal. He kept an urn at the bottom of his clothes chest engraved with the same name. Besides Demitre, no one knew about it or whose ashes were inside.

He clutched the amulet in his fist. "Very soon *Consul* Clovius Longinus will know what it feels like to lose *his* son. I will have my revenge, as will you, Aurelius. I promise you!"

After being dismissed, Adas closed the office door behind him and started to cross the main quad toward the officers' quarters. Cassius was waiting.

"What happened? Did Valentius believe you?"

Adas took three strides before he could bring himself to answer. "Apparently he does believe me, which is why he devised his own version. He says if I don't 'admit' I was falling down drunk, he will round up the followers of Yeshua. He will order their interrogation under torture for 'attacking me' when they 'stole Yeshua's body.' His words. Octavean truly does stand behind Valentius's shield."

"Adas, this makes no sense. Your father is the minor *consul*. He stands only a few men from the emperor. How can Valentius get away with this? When Salvitto hears of this. . ."

"He's counting on me not telling my father or Salvitto."

"So he's blackmailing you into withdrawing your accusation?"

"I have to write an apology, confirming his version, which will make it official."

Cassius stopped in his tracks. "Is he making you read it in general assembly?"

"No. He's not. I wonder why?"

"Perhaps he doesn't want to push his luck."

"He threatened me with *fustuarium*."

Again, Cassius stopped and stared in astonishment. "Now I know he's lost his mind. A centurion has to nearly kill off his whole *centuria* before *fustuarium* is declared. What has set him against you with such vengeance?"

"I don't know. He did make an odd reference to my family. I have no idea what he was talking about. Whatever is going on, you have to promise me you won't say anything about the man who came for you, not to anyone. His life would be forfeit. Valentius knows I have witnesses out there. He may try to find them."

"I understand, but what about you? Adas, I know you and your father have your differences, but maybe you should tell him."

"No. He taught me to stand up for myself, so I'm not going to disappoint him anymore than I already have. Besides, he was furious when I joined the army. If I tell him about Valentius, it will confirm he was right, and I was wrong. I hope you don't get dragged into this further."

"I'll be fine. Go, you look like you're about to collapse."

The two men continued across the quad. Cassius headed for the common room. Adas went to his quarters. As he turned down the lane, he thought he saw an odd shadow near his door. Someone was crouching in the dark, waiting for him.

Chapter 12

⸺⸺⸺

Adas slapped a hand to his belt, forgetting he was unarmed. He braced himself for an attack, but the figure stood and spoke. "Sir, you are injured. Do you need medical attention?"

It was Demitre, the slave trained as a *medicus* in Rome. He was fifty-four years old, but looked much younger due to his dyed, black, wavy hair and short-cropped beard. It was not vanity, but rather secrecy that motivated the disguise. Any aging around the eyes and mouth were shielded from casual observation by his hair and beard. He rarely revealed his true feelings. His jet-black eyes were shiny with intelligence, but the irises seemed too large for his eyes giving him a disconcerting stare. People often felt uncomfortable under his gaze, and would complain about Demitre's disrespectful scrutiny. Valentius would angrily rebuke them. Demitre maintained a subservient manner, yet he watched for the faults and vices in others to use for his advantage.

Demitre padded closer, silent as a cat. "Centurion Longinus, I did not mean to startle you. Do you wish for me to check your injuries?" Adas hesitated, knowing Demitre would report to Valentius, but decided he might learn something as well.

Adas responded in Greek, "Fine. Come in." Adas was surprised to find an oil lamp already burning. He shot a withering glare of reprimand at the slave.

"My master told me to put your possessions in your quarters. I left my lamp there for you." Demitre used the lamp to light the others. He set his medical kit on the table.

Adas saw his knapsack lying on the bed. He opened it to see if his sword and dagger were undamaged. He slumped into a chair at the table, and gestured for Demitre to sit.

Demitre remained standing. "Sir, you will need to remove your armor. Let me help you." The slave helped him out of the armor and set it on top of a wooden chest. "And your belt, Sir?"

Adas realized that when Lucius took his knapsack and weapons; he might have taken Dulcibella's eilat stone. Before he unfastened his belt he pressed his fingers around the coin pouch. He relaxed when he felt for the eilat stone in the pouch. He unfastened the belt and hung it off the back of his chair. Demitre saw the gesture and wondered what was in the pouch.

Demitre held an oil lamp to the head wounds and inspected them. He fumbled through the vials in his kit. Adas watched without really seeing; his vision was blurred with fatigue. He couldn't remember ever feeling more exhausted.

"Demitre, how long have you served Centurion Valentius?"

"Many years, Sir," Demitre answered in Latin.

"Greek, if you would, Demitre. I need the practice."

"Yes, Sir. I was a young man when I came into his possession. If you'll put your head back, Sir, I don't want the vinegar to get in your eye."

Adas was about to tell him his rescuers already applied *acetum*, but thought better of it. Demitre poured a small amount in the gash. Adas grimaced and squeezed his left eye shut.

"I am sorry, Sir. The vinegar has a powerful sting, but it prevents infection and aids healing." He patted the wound dry with a clean wool cloth. He then applied willow powder.

The willow stung, but Adas managed to talk. "Did you serve his family?"

"I'm sorry, Sir. The willow is unpleasant, but it also prevents infection." He put the vial back in his kit. "You asked about my master's family. Once his parents died, he had no family, not really. He was the youngest of the children, but they were much older and he has lost track of them. In fact, I never met them."

Demitre put a patch of wool over the wound. He took a clean strip of linen, wrapped it around Adas's head and tied off the bandaging. He felt the knot on the back of Adas's head, but said nothing. He followed the same procedures for the neck injury, but did not apply bandaging.

Demitre picked up a lamp. "Please, keep your eyes straight ahead. Something I learned at the Army *Medicus Schola* in Rome." He moved the lamp back and forth close to Adas's face. "Ah, a good sign. Your eyes are equally reactive. May I remove the bandage on your hand, Sir?" Demitre didn't wait for an answer. His eyebrows shot up in surprise and a hint of pleasure on seeing the cross. "Sir, may I ask—what caused these cuts?"

"My dagger."

The corner of Demitre's mouth twitched. "I'll clean the wound, Sir. These cuts are deep. You must have a high tolerance for pain." The vinegar burned like the sting of hornets.

"Forgive me, Sir." The *medicus* firmly pushed Adas's fingers down and pressed his own fist over them while the acid sterilized the wound. "I am sorry, Sir. I will wash away the vinegar in a few moments."

Adas thought it was much longer than a few moments before Demitre brought the water pitcher and basin from the pedestal table to wash the cuts. Again, he apologized.

"Demitre, stop apologizing. You're just doing your job." Adas was surprised to see a sly smile on the man's face, but it vanished quickly. His face was again an impassive facade.

"I'm almost done. I will apply the willow to help the vinegar. They work better together. And I will apply henbane seed for the pain."

"No, nothing for pain."

Demitre eyes narrowed. "Why do you refuse it? Do you doubt the quality of my medications?"

"Should I?" Adas shot back. "Have there been complaints?"

Demitre lowered his gaze. "No, Sir. Please forgive my insolence. It was inexcusable."

Adas closed his eyes and leaned his head on his hand. Demitre quickly took a roll of bandaging from his kit. There were several rolls, some tied with white string, some black. He stuffed a black string out of sight in the kit, and wrapped Adas's hand. He selected another vial containing opium. "Take this, Sir; it will help you sleep and ease the . . .it will help you sleep."

"What is it?"

"Just a bit of new wine." Demitre watched with relief as Adas drank the liquid without argument. "Sir, if you will tolerate my curiosity, may I ask why you cut a cross in your hand?" Adas could barely focus. "Sir, perhaps I should help you to bed?"

"I will answer you first."

"Perhaps you are too tired." The opium was affecting Adas too quickly. "Come, let me help you to your bed while you can still stand."

"This scar is a reminder."

"A reminder of what?" Demitre put a shoulder under Adas's arm and helped him stand. "To refuse . . .immoral commands." He collapsed in his bed.

"Sir, you would refuse a direct order from a superior?"

"Will not . . .execute . . .innocent man."

"Are you speaking of Yeshua, the Nazarene?"

Adas could only manage a nod. Demitre unlaced the centurion's *caligae* and pulled a blanket over him. Adas still wore his blood-stained tunic, but Demitre didn't try to remove it. He peered into Adas's eyes. The centurion's pupils, despite the low light, were small, nearly pinpoints. The opium had taken effect.

The slave repacked his kit. "I know who you speak of. It's a shame he's dead."

"Wrong."

"What do you mean?"

"Not dead. He smiled . . .today."

"*What*? You are confused, Centurion. Your head injuries are worse than I thought. You executed the man yourself!"

"Yes. Split heart . . .with spear. He's ali . . .." Adas fell asleep.

"Sir? Sir?" Demitre shook Adas by the shoulder. He cursed himself for offering the opium too soon. Valentius would want to know more about the centurion's hallucinations. Demitre decided not to waste an opportunity. He opened Adas's coin pouch and tapped the contents into his hand. Along with a few coins, the eilat stone dropped out. It was a common item in Judea, but evidently, the centurion valued it. The stone must be a gift from a loved one, perhaps a girlfriend. Valentius would value this information.

Demitre put the eilat stone back in the coin pouch. He picked up the body armor and cleaned off the dried blood. There was no display holder for the armor. He opened the clothes chest and carefully set the *lorica musculata* in with the rest of the armor and clothes. The fact Longinus kept his armor out of sight would interest Valentius. Most officers liked to stroke their egos by displaying the quality and quantity of armor they could afford.

Demitre padded to a chair and sat down. His thoughts turned to his own life and the many luxuries he once could afford. His black eyes dulled with bitterness as he thought about the event which forced him into slavery. Even though Valentius caused him to suffer, the Roman had saved his life. However, over the last few years his master had become increasingly unstable. Demitre worried that Valentius's obsession would be his undoing.

The *medicus* needed to report to his master. He retrieved his medical kit and blew the lamps out. Automatically, he picked up the water pitcher and set it outside the door. A slave would refill it early the next morning. He walked down the lane between the rows of officers' quarters and crossed the quad. Demitre paused and beheld the night sky. A bright light tore a path through the darkness. There was a faint hissing as the light changed from white to yellow, and then orange. It broke off into several separate trails of light and disappeared. Demitre stood very still, wondering what the appearance of the streaming light meant. He waited, but when nothing else happened, he padded up to his master's door and knocked with his personal signal. The door opened and Demitre disappeared inside.

Chapter 13

The next morning, Adas stiffly sat up. Slowly, the events of the previous day started to come back to him, but in a jumbled order. The room seemed to rotate. He groaned and sank back on the bed. Much more slowly, he sat up again, but had to wait for the room to stop moving. Carefully, he nudged his feet to the floor. His vision corrected and he stood. Without thinking, he opened the door and picked up his water pitcher.

Adas took the copper mirror off the wall. Turning it over, he read the inscription on the back. "Never Relinquish Your Dream." He thought of the day his mother gave him the mirror, many years ago.

"Adas, I have something I'd like to give you," said Marsetina as she gestured for her young son to follow her.

"What is it?" Adas was excited that she had a gift for him.

"It is a *speculum cuprinus*, and I'm giving it you." She handed him the polished copper mirror. "For generations my family has passed this mirror from father to daughter, and mother to son. Some say the first owner gave the mirror to her eldest son because he was very handsome, but he had a mole on the side of his face. She wanted him to remember he was not perfect and to embrace humility. With humility comes wisdom."

"What does humility mean, Mother?"

Marsetina knelt on her knees and re-laced his sandals. "Even though this is a job for a slave, I do this for you out of humility, Adas. There is no love more powerful than to put the needs of others before your own, even if the task is lowly."

"Is this why Misha is my nanny? Because she has humility?"

"Yes, Misha loves humility, but she loves you more."

"Why does she love me?"

"Because Misha has a pure heart. She loves you and me more than she loves herself. She gave up everything to be with me. More than once, she would have sacrificed her life to protect me. Only the purest of heart are willing to die for someone."

"Did she almost die?" The thought scared Adas. "Who saved her?"

"Your Father saved both of us at great risk to himself. Your Father is the bravest man I have ever known. Never forget that, Adas. He loves both of us very much."

"Does Father have humility, too?"

Marsetina's eyes twinkled. "Not as much."

"Does he have wisdom?"

"Yes, he has wisdom because he has courage. Not only did your father rescue me, he rescued my heart. If your father had not saved me, you would never have been born." She showed him the back of the mirror. "What does it say, Adas?"

"Never relinquish your dream. What does it mean?"

"Never accept less than your goals. Don't settle for something because it is easy."

"What is your dream, Mother?"

"My dream now is for you to love and be loved. There is no greater treasure than those we love."

"Is Father your treasure? Are you his treasure?"

Marsetina smiled. "You do understand."

Adas jumped to his feet to run from the room. "I'm going to show Father my beautiful mirror."

Marsetina's smile vanished. "No, Adas. Don't ever tell your father about the mirror. He won't understand why I kept it. This is our secret. Not even Misha knows I kept it."

Adas put the mirror back on the wall. He longed for the day his mother would meet Dulcibella and know her dream had come true. Adas studied his reflection and frowned. His four-day-old beard could not hide the evidence of violence. Under his left eye was the beginning of a purple bruise which extended across his entire cheekbone. The cut along the underside of his jaw was long and surrounded with bruising. The bandage across his forehead revealed the wound had bled in his sleep. Tentatively, he pulled the bandaging off. There was a gash above the left end of his eyebrow and across his temple. Dark purple bruising fanned away from the injury and disappeared into his hairline. He tossed the bandage in the fireplace.

Adas remembered that Valentius wanted an apology before the third hour, but it was close to noon, judging by the shadows from the window lattice. Adas pulled his ruined tunic off and threw it on the floor. He put on a fresh tunic. He found papyrus, a pen, and a clay inkpot, which was almost empty. It would have to be a short "apology."

Five minutes later he left his quarters and crossed the quad to Valentius's office. He knocked and Valentius called out to enter. Adas stood at attention while Valentius stamped documents with his seal ring, carefully placing each one in a neat line across the top of his desk. He would adjust a sheet, study it, and re-adjust it. Finally he blew out the sealing wax and put his ring on his hand. He scowled at Adas. "What did I tell you last night?"

"Sir, you told me you wanted a written apology on your desk before the third hour."

"Yet here you are after the fifth, with an excuse I'm sure."

"I have none, Sir."

Valentius circled around his desk. "You don't offer an excuse when I know you have a perfectly good one. Why don't you say it? Afraid of getting my slave in trouble? How touching. Demitre told me he gave you a dose of his sleeping potion. A man will sleep through a battering ram at his door with that potion." Valentius put his hand out for the scroll. "Go check the duty wall. You have today and tomorrow to recover. Report for duty Wednesday. Dismissed."

Hiding his surprise at the leniency, Adas turned to leave.

"Oh, one more thing, Longinus. You got a letter from your father." Valentius reached into a set of shelves and pulled out a scroll. The wooden spool was damaged and the seal was broken. Adas took the letter without comment and turned to go.

"Aren't you going to ask why it's broken?"

"No, Sir. Will that be all, Sir?"

"No, it will not. I'll tell you anyway. The *tabellar* swears he received the letter in that condition. Isn't this your father's personal seal?"

"Yes, Sir." Aquila had never written to him before now. How did Valentius know what *Consul* Longinus's personal seal looked like? His father had sent only one other letter to the Antonia, addressed to Tribune Salvitto, to request Adas be transferred to Jerusalem.

Do you wish to file a complaint against the *tabellar*?"

"No, Sir"

"Why not? Are you afraid of getting *him* in trouble?"

"No, Sir. It is not worth the effort. Sir."

"Does your father know his letters are 'not worth the effort,' Longinus?"

"You would have to ask *Consul* Longinus, Sir. Would you like me to request his presence? Then he could answer your questions, in person. Sir."

A red flush started up Valentius's neck. "Are you threatening me?"

"No, Sir. Why would my father's presence be a threat to you? Sir."

"Go!" Valentius thrust a finger at the door. "Get out of my office!"

Once outside, Adas smiled to himself. Apparently, the commander was not unmindful of *Consul* Longinus's authority, after all. He crossed the quad to the officers' *cafeteria*. When he entered the building, most of the conversation stopped, but he was too hungry to care. Ignoring their stares, he sat at his favorite table. After seeing Adas, the men were growing suspicious of the report presented by Valentius. They certainly knew the difference between injuries from drunkenness and injuries from a fight.

Several men walked over to Adas. "Mind if we talk with you?" asked one of the decurions. Adas gestured to the empty table and they sat. "Valentius said you were drunk yesterday and hit your head. Hitting the ground didn't make that cut under your jaw, and none of us have ever seen you drunk. What's the real story?"

Adas took a slow breath. "I wish I knew the real story. Something hit me, and the next thing I knew, I came to alone."

The men grumbled vague comments. They rejoined the others to add fuel to the rumor mill. A young slave approached and asked for instructions. The boy tried to ignore Adas's injuries, but was forced to confront the eyes of a wolf.

"You must be new," Adas addressed the child. "How old are you? What is your name?"

"I am nine, Sir. My name is Onesimus, Sir."

"Onesimus, a fine name. Who is your master?" Adas noticed he had no obvious injuries or signs of starvation.

"My master is Tribune Salvitto. He assigned me to the officers' *cafeteria*." He kept his eyes downcast, but glanced up every three or four words.

"Have you ever worked with horses?"

"Yes, Sir. I helped with our horses before my father was forced to sell me."

"Did you like working with the horses?"

The child's eyes lit up. "Yes, Sir. Horses are magnificent creatures."

"Bring me ale and whatever you can find. Find something that actually tastes good, and I'll share with you." Onesimus saw Cassius approaching, but hurried away.

"Why do you coddle them, Adas?" asked Cassius as he sat at the table.

"Can you think of a better way to insure a slave won't spit in your food?"

"Precautionary lashes would do the same thing and cost less."

"Yes, and you would have an enemy instead of an ally."

Cassius shrugged. "They're slaves. Who cares? By the way, you look terrible, but I have news that'll make you feel better."

Onesimus set a mug of ale, a bowl of stew and half a loaf of bread on the table. Adas tore off some bread and handed it to the child. Onesimus beamed and stuffed it in his mouth. The boy took Cassius's order and left. Adas noticed he did not hurry this time.

Cassius watched as Adas devoured the stew. "When was the last time you ate? You even eat like a wolf." Adas kept chewing. "Right, so you might want to go by the officers' common room and check the duty wall. There's a few interesting entries at the end of the list. Do you have any idea why Valentius is after you?"

Adas swallowed a mouthful of warm ale. "It must have something to do with my father."

"Why?" Cassius asked.

"Everything in my life has to do with my father. But listen, in case you thought I forgot about Tigula, I'll come to your quarters when you get off duty."

"You can get my tool set then. Are you going to need a new bolt on your door?"

"Probably." Adas raised his chin in the direction of the kitchen. "There's your food." The slave set the meal down and waited for further instructions. Cassius waved him off. Adas patted Cassius on the shoulder. "It was good eating with you." He left the officers' *cafeteria* and went to the common room.

When he entered, the conversation stopped. Adas walked over to the duty wall, a smooth white section of wall marked with charcoal. Every week, a slave whitewashed the writing, and the new duties were posted for each of the sixty centurions. Contrary to common practice, a specific assignment was posted for three legionaries. Lucius, Hektor, and Falto were assigned to *latrinae* duty. Water ran continually through the *latrinae* channels, but they had to be scrubbed with pumice stone, which left the hands raw. This was a backbreaking job reserved for rebellious slaves. It was an extremely humiliating punishment for a soldier.

At first, Adas thought this punishment would contradict the cover story Valentius presented at the morning briefing. Then he realized the punishment was appropriate for abandoning a ranking officer too drunk to defend himself.

Adas glanced around the room. The men had gone back to their previous activities, but now a few of them spoke in hushed tones. A group of soldiers was gambling with dice in a corner of the room. One of them cheered, elbowed the man next to him and gathered his winnings off the floor. Several men were exercising on the pull-up bars set in the walls. Other men talked as they exercised with free weights. A few men sat on benches talking and, occasionally, looking at Adas. Two men had a chess board between them. The man playing with red pebbles was beating the man using the white pebbles. A group playing Twelve Lines had neglected to put the board and dice back in the game shelves.

A decurion named Corvus walked over to Adas. "You look terrible, my friend."

"Yes, I've heard."

"We're playing soccer Saturday and could use you on the team if you're up to it. Drusus had his slave make a new soccer ball with a pig bladder. They bounce better than goat bladders."

"I doubt I will play, but I'll be there. What time?"

"Ninth hour."

The men working out seemed to be resting, and the dice sat idle in the corner. Every man in the room was watching him.

"Adas, we were wondering how you got the cut on your neck?"

Adas sighed and shook his head. "Honestly, I don't know."

"Listen, if you were attacked by zealots, why haven't they been arrested?"

"I didn't see any zealots. I only saw my men—no one else." Adas pointed to the last three names on the duty wall. "Those three."

"Right, well, don't forget the soccer game." He excused himself and left.

The men went back to what they were doing. He left the common room and headed for his quarters. Hopefully, no one else would question him. His pride was making it difficult to keep the truth to himself, but if he didn't, others would be in danger.

A voice sounded behind him and Adas turned to face the man. "Sir, may I speak with you?" It was Faustus Tertius Victorius, his *optio*, second in command.

"Of course, what do you need, Victorius?"

"Centurion, the men asked me to say that your *centuria* stands with you."

"I deeply appreciate their loyalty and courage. Thank them for me, Victorius." Adas gave his *optio* an approving nod and continued toward his quarters. When he turned to go down the lane, a group of men blocked his way. They were centurions from different cohorts. The scowls on their faces were not encouraging. Centurion Plinius from the 3rd *Cohors* stepped forward.

"Not so fast, Longinus! We want to talk to you," said Plinius. "Some of us actually survived sixteen years of warfare. None of us were handed our titles on a silver platter like you." The other centurions muttered in agreement. "You were a *veterinarius* in Caesarea. *Ohe*, such terrible dangers you must have endured! Horses can be quite deadly when they're eating grass." The other men laughed contemptuously.

"You are incorrect. I *still am* a *veterinarius*. And you are centurions who have earned your titles honorably." Adas looked each man in the eye. "I have seen your courage and skill as true leaders, men who stand their ground."

"You dare mock us?" Plinius stepped closer as he squared his shoulders.

"No, I agree with you. I do not deserve the title of centurion, nor did I want it. I wish it could be taken from me and be left as I was."

"You won't even defend yourself. You're not worth our disgust." Plinius pushed past Adas. The other men glanced at each other, confused at his humility, but walked away without comment.

Adas reached his quarters and went inside. He closed the door, leaned his back against it and sighed. When he tried to lock the door, the antiquated bolt resisted his efforts. He had to force the lock. He pulled the scroll from under his belt and sat down. Even though the seal was ripped open, he could still see it was his father's personal stamp in the wax. Again, he wondered why Valentius recognized it.

To: Centurion Clovius Longinus
10th Legio, Jerusalem, 10th Cohors, 6th Centuria

Greetings Adas,

It gives me terrible grief to tell you a tragic thing has happened. Your mother became very ill. The doctors could do nothing. She wasted away before my eyes. It distresses me to have to tell you she did not survive her illness. This letter will not get to you in time for her funeral. There is no need for you to come home. Please do not worry about me. I hold on to my memories to survive. But take heart, Adas, for I plan to marry before the end of the season and you will have a step-mother. I am confident you will approve of this marriage. She is young, strong, and healthy, and will bear me children. You will finally have brothers and sisters, something your mother wished to give you. I will inform you of the wedding date as soon as we set it and I will hope for your arrival then.

Your father,
Consul Clovius Longinus

Chapter 14

⊖⊗⊗⊖

Devastated, Adas stared at the letter. He couldn't breathe. He couldn't move. He remembered the premonition he had at Golgotha about never seeing his mother again. Hot tears blurred his vision. Marsetina was more than his mother; she was his confidant and guide. She had encouraged him to pursue his ambitions. When his last two letters went unanswered, he should have set aside his pride and written to his father. Adas lived far away from his parents, but it was always a comfort knowing they were reachable. It was only a matter of distance and time. When it was his choice, he was content to stay away. The finality of death eliminated that choice forever.

Adas analyzed his father's choice of words. The formal tone was indifferent, at best. The apparent dismissal of his mother's death amplified Adas's lifelong resentment toward his father. With all his strength, he hurled the scroll at the wall. Pieces of it clattered to the floor. He snatched up the letter and shredded it. Taking hold of the broken spool, he jerked the bolt in the lock, opened the door, and threw it out. It hit the wall of the officer's quarters across the lane. Two centurions walking down the lane abruptly stopped their conversation and looked from Adas to the broken pieces. He slammed the door so hard; the window lattices shook. He rammed the door bolt into the casing so violently something cracked. He managed to get to a chair and fell into it. Immediately he jumped to his feet, grabbed the chair, and raised it over his head. With a consuming fury, he smashed it against the door repeatedly until the wood frame and reeds shattered. Bits of splintered wood pelted him. Adas stood, panting with exertion and rage. He had contemplated his own demise, but never considered his mother's death.

He stumbled back until his bed forced him to sit. He looked at the scraps of papyrus on the floor. Aquila had described Marsetina's death like it was an inconvenience. He had the audacity to announce he had already selected a new wife to bear him children. The memories of bitter disputes with his father, his guilt over Yeshua's execution, the attack by his men, Valentius's hatred, and now the death of his mother bonded into an overwhelming cascade of despair. Adas wanted to scream.

An icy chill went up his spine. Valentius must have read every word. Adas remembered the sneering look on the centurion's face when he handed him the broken scroll. No doubt, he must have smiled at the calculated wording of the letter. He pictured Valentius savoring Marsetina's death. Valentius's mockery of his loss and exploitation of Adas's privacy ignited a passion he had never experienced.

Adas snatched his knapsack from the floor. He grasped the dagger and pulled it from the sheath. The yellow wolf eyes gleamed at him from the handle. The weapon felt good in his hand. Valentius had endangered his life at every opportunity for two years, and he set Adas's own men against him. Like the wolf, Adas would go for the throat.

Striding across the room, he pulled on the lock bolt, but it wouldn't move. He pulled again. It still wouldn't move. In frustration, he jammed the dagger into the wooden door, grasped the bolt with both hands, and pulled as hard as he could. It twisted slightly. He repositioned his hands and tried jerking the bolt. Pain tore through his right hand as it slipped. Adas cried out and cradled his right hand against his chest. He stood panting, his heart thundering as he leaned against the door. The injury had reopened. The intensity of the pain snapped him out of his fugue. His breathing slowed. His fury ebbed. Despair took its place.

Adas had never felt such anguish. Even the heartache of leaving Dulcibella behind in Caesarea did not equal the pain he felt now. His mother was dead and dismissed by her husband of twenty-seven years. His father hadn't even bothered to call her by name. All he cared about was continuing the clan of Longinus.

Adas stared at his bandaged hand. If he had not already taken the dagger to his own hand, he certainly would do it now. Somehow, the physical pain helped to lessen the misery in his heart. It was only a distraction, but one he welcomed. He threw himself on the bed and sat with his back against the wall. He wasn't sure how long he stayed there, but the shadows had shifted through the windows when his emotions were finally spent. He got up and examined the door bolt. In his fury, Adas had caused the bolt to be jammed in the casing by a broken nail.

With his anger drained, Adas shuddered to think how close he came to ruining his life. There would have been no going back. He would have been executed for murdering Valentius. Adas pulled his dagger from the door and pried the damaged metal casing from the frame. The pain in his hand forced him to stop. The edges of the gashes were red and hot. He poured water over his palm into the basin. Adas picked up his ruined tunic still lying on the floor and tore a strip of linen from it. He re-bandaged the wound.

He thought of Mary witnessing Yeshua die on the cross. Her heart was torn into pieces as Adas's was, but she blamed no one, cursed no one, not even God for allowing such a cruel death. She only grieved. Jamin had told him to go to the market place.

He resolved to find the young man who helped save his life. There was something he wanted Jamin to do.

Adas picked up his knapsack, dumped everything out on the bed, and slipped the strap over his shoulder. He left his quarters to find Cassius, who would be on duty in the main hall. Adas found him sitting at a desk writing out duty rosters on slate tablets.

"Cassius, I need a favor."

"Sure. What is it?" Cassius set a tablet aside.

"Could I borrow Draco? Venustas's hoof is still infected."

"Sure, he's probably bored." Cassius looked up. "Adas, what's wrong? Did something happen?" Adas shook his head. "Take the beast for a stroll. I think you both need one."

Adas hurried to the stables. The newest member of Nikolaus's team ran over when Adas entered the arena. He asked for Draco. The boy brought the stallion and dropped to his hands and knees next to the horse. It was customary for a slave to 'back up' a rider. Roman saddles had four saddle horns, but no stirrups.

Adas put his hand out to the slave. "Get up," he said as he gripped the child's wrist, and pulled him to his feet. He gaped at the centurion. Adas tied the strap of his knapsack on a back saddle horn. "You're new. What is your name?"

"Calais, Sir," He kept his eyes respectfully lowered.

"Is Nikolaus back there?"

"He is, Sir. Here he comes now." Nikolaus emerged from the stables leading a couple of saddled horses. Two decurions stood nearby, talking while they waited. "I'll get him." The boys hurried back to Adas.

"Nikolaus, if Tribune Salvitto approves, I might add a new kitchen slave to the Saturday morning class. Calais, how old are you? Do you work well with horses?"

"Eleven years, Sir. Yes, Sir. I love horses. They are big, but they never hurt me."

Adas managed a smile. "You are old enough to be in the class. Would you like to join?"

The child was speechless. Nikolaus elbowed him. "I—I would like it very much. Yes, Sir. Thank you, Centurion Longinus, Sir."

"I will speak to Tribune Salvitto about you as well. Nikolaus, tell me if any stallions get rough around Calais, since he's new here."

"Yes, Sir."

Adas grasped a front saddle horn, jumped, and threw his right leg over the saddle as he pulled himself up. "Nikolaus, could you get someone in maintenance to replace the lock on my door? Remove the broken chair, too."

"Of course, Centurion, I will see to it."

"Thank you." Adas reined Draco around into a brisk trot.

Calais stared after him. "Does he always get on his horse without help?"

"Yes. He is—unique."

"What did he mean about the stallions?"

"That's his code for, 'Tell me if anyone is abusive,' in case anyone overhears us. Since he came to the Antonia, no one on my team has been beaten. Centurion Longinus 'put' us behind his shield. Now, you're included, Calais."

"Does he always thank you when you do something?"

"He does. But he's the only one."

Outside the fortress, Adas slowed Draco to a walk. He was aware of a few gawking pedestrians. He assumed the local citizens were amused to see a battered Roman soldier. He was wrong. It was because Adas wore the *caligae* and belt of a centurion yet was unarmed. It was a rare sight to see a Roman dare to venture into Jerusalem without weapons. When Adas reached a scroll shop, he dismounted and dropped the reins. Draco snorted, but did not move away from where the ends of the reins lay in the street. He patted the horse's neck and walked in the shop.

"Ah, Centurion, what may I do for you?" asked the shopkeeper, literally dropping what he was doing to assist. The man hastily picked up the bundle of papyrus he had been carrying.

Normally, Adas would have apologized for startling the man, but not today. "I'd like several letter-sized scrolls and a pot of ink," he answered in Hebrew.

The man's eyebrows shot up. "Your Hebrew is very good, Sir. Here's my selection."

Adas selected several scrolls and an ink pot. He paid for the items and left. Draco pawed the ground while Adas put his purchases in his knapsack. Once in the saddle, he tried to clench his fist, but it was too painful. He decided to find Demitre when he got back to the Antonia.

He rode down Market Street scanning for Jamin. Adas dismounted to buy peaches, apples, apricots, figs, and dried meat from several vendors. They were impressed when he haggled over the prices in Hebrew. He found an exquisite silk scarf colored like the tail of a peacock. It reminded him of Dulcibella's eyes. For the first time since he read his father's letter, he relaxed. The price was more money than he had with him. He told the vendor he would return tomorrow and pay her extra for the scarf. The vendor, a middle aged woman with a broken front tooth, promised to be in the same spot so he could easily find her.

Adas stepped back to leave and bumped into someone. The man spoke in Hebrew. "I've been here all day looking for you."

"Jamin, is there somewhere we can talk?"

He nodded and started off down the street. From the height of Draco's back, it was easy to keep track of Jamin's progress. Minutes later, they were out of view in an alley.

"Centurion, you look awful."

"I've heard. I wasn't sure I'd find you today." He slid from the saddle.

Jamin handed Adas a small scroll. "This is for you."

"What is it?" Adas unrolled it, but he didn't need an answer. He smiled when he read the first few words. "This is from The Book of Psalms. Thank you. I will treasure it."

"I wrote some more quotes I thought you should see. Look at the first one."

Adas read aloud. "*The enemy shall not outwit him, nor the son of wickedness afflict him. I will beat down his foes before his face, and plague those who hate him.*" Adas took a slow deep breath. "I can use this kind of help."

"I can't believe it was just yesterday when the whole world turned upside down."

"Yes, it has in more ways than you know. Could you arrange a meeting for me with Peter and John. Perhaps, at the garden of the tombs tomorrow."

"I'll see what I can do, Centurion. Do you want to talk to them about Yeshua?" Trusting a Roman soldier, even one Jamin risked his life to protect, did not come easily. The last thing he wanted to do was lead his friends into danger.

"Yes, I want to know everything I can about Yeshua. Perhaps there is something I can do for them as well. Tell them I'll be at the tomb at the sixth hour. I will be alone, but they are welcome to bring others. And call me Adas. You did yesterday."

"Adas it is, but not if unfriendly ears are close by. It would be dangerous for both of us. Speaking of danger, what happened to the soldiers who attacked you?"

"In short—not much. My commander refused to accept my charges. The situation is complicated and dangerous. It is best if you do not know the details."

"Understood. We probably should go. You will recognize John if he meets with us. He was the one at the crucifixion, standing with Yeshua's mother."

"Then he will also recognize me. Perhaps he will want to knife me rather than talk."

"Violence is not our way. John will not welcome you, but he will listen to you. Whether they come with me or not, I'll be there."

Adas thanked him and leaped into the saddle. He clicked his tongue and the big bay sprang into a trot. He headed for his favorite furniture shop, *Serapio's Suppelex*. The two-story building sat at the intersection of Commerce Road and Sheep Gate Street. It was also the home of Serapio and his wife, Fabiana.

Serapio was a former *gladiator* who had survived the arena long enough to buy back his freedom and pay off his debts. His name was Regulus Novius Serapio, but he preferred his *nomen*, Serapio. Hard times had forced him into the arena when he was a young man. Now at the age of forty-two, he was prosperous. His furniture was the most sought after in Jerusalem. He was built like a bear with huge hands and heavily muscled arms and shoulders which gave him a fearsome appearance. There was a plowed furor of a scar that ran from the top of his forehead to his jaw. While in the arena, Serapio survived the force of a short sword across the face, blinding the eye. Children stared in fright at first sight until Serapio's hearty laugh put them at their ease. He was not only skilled with weapons. Serapio worked wonders with reeds, leather, and wood.

Serapio and Fabiana had two adopted sons, an Egyptian, named Nebetka, and a Greek, named Dorrian, who worked as his apprentices. Nebetka and Dorrian were once slaves owned by a *gladiator* trainer. When Serapio neared the end of his slavery contract, he arranged to stay on an extra month in exchange for the boys' freedom. Serapio and his wife adopted them, and they grew up with their other children who now had their own families. Nebetka was unmarried, but he vowed to stay with Serapio as his assistant even if he should wed.

Adas first met the boys when he was a teenager in Rome. Aquila expelled him from home after a series of heated arguments. Serapio took Adas in to work as his apprentice. It wasn't long before Serapio and Fabiana loved Adas as a son. He found acceptance and encouragement in their household. He missed the companionship of his mother, teachers, and favorite servants. However, the friendship Adas and Serapio developed offset the pain of his estranged relationship with his father. Having brothers and sisters for the first time in his life was an adjustment, but he learned to cherish the companionship and good-natured teasing. Adas and the two young men had known each other for nine years now, and he considered them good friends, especially Nebetka.

"Adas, my friend!" exclaimed Serapio as he clapped a huge hand on his shoulder. "Ah, it does my heart good to see you, but it troubles me to see the state you're in. What does the other fellow look like?"

"It's always too long since I've seen you last, Serapio. To answer your question, the three of them look fine." The two men sat down at the back of the shop. "I find myself in need of a new chair. It seems my old one threw itself against my door and made a mess. You should teach your chairs to behave better."

"Well, you pick one out and I will give it a stern lecture. Agreed?" Serapio moved a few chairs out of the back room. Selecting one, Adas sat down in his new chair in no hurry to leave.

"You would pick that one. Rosewood is my most expensive wood. I receive a shipment every so often, paid in full. Yet, I do not know who sends it."

"Really? Interesting." Adas inspected the chair more closely.

Serapio threw his hands in the air. "It's a mystery! Does a certain centurion I know pay for them? You've already invested enough for me."

"Honestly, Serapio, it's not me."

"It's not often, but it started as soon as I opened this shop. I've saved the receipts. The total has come to quite a high figure." Their conversation moved on as they watched people pass by the open door. Occasionally, Serapio would tend to a customer.

Fabiana returned from the marketplace and greeted Adas with a hug and an offer of wine. He happily accepted the hug, but declined the wine. She was a slender, Greek woman with coal black hair and dark, long-lashed eyes. She gently touched his bruised face and frowned.

"I should like to tie a block around the neck of whoever did this and toss him in the sea." She turned his injured hand palm up. She removed the bandage and examined the injury. "These cuts are infected. How did this happen?"

"I put them there, but I didn't think about infection. All I could think about was, well, it's done now. It is a . . . reminder."

"Drastic measures may be required now." She looked at him with dread.

"Surely, it won't come to that. But if it does, would you do it?"

"Not me! Serapio can do it. He's done it before."

Serapio looked over Adas's shoulder. "You get over here tomorrow morning if it has not improved. Otherwise you could lose your hand if we don't cauterize it. A tattoo would have served better than this injury."

"You're right. I acted on impulse."

Fabiana re-bandaged the injury. "When you get back to the Antonia, get your *medicus* to try vinegar and willow. Soak your hand in the vinegar for a while. The infection is in the early stage and it could improve."

Adas gave her a reassuring smile and reached inside his coin pouch. "I know your stubborn husband will try to refuse payment for my new chair." He reached for her hand and gave her more than enough coins. "Use it to buy Nebetka a silk tunic and matching robe. Maybe it will catch the eye of a beautiful girl."

She chuckled. "Apio does have this annoying habit of forgetting to get payment from certain customers, but I can't seem to reform him. Do you think I should keep him, anyway?"

"Probably, It would be hard to train a new husband."

"What makes you think he is *already* trained?" She chuckled at Serapio's pretend annoyance and left the room.

Serapio gave Adas a good-natured grin. "I let her think she can boss me around *Ohe*, I have news. Dorrian and his wife found a house for sale just down the street. You should have been there when they moved in. There was so much commotion; I was surprised the whole *legio* didn't investigate. It's good he lives close to the shop. Fabiana enjoys his wife's company. Of course, it is hard for my Ana to meet someone she doesn't like."

Adas grew quiet. Thoughts of his mother surfaced, but he wasn't ready to talk about her yet, even to Serapio.

Serapio could see that Adas was troubled. "You know you can talk to me about anything, Adas. I know you. You are not one to pick fights, especially three against one. So I doubt the usual story will explain your injuries. If you are in trouble, you know I have no love for the Roman Army. You will tell me if you need help?"

"I will and I thank you. Yes, there is a problem and I don't even know the reason for it. So keep your battle ax handy. I may yet have need of it." Adas gazed out the open door. Occasionally, Draco would stomp a foot and twitch a fly off his sleek hide.

"Venustas still have a bad hoof?" Serapio didn't wait for an answer. "Valentius is the problem, isn't he?"

Adas was startled. "How did you know?"

"Easy guess. Valentius is known for targeting people for petty reasons, but he is a man of two hearts. He will take pity one day and flog the same man on the next. They say he was traveling to Jericho with a few squads of *sagittarii* when he came upon legionaries about to crucify a runaway slave. According to the story, Valentius ordered the legionaries to untie the slave. Valentius sat on his horse, watching. The slave took off at a run. Valentius dropped him with a single arrow before he got five paces away. He walked his horse up to the slave, retrieved his arrow, and rode off without a word."

"So, what was that about? Saving the man from a slow death or enjoying a little target practice?"

"The arrow didn't kill the slave. It did hasten his death, however."

"So, was it kindness or cruelty?"

"Who knows?" Serapio shrugged. "Maybe both."

"Can a rational man act on both motives at the same time?"

"I have no idea, my friend."

Adas thought about the two days off Valentius gave him. Was it fear of breaking protocol, or the loss of his mother? Was it neither or both reasons?

"I've been in Jerusalem two years. I've never given Valentius reason to hate me. Yet, his behavior has become increasingly hostile. I think it has to do with my father."

"It might, but do not dismiss Valentius's personality. His nickname is self-explanatory."

"What is it?"

"I'm surprised you haven't heard it. They call him Cerberus, the three-headed dog of Hades. Like Cerberus, he is vicious, but lacks imagination."

Adas thought for a moment, and then laughed. "I have heard a few centurions refer to Centurion Tacitus as Hercules when they're discussing Valentius. Now I understand why. Hercules overpowered Cerberus, stole him, and then returned the humiliated dog to Hades. You think the men are hoping 'Hercules' will repeat the last of his twelve labors?"

"I'm sure that's what they're hoping for."

"I may have to set my 'pack of wolves' loose on this 'dog' someday."

Serapio threw his head back and roared with laughter. Adas was referring to his weapons. It made Adas smile to hear the big man laugh. No matter what was wrong, he always felt better around Serapio.

"If your 'wolves' go on the prowl, don't forget to tell this old *gladiator*. I will not allow my generous investor to face Cerberus without me."

"Generous? Not me, I was only thinking of myself. How else would I find a decent chair in this town? I guess I should get back." He picked up his chair. "This is a fine chair, Serapio. I'm sure it will behave much better than the last one, especially since it is made of the mysterious rosewood."

"Rosewood or not, it better behave! I would chop it up if it mistreats you."

Adas hung the chair from a back saddle horn and jumped on Draco's back. They said their farewells and he turned Draco toward the Antonia. When he entered the arena, one of the stable slaves told Nikolaus his favorite centurion was back.

"Sir, I'll take Draco for you," called Nikolaus, hurrying from the stables building.

Adas handed him the reins. "Was there any problem with the door bolt?"

"No, Sir! The *primus opifax* told me to fix it. He said the other mechanics were busy. Since he is the prime mechanic I did as he told me. I also removed the chair."

"Well done, I knew I could depend on you."

"Thank you, Sir."

Adas took some of the fruit from his knapsack. "Here's for your trouble." He handed Nikolaus peaches, apples, and figs. The boy's hazel eyes lit up as he thanked him. He dropped the fruit down the inside of his tunic, except for one of the apples. Adas grinned to see the boy eagerly bite into the fruit.

From the stables, the centurion went straight to his quarters. Adas noticed the broken spool pieces were gone. He assumed Nikolaus must have removed those as well. He set the new chair down at his table and saw that the new lock was properly installed. The bits of papyrus were still scattered on the floor, but he left them.

The pain in his hand was getting worse. Adas knew he should find Demitre, but instead he sat, staring at the bits of torn papyrus. If he threw them away it would be like throwing his mother away and confirming the irrevocable reality of her death. If he left them on the floor, they would only be silent bits of paper. It was the same as not telling Serapio and Fabiana about her death. He simply couldn't bear acknowledging the fact to anyone else.

Trying to think of anything besides his loss, he remembered Tigula. He left his quarters and headed for Cassius's quarters, the last on the row. When he knocked, he heard a loud sniffing at the base of the door. "Tigula, is that you?" The mastiff barked and pawed at the door. "Where's your master, Tig?"

"Right behind you," answered Cassius.

Adas spun around. "Did you *have* to do that? For somebody who has such a bad limp, you certainly are stealthy."

"And for someone who has the eyes of a wolf, you certainly don't have the ears of one. You need to brush up on your skills, my friend."

When Tigula saw both his master and Adas, the big dog wagged his tail so hard it shook his whole body. After greeting his master, the dog went to the centurion. Adas signaled for the mastiff to lie down. Adas listened to the dog's heart and rate of breathing, as well as checking his eyes, tongue, teeth, gums and skin. Then he pressed around the dog's stomach, watching Tigula's eyes to see if he gave any sign of distress.

"I don't find anything wrong. Maybe he's just bored."

"I hope that's it, but I'm stuck at a desk for the rest of the week. I'll take him to the game Saturday. Did they tell you about the soccer game?" Adas glanced up, but didn't answer. "*Ohe*, I'm sorry, Adas. I'm acting like yesterday didn't happen. What are you going to do about Valentius? Everyone's talking about it. They think he's hanging you out for target practice."

"Apparently, my own men are his arrows."

A shadow moved outside the window. Cassius put a finger to his lips and pulled the door open in time to see Demitre disappear around the corner.

Adas started to go after him. "Slow down, my friend," said Cassius. "You won't get anything out of him. If he was listening, then so be it. Come on, let's get some dinner." Cassius headed up the lane. Adas glanced in the direction Demitre had gone, but decided his friend was probably right. He caught up, and Cassius continued, "Valentius will know the rest of us don't buy his story, and I mean 'us' as in most of the decurions, your *centuria*, and many others. Besides, you don't want to go after that little sneak. Valentius may talk tough to Demitre, but as long as I've been here, nobody mistreats Demitre. He may be a slave, but he stands behind Valentius's shield more than anyone at the Antonia."

"There seems to be quite a crowd behind that shield."

"It's not just Valentius's protection you need to consider. If you get crosswise with Demitre, you better not get sick or injured. In his defense, he's the best *medicus* I've ever known. The only reason I can still walk is because of him. If he likes you, you'll get the best medical care possible, but if you've crossed him or Valentius, you're in trouble. I don't care how anyone treats a slave, but I'm careful how I treat Demitre."

"Wasn't there something else you were going to tell me about him? You mentioned something at Golgotha."

"Yes, since Demitre did this leg surgery on me, he's been trying to get me to take opium water to help me sleep. If I didn't know better, I'd wonder if Demitre saved my leg to get me addicted to his concoctions. I hear he charges handsomely. I took his opium before the surgery, of course, but I don't want it now."

"You're having trouble sleeping?"

"No, and I've never mentioned a problem to anyone. I keep refusing because opium doesn't settle well with me. I'd say something to Valentius about it, but there's no way to know how he would react. I've heard of him punishing a soldier just for shouting at Demitre. Besides, if I should get injured again, I don't want to burn any bridges. Have you noticed Demitre never relaxes except when he's in his master's presence? I find it odd behavior for a slave. They must have a complicated history."

They reached the officers' *cafeteria*. Adas tried to ignore the stares and whispered comments. He was beginning to think the men had nothing else to discuss. After they finished eating, Cassius left for the common room, leaving Adas alone at the table.

Onesimus appeared to clear away dishes. "Sir, do you need anything?" he asked eagerly.

"Do you know Nikolaus who works in the stables?"

"Yes, Sir. I know most of the stable boys. Calais and I came here together. We both belong to Tribune Salvitto. He allows us two meals every day and gives us a new tunic every year. We are most fortunate to belong to him."

"Nikolaus is the leader of my team of stable boys. I'm looking for some more boys to join my class. You told me how much you love horses. Would you like to join?"

Onesimus gaped at Adas with round eyes. "Sir! Are you *asking* me?" Immediately, the boy ducked his head and apologized. "I will do as my master wishes."

"You have nothing to apologize for, Onesimus. I did, indeed, ask if you would like to join my apprentices. I do not waste my time training someone who is not interested."

The boy raised eyes bright with eagerness. "Yes, Sir, I would like it very much. I will work hard for you!"

"Fine, then." Adas stood to leave. "I will request adding you to the class when I speak with Tribune Salvitto. Horses need patience and a kind hand, even if they try to hurt you. You have to be firm, but never cruel. Do you think you can give it a try?"

"I will do my best, Sir."

"Your best is all I will ever ask of you, Onesimus."

"Yes, Sir! Thank you, Sir!"

"If your father taught you any special techniques, I would like you to show them to me."

"Thank you, Sir!" Onesimus scampered back to the kitchen before anyone could see his broad smile. He did not want someone to suspiciously demand why he looked so happy.

Adas left the *cafeteria* and went to his quarters. Once inside, he stepped around the bits of papyrus on the floor. He sat at his table to write a letter to Centurion Cornelius. He wrote for nearly two hours. By the time he finished, it was getting dark. He planned to write a letter to Dulcibella in the morning, but he would leave out many details, especially his injuries. Using his iron fire starter and flint, he got a spark to take flame on a bit of tender and lit his oil lamps. Now the problem would be getting the letter to Cornelius. He didn't think he could trust any postmen at the *cursus publicus*, even if it was the fastest mail service. Perhaps Serapio would know of someone who could be trusted or maybe he could hire Jamin to take the letter. Adas rolled the scroll up and sealed it with wax. He pressed his wolf ring into the wax and blew on it until it set. He put the letter in his knapsack.

Adas looked at his bandaged hand. It felt much more painful than it did the day before. He hoped it was from holding a pen for so long, but he knew Fabiana was never wrong about injuries. Carefully, he unwound the linen and contemplated the cross. The cuts were indeed enflamed, but Adas was too tired to search for Demitre. He washed the cuts at the basin and tried to straighten his fingers out, but the pain intensified. He decided to let the injury air out and tossed the used bandage in the fireplace. A shadow passed through the moonlight streaming into the window to the left of his door, but no shadow appeared from the window to the right. Someone was outside his door. Slowly, the door handle began to move.

Chapter 15

Adas grabbed his dagger off the bedside table. He stood in front of the door, but the handle moved back in place. A knock sounded. Holding his dagger behind his back he unbolted the door and opened it. Demitre stood outside, his medical kit in his hand.

"I beg your forgiveness for intruding, but my master sent me to check on you, Centurion. I was going to wait for you inside, as my master instructed me to do, but your door was locked. I came by earlier, but you weren't here. My master berated me for not finding you even though I looked all over the Antonia."

Adas ignored the hint to explain his absence. "You might as well come in."

"A wise decision, Sir. It would be dangerous to leave an infection untreated."

"An infection?" Adas narrowed his eyes. "Why would you make that assumption? Do you distrust your own skills?"

Demitre hesitated. "Injuries to the hands often become infected. It is simple logic. A quick examination is all I need to be sure. To prevent amputation later, of course."

Adas backed away to let the *medicus* enter. Despite his reservations, Demitre's skills surpassed Serapio's limited abilities. He sat at his table and gestured for Demitre to sit. The *medicus* removed the bandage and studied the cuts.

"Sir, this is not good. As I feared, these cuts are quite infected. It is not too late for treatment, but it soon will be."

"What do you think caused the infection?"

"I can think of two ways. You did not put your dagger in boiling water or run it through fire. Or you did not use freshly washed linen when you bandaged it. Experience has taught us to heat surgical instruments before each use to avoid disease, even on the battlefield."

"What do you recommend? Vinegar and willow powder?"

"Sadly, no. I'm afraid the *contagio* is too advanced for potions. There's only one thing left to do to avoid *gangrena* and amputation."

"Cauterize my hand?"

"Yes, I am truly sorry. It will be exceedingly painful." Without waiting for approval, Demitre pulled a leather strap from his kit. "I will need to use a restraint. No man can resist the urge to avoid such agony."

"What will you use to make the burns?" Asking the question offered a fleeting illusion of control. Demitre presented a short L-shaped iron rod with a thick wooden handle. "You'll need to burn it in sections?"

"Yes, I'll treat the longest cut first, hopefully with no more than two applications. The shorter cut will only require one."

"I let the fire go out, but the lamps are full." Adas accepted the pain he was about to endure. He thought about the men he had crucified. Their guilt did not erase the images. A skillful swipe of a sword would produce the same result without the prolonged agony.

"Will you take the opium first, Sir?" Adas shook his head.

Demitre put more wood in the fireplace and used a lamp to light it. He stared intently. The twisting flames reflected in his black eyes. He shook himself as if from a trance and set the iron rod in the fire. Demitre allowed himself to smile as the fire embraced the iron rod.

Adas pulled his chair closer to the table and lay his right arm out flat. Demitre picked up the ruined tunic on the floor and folded it into a thick pad. He saw the bits of shredded papyrus on the floor. He knew they were pieces of a letter from *Consul* Longinus. His master would be amused. He placed the pad under Adas's hand. Apologizing, Demitre wrapped the leather strap around Adas's wrist several times, pulled the strap tightly around the table and tied it underneath. Using a strip of linen, he wrapped the cloth around Adas's fingers and thumb to keep them out of the way. Forcing his hand to lay flat caused the cuts to open. Adas grunted from the pain.

Demitre stepped back and clasped his hands together. "Do you wish for me to stop?" Adas wearily shook his head.

The rod began to glow red. Demitre took the rod from the fire. He held it close to his face to feel the heat radiate from the iron as the red glow slowly faded. Adas felt his mouth go dry. He swallowed hard and looked away.

Demitre pulled the other chair away from the table. He took a short multi-layered leather strap from his kit and handed it to Adas. "Sir, you will want to put this between your teeth. I will do this as quickly as possible. Lean against the table as best you can in case you pass out. Let us hope you do. Will you take the opium water now? The pain will be unbearable."

Adas ignored the offer, put the strap in his mouth, and pulled his chair in closer. He put his left hand over the crook of his outstretched right arm and laid his head down on his left forearm. Demitre placed his fist over Adas's cloth-wrapped fingers and pressed down with his weight. There would be an involuntary urge to clench the hand into a fist. He brought his knee up and pressed his shin down on the wrist.

"I will hold this position until your hand goes numb. Then I will say 'now.' Understand?" Adas nodded and took a deep breath. Demitre shifted his weight. "Now."

Savage white-hot agony shot through Adas's hand. His jaw muscles jumped as he bit into the leather. A tortured groan caught in his throat. His back muscles constricted. He felt a wave of nausea as his whole body broke out in sweat. There was a sizzling sound. The air smelled of burnt flesh and hot metal. The agony seemed to go on for eternity.

"Now," said Demitre again. He pressed the rod into the same cut, but closer to the wrist. The pain was overwhelming. As Adas bit into the leather strap, he struggled to breathe. Finally, Demitre lifted the rod. He put the rod back in the flames to burn off the infected tissue.

Adas took the leather strap from his mouth and looked at the charred line along his palm. Sweat ran into his eyes, but he barely had the strength to wipe his forehead. Demitre waved the rod in the air until the red glow disappeared.

Again, Demitre pressed down with his fist and shin on Adas's fingers and wrist. "Now." He pressed the rod in the remaining cut. The excruciating pain seemed even worse than the first two burns. As he clamped his teeth on the strap, Adas struggled to maintain control. This time, along with the nausea, he felt faint. He clenched his arm so tightly his left hand cramped. Adas kept his head down, fighting to get enough air. Panting, he tried to focus his attention on his good hand as he squeezed his arm. It seemed Demitre would never remove the burning rod.

Then the pressure on his wrist let up. Demitre raised the rod and set it on the floor. He kept his fist pressing down on Adas's fingers. "Do not try to close your hand. Keep the leather strap in your mouth. We're done with the rod, but there's one last thing to do." Slowly, he let up the pressure with his fist on Adas's fingers. He took a small wine skin from his kit, and pulled the stopper out. "This is vinegar."

Again, Demitre pressed down hard with his fist over Adas's fingers. "Now!" he said as he poured a generous amount of vinegar on the burns. The acid bubbled making a low hissing sound. A new wave of nausea slammed Adas as violently as the sting of the acid. His vision faded until he slumped to the table unconscious. Demitre turned Adas's head sideways to take the leather strap out of his mouth.

"Centurion? Sir! Can you hear me?" Demitre snapped his fingers in front of Adas's face. When there was no response, he knelt down to eyelevel. Watching his face closely, Demitre grasped Adas by the hair and lifted his head a few inches. "You're such a fool. You think Valentius is the only one to fear. You're dead wrong." A mirthless laugh sounded in the room, and he let go. Adas's head dropped onto his forearm. "You *will* take the potion tonight. Truthfully it will *not* ease your pain, but it will make your night—interesting."

Adas groaned, and the slave's face morphed back into a mask of indifference. He took off his robe and rolled it up into a makeshift pillow. He lifted Adas's head carefully, straightened his left arm out, and slid the pillow under his head. Demitre arranged his face into a sympathetic expression, hovered unblinking, and watched. Only when Adas tucked his left arm protectively against his head did Demitre remove the leather strap from his wrist. The bright red area around the centurion's wrist and the crook of his arm would soon be dark with bruises. Demitre used a clean cloth to soak up the vinegar from the burns. He removed the linen strips from the centurion's fingers.

Adas tried to lift his head. Demitre cautioned, "Do not move yet. I'm going to bandage your hand."

"Did I pass out?"

"For less than a minute, Sir. You tolerated the treatment better than most. Now try to be still. It's almost over. I'm sure you are sorry this extreme treatment was necessary, but I appreciate your trust in me." Something in the slave's tone was odd.

The *medicus* moved several rolls of linen bandaging aside, selecting one tied with black thread. He threw Adas a stealthy glance and pulled the thread off. He bandaged Adas's hand, weaving the linen strip around the palm and wrist.

Adas thought of his order for Octavean to drive the spikes in Yeshua's hands and feet. Shame burned in his soul ten times hotter than the cauterizing rod. Yeshua said, *"Father, forgive them."* Why couldn't he accept it? He embraced the pain as a just punishment.

Slowly, Adas raised his head. Demitre was next to the table clutching his arms across his chest as if he were cold. But his eyes were fixed on Adas with an unblinking stare. Demitre neither moved nor spoke.

"Demitre, surely you have neutralized the infection."

"Yes, surely. One can hope. It is possible the burns will become infected. I must monitor the wound closely." Demitre placed the rod back in the fire to clean it. He set the rod on the hearth to cool. A satisfied smile spread across his lips, but when he turned around, his face was once again a passive veneer. He went to his kit and pulled a vial from it.

"Please, Sir, take the opium water. It will ease the pain."

"No."

Demitre pulled the leather stopper out. "Sir, my master will be displeased with me if I leave you this way." He held the open vial closer. "Surely, you don't want me beaten."

"How would he know? I'm not going to tell him. Are you?"

Demitre had overplayed his hand. He pressed his lips together in frustration. He resealed the vial and turned away. He helped Adas to the bed, removed his *caligae*, and covered him with a blanket. He retrieved his robe from the table. "Sir, will you reconsider the opium water?"

"No, you have done your job well."

"You are most kind considering the violence done to you."

Adas eyed Demitre sharply. "Odd choice of words, Demitre."

"The cauterizing, Sir. That's all I meant. Nothing more." Demitre sat by the bed without waiting to be invited.

"Demitre, were you outside Decurion Quintus' door earlier today?"

"Yes."

"Why?"

The *medicus* got up and poured water from the pitcher into a cup, stalling to think of a good answer. He helped Adas sit up to drink. "My master sent me to find you. I saw you and the decurion go into his quarters. I was about to knock when the door opened. It startled me. I ran off. Old habits, I suppose. There was a time when I did not belong to Centurion Valentius. He rescued me from others less—tolerant. He is a good man, but I fear he is ill. Please do not judge him for what he has become."

"What has he become?"

"Obsessed."

"How so?"

"I have said too much." The slave licked his lips nervously, but inwardly he smiled, when his focus on Valentius distracted Adas from his original question. "I will check on you in the morning." He blew the oil lamps out. He took up his medical kit, but paused at the door. Adas had turned on his side. Demitre deftly slipped a small wooden shank in the lock casing. He left and shut the door softly behind him.

Adas heard the door close. A soft breeze crept through the window lattices, making the fire toss flickering shadows across the room. He reached for the cup of water on his nightstand and saw something which did not belong there. It was the vial of opium water.

Chapter 16

Adas woke to find his mother sitting on his bed. It was dark, but moonlight streamed in through the lattice in the windows, cutting two shafts of misty white across the room. He could see her plainly, dressed in a long flowing gown of iridescent white. She leaned down and gazed into his eyes. The copper color of her eyes was gone, replaced by a kaleidoscope of hues and shapes. Adas tried to pull away from her, but he couldn't move. She touched the injured side of his face and he gasped. Her hand felt so cold it burned. Her pale lips were stretched tightly over her teeth as if they were too small for her mouth. Her teeth were squares of swirling iridescence.

"Having bad dreams, my son?" Her voice echoed as if it came from a great distance. "Does Aquila stalk you in your sleep?" Marsetina reached for his bandaged hand lying next to his head. She clasped his wrist with frozen hands. "I see I'm too late. He's already done his work. The Eagle has driven his scepter through your hand. *What did you do to deserve this?*"

Marsetina looked at the scraps of Aquila's letter on the floor. She released his wrist and snapped her fingers. The bits of letter lifted from the floor. They danced in the air and wove themselves together over the palm of her hand. The last piece attached itself. Rippling with vivid colors, the paper floated to her hand.

"Adas, why did you leave your father scattered all over the floor?" She kept her eyes fastened on his face, but moved her head back and forth. She let go of the letter, but it remained floating in the air. Slapping her hands down on either side of his head, she lowered her face to his. Her multi-colored eyes began to shift to a solid golden glow. "Is this how you show your loyalty? Leaving your father to be trod upon?" She crouched over him like a spider. Her lips curled back revealing shiny silver fangs.

Adas felt his heart thundering as if it were about to burst. The sound filled the room, making the walls expand and contract with each beat. Marsetina moved closer. He could feel her cold breath on his face. "For three full moons I waited for you. Where were you?"

Without taking her eyes from his face, she took hold of the floating letter. It turned into a spear of writhing flames with a glowing red-hot blade. She held it in front of his face. "Only a coward would assault the dead. Were you proud of yourself when your sin pierced the heart of God?" He could feel the heat of the blade and smell the hot metal.

"Look at this!" she demanded in her far away voice. "Think upon your handi-work, and despair." She raised the spear and let go; it hovered in the air. She grasped the fiery shaft in her fist like a dagger. She dragged the point of the spear over his heart. A sizzling hiss sounded as the blade sliced his tunic. The edges of the burnt linen peeled back, bubbling and black, as the hot blade consumed the cloth. Adas could feel the heat of the metal. Marsetina pressed the point between his ribs. Her eyes erupted into flames. "I should split your heart in two!" Then she was gone, but someone else was there.

A man wearing a robe made of tiny, writhing snakes materialized from the wall. He floated across the room to hover over Adas. His face was shrouded with a long white beard and long shimmering white hair. The filament-like hair floated about the head as if repelled by waves of heat. His eyes were glossy, jet-black ovals. Within each eye was a reflection of a terrified face—Adas's face. The ghoulish figure bent so close, Adas caught the stench of foul breath. When the man reached for him, Adas cried out with all the strength he possessed. His eyes shot open. He pushed himself up on his elbows in time to see his door shut. A figure passed, interrupting the moonlight streaming through the window lattice.

Adas slapped his hand on his chest. The tunic was intact, but the pain in his hand was worse than ever. He felt his forehead. His skin felt sensitive, hot and dry. His mouth was as dry as chalk. He wrestled his tunic off and threw it on the floor. The torn pieces of his father's letter swirled away from the rumpled garment. In panic, Adas thought the horrific nightmare was starting over, but the bits of letter were only reacting to the air stirred by the tunic. He examined his chest and side. There were no injuries. With a sigh of relief, his breathing slowed but his heart was still racing.

Another fearful thought seized him. He went to the copper mirror and snatched it off the wall. He was terrified he would see the same face as the one reflected in the eyes of the nightmare apparition. Much to his relief, it was his natural expression. But something caught his attention. The pupils of his eyes were unnaturally dilated, even for the dark. He retrieved an ember with the fireplace tongs and held it close to his face. The mirror revealed that light or no light, his pupils remained fixedly dilated.

He sat down on the bed. There was a bitter taste on his tongue. He drank from the cup he kept on the bedside table, spilling half of it. In the light of the moon, he saw the vial of opium water Demitre left behind. The stopper was off and the vial lay empty on its side. Using the tip of his finger, he tasted the contents. It was bitter. Adas couldn't remember drinking the contents of the vial, but he did remember refusing it, repeatedly. He stumbled to the door and tried to lock it, but something was jammed in the casing. Too exhausted to care, he returned to the bed. He pulled the blanket up over his head, a childhood habit, and fell asleep again.

A banging sound woke him. Someone was knocking on his door. He threw the blanket off and called out, "Come in." The door slowly swung open to reveal Onesimus.

"Centurion Longinus, should I come in?" Adas waved him in as he got out of bed and pulled another tunic from his clothes chest. Onesimus set a tray down on the little table. "Sir, I was worried when you didn't come for breakfast, so I brought it to you. Cook gave me permission. Demitre was outside your door when I turned the corner, but he left without knocking. I hope I have not disturbed you, Centurion." The boy glanced up before he fastened his eyes on the floor again. "And Tribune Salvitto is back."

In spite of the lingering effects of his terrifying night, Adas smiled at the subtle reminder of his offer to join his Saturday class. "Thank you for the food, Onesimus. Tell me, did you see anyone leave the slave quarters last night?" Adas took his belt off the back of the chair and tried to fasten it, but the buckle touched the palm of his right hand. He winced and let go of the strap. He tried to flex his fingers, but his hand was stiff with pain.

"Sir, may I assist you?" He fastened the belt carefully, asking if it was too tight or too loose. He stepped back, keeping his eyes lowered. "May I assist you with your *caligae*?"

Adas sat down. "Thank you, Onesimus. It seems you have come to my rescue this morning. I'll be sure and tell Tribune Salvitto when I ask about you joining my class. He'll be pleased with your service. Tell me about last night. Did someone leave?"

"Yes, Sir."

"Could you see who it was?"

Onesimus ducked his head lower. He concentrated on methodically lacing the boot sandals. "I might be mistaken."

When Onesimus finished lacing the boots, Adas gestured for him to sit. He saw the gesture, but couldn't believe he was invited to sit in the centurion's presence. Adas scooped up a mouthful of stew. "You even brought a utensil for eating. You are most efficient. This is very good. I think I'm hungry enough to eat a herd of sheep, bones and all."

The child smiled shyly, keeping his gaze to the floor. Adas nodded his head at the chair. "Go on. Sit. The chair won't bite, and neither will I." The boy obeyed. "I understand your reluctance to answer my question. I know you have to live with the other slaves in close quarters, especially at night when you are locked in. But I assure you, this person will not get in trouble and neither will you. This will stay between the two of us."

Onesimus swallowed nervously. "Sometimes I can't sleep. It was dark, of course, but there was a good moon. I could not see his face, but I saw the outline of him as he slipped out the door. It was Demitre. I don't know how he knew the door would be unlocked. When I woke up this morning, he was back. We had to wait for someone to unlock the door."

"Onesimus, you must not tell anyone you have told me this. It is very important."

"I understand, Sir. I will do as you say."

"Excellent. And so is this stew. Are you helping with the cooking? It seems the food has improved since you came here."

Onesimus beamed with pleasure. "I do help with the seasoning. My mother taught me how to use herbs and spices."

"Your mother taught you well." Adas ate a few more mouthfuls, but then set the bowl down. "But, I don't think I can eat anymore. Perhaps you can finish it for me while I shave." Adas set the bowl in front of the child and handed him the utensil. Onesimus stared at him in disbelief. "It is wrong to waste food, especially stew this good. If you take any of it back to Cook, he'll be insulted."

The boy ate as if it were his last meal. When he thought Adas wasn't looking, he licked the bowl clean. It was a struggle, but Adas managed not to laugh out loud.

"I need you to find Decurion Quintus. Ask him if I might borrow Tigula today."

"Yes, Sir." Onesimus picked up the tray and scurried out the door.

Adas took some of the fruit from his knapsack. He was still hungry. After he finished eating, he used his dagger to remove the stick jamming the door bolt. Only Demitre had the opportunity to jam the lock. But why would Valentius order Demitre to take such risks? However, Adas had never experienced images as vivid and terrifying as that dream. Obviously, there were other ingredients in the opium water. Perhaps Valentius was hoping Adas would complain so he could accuse him of paranoia. Or maybe Valentius wanted him to see how vulnerable he was. Whatever the reason, it was more than disturbing. Adas remembered his oil lamps were full before Demitre cauterized his hand. The slave blew them out when he left. Adas found each one was nearly full, except for the one on his bedside table. It was nearly empty. His skin crawled at the thought of Demitre creeping into his room, forcing him to drink the potion, and watching him while he slept.

Adas caught sight of his reflection in the copper mirror. The bruising across his left cheekbone and temple area had taken on a greenish purple color. There was dark purplish blue bruising around his right wrist and upper forearm. Even his fingers were bruised. The pain in his hand was a constant reminder of the possibility of amputation. In spite of his fear, he would not have to face it alone. Serapio and Fabiana were more like parents to him than just friends. Also, his three unexpected rescuers were not far away. Jamin, Cleopas, and Malchus risked their lives to help him although he was a stranger and a Roman. Even after all their questions were answered, they did not desert him.

He opened his door and stepped outside. Judging by the length of the shadows, it was after the fourth hour. He thought about his upcoming meeting with Jamin and, hopefully Peter and John, with anticipation and a bit of dread. He only had an hour to get to the garden if he wanted to be early. Deciding not to wait for Cassius to bring Tigula, Adas headed toward his quarters. Lucius Octavean was walking toward him directly in his path. Adas stopped, forcing Lucius to give way. His pale eyes glinted with animosity, but his face remained impassive.

"Excuse me, Centurion Longinus. I didn't mean to get in your way."

Adas said nothing, but never took his eyes off the man's face. Lucius stepped past. Adas rounded on him. "Octavean!" The legionary slowly turned. "That shield you're standing behind won't be there for long. Do you really think he will protect you forever? He will dispose of you when you cease to be useful. Consider what he's doing to me, a centurion and the son of the minor *consul*. What do you think he'll do to you, a mere legionary?" Adas walked away. He could feel Lucius staring after him. The smirk evaporated from the legionary's face.

Adas reached Cassius's door and knocked. The decurion ushered him inside. "So the kitchen boy says you'd like to borrow Tigula for the afternoon. I was about to bring him."

Lucius rounded a building, stopped, and peered back around the corner. He watched as Adas went in Cassius's quarters. He leaned back against the wall and scowled at the raw skin of his hands. Scrubbing the latrine channels was the most humiliating punishment he had ever endured. Even worse, his punishment was scheduled for two weeks longer than Hektor and Falto. The message was clear; Valentius owned him.

Tigula bounded out of his master's quarters, wagging his tail, and barking excitedly. Lucius peeked around the corner again. Adas knelt down, scratching the dog's ears and neck as Cassius attached a leather leash to the collar. "You two have a good walk. *Ohe*, here's his favorite toy." Cassius handed Adas a short stick covered in leather. "You know how he loves to play." Adas thanked him and left with the big mastiff excitedly wagging his tail.

Lucius watched Adas cross the quad, but didn't follow. He remembered two years ago when Valentius first ordered him to spy on Longinus. Lucius thought the commander wanted to see if the untested centurion could do the job. However, in the last few months, Valentius's orders became more aggressive. Lucius was in a dangerous situation. He had no proof he was acting under orders. Even worse, assaulting Longinus and forcing Valentius to cover for him had cost him any leverage he might have had. He was trapped with no conceivable escape.

Adas left the Antonia with Tigula and took the main road to the market place. He found the same woman selling silks and bought the peacock-colored scarf. He paid extra as he promised. Afterward, Adas took side streets until he reached the east gate and passed outside of the city. There was Golgotha, Misery's playground. Adas stopped at the sight of several crucified men hanging lifeless from their crosses, their corpses left to decompose in the elements. The banners announcing their crimes fluttered in the breeze. Tigula whimpered, but waited for Adas to move. The dog nudged his hand, drawing him back to the living.

"You're a good companion, Tigula," The mastiff woofed and wagged his tail. There were other people passing along the road, but they gave the mastiff a wide berth as Adas and the dog continued along the road.

Adas entered the garden and tied Tigula's leash to a tree. He entered the tomb. The burial linen was gone, but nothing else had changed. He found where the pearl was buried and uncovered the pouch. The pearl was inside. Adas sighed with relief. He tied off the drawstrings, put the cord around his neck, and slipped the pouch under his tunic.

When Adas stepped out of the tomb, Tigula stood up, wagging his tail. Adas grinned at the dog's eagerness to play and disconnected his leash. He hurled the stick toy up the garden path. Tigula tore after it, almost skidding past it as he snatched it up. Adas put the dog through his paces, praising him when he obeyed a command. When Tigula was tired, Adas gave the panting dog handfuls of water from his wineskin. After Tigula had his fill, Adas took a long drink and sat down.

Jamin, Peter, and John watched from behind the hillside boulders above the garden. Jamin whispered, "How long are we going to sit here? He's been waiting at least an hour."

"Patience, Jamin," said Peter, "we will sit as long as it takes."

"As long as what takes?" Jamin checked his stick sundial again.

"As long as it takes to watch him."

"Well, I've watched long enough," said John. "Any man who gives water to his dog before he takes water must have some goodness in him." John started down from the rocks as Jamin called to Adas, waving a hand. Adas waved back.

The three men descended, picking their way around outcrops and loose gravel. Jamin made it down first and welcomed Adas. Tigula stepped between the two men. He didn't growl, but made a low woof sound deep in his throat. Jamin stopped abruptly.

"It's all right," Adas assured them. "Tigula doesn't like many people, but he won't do anything unless he feels threatened. . .or you make sudden moves. . .or you raise your voice. . .or you pick up a rock. . .or. . ."

"We get it! If we don't move, the big dog stays happy." Jamin kept a wary eye on Tigula. He saw Adas flinch as the dog nosed his bandaged hand. "Has your hand gotten worse?"

"It'll be all right, I hope." He focused his attention on Peter and John as they slowly approached. Jamin introduced Adas to the men. Both men had dark eyes, dark brown hair and beards, but Peter was taller and huskier than John, who had a slender, more athletic build. They both wore the long tunics, robes, and sashes common to men from Galilee. Adas nodded recognition at John. The Galilean studied the centurion for a moment, but finally dipped his head once. They walked to the shade of several terebinth trees and sat down. Peter sat where he could keep an eye on the garden entrance. Tigula lay down at Adas's feet, but kept his eyes on the men.

Peter spoke first, "Why did you summon us here, Centurion?"

"Please, call me Adas. Only a man, like yourselves, asked you here today not a soldier. I have two reasons, the first being I want to learn everything you can tell me about Yeshua. To my shame, I knew he was innocent of any charges, but I followed orders anyway. Jamin, Cleopas, and Mal. . ." Jamin coughed loudly and shook his head. ". . .they explained it was God's plan to allow Yeshua to die, but I wish I had not been the executioner. This unrelenting guilt gnaws at my heart. I can't let it go."

"The Lord forgave you, Adas," said John. "I heard him say it. And he didn't mean just you and your men. Yeshua asked God to forgive everyone who was there."

"At the time, I didn't even consider asking for forgiveness, but Yeshua did so much more than forgive me. He appeared to me days later. He made sure I knew he was alive. I saw him right here in this garden. I watched him greet a few women, including his mother. Did Jamin tell you?" Peter and John nodded. "I know he is the Son of God. Will you teach me *HaDerech*?"

Peter scrutinized Adas with a critical eye. "We can teach you the Way, but what if this is a scheme for you to pass on information about us to your superiors or the Sanhedrin? What assurances can you give us?"

Adas shook his head. "None. I can give no proof of my motives, but does God not protect you? Even if I were here by deceit, wouldn't God turn my actions to your advantage? Doesn't he have a plan for you? I don't know as much about God as I want; but until now, I have never seen a force powerful enough to bring the dead back to life. God is not a complete stranger to me. I was taught as a child."

Peter and John exchanged quick looks. John arched an eyebrow and gave Adas an appraising nod. "As for God's protection, you are correct. If you try to thwart God's plan, you will never succeed. You may win a few battles, perhaps for a long time, but the final victory is always God's. Jamin says you carved a cross in your hand." John glanced at Adas's bandage.

"Even before the angel appeared and took the stone away from the tomb, I knew that Yeshua was not an average man. I did not want to ever forget him or forget my vow to never again execute the blameless. I cut my hand as a reminder."

"I can see you're paying a great price for that reminder," declared Peter. "It appears the wound had to be cauterized. I see the bruising from straps. But I suspect you left out one of your reasons. Did you also hunger for the pain?"

Adas saw the same haunted expression on Peter's face as he saw in the copper mirror. "How did you know?"

"I also felt the same need. You are not the only one who did a great injustice to Yeshua."

"As did I," said a man who stepped out from around the trees. Tigula leaped to his feet, growling. He lunged at the newcomer, but Adas grabbed his collar.

"What are *you* doing here?" Peter demanded. He glared at Adas. "Is this your doing?"

"No! It is *my* doing," exclaimed Jamin. "I invited Malchus to join us."

Peter pointed at the temple guard. "He works for Caiaphas! He was there to arrest Yeshua. Why would you defile us with this man's presence?"

Adas struggled to hold Tigula back. The dog was now snarling at the other men. "Please, everyone needs to lower their voices," Adas implored. He coaxed the agitated mastiff to sit. Peter and John kept a suspicious eye on Malchus who moved as far from Tigula as he could.

"Malchus risked his life to save mine, even though I was a stranger to him. He stopped a formidable soldier from killing me when I was defenseless. There were two other legionaries who could have shown up at any moment. Still, he challenged Octavean."

"Peter, listen to him," pleaded Jamin. "This legionary would have given Sampson a good fight, yet Malchus stood up to him, alone."

Peter turned doubtful eyes on Malchus. "So, you took on Sampson, did you?"

"Not exactly. I did have one advantage."

"What was that?" asked Peter warily.

"The man was falling-down drunk." Malchus shrugged. The anger went out of Peter's dark eyes. Jamin and Adas exchanged amused looks.

"Drunk or not," said Jamin, "the big legionary was big trouble."

"Malchus intervened because he wanted to know what I saw here when the angel appeared and opened the tomb. Would he take the risk of confronting Octavean if he didn't care about the truth?"

"Peter, Adas is right," John said, "our Lord has forgiven all of us. What right do we have to not do the same?" He gestured at Malchus. "How can you judge this man before you even know why he's here? Did not Yeshua heal his ear, the one you cut off? We have all failed Yeshua at some time. I presumed I should sit on the right hand of his throne in God's kingdom. You pretended you didn't even know who he was when the Sanhedrin took him."

"I accused him of being a liar." Jamin, looked away as he folded his arms across his chest. "I almost shouted insults at him as he was dying."

"Not one of us is innocent," said Adas. "But we have all answered Yeshua's call. He has forgiven us, but the hardest part is to forgive ourselves, which is something I find impossible to do. Nightmares haunt my sleep, and guilt gnaws at me when I'm awake. I need to understand. I hope you can find it in your hearts to tell me about him. Maybe then I will understand why God selected me to be the executioner."

"You speak well, Adas," said John, "and I don't just mean your excellent Hebrew." Adas felt the tension relax and loosened his hold on Tigula's collar. Malchus moved to shoo away a fly. The big dog snarled a warning at him.

"Good dog," Peter muttered under his breath.

Malchus gave an annoyed look at Peter. "Let me explain. When Yeshua healed my ear, he didn't just heal my physical being. Something else happened, which I cannot explain. I could not deny any longer he is the Christ. I wanted to leave Jerusalem and be done with Caiaphas, but then I knew I must serve God first. I have come to warn you. The Sanhedrin is talking about you two. They thought you would have gone back to Galilee by now. It bothers them that you're still here. The captain of the guard was instructed to bring you in if you ever talk to the people about Yeshua and his resurrection. I am only warning you to be aware of their plans. As for me, I will only work for Caiaphas as long as I can help you. When my usefulness is over, I am leaving Jerusalem. Every Sabbath when Yeshua was in Jerusalem, I was ordered to spy on him. But I also listened to his teachings. Caiaphas accused me of being deceived because I said I had never heard anyone say the things he did. Yeshua spoke to my heart and my soul. Now, Caiaphas watches me with a wary eye. I don't know how long I will be useful."

Adas asked, "Won't we all be useful as long as God wishes it?"

John laughed softly. "Peter, do you remember what Yeshua said about the centurion in Capernaum? He had never seen such faith in all of Israel like the faith that man possessed. Perhaps Yeshua would say the same of Adas."

"Centurion Claudius Januarius," Adas volunteered.

"Who is Claudius Januarius?" asked Peter.

"He is the centurion John is talking about, the one in Capernaum with the servant who was dying. Claudius told Yeshua that he didn't need to come to his unworthy home, but could just say the word and his servant would be healed. And he was. The servant's name is Andreas."

"How did you hear of it?" asked John.

"Another centurion, Marcus Claudius Cornelius, my superior in Caesarea, was friends with Claudius. Marcus told me about it in a letter."

"Yeshua's miracles have touched more lives than we know," said Malchus. He stood up. "I must go before I am missed. Jamin, we will talk later."

Jamin nodded eagerly. "If you need to find me, I will be staying with Cleopas and Mary. In the meantime, I will figure out a way we can communicate."

"Do either of you know of anyone who would take a letter to Caesarea, to Centurion Cornelius? I do not trust the couriers at the Antonia and I will pay the asking price."

"I have business in Caesarea," said Malchus. "I can carry it."

"When will you leave?"

"Sunday, after Sabbath."

"If you're not leaving until then, I have time to write another letter. Both can be delivered to Centurion Cornelius. When should I bring them to you?"

"Any time before Sunday morning. We will leave very early."

"Will you be there long enough in case they have letters for me?"

"I'll be there at least a week. I'll make sure the centurion knows. Bring me the scrolls on the Sabbath, outside the temple. I will find you at the Gentile fountain around the seventh hour."

"Thank you, Malchus. I appreciate this." Jamin and Malchus said their farewell to the group. They left the garden and headed for the city gate.

Peter and John stood up to leave, but Adas held up a hand. "Please, there was a second reason I wanted to meet with you. John, I heard Yeshua entrust you with the care of his mother, Mary. Does she live in your home?"

"Why do you ask?"

"I want to give her a gift which will provide unlimited security and comfort. I am giving it to you so you can present it to her. She is free to do with it as she pleases." Adas handed John the pouch. "I want her to have this."

"What is it?" He opened the pouch and tapped it on his palm. The blue pearl rolled out. Peter and John gasped. Both men were struck speechless.

Peter finally tore his eyes from the shimmering gem. "Where did you get this treasure? I didn't know such magnificence was possible."

"A tax collector in Jericho named Zacchaeus gave it to me." Adas told them what transpired on that day.

"I remember Zacchaeus," said John. "Yeshua went to his house and stayed all day. We didn't go, since some of us have relatives in Jericho." John handed the pearl to Peter. "Adas, you do realize this pearl is worth a kingdom. Are you sure you want to give this to Mary?"

"Yes, more than anything. Will you do this for me?"

John and Peter exchanged glances. Peter said, "Adas, I take it you do not want her to know it is from you. We have too much respect for Mary to not tell her the truth. If you want us to give this treasure to her, you must trust us to do the right thing."

John handed the pouch to Peter. He carefully put the pearl back in the pouch. "She will want to talk with you."

"I have faced rebels, criminals, and even rogue *gladiatoris*, but I shudder at the prospect of facing her."

Peter nodded. "Believe me; I understand."

"However, I will obey her wishes. How will you get word to me?"

"Since you're going to meet Malchus on the Sabbath, we will find you there," said John.

"And bring your dog," said Peter. "I like him. He is a good judge of character."

Adas grinned. "Tigula does not belong to me, but I like his company."

"He's not your dog?" asked Peter. "Yet he protects you without hesitation. Usually a dog is only that loyal to his master. Why does he do this for you?"

"It's always been this way for me with animals. They trust me, and I trust them, which is why I trained to be a *veterinarius*."

"You did not plan to be a soldier?" asked Peter.

"No, becoming a centurion was my father's doing even though, ironically, he was furious when I enlisted. I only did it to further my studies with the *veterinarii*."

"God has given you this gift. Surely, one day you will set aside your sword. For now, there is one more thing to do before you go." Peter clapped his work-roughened hands on the centurion's shoulders. "Adas, I pray for the Lord God to heal you, body, heart, and soul." Peter let go and stepped back. "I look forward to teaching you the Way of Yeshua. Now we must go. We will see you on the Sabbath."

Soothing warmth came over Adas, but it quickly passed. He wondered at the sensation, but dismissed it as he watched them walk away. On the way back to the garrison, Adas replayed the events of the meeting. He expected them to be more guarded. In fact, their acceptance of him seemed too easily given. But then he reasoned they had faith, which no doubt gave them courage. Adas only hoped they would not trust their safety to the wrong people. Even the most skilled soldier wore armor.

Adas approached the gate to the Antonia and felt the suffocating anxiety of its atmosphere. He crossed the quad to the officers' quarters. Without thinking, he switched Tigula's leash to his right hand, looping it loosely around his palm. When he turned down the lane, the mastiff suddenly threw his head up, barked once, and leaped into a run. As the leash jerked from his hand, Adas realized he felt no pain. He stared at his hand as if he could see though the bandaging. The dog barreled down the lane and excitedly pranced around Cassius.

"*Ohe!* You men have a nice walk?" asked Cassius.

"What men?"

"You and Tigula. Who else would I mean?"

"Of course, yes, we had our exercise for the day. *Gratias* for letting me borrow your 'man.' Did you know he's a good judge of character?"

"What?" Cassius wrinkled his nose in doubt.

"I'll meet you later for dinner," Adas called as he hurried to his quarters.

"Fine, and you're welcome. Come on, Tig. I think our friend is done with us."

Adas retreated into the privacy of his quarters. He unwrapped the bandaging as he sat on the bed. With the linen off, he stared at the square of folded cloth, almost afraid to look. Gingerly, he peeled it away. The cauterized skin was no longer black. The angry red lines of infection were gone. The scars were wide, but they were healed, and the pain was gone. He got up to look in the copper mirror. The gash over his eye was healed, leaving only a scar. The bruising across his temple and cheekbone was gone. He clenched his hand into a fist. Still, there was no pain.

Adas shook his head in happy disbelief. Peter prayed for him to be healed and he was. Adas bowed his head. "I did nothing to deserve your forgiveness. I deserve to suffer, yet you healed me. Thank you, Lord God." Adas would be sure to thank Peter for his healing prayer.

Chapter 17

It was Saturday, a day of rest for the citizens of Jerusalem and the soldiers of the Antonia. Adas awoke early, judging by the low light streaming through his window lattice. A shadow appeared on the wall within one of the squares of light. Someone was looking through the lattice. Adas stiffened. Who would dare to be so invasive? He threw his blanket off, and the shadow moved away. There was a knock on his door. Adas opened it to find Demitre standing outside. He held his medical kit to his chest.

"Centurion, please pardon me. My master sent me to check on your injury." He bowed his head. When Adas didn't respond, he looked up. He clutched the leather kit tighter as if it could escape his grasp.

Adas held his right hand out. "You mean this injury?" The shock on Demitre's face was unmistakable. "You can tell your master your services are no longer needed."

"Impossible!" snapped Demitre. He dropped his medical kit and took hold of Adas's hand. His astonishment gave way to fear as he inspected the newly formed scars. His eyes darted to the new scar over Adas's eye. "How could you heal so quickly?"

Adas pulled his hand away from Demitre's grasp. "A follower of Yeshua prayed for me. I told you; Yeshua is alive. If God had not healed me, I'm sure—especially now—I would have lost this hand. Judging by the heavy thud of your kit when it hit the ground, you brought your amputation saw. You came prepared."

Demitre's eyes narrowed in hostility. "I must get back to my master." He grabbed his kit and hurried away, not waiting for the customary dismissal. Adas stared after him. Cassius was right. Demitre was a deadly weapon in Valentius's arsenal.

Adas headed for the officers' *cafeteria*. As he was crossing the quad, an aide to Salvitto approached him. "Sir, I have a message from Tribune Salvitto. He has granted permission for the slaves Onesimus and Calais to be in your Saturday class." Adas thanked the aide and continued on to the *cafeteria*. He was pleased the two boys would be included.

Adas entered the *cafeteria* and sat at his usual table. Onesimus promptly appeared to ask for instructions. "Good morning, Centurion. We have boiled eggs, goat cheese and bread available." Onesimus glanced up every few words, as usual.

"That will be fine. Tribune Salvitto has approved your attendance in my Saturday class. I'll tell Cook." Onesimus smiled so broadly Adas almost laughed at the transformation in the boy's face. After he finished eating, they headed for the stables.

Nikolaus saw them and hurried over. "Are we going to have a lesson, Sir?" Nikolaus smiled briefly when Adas confirmed it. In two years, he had rarely seen Nikolaus express any emotion. He was only sixteen, but he had been with the Jerusalem garrison four years. His slavery contract indicated that Tribune Theo Camillus Salvitto owned him, but the money came from the garrison's budget. Technically, he belonged to the emperor.

"Let's talk before you round everyone up, Nikolaus. I understand we have some new horses. Tell me about them."

"Yes Sir. We have twelve new ones, seven mares, three geldings and two stallions. One of the mares is difficult to saddle."

As Adas and Nikolaus walked into the barn, Lucius Octavean leaned against a wall, watching. He knew Adas gave lessons to the stable slaves. Valentius would want details on the centurion's interaction with them.

"Why is this mare difficult to saddle?"

"She bites when you cinch the saddle."

While they waited for the other boys to finish their tasks and join them, Adas checked on Venustas. She was an Arabian, dapple-gray mare with black socks, muzzle, mane and tail. Her black coloring slowly lightened into silvery gray and her spots were pale silver. She had the arched neck, lean flanks, long legs, good endurance, and gentle disposition of an Arabian. She nickered at the sight of Adas. He gave her a hand full of oats and checked her hooves. The previously infected hoof was healed. He breathed a sigh of relief.

When the other boys joined them, Adas gave instructions. "Nikolaus, bring the new mare out to the arena. Onesimus, ask Cook for a few bunches of overripe hyssop and carrots. Get the yellow ones. They're sweeter. Calais, get my saddle."

"Today we're going to work with a biter. Horses bite if they feel threatened or to exert dominance, but sometimes they're just being playful. However, I think this mare bites from a bad habit and needs to be retrained. First, what are my three rules?"

In unison, the boys recited, "Never do harm, be patient, be consistent."

Adas tied a handful of hyssop on Nikolaus's left shoulder. "Since hyssop is used for seasoning, it is not harmful, but overripe hyssop is bitter. Try to saddle her. When she reaches to bite, make a loud hissing sound like a cat. If she bites, she'll bite the hyssop. When she doesn't bite, praise her and give her a carrot."

The lesson progressed well using the bitter herbs and a hiss. Eventually, just hissing made the horse refrain from biting. The boys rewarded the mare with praise and carrots.

"It's easy to see what we're doing, Sir," said Nikolaus. "We're training her to remember the bitter taste of the hyssop when she hears hissing."

"Well done, Nikolaus! Remember, the training goes both ways. When people are properly trained, horses can be properly trained. The best way to train an animal is with rewards and praise, not punishment. The worst thing you can do is intentionally injure a horse. It makes no sense to mistreat anything you must depend on. You boys have done well." Adas handed out apples and apricots from his knapsack. They eagerly took the fruit. Adas handed the mare's lead rope to Nikolaus. "Take the mare back to her stall."

"Yes, Sir. Thank you, Centurion. I learned a lot today."

"That's because you're a good student, Nikolaus."

Adas left the arena for his quarters to write Dulcibella a letter. After the lesson was over, Lucius slipped a bit of papyrus under Valentius's door. He would be interested to know the centurion favored the slave called Nikolaus.

To: Dulcibella Cornelia Minor Cornelius,

Dearest Dulcibella,

I cannot express how much I miss you and your family. I hope they are doing well. So much has happened. When we're together once again, I'll tell you everything. For now, I want to tell you about Nikolaus. He is a fine apprentice. I would like to think the apprenticeship is a positive influence on him. He is strong. A weaker person would have succumbed to his tragic experiences. He came from a large family in Greece, supported by his father who was a successful engineer in charge of constructing public buildings in Corinth. Due to his father's expertise, Tiberius offered him a villa in Caesarea and a contract to build a complex of bath houses and shops for the families of government administrators. Nikolaus and his family were traveling by ship from Greece, but disease broke out. A Roman medicus in Caesarea tended the family for many days, but only Nikolaus and an older sister, Dionysia, survived. He was twelve years old; she was fifteen. They did not have enough money to pay the medicus for his services so he claimed his right to sell them into slavery. Nikolaus was sold to Tribune Salvitto, who told me the boy's background. Instead of giving into defeat, Nikolaus devoted himself to caring for our horses. He assists me with all the mares when they birth their foals and takes instruction well. The primus veterinarius is only months from retirement and is quite content to let me monitor the care of the horses. Therefore, Nikolaus gains more experience and knowledge with each injury, sickness, or birthing. Dulcie, I hope to purchase Nikolaus and free him some day. Perhaps, we will become friends. I'm sure he will want to see his sister, if he can find her, but there's no guarantee she is still with her original owners in Rome. When I go for my father's wedding, I will try to locate her.

Also, my efforts at winning over the men of my centuria have come full circle. I have tried to treat them in the manner I want them to treat me, but I first had to set the example. According to my second-in-command, Optio Victorius, my legionaries have accepted me as their commander. I believe he has encouraged the men on my behalf ever since the incident in Bethany. I was close enough to distract a horse that nearly trampled Victorius when the poor beast was bitten by a viper. It must have been a dry bite since the horse recovered quickly. Victorius sustained only minor injuries, which I was able to treat. Since then, Victorius has proven his trustworthiness many times.

I also count Nikolaus as an unofficial member of my centuria and one of the most dependable. It would grieve me greatly if any harm should come to him. If I had a brother, I would want him to be like Nikolaus.

Dulcie, if you still wish it, and the timing pleases you, I think this would be a good time to announce our engagement. I want nothing more than to take your hand in mine, not just the required three times but every day for the rest of our lives. I await your answer eagerly.

Dulcibella, I count the hours until I can hold you in my arms again. I dream of your smiling eyes and sweet lips. I yearn for the sound of your voice. I crave your touch. Know this, Sweet Beauty, I carry you in my heart, and your love carries me through each day.

Yours forever,
Centurion Adas Clovius Longinus

Adas put the letter in his knapsack and left to meet with Jamin and Malchus. He headed for the stables and whistled his personal signal for Nikolaus. The teenager brought the mare out.

"Thank you for taking such good care of Venustas, Nikolaus. This horse means much more to me than I can say. She was a gift from a family in Caesarea."

"Yes, Sir. I understand." He turned away to hide his surprise. It was the first time the centurion had shared any personal information with him. He watched as Adas easily jumped into the saddle without assistance, but before he left, Adas pulled something from his knapsack.

"Why don't you take this?" Adas held a bundle of dried mutton tied with string. Slaves were not given meat, so he always bought an extra amount when he was on Market Street. The boy gratefully took the meat.

"Are you working at the soccer game today?"

"Yes, Sir, I'll be keeping score."

"Good, then I'll see you there." Adas tapped Venustas's flank. As he rode to meet with Jamin and Malchus, Adas hoped Mary had accepted the blue pearl. He expected nothing from her in return, not even her forgiveness. When he reached the Gentile Fountain in the temple's public courtyard, he glanced around. Judging by the length of the shadows, he was early.

"Centurion! Over here!" Jamin was waving a hand. Malchus was standing next to him. Adas clicked his tongue and Venustas tossed her head as she set off at a trot. Adas dismounted. The three men greeted each other. Jamin noticed Adas scanning the crowd.

"You're wondering if Peter and John are here. They're here, but they're still a little cautious. No offense."

"None taken."

Malchus snorted. "I think it's more likely they're hanging back because of me. I don't blame them. I wouldn't want to be seen with me either."

"Well, I'm glad to see you." Adas pulled two scrolls out of his knapsack. "Here are the letters." Adas opened his coin pouch, but Malchus held a hand up.

"There is no need to pay me, Adas. I may ask you to return the favor someday. Would Cornelius's daughter be the one who gave you the eilat stone?"

"How did you know about the stone?"

"I found it with a few coins and an empty money pouch in the garden when you were unconscious. I assumed it was Octavean's doing, and they belonged to you since there was no pouch on your belt."

"Thank you. You're right. Dulcibella gave me the stone. I would have sorely missed it. I must tell her how you 'rescued' it."

"She must mean a great deal to you, Adas," commented Jamin.

"She means everything to me." His expression grew pensive. "I miss the whole family. I wish I was going with you, Malchus. Thanks for doing this." Malchus took the scrolls. His smile suddenly faded and he walked away.

A baritone voice spoke behind Adas and Jamin. "Centurion Longinus, it is good to see you," said Simon Peter. Adas greeted Peter and John. "We need to go to a different location." The two men abruptly turned and walked off. Several chief priests who were standing nearby eyed them and then glared at Adas.

"Is there a problem?" Adas whispered.

"Hopefully not, but we are always careful. We don't want to get you in trouble. Also, you're invited to lunch. Go to Ficus Street in the heights. I will find you there." Jamin quickly blended into the crowd. Adas jumped back on his horse and started off in the opposite direction.

After a few twists and turns, Adas found Ficus street. He could see how it was named. Jamin was standing in front of a courtyard under the shade of a giant ficus tree. Venustas trotted up the street. Adas dismounted. Anxiety twisted inside him at the thought of meeting the mother of Yeshua.

Chapter 18

———⌘———

J amin indicated the chairs set out under the tree. "Welcome to the home of Mary, mother of John Mark. Yeshua's mother, Mary, is here. She wants to meet you."

Adas studied the surroundings. It was a simple neighborhood with two-story houses built of whitewashed adobe brick. The shade of the ancient tree cooled the air and softened the bright sunshine. Despite the peaceful setting, Adas felt as if he faced a court-martial instead of a lunch invitation. When Jamin and the others came out to greet him, he stood and lowered his head.

Jamin introduced John Mark and his mother, Mary. They exchanged a formal greeting. Adas caught the surprise in their eyes when he responded in perfect Hebrew. Mark stepped back, allowing two women to come forward, Salome, the mother of John and James, and Rhoda, a young servant girl. Salome coldly studied Adas while Rhoda kept her eyes downcast. They moved aside, and Jamin motioned for Joanna. Adas recognized her as the wife of Chuza, Herod's business manager. He had seen her when he supervised security during festivities at the palace.

Another woman stepped forward. Adas recognized her as the first person to see Yeshua alive that Sunday morning. "I remember you at my Lord's crucifixion. You gave him drink when he was thirsty. You rebuked the soldiers when they were dis-respectful. You announced, 'He must have been the Son of God,' so everyone could hear. You were God's chosen servant to shed his Son's blood for atonement. My name is Mary of Magdala." She stepped aside and touched the shoulder of an older woman. "This is Yeshua's mother, Mary, widow of Joseph."

Adas needed no introduction. He would never forget the woman who grieved for Yeshua. His eyes began to water and his heart hammered in his chest. He dropped to one knee and lowered his head as cascading emotions flooded his heart. He tried to speak, but could make no sound. A reassuring hand lighted on his shoulder.

Peter leaned down. "Adas, she understands more than any of us. Just speak your heart."

"I-I am so sorry for what I have done. . .for the misery I caused." Adas could say no more.

Mary stepped closer and lightly touched his face. Slowly, Adas met her eyes as she gently lifted his head. "Stand up and look at me, Adas. *Yeshua HaMashiach*, the Messiah of all people, forgave you. I heard him say it. How could I not do the same? It was his life to give, and no one could take it without his permission. Yeshua could have called all the angels of heaven to rescue him, and you would have been powerless. Yeshua *gave* his life; you did not *take* it!"

Adas felt overwhelming relief. Mary took his right hand and cradled it in her hand. "Jamin told me what you did and why. You cut this cross as a vow to never again execute an innocent person. I see the cuts have already healed."

"Yes." Adas glanced at Peter. "God healed me through Peter."

"There is your proof of God's forgiveness." Mary pulled a leather cord from under the neck of her tunic and placed the pouch in his hand. "You made a generous gesture by giving me this *pninah*, but I am not the one who should have it. Remember the parable Yeshua told Zacchaeus about a pearl of great price. The pearl in the parable represented the kingdom of heaven. This blue pearl is more than a spiritual symbol because it has earthly value. God has set this pearl on a journey, and it must continue just as your journey must continue. For now, it belongs to you. Keep the pearl close to your heart. When it is time to let it go, God will show you." She curled his fingers over the pouch. "However, there is something I want from you, something you must do for me. If you are truly repentant for executing Yeshua, you will do what I ask."

"Anything, Mary, ask anything of me and I will do it." He waited for her answer, entranced by the serenity of her face.

"I believe you. I will tell you what you must do. Then there will be no debt. Once you do what I ask, it will honor the life Yeshua sacrificed willingly. Do you understand?"

"Yes, what do you wish of me? I will do it."

"I want you to forgive *yourself* for executing Yeshua. God chose you for a reason, a wonderful reason, but you cannot fulfill God's purpose for you until you forgive yourself. Will you keep your word as you promised me? You must say it aloud so I can hear you."

Adas tried to speak, but couldn't. The words caught in his throat. Then he looked into her gentle eyes and saw unconditional love. "I forgive. . .," he closed his eyes and forced them open again. "I forgive—myself. I forgive myself!" A peaceful release passed through him. The weight on his heart vanished. He took a deep breath. Mary saw relief alter his expression and she smiled. He returned her smile. "I really do forgive myself. I-I didn't think it would be possible." Adas put the leather-corded pouch around his neck.

"Adas, you must remember this moment of forgiveness for the rest of your life. At times, you will be tempted to take back your guilt. Others may even encourage it. Do not give into that temptation. You followed orders not knowing, *truly* not knowing, who you were crucifying."

Adas wiped at his eyes with the back of his hand. Apprehensively, he glanced around at the others. He saw compassion in their eyes. Mary reached for him. He welcomed her hug.

"Mary, I offered you a small gift from the sea, yet you have given me a far greater gift from your heart." She took his face in her hands and smiled. With a light pat, she released him.

Peter clapped his hand on Adas's shoulder. "Let's eat. I'm starving!"

The others laughed and wiped at their eyes. They sat under the tree and ate their fill. Adas couldn't remember feeling so relaxed since he left Dulcibella and her family. The others found themselves marveling they could feel so comfortable in the presence of a Roman centurion.

"Adas, the pearl is a priceless gift," said Mary, "but it is true what I said. God has another purpose for it. You must keep it near your heart until he reveals it to you."

"Did Yeshua tell you himself?" Adas honestly wondered if she had discussed it with him.

"Not in so many words, but I know his wishes. I want for nothing. I have raised many children and was married to a good man. I do not need much. But I do thank you for offering such an extraordinary treasure freely and for trusting Simon and John." Her eyes twinkled mischievously. "Even if they initially did not trust God with your gift."

Simon Peter and John glanced at each other. Adas was surprised to see embarrassment cross their faces. "It is true," Peter said. "We were afraid of being found with such a priceless thing." John nodded agreement.

Adas looked from one to the other. "I don't understand?"

"Adas, we knew that your motives were pure when you gave us the pearl," said Peter. "No one acting under deception would ever let go of a treasure like that. However, we reasoned that you may not be aware of how often legionaries search us and steal what they find. They never do this in the presence of an officer. The pearl is beyond price. If we had been stopped, the soldiers would have killed us to steal the pearl. So we hid it. We immediately spoke to Mary and she instructed us to bring it to her. We retrieved it. I wore the pouch in plain sight. I made no effort to avoid any soldiers, trusting in God's protection. We passed. . .how many soldiers, John?"

"Dozens. They never even glanced at us."

"But we must be careful," added Peter. "Yeshua warned us that he was sending us out as sheep in the midst of wolves?"

John gave Peter a slight shake of his head. The others glanced quickly at Adas.

"What?" Adas looked at them questioningly. "Did I miss something?"

Jamin answered for them. "Well, Adas, you do, kind of, have. . ."

"Wolf eyes? You're not the first to notice. When I was a child, our neighbors kept their children away from me. They called me *versipellis*, one who can change into an animal, usually a wolf. When I was seven years old, I overheard a woman tell my mother, jokingly, of course, that a *versipellis* must have stolen her baby and left me in his place. Mother was not amused. When she told my father about it, he laughed and said it would explain why dogs liked me so much. She did not appreciate *his* humor either."

Adas frowned, thinking of the childhood memory that came to him the day of the crucifixions. "There was another incident. My father and I were in the market place and I was angry because he kept his hand on my shoulder so I couldn't run off. I was only six or seven, but I resented his protectiveness. I dodged away from him and ran right into this big, ugly man. He called me a name and shoved me with his knee. I landed flat on my back. My father hit the man, just once, but it knocked him down. It was the only time I saw my father hit anyone."

"What did the man call you?" asked Jamin.

"He called me a *dhampir*." The others looked at him questioningly. "A *dhampir* is born of a human, but fathered by a *vespertilio*, a vampire, basically a half-breed *daemon*." They shook their heads in sympathy. "My father's display was embarrassing. Everyone was staring at us."

"Your father was defending you, Adas," said Peter.

Adas nonchalantly waved a hand. "I suppose he was, but I grew accustomed to the name-calling. Maybe it was for the best. It made me quick to defend someone being mistrea. . ." He frowned and looked at the scars on his hand.

"Adas," said Peter softly, "All of us mistreated Yeshua in some way."

"I suppose so, but it doesn't make it any less shameful."

Peter lowered his eyes. "No, it doesn't."

There was an uncomfortable silence until Yeshua's mother asked, "You must have been quite lonely as a child. Did you have any friends?"

Adas smiled, grateful for a change of subject. "I did—the four-legged variety. I suppose my lack of human friends was why I enjoyed the companionship of animals. They never make fun of you, or betray you. If you're good to them, they love you without question. I understand animals—people—not so much."

Joanna declared, "Trust is the hardest emotion to earn, even harder than love. It is also the easiest emotion to destroy, I think."

"But it is possible to rebuild trust and love," Peter added. "Yeshua taught us that."

They described their first encounters with Yeshua. Adas wanted to hear more, but time was getting short, and they still had business to discuss. Jamin wanted to tell them about the communication system he devised.

"We need centrally located homes. Cleopas' house is one, this is two, and we need one more spot. When we need to meet, locations will be announced by displaying a different decoration for each specific spot and time. Adas, do you know of a place?"

"Are you familiar with Serapio's *Suppelex*, the furniture shop at the corner of Commerce Road and Sheep Gate Street?"

"In the last few years," said John, "Yeshua left some items there on consignment."

"What! Serapio knew Yeshua?"

"Oh, yes," said Peter, "they talked often whenever we came here."

"Did Serapio know Yeshua could heal any ailment?"

"Serapio was standing in the door of his shop when a woman with a flow of blood was healed simply by touching the hem of Yeshua's robe."

"Yeshua praised her," John added, "saying her faith made her well. Serapio watched and heard every word."

"Then why didn't Yeshua heal Serapio's eye?"

"Serapio never asked to be healed," said John.

"I don't understand. Why would he want to stay half blind? Anyway, I'll ask Serapio about the decoration display. I know I can trust him. He saved my life once."

"Really? What happened?" asked Jamin eagerly.

"When I was sixteen, my father took me to a birthday celebration of the son of his colleague. I didn't want to go. Out of spite, I got drunk and decided to walk home alone. I got tired and stopped to rest under a tree. I woke up the next morning with a skull-cracking headache. So I started for home, and then some men attacked me. They weren't armed, but they definitely had fists. Serapio was suddenly there and he *was* armed. They scattered like roaches."

Adas pressed his lips in a line. "Then the worst happened. Instead of thanking him, my father accused Serapio of setting the whole thing up for a reward. My mother intervened, and she insisted Serapio stay for breakfast. While they were talking over breakfast on the terrace, my father and I were in the house exchanging hateful words. I honestly don't remember what I said. Something very ugly, I'm sure. Then my father ordered Gregos, his personal servant, to 'escort' me out of the house, which he did with sorrow. I ended up living with Serapio and Fabiana for a while. I worked as his apprentice, but I was treated like a member of the family. Along with teaching me carpentry, he taught me every *gladiator* trick he knew. By the time I left Serapio's, I was fit for the army. But I didn't leave his home willingly. My father ordered me to come home on my seventeenth birthday. The next day, I enlisted. My father was furious, and it broke my mother's heart." He sighed and looked away.

"What is it, Adas?" asked Jamin.

"The pearl—I had planned to give it to my mother."

Joanna frowned. "Why can't you give it to her now?"

"My mother died. I found out a few days ago in the first letter my father ever sent me."

The others expressed their sympathy. They had also lost parents, children, or spouses.

Peter asked, "You said your father's servant turned you out? He wasn't a slave?"

Adas shook his head vehemently. "No, we never owned slaves. Gregos begged me to apologize. He swore my father would regret getting so angry. Gregos was with my father even before he married my mother. He knows him better than anyone. But I was angry, too, and full of myself. The argument wasn't just about Serapio. As for not having slaves, that was my mother's doing. Our servants were once slaves. My father bought their contracts, freed them, and offered them jobs. Even my teachers were paid. All the children I knew had slaves for teachers. They *treated* them like slaves, too, which I was never allowed to do. I was punished if I was disrespectful to my teachers or the servants."

"How so?" asked Joanna.

"I would have to do their job. My teachers also taught the servants' children so I would have to teach the kids. That punishment backfired since I enjoyed it. Knowing how clever my mother was, she was probably hoping I would. She could always bring the best out in me, even when I didn't know it was there." They grinned at his honesty.

"If I was rude to a servant, I had to do the cooking, or scrub the floors, or wash the clothes. I know what you're thinking. I must be a slow learner, right?" They smiled and chuckled. "I could be quite a brat when I set my mind to it. Once, I was very rude to Gregos, and he reprimanded me. I tattled on him to Father. *Ohe,* I never did that again!"

"Why? What happened?" asked Jamin.

"Father made me work the vineyards for a solid week. I was pruning and digging out weeds from sunrise to sunset. Gregos kept bringing me water and food when Father wasn't looking. Father told me if I ever treated Gregos disrespectfully again, I would be a slave for everyone in the household for a month. He wasn't bluffing. He never did. I could never outsmart him. Sometimes I thought I had outsmarted Mother, but I think she knew. One time, she decided we needed a bigger *furnus* in the kitchen. My father hired a crew to do the masonry work. I had an idea which would make the *furnus* hotter, but use less wood. My father refused to try the idea, but he left that day for a business trip in Ostia. After the workmen hauled the rock into the kitchen I berated them for no reason. My mother paid them for a full day's work, but sent them away. My punishment was to build the *furnus* by myself, which was my plan, of course."

"Did it work?" asked John Mark.

"Absolutely, if you like burned bread. The cooks weren't used to the *furnus* holding more heat so it took a little experimenting before they figured it out. Naturally, I got to eat the *experimenti* for the rest of the week." They hooted with laughter.

"What did you do to make the *furnus* hotter?" asked Jamin.

"I used black slate to line the baking chamber."

"Clever," said Peter. "What did your father say?"

"Nothing. I don't think he ever found out. Besides, I'm not sure my father even knows where the kitchen is, so it wasn't a problem." He shrugged as they chuckled.

"But real punishment was getting exiled from the stables. I hated being separated from the horses, or my dogs, or my pet donkey."

"A *pet* donkey?" asked John. "That pet could have pulled a poor man's cart."

"She did for many years, until her leg was mangled in an accident. The man who owned her barely had enough money to feed his children, so he could not afford to feed a useless donkey. I bought her. Using my own recipe for a sedative, I was able to amputate the damaged part of her leg, but saved the knee. My mother brought food out to the stables for me. I refused to leave the donkey until she completely recovered. Gregos brought me a mattress and I slept in the stables. Actually, Gregos helped a great deal. For weeks he brought me anything I needed. I'm surprised my father allowed it, now that I think about it." Adas paused for a moment, lost in the memory. "I nursed the donkey back to health and made a wood and leather stump for her. It fit under her knee and had a harness to strap around her torso. She could walk fairly well, but would never work again. She followed me everywhere. I called her Musculus."

Jamin grinned. "You called your pet donkey Little Mouse?"

Adas nodded. "Mus, for short. The little thief would steal treats from my knapsack when we would go for walks with my dogs." The others tried to imagine this battle-hardened centurion out for a stroll with his crippled donkey.

"Did you take Musculus with you when you lived with Serapio?" Jamin asked.

"Mus was gone by then. It was the happiest time of my life when I lived with Serapio's family. His daughters laughed at my first attempts with wood working, but their teasing was in fun. It was tricky work, but I began to enjoy it."

Peter studied Adas's hands and arms. He saw the occupational trademark scars similar to those on the carpenter from Nazareth. Adas felt Peter's eyes on him and met his gaze. They studied each other with mutual curiosity. They represented men living on opposite sides of life, yet there was the beginning of a bond.

Peter asked, "Were you surprised when you found Serapio had opened a shop here?"

"No, he set up shop after I came here. They left Rome while I was in Caesarea. When I learned he wanted to open his own furniture shop, I invested a little with him. He did some commissions for Tribune Aquillius, and his reputation as a skilled craftsman became established. He wanted to pay me back, but I wouldn't let him. So Serapio outsmarted me. He commissioned my sword and dagger. He knew I would not turn down such gifts, nor would I insult him by trying to pay for them. Serapio didn't only want to cancel a debt. He wanted to remind me that I am the son of my father no matter how I feel about him. Serapio never held any grudge against him. In fact, he refuses to listen if I speak ill of him. He tells me I should be thankful I have a father, even if he is Aquila Clovius Longinus." Everyone gasped.

"What!" Jamin exclaimed. "Is your father *Consul* Clovius Longinus? *That* Longinus?"

"Uh, you've heard of him?"

Peter coughed. John shook his head. Incredulously, John Mark asked, "So—your father plays chess with Emperor Tiberius?"

Adas laughed, trying to imagine his father bent over a game board with the old man. "I don't think they're *quite* that close. My father goes to great pains to avoid Tiberius. But being Aquila's son has never made things easy, just the opposite."

Peter remembered Adas saying that he was no different than any other man. "Adas, you are full of surprises. You are a type of Roman we have not met, other than Centurion Januarius in Capernaum."

"I imagine you have, but just didn't know it. My former commanding officer in Caesarea, Centurion Cornelius, is a man of honor. He, too, is learning about God from teachers at the temple. There are others. But people rarely hear about them."

Time passed while Adas listened to stories about Yeshua. The shadows were lengthening, and Adas had promised Nikolaus he would be at the soccer game. He thanked them for their hospitality. They promised to meet with him again soon. Adas asked Mary if she would talk with him about Yeshua. She promised to share her stories.

"There is nothing I enjoy more," said Mary. "He is always with me." She placed her hand over her heart and forehead. "Here and here. My prayer for you, Adas, is to have the same connection to Yeshua as I do. Will we see you next week?"

"I will do my best," declared Adas.

Jamin walked with Adas out to the street. They made arrangements to meet at Serapio's shop the next day. The men clasped hands. As they talked, Cassius watched from around the corner of a courtyard. He saw Adas clasp hands with a young Hebrew man. Adas climbed on his horse and left at an easy canter. Cassius quickly turned his back to the rider and waited until Venustas was gone before he walked to his horse. He found this meeting to be disturbing. He wondered if Adas sympathized with the zealots or if they were using him. Whichever it was, Adas's activities might mean trouble for his friends, as well as for himself.

Chapter 19

---⧬---

Adas arrived at the game just before it started. Cassius was sitting on the bottom tier of the stands with Tigula lying at his feet. The mastiff sprang to his feet when he spied Adas.

"*Ohe*, I was about to give up on you. Where have you been all afternoon?" asked Cassius.

"In town, mostly. Why?"

"Just curious."

The two men watched as players began to arrive on the field. They were stripped down to their *caligae* and *campestre*, the leather loincloths worn for sporting events. Depending on their team, the players wore either white or red sashes around their waists. Nikolaus, carrying a wax tablet and stylus, talked with the team leaders briefly before taking up position near the stands.

"Nikolaus!" Adas called out. "Come over here and sit."

He trotted over, but stood hesitantly. "I don't think I should sit down, Sir. Some people might think it improper."

"Don't worry about 'some people.' Sit with me. Besides, I can help you keep score."

The referees signaled for the game to begin. After a few plays, the red team scored a goal. Half the crowd jumped to their feet, cheering and clapping. Cassius pointed out a foul that went unnoticed by the referees. Adas disagreed it was a foul. He was quoting the rule when someone blocked his view. It was Lucius Octavean.

Lucius stumbled in front of Nikolaus. "You clumsy oaf! You tried to trip me!" He grabbed Nikolaus by the tunic and yanked him to his feet. Nikolaus dropped the wax tablet, his eyes wide with fear. The spectators shouted, not at Lucius; but at the referees for another questionable foul.

Adas came to his feet. "Legionary Octavean, release him."

"Or what, Centurion? You'll report me to Valentius?"

"Yes, his pet spaniel has been a bad dog, and should be leashed to a latrine."

Lucius pushed Nikolaus away. The legionary rounded on Adas. His huge hands curled into fists. Adas stepped closer. "Go ahead, Octavean. Just pretend I'm unconscious."

"You think you're better than the rest of us, yet you seek the company of slaves. You enjoy how they idolize you and fall all over themselves to do you favors."

"Did you figure that out by yourself? I'm impressed."

Lucius pulled his fist back. Adas didn't blink as he stared into the legionary's eyes.

"*Octavean!* My office! Now!" Lucius dropped his fist. Adas turned around to find Tribune Salvitto standing behind him. "You, too, Centurion."

Bewildered, Nikolaus stared after the men as they walked away. The spectators had not noticed any problem until the legionary raised his fist. It worried Cassius that Octavean continued to challenge Adas, but he would not have interfered with disciplining the slave.

"Better get the last score, boy," said Cassius. "Pay attention. And go stand over there."

Inside Tribune Salvitto's office, Adas and Lucius stood at attention while the tribune sat behind his desk. Theo Salvitto was in his early fifties. He had an athletic build, gray-streaked black hair and green eyes. He rarely raised his voice since his presence commanded silence.

"Octavean, you threatened a superior officer and attempted to harm my slave," Salvitto declared without emotion. Lucius started to speak, but the tribune raised a warning hand. "Centurion Longinus, were you harmed in any way?"

"No, Sir."

"Did the boy do anything to warrant Octavean's behavior?"

"No, Sir."

"Why did you attack my slave, Legionary?"

Lucius hesitated. "Sir, I thought he tripped me."

"Centurion, did my slave trip Legionary Octavean?"

"No, Sir."

Salvitto glared at Lucius. "Nikolaus is my property. He answers to me. He also belongs to the Emperor since he was paid for out of the Antonia's budget. If he is harmed in any way, *by anyone*, you will suffer the same. Do you understand me?"

"Yes, Sir!"

"For threatening a superior officer, you'll have forty lashes."

"Sir, may I speak?" asked Adas. Salvitto nodded. "If it pleases you, Sir, may I recommend forty days in the pit, instead of the whip?"

"So be it. Report to the pit, Legionary. Now."

"Yes, Sir!" Lucius spun on his heel and fled the room.

"What in Hades is going on here?" Salvitto demanded.

Adas had to choose his words carefully. "Sir, there was a misunderstanding when we were guarding the tomb of Yeshua. Valentius ordered latrine duty to the men as punishment. Apparently, Octavean's resentment fueled his infamous temper."

"To what misunderstanding are you referring? I've seen no such report from Valentius. And why were you guarding the Nazarene's tomb? I know for a fact that Governor Pilate gave no such order. You look confused, Centurion."

"Sir, I was ordered by Centurion Valentius to seal and guard the tomb for three days. I do not understand why. . ." Adas suddenly understood perfectly.

"What is it Centurion? What are you not telling me?"

"Sir, I have no provable explanation. I obeyed my orders. As for Octavean, his behavior has become erratic."

"Why don't you want Octavean under the whip?"

"I think isolation might rehabilitate him, Sir." In reality, Adas wanted the legionary taken away from Valentius's control.

"You're dismissed, but I will need your official statement for my investigation." Adas started to leave. "Centurion, hold on. Apparently congratulations are in order for your father. He sent me a letter requesting your presence at his wedding. The date is not yet determined, but you may have four months leave when it is announced. Minus travel time, that will give you over a month in Rome. You have not taken leave since you've been here."

Adas tried to keep his voice neutral. "My father sent a leave request? *He* sent it *for* me?"

Salvitto hesitated, "Yes, it is unusual for a family member to request leave for a soldier, especially a centurion. I'm sure you must feel awkward, but it will stay between the two of us. Your father never served in the military. Did he?"

"No, Sir, he did not."

"I did not realize he was a widower."

"I didn't either until a few days ago, Sir."

"I see. Adas, I'm sorry."

Adas was surprised Salvitto used his *praenomen*. "I appreciate that, Sir. Thank you for the four-month leave."

"Please extend my condolences to your father, and my congratulations on his marriage." He frowned at the paradox.

Adas struggled to keep his composure. "Yes, Sir, I will." He left the office, and went straight to the stables. Preparing Venustas himself, he led her out through the arena gate and vaulted into the saddle. He needed to talk to someone who always understood. He needed Serapio and Fabiana. Adas left the Antonia for Serapio's shop.

Once there, he found Serapio busy with a customer; Fabiana was at the marketplace. Serapio gestured for Adas to wait. After the customer left, he demanded to inspect Adas's hand. He was amazed to see the healed scars.

Adas finally told him about Marsetina's death. Serapio expressed his profound grief. "Your mother was an amazing woman. She did not take the easy way by pampering you. She expected you to be your best even if it was hard on you."

"I know. I know how hard she worked to knock some sense in my head. She was strict, but I never doubted her love."

"I am curious why your mother refused to own slaves? That was very unusual."

"I know, but she never explained why. My mother would occasionally go to slave auctions to observe. Once she came home with a young girl who was terrified and starving. After she nursed the child back to health, a few of our servants took her away. Months later they returned without the child, saying the mission was successful. She was happy about it for weeks."

"You think they found the girl's family?"

"Probably. It would explain why they were gone so long. My mother never mentioned anything about her parents, or her childhood. I asked her, but she would always leave the room without answering. It worried me, but I learned that I could either ask personal questions or be alone. She and Misha, my nanny, would speak Parthian sometimes so I wouldn't understand what they said. Misha taught me Hebrew and Greek, and my mother taught me Egyptian. But they never taught me Parthian."

"Maybe she never knew her parents. I can understand her not wanting to tell you."

"My childish imagination conjured all kinds of terrible possibilities when she ignored my questions. But I know she never lied to me."

A customer came in to order a jewelry box. They discussed the design and the woman left. Adas continued, "I don't know how my parents met or where. Neither one ever spoke of it."

"Your mother was a striking woman, with her exotic, copper eyes and graceful beauty. It is easy to see how you came by your eye color. Maybe she was originally from Parthia."

"I don't know. Maybe." He watched a group of children troop past the doorway. One child was carrying a dodge ball. "Parthian was one language my mother did *not* want me to learn. She only used it with Misha. She and Misha were not native Latin speakers. Mother had a slight accent, Misha more so. They made Latin sound exotic. I could sit for hours listening to them talk. I know very little about my parents. I don't even know where they were married. Misha said the stories she told me were the same stories she told my mother when she was a child. She called them 'stories of the Israelites,' but she was not Hebrew; at least, I don't think she was. I could be wrong. She spoke fluent Hebrew and had a Hebrew name, but she said her father was Greek. I remember asking Misha if she taught Hebrew to Mother. She said my mother rarely needed to be taught anything—she just learned."

"And there's your *praenomen*," added Serapio. "It is a Hebrew name. I would think Roman parents would only give their child a Hebrew *praenomen*, to honor a Hebrew relative."

Unexpectedly, the dodge ball sailed in the open doorway, bounced against a wall, and rolled against Serapio's chair leg. He picked the ball up with one hand and tossed it out the door. Someone ran close to the door, paused, and ran off. "Thank you, Serapio!" a child called out.

"It sounds like Marsetina and Misha were very close."

"They were. They didn't interact like mistress and servant, more like friends. I was told she was a servant and never questioned it. Looking back, I realize the relationship was unusual. My father had a great respect for Misha. If I talked back to her, Father made me scrub the floors the rest of the day. Our floors were spotless. I could be really stubborn when I was a kid."

"You say that as if you've changed."

Adas chuckled. "You know me too well."

"I share the same trait, my friend. Tell me—how old was Misha?"

"Older than my mother, but I don't know how much older."

"Could she have been Marsetina's mother?"

"*What?* No! They would have told me. Why keep such a thing secret?"

"Adas, could they have been slaves? Maybe your father freed them?"

"Not possible! At least, not probable. I've never seen a slave with a volatile temper. My mother didn't show it very often, but one time this man was beating this old street beggar who was in the same spot every day. Mother often gave him food. She went up behind the attacker, and kicked him in the back of the knee. When he went down with a howl, she kicked him in the back, and knocked him flat on the ground."

"No! Not Marsetina! How old were you?"

"Maybe five or six. Anyway, I thought she was done. Not even close! She went down with her knees on his back and whipped out this knife. I didn't even know she had a knife. She grabbed him by the hair and showed him the blade."

Serapio bellowed with laughter. "*Ohe,* definitely not a slave. She must have been a *gladiatrix* in another life. You're not making this up, are you?"

"No, I'm serious! She said something in his ear and stood up. She kicked the fellow again for good measure. Then she grabbed my hand and took off with me in tow. I looked back, and the man was still lying in the street. He *and the beggar* were staring after us in shock. When we were a few blocks away, Mother said, 'Adas, do you know what's worse than a bully?' I shook my head. She said, 'Not much.' We never spoke of it again."

"Did Aquila ever find out?"

"Not from me. Are you kidding? That night at dinner, my father said, 'Tina, did you have a good day? What did you do?' She just smiled, 'Went shopping in the marketplace. Not much else.' Her expression never faltered. Later, I thought I imagined the whole thing, until I found the knife in a jewelry box."

"Adas, I don't think your father feels as unaffected by her death as the letter implied." He folded his muscular arms across his broad chest. "Maybe your father is in some kind of denial. Maybe he has a hard time communicating his feelings. I do."

"Perhaps you're right."

"What? Did I hear correctly? Did you actually give your father the benefit of the doubt?"

"I guess I did. I'm so used to assuming the worst. I didn't even consider that he is struggling with his grief." Serapio wanted to discuss Aquila further, but Adas abruptly changed the subject. "My friends told me you knew Yeshua, and that you took in his work on consignment."

Serapio eyed Adas at the sudden change of topic, but went along with it. "Yes, a few items here and there. We talked often. He had such a powerful presence. I saw him heal a sick woman once just by the touch of his robe. It was a miracle in every sense of the word. His execution was a terrible injustice."

Adas looked at the palm of his hand. "I have to tell you something."

Serapio listened as Adas confessed his role in Yeshua's death. The pain in his expression and voice was undeniable, but Serapio couldn't look at him. He was deeply grieved to hear what Yeshua suffered and how Adas was involved. However, when Adas described the miraculous events which occurred on Sunday, Serapio fastened his eyes on him and listened intently. He didn't speak for a while after Adas finished.

"I heard you," Serapio finally said, "but my mind is still trying to understand it. I have heard the rumors that Yeshua is alive, but Fabiana and I have not heard these claims from anyone who actually saw him. You are telling me you saw him with your own eyes?"

"I did. Many others have seen him as well. I have asked to study his teachings with Peter and John. I want to know why he appeared to me since I'm the one who killed him."

"It's not easy to say this, but I believe you. I really do believe you. There was something so unique and compelling about him. His teachings were not like anything I've ever heard. That miracle I saw; it wasn't the only one that day. There was a greater miracle. A man called Jairus wanted Yeshua to heal his daughter. He said she was near death. Yeshua agreed to go with him. Then these men told Jairus it was too late; she had died. Yeshua told him, *'Do not fear, only believe and she will be made well.'* The next day, Jairus came in here with his little girl, very much alive. I just assumed she hadn't really died. Jairus told me she *had* died. He told me how Yeshua brought her back to life. That's why I believe you."

"Serapio, why didn't you ask him to heal your eye?"

"Because I knew he would."

"I don't understand."

"Why do you have a cross branded into your hand? You're not the only one who wants to be reminded to never again take an innocent life."

"What happened?" Adas wasn't sure he really wanted to know.

"Maybe someday I'll tell you, or maybe not. In fact, you might even have to be dead before I tell you."

"Serapio, you do realize how unsporting that is." The two men laughed.

A woman carrying a bulging knapsack appeared in the doorway. Serapio greeted her by name as he rose to his feet. She was trailed by five young girls. Adas noticed that none of the children resembled the woman or each other.

"Hannah, it is good to see you," declared Serapio. "And how are my little weavers this fine day?" The children greeted him. Hannah pulled baskets from her knapsack and placed them on the counter. Serapio selected several and paid her.

"Bless you, Serapio," Hannah said. "Your generosity is most welcome. God sees what you do for them." She glanced down at the children.

"As God sees you, Hannah." Serapio waved at the little girls. "Be well and be safe, little weavers." They waved good bye and left the shop.

"Why did you pay so much for the baskets?" Adas asked.

"The money Hannah earns with her work feeds and clothes those orphaned girls. She was denounced as an adulteress and nearly stoned to death in the street. At the time, Yeshua was teaching in the temple. Some Pharisees dragged her before him, demanding to know what should be done with her. According to Mosaic Law she *and the man* should be stoned, but they only had the woman. Of course, Roman law prohibits executions without trial."

"They were trying to trap him. What did Yeshua do?"

"First, he wrote something in the dirt. When they again demanded an answer, he said, *'Let him who is without sin among you be the first to throw a stone at her.'* Then he wrote on the ground again. As each accuser looked at what he had written, that man slipped away. Yeshua asked the woman where her accusers were. She said they were gone. He said to her, *'Neither do I condemn you; go and sin no more.'* Hannah's husband divorced her. No one will marry her. Now she takes in homeless girls and teaches them how to weave. Those children faced starvation or slavery before she took them in. Hannah is a skilled weaver. She wove a tunic for Yeshua that was seamless from top to bottom. He was wearing it the last time I saw him."

Adas looked away. "Yes, I remember the tunic."

"Adas, you know what happened was meant to be. God would never have allowed it otherwise. What matters now is what you do about it. You cannot change the past, but you can do as Hannah has done. She broke the law, she was forgiven, and now she gives orphan girls a home. Did he not also forgive you?"

"Yes, he did. John and Peter have told me if I can't forgive myself, then I crucify him all over again."

"That is true. You must honor the price he paid. It is an arrogant man who thinks his sin is greater than God's forgiveness."

"I never thought of it that way, but you're right. This is why I keep coming back to talk with you, my friend. Your wisdom is invaluable."

"My wisdom, you say! Ha! It was my Fabiana who said it to me first."

"So tell me, what do you do with the baskets? Fabiana must have quite a collection."

"She has a few, but I usually give them away to my best customers." Serapio put them in Adas's knapsack. "Enjoy, my friend." Adas thanked him. He knew Dulcibella and her mother, Iovita, would like the intricate design and fine workmanship. The two men clasped hands as they said their farewells. Adas realized his grief seemed easier to bear now.

Filigree clouds floated across what little moon there was, making it dangerous to navigate the streets. Adas slowed Venustas to a walk. He was glad when he saw the torches of the garrison gates come into view. He whistled when he approached. A guard in one of the towers demanded the password. Adas responded. One of the two gates swung out far enough for horse and rider to pass through.

It was customary for two guards to be stationed at each of the watchtowers throughout the night. It was boring work. The soldiers entertained themselves with conversation to pass the long hours. Legionary Ennio watched Adas enter the fortress. He turned to his fellow guard to continue his conversation.

"So, that's why I've been in Jericho the last few months. Can't say I'm glad to be back here. At least, I missed the Passover. Anything interesting happen? The usual riots, I suppose."

Legionary Hilarius snorted. "Interesting? What an understatement! There was this strange darkness in the middle of the day. It went on for hours, which is completely *impossibilis!* Did it happen in Jericho?"

"Yes, it scared everybody, me included," said Ennio. "There was no color; everything looked gray. The gods were surely angry about something. Then the earthquake hit. I was expecting Jupiter's thunderbolts next. Did you feel it here?"

"Shook like the end of the world. Did you hear about Barabbas?"

"Tell me he was crucified!" Ennio angrily demanded.

"No, Pilate released him for the Passover pardon."

"You've got to be joking!" Ennio grimaced angrily. "We lost two men in that riot he started. One of them was a good friend of mine. I wish I could crucify him myself."

Hilarius shrugged. "The crowd wanted Barabbas released, but you will still get your chance. The fool got drunk and got in a fight over a woman. Our patrols intervened, but too late. Barabbas had already knifed the husband. Turns out the dead man was the son of a Sanhedrin chief priest. The pardon was wasted on Barabbas."

Ennio started to comment, but had a sneezing fit instead. He rubbed his nose with the back of his hand. "I hate night duty. It gives me the *allergia.* Speaking of night, I thought you were on day shift."

"I was, but after the Nazarene's crucifixion, I got reassigned. Once those two thieves were scourged, we were ordered to bring out the Nazarene. Then this tribune approached us. He claimed to be from Rome, but I could swear he looked familiar. He had this strange, grating voice. He told *Optio* Blandus he wanted to observe."

"Didn't he have better things to do?"

"Guess not," said Hilarius. "He looked like a costumed skeleton. He suggested the King of the Jews should have royal trappings—his words. *Optio* Blandus thought that was a great idea. He sent me to find a reed for a 'scepter' and he made a 'crown' from thorns. His hands were all torn up by the time he finished. What an idiot."

Ennio snorted. "All of you were idiots. Crucifying a man is punishment enough."

"It's boring. Why shouldn't we amuse ourselves?" Hilarius demanded resentfully.

"Sounds childish to me," said Ennio. "They say the Nazarene was a great healer. Why go to so much trouble to torment someone like that? He was no threat to us."

"It wasn't my fault. I just did what I was told. Blandus did whatever that tribune suggested. The tribune looked like he enjoyed it. He made my skin crawl. I saw the Nazarene lock eyes with the sniveling little rat, as if they knew each other. You'd think the tribune's eyes caught on fire, he looked away so fast. Then he was gone, but I didn't see him leave. Then I saw him again in the crowd at the Nazarene's crucifixion when my squad leader stopped to talk to Longinus. He introduced himself as a silk merchant to a group of Pharisees. He didn't mention being a tribune. If I were a tribune, I'd want everyone to know."

Ennio laughed. "If you could be a tribune, I could be an eagle and fly to the moon."

Hilarius scowled at the insult, but could think of nothing in defense. "That scrawny tribune got us in trouble. He made us waste time on the Nazarene."

"Waste time? Who would care?"

"Cerberus cared!" exclaimed Hilarius. Ennio eyed him quizzically. "Centurion Valentius. They call him Cerberus. He was furious. He shouted at Blandus for intentionally delaying the crucifixions."

Ennio smirked. "I bet I know why. A delay would put the executions on day shift. Longinus was coming in from night patrol. He wanted Longinus to crucify the Nazarene because he expected a huge riot. Valentius is out to get Longinus. That's what *Optio* Victorius told me."

"Then Valentius has it in for Blandus, too. Valentius threw us in the pit, as if we'd insulted his precious slave, or something. I swear the man has lost his mind."

"How long were you in the pit?"

"About an hour. Centurion Tacitus found out and went after Valentius right there in the quad, or so we were told. Tacitus really hates Valentius."

While the tower guards were discussing the Passover events, Adas walked Venustas into the arena and back to her stall. It was easy to find the way since a torch was still burning nearby. Adas found Nikolaus asleep on a blanket. His heart went out to the teenager knowing he was probably worried about the incident at the soccer game. Venustas stomped her hoof impatiently, waking Nikolaus.

"Centurion Longinus, I'm glad to see you," He pushed himself to his feet. "I deeply regret causing you trouble. I don't understand why the legionary thought I tripped him." Nikolaus opened the stall gate and led Venustas inside.

"It's not your fault. Octavean did it to provoke me."

"He sees that you treat me well and used that against you. I wish I was your slave."

"My mother once said, 'Anyone who thinks he can own another human being has enslaved himself with ignorance and delusion.' I think she's right." Adas sighed and bowed his head. "No one should be a slave." When he looked up, Nikolaus was watching him anxiously.

"Sir, are you all right?"

"I'm fine. Listen, Nikolaus, I will never own a slave, but if it should ever be possible, I will find a way to free you. Thank you for keeping a torch burning for me. But you should get to the quarters before they lock the doors."

Adas left before the boy could say anything. He was immediately sorry he had impulsively made such a promise. He may have given Nikolaus false hope.

Chapter 20

─────◦◦◦◦◦─────

Sunday morning started with a bright cloudless sky. Adas woke up to sunlight streaming through the windows. Dust motes, looking like tiny pixies, fluttered in the air. A small bird with glossy blue and gray plumage sat on the lattice of a window. It blinked at Adas, seemingly unafraid. When he threw his feet over the side of the bed, the sunbird let out an alarmed chirp and flew away. Adas pressed his hand over the leather pouch around his neck. He was still shocked that Mary gave the pearl back. Her forgiveness made Adas ashamed of his disrespect toward his father's letter. He collected the pieces and set them in the fireplace. Serapio was right. He should be grateful to have a father, even if he didn't understand him.

Adas went to the officers' *cafeteria* for breakfast. Onesimus, sleepy-eyed and a little slower than usual, brought the centurion a breakfast of bread, olive oil for dipping, and fruit. "When is the last time you had wheat bread, Onesimus?"

"When I was still in Greece before. . .it's been awhile, but I don't mind the barley bread. Tribune Salvitto told Cook to let me have as much as I want. I am grateful. Many slaves never have enough to eat." Someone called to him, and he hurried away.

Adas wondered how well Octavean would fare on barley bread for forty days. The legionary deserved an even worse punishment than the misery of the pit. Adas smiled at the image of Lucius sitting on the slimy stone floor. Then the crucified image of Yeshua sprang into his mind, as did the memory of Mary forgiving him. The smile faded.

The pit was situated in the center of a large stone building, called the Pit House. The only windows in the building were large, barred openings above the huge double doors. Interrogation rooms lined three of the walls along with brackets for torches. The pit, lined with mortared rock, was six paces deep and twenty paces in diameter. Prisoners had to climb in or out by a removable ladder. There were no beds or benches. The pit stank of human waste. Roaches and rats burrowed between the stones. The vermin made nights agonizing. The absence of privacy was dehumanizing. Boredom and buzzing flies were a constant torment. Mosquitos and gnats weren't just unpleasant, but were also a source of disease. Prisoners could only pace mindlessly, or sit on the filthy stone floor. Other than execution, confinement in the pit was the most grievous punishment, and was usually reserved for prisoners of war and rebellious slaves. Even a few lashes with the whip were less dreaded than days or weeks in the pit.

After breakfast, Adas stopped by maintenance and asked for a few supplies. His project didn't take long to complete. After picking up a loaf of bread at the officers' *cafeteria*, Adas walked into the Pit House. He looked over the edge of the pit. Lucius was alone. Adas stood so the light from the open door was behind him, putting him in silhouette. He backed up until he could barely see Lucius's head and whistled. Lucius looked up as Adas tossed the bread. It never hit bottom. Then he tossed in his project. It hit the floor. Lucius picked it up. Adas smiled to himself when he heard the legionary mutter, "Thank the gods—a flyswatter." Adas left the Pit House to find Nikolaus in the stables.

"Good morning, Centurion," Nikolaus called out. "Do you need Venustas?"

"Yes, but we need to talk first. Listen, what I said last night about your freedom. I will do my best, but your ownership is complicated."

"Sir, I understand. Just to hear you say it made me happy." He saddled Venustas and led the horse out of her stall. Adas thanked the teenager, and vaulted into the saddle. He headed for Serapio's place.

Jamin had already arrived at the shop. Fabiana remembered the young man who often came with Yeshua. Serapio appeared from the back entrance and greeted Jamin by name.

"So, you remember me?" exclaimed Jamin, surprised but pleased.

"Yes, especially since you came with Yeshua."

"No one could ever forget Yeshua." He gave Serapio a sidelong glance. "Adas met with a few of us yesterday."

"He told me. He's looking forward to meeting with Mary, and the others, again."

"He told us about how you saved his life, took him in, and bought his weapons as repayment for investing in your shop." Jamin eyed Serapio closely, hoping he would confirm what Adas told them.

"He exaggerated a bit. I didn't save his life. I doubt those men would have killed him. As for his weapons, the cost doesn't even come close to repaying him. Adas paid for this whole building. I think he gave me all his savings. He'd only been a centurion a short time, so he did not have money to waste. We call the weapons his 'Wolf Pack.' Perhaps I will be able to pay him back another way, someday."

"There are many things a man can do for a friend."

"Ah, I do believe I hear the hoof beats of a certain Arabian. Did he ever tell you how he came by his horse?"

"No. Sounds like there's another story to be told."

Serapio grinned, making his scar wrinkle. "Venustas was a gift from the Cornelius family, but it was the younger daughter who selected the horse. Needless to say, Adas treasures that horse. He taught Dulcibella, Greek and horsemanship, but he refused any payment other than invitations to stay for dinner. Centurion Cornelius was his highest commanding officer in Caesarea, but he is more like a father to Adas."

Venustas stopped at the open doorway. Adas dismounted and greeted his friends. When Fabiana came out to greet him, he asked her to join them. Serapio found the best chair for her. Fabiana looked rather pleased to not have to listen from the top of the stairs.

"Let me see your hand," said Fabiana. "Serapio told me what happened." She was delighted and asked Adas for all the details of the healing.

Then Jamin explained how the communication system would work. Many people hung banners from their rooftops, so the signals should not arouse suspicion. After the communication system was discussed, Adas left to report for duty.

Nearly two weeks later, Adas was on patrol when he saw a wide leather strap hanging from Serapio's rooftop. It was a non-emergency signal, but Adas was eager to learn the message. When Venustas appeared outside the open door, Fabiana waved for him to wait. She disappeared up the stairs and returned with two scrolls.

She smiled up at him as she stroked Venustas's neck. "Your friend just brought them."

Adas thanked her. When he got back to his quarters, he ripped open the scroll with the Greek symbols for Alpha and Omega, Dulcibella's pet greyhounds.

To my dearest Beloved,

I cannot tell you how glad I was to receive your letter. It was wonderfully long. Reading it over and over warms my heart. I will start with the end. In answer to your question: how many ways can I say yes? YES! YES! YES! There you have it three times, one YES for every time you must take my hand in yours for all to see. I was just a child when I first saw you jump off your horse and come to attention before my father, but I knew then I would have none other than you, Adas. And, yes, I agree the time will be perfect for us to reveal our engagement when you take ship to Rome. Have they set a date yet? That question brings me to a more important matter. Adas, I am crushed to hear of your mother's death. My whole family grieves with you. I cannot imagine how devastated you must feel to not be able to see her one last time. Why does life have to be so sad at times? When I see you next, I will hold you to my heart and grieve with you since I have also lost my mother-in-law. I never got the chance to tell her what a wonderful son she has. If the loss of your mother wasn't awful enough, Father seems worried about you for another reason. Is there something bad going on at the Antonia? He will not share it with me, but says it needs to come from you. I fear something is terribly wrong and it worries me, but Father also reminded me of how resourceful you are. You will laugh, but he said, and I quote, "The wolf is cunning, not easily caught, and if cornered, beware all the more!" He said this to me with a stern face and then gave me that reassuring little smile. It lightened my heart. My mother, sister, and brothers also send their love to you. I think my sister suspects you will ask for my hand when you come to Caesarea. She asked in a letter if I might have need of her wedding veil. But now, on to the other things you wrote to me. I cannot wait to discuss what you have learned about the Galilean named Yeshua. I, too, want to know more about him; in fact, the whole family does. For now, I long to hear your voice, to gaze into your eyes, and feel your arms around me.

Yours forever, Dulcibella

Adas was greatly relieved to know Dulcibella still wanted to be his wife. He picked up the scroll with the letters MCC stamped in the sealing wax. Adas broke the seal and read:

To: Centurion Clovius Longinus
Jerusalem, 10th Legio, 10th Cohors, 6th Centuria

Adas, I am extremely concerned about the events you have described in your letter. Valentius is more irrational than I remember. The fact that three legionaries conspired against you, claiming protection from Valentius, is deeply disturbing. You suspect this has something to do with your father, but it is possible it stems only from the unstable mind of Valentius. I know this from experience. Centurion Tacitus was forced to present charges against Valentius during the Samarian rebellion. I sent an official request the same day I received your letter, to have you come to Caesarea to train my decurions as a medicus veterinarius. You were wise to correspond with me through private channels. When the tribune receives my request, he will not know we have communicated. I suggest you burn this letter. I have sent my request with a squad and my personal servant, Andreas, the one I told you about who was healed by Yeshua. If Tribune Salvitto approves your leave of absence, they can escort you here. In truth, I really could use your help with the horses. As for the healer called Yeshua, I also want to discuss him. I want to hear everything you can tell me about him. I will try to learn more before you (hopefully) arrive. Iovita sends her love and Dulcibella does most of all. Also, please know all of us grieve with you for the loss of your beloved mother. No man as young as you should lose a parent. I am very sorry Iovita and I will never get a chance to meet her. I would have expressed my best praise to her for giving such a fine son to us. Be safe, my friend.

Your Fellow Soldier-at-Arms,
Primus Pilus Centurion Marcus Claudius Cornelius

Adas read the letter again before burning it in the fireplace. He stirred the charred papyrus until only ashes remained. Adas left his quarters and walked to the officers' *cafeteria*. He found Cassius and sat down.

"Glad to see you, Cassius. I won't have to eat alone."

Cassius mumbled around a mouthful of bread, "Where have you been? I haven't seen you in weeks." Cassius offered Adas a section of his bread. "Have you joined up with the followers of that Nazarene? They're nothing but trouble, you know."

"Yes, I've joined them. We're planning to sack Rome. Want to come along?" Adas laughed at the stern look on his face. "What! I was kidding."

"I'm serious, Adas. What's going on with you?"

"If you really have to know, I've been seeing a woman. She's fascinating. She tells me the most amazing stories about her son." He managed to change the subject, but Cassius remained unusually sullen. When Adas left, the decurion stared after him.

Adas strode across the quad. He was concerned by how often Cassius questioned his whereabouts. He had to be careful since his activities could affect the lives of others. He wondered if Cassius was reporting back to someone, or if he was just a concerned friend. He headed for the stables to find Nikolaus. The boy was cleaning stalls. "Nikolaus, have you noticed anyone leaving as soon as I do when I'm off duty?"

"Yes, Centurion, just in the last few weeks, I have noticed that Decurion Quintus seems to want Draco right after I saddle Venustas."

"Be watchful. It is important, but keep this to yourself."

"Of course, Centurion, whatever you ask, I will do my best."

"Good. Speaking of Draco, I think one more dose of *Nikotiana tobacum* will kill off the worms in his gut. I should take care of that now."

"I'll help you, Sir."

They found the dried tobacco leaves in the tack room. Adas crushed a leaf and, using a little water, made a ball of paste. They went to Draco's stall and coaxed the horse to swallow the paste. After Adas left the stables, an aide told him that he was needed in Tribune Salvitto's office. Adas knocked on the door and entered.

"Take a seat, Centurion," Salvitto ordered. "Centurion Cornelius has requested your assistance with a situation they're having with their horses. He sent an escort, asking if I could spare you for as long as possible. The problem is I have already granted you four months of leave for your father's wedding."

"Yes, Sir, but my duty comes first. My father will understand."

"Well then, you will leave with the escort tomorrow morning. Since I already approved a four-month leave, you can stay in Caesarea for the same time." He pressed his signet ring to the document, and handed it to Adas. "Please give my regards to Centurion Cornelius. We have known each other a long time."

"Sir, if I may—I believe I can accomplish two goals in Caesarea."

"How so?"

"Allow me to take the slave, Nikolaus, with me. I will be able to accomplish more and better train him."

"My only concern is he belongs to the Antonia."

"Sir, allow me to pay for his services."

"Agreed. I will make the proper notation for the pay deduction next month. Of course, you will have to pay for his replacement if he should run away. And when he is caught he will be crucified, as per the law. Are you willing to subject him to temptation?"

"Nikolaus is an intelligent, educated young man. He has served us by his own high standards. I think he is worthy of the test. If Nikolaus runs, I will take responsibility."

"You have a great deal of faith in this slave."

"I don't see him as a slave. He was born free and cherished by his family for twelve years. It was an accident of circumstances which forced him into slavery. For two years I have watched him do the right thing even when he thought no one would notice. Centurion Cornelius will be most pleased with your support on his behalf. Thank you, Sir. It is a pleasure and an honor serving you, Tribune." A hint of a smile crossed Salvitto's face.

Adas wanted to shout out loud, but managed to restrain himself. He headed for the barracks to find his second-in-command, *Optio* Victorius. Adas explained the reason for his summons to Caesarea and that Victorius would be in charge of the men until he returned.

"This is a great honor, Sir," said Victorius. "I will do my best."

"Thank you, Victorius. This is also a good opportunity for you to qualify for promotion. Summon the *centuria*."

Victorius used the ram's horn in the quad to summon the men. Adas explained the situation to them. After he dismissed them, he offered his hand to Victorius. "Take care of our men." Victorius squared his shoulders with pride at his commander's trust.

Adas headed across the quad to the officers' common room to inquire about the escort from Caesarea. A young man approached him. "You must be Centurion Clovius Longinus. I am Andreas, personal servant to Centurion Claudius Cornelius. It is good to meet you, Sir."

Adas shook hands eagerly. "It is good to meet you as well. I am looking forward to my assignment. I will be ready to go at the first hour. And call me Adas."

Andreas introduced Adas to the other four men. They went to the officers' *cafeteria*, and ate while they traded news about Caesarea and Jerusalem. By the time they left the *cafeteria*, it was nearly sunset. Adas directed them to the visitors' quarters. He went to the stables to look for Nikolaus and his team. He found them sitting on bales of hay eating their dinner of barley bread, squash, and carrots. Adas told them he would be gone four months, but promised to make it up to them when he got back. The boys were sad, but Nikolaus was the most depressed. Adas motioned for Nikolaus to follow him to a stall.

"Nikolaus, what do you think of this horse?" The boy refused to look Adas in the eye.

"Sir, he has the fine look of an Akhal-Teke, but also the typical aggressiveness. He needs much work with firm handling. He will improve if the rider can win his trust. He has endurance, but possibly not as much speed as your horse. I don't think he'll make a good war horse. He is skittish around loud noises."

"I see. Not good for battle. What do you think of his color?"

"He does have the yellow metallic sheen of his breed. He lives up to the term 'Golden Horse.' I would use black tack to match his mane and tail."

"Is there a black saddle and bridle not being used?"

"Yes, Sir. There are a number of sets, in fact," Nikolaus said as he rubbed the horse's forehead. The buckskin turned his head toward Nikolaus.

Adas couldn't resist grinning. "Well, then, you'll have to decide on which set to use, since you'll be riding this horse for a while."

Nikolaus blinked in shock. "Sir, you know slaves are not allowed to ride the horses."

"You're going to have to ride this horse if you are to be my assistant in Caesarea."

Nikolaus's eyes fairly popped as his jaw went slack. "I am going with you *to Caesarea*? Four whole months?"

"Do you want to come?" Adas already knew the answer.

"More than anything in the world, Sir. I will do my best for you. When do we leave, Sir?"

"First hour, tomorrow. There are five other men who will be traveling with us. I want you to gather your belongings. I'll go with you. I need to tell the legionary on duty that he will be short one in his count tonight. I want you to stay in the guest quarters."

Nikolaus rolled the only spare tunic he had in his blanket. Together they went to the visitors' quarters. Adas found the five men sitting at a table playing *Tali,* a board game played with dice. Adas greeted them. "Andreas, I would like you to meet Nikolaus, my assistant. Nikolaus this is Andreas, Centurion Cornelius's personal servant." Andreas greeted the teenager. Adas pulled Andreas aside. "I would like Nikolaus to sleep here tonight. I don't want a particular slave to know our plans."

"Of course. There are more than enough cots. We will be ready at sun up. I know you are eager to get on the road."

A corner of Adas's mouth curved. "You have no idea."

"Actually, I think I do. Dulcibella has talked of no one else since her father announced he was sending for you."

Adas bid good night to the men, acknowledging each one individually. He looked over at Nikolaus. "Sleep well."

"And you, Sir," Nikolaus had to bite his lower lip to keep from shouting with joy at the prospect of "escaping" from the Antonia Fortress even if it was temporary. To have adventures in an imaginary world was a fleeting escape from the drudgery of slavery, but it was all Nikolaus had—until now. He was sixteen years old and had been a slave four of those years. The first twelve years of his life seemed to have happened to someone else.

Nikolaus's first memory of the centurion was when he led a stunning horse through the arena gate. He was weighed down with several knapsacks. There were more hanging from all four saddle horns. The soldier was medium in height and powerfully built. Nikolaus thought he must be more than a legionary since his horse was high bred, yet he appeared to be too young for an officer. Nikolaus hurried over to the stranger to offer his help. When he approached, the soldier looked him directly in the eye, which was highly unusual. Nikolaus blinked in alarm at the centurion's wolf-like eyes.

"What is your name?" the stranger asked. No soldier had ever asked for his name. They always called him "boy" or "slave." Nikolaus gulped when he saw the *caligae* and belt of a centurion. He respectfully lowered his eyes. "Sir, my name is Nikolaus. I wait for your instructions, Centurion." When there was no response, Nikolaus glanced up. The young man was watching him, not with distaste, but with curiosity.

"Nikolaus is a fine name. Do you have a *nomen*?"

"Yes, Sir. My clan name is Kokinos."

The centurion looked startled. "Nikolaus Kokinos. Your initials are NK." He acted as if he had heard something remarkable.

"Is there something wrong, Sir?" Nikolaus was bewildered at his reaction.

"No, nothing is wrong. Just—interesting. I am Centurion Clovius Longinus. I'll leave my horse in your care, and return shortly." He handed the reins over. Gathering his knapsacks without ordering the boy to assist, he walked out of the arena. Nikolaus stared after him. He was surprised at the centurion's unconcern. Undoubtedly he cared a great deal about such a beautiful horse, but it seemed he was putting an equally great deal of trust in him. Nikolaus led the Arabian back to an unused stall. He spent more time tending to the centurion's horse than even the most demanding officers expected.

When the centurion returned he scrutinized his horse without comment. He was carrying a small loaf of wheat bread. "You have done an excellent job, Nikolaus. Venustas looks well groomed. It pleases me that you brought her fresh hay and water. You even cleaned the mud out of her hooves." He handed the bread to Nikolaus. "I think you've earned this." The boy only hesitated a moment before he took the bread.

"Thank you, Sir, but slaves are not allowed wheat bread. I do not wish to get you in trouble. Besides, it is my job to care for the horses."

"It is the way you have done your job that deserves reward. As for the bread, since I am breaking the rules, I suggest you eat it quickly. From now on, I don't want anyone else to tend to my horse. Can that be arranged?"

"Yes, Sir, if you request it with Tribune Salvitto."

"Then I will make the request, Nikolaus."

Being selected to assist Centurion Longinus in Caesarea was the first reward Nikolaus had received since he was forced into slavery. His perseverance and hard work had finally paid off. Adas had befriended him, even though he was a slave. He began to look forward to the Saturday classes as his trust and faith in the centurion grew. Sometimes, when Centurion Longinus asked him to assist with an injured or sick horse, Nikolaus felt hope again, hope for a future.

Chapter 21

———— ⌘ ————

Nikolaus woke up with a start and looked around. Soft light through the window lattices was chasing away the darkness. Today he would leave the Antonia for the first time in four years. He hadn't felt such happiness since his family was alive. While the other men slept, he slipped out quietly, went to the officers' *cafeteria,* and asked Cook if he could take breakfast to Centurion Longinus. With a tray bearing a substantial amount of food, Nikolaus went to the centurion's quarters and knocked. The door opened quickly.

"Sir, I hope this meets your approval. I thought it might save time."

Adas was already shaved and dressed. He gestured for Nikolaus to enter. "I definitely approve. I'm starving." He set his other chair at the table. "How did you talk Cook into all this?"

"One of the kitchen slaves loaded the tray, Sir. I told him it was for you." Nikolaus set the tray down, but remained standing. "What are your instructions, Sir?"

"Help me eat all this food," Adas motioned to Nikolaus to join him. He obeyed, but ate sparingly, watching Adas carefully for any hints he was overstepping. Leaving several boiled eggs, fruit and half of the bread, Adas got up to make a final check of his knapsacks. Adas gestured at the tray. "Don't waste that food."

The boy eagerly finished off the remaining items. Adas turned away to hide an amused grin. Nikolaus ran the tray back and joined Adas in the stables. Andreas and the soldiers were fitting their knapsacks and waterskins on the pack horses. Adas added his belongings. When the stable boys led the saddled horses out, Adas told them Nikolaus was going with him. They kept their expressions neutral, but when Nikolaus led the buckskin gelding out and tied his knapsack on the saddle, their expressions changed to resentment. Adas decided it might be beneficial for both of them if he trained Nikolaus to be his sparring partner.

The men mounted up and headed down the avenue which would take them to the Valley Gate. Then they would head west through Emmaus and on to Joppa. From there, they would travel north along the coastline to Caesarea Maritima.

Before they left the city, Adas told the others he would catch up with them. He signaled for Nikolaus to go with him and headed for Serapio's *Suppelex*. Serapio and Fabiana were sitting by the door enjoying the cool morning breeze.

"Well, what brings this grand soldier to our shop so early?" Serapio exclaimed.

"I wanted you to know I'll be in Caesarea four months, to help Centurion Cornelius with some sick horses. I also wanted both of you to meet Nikolaus." He motioned the teenager forward. "Serapio, Fabiana, this is Nikolaus."

The boy bowed his head respectfully keeping his eyes on the ground. Serapio clamped a bear-paw of a hand on Nikolaus's shoulder. The boy looked into Serapio's ruined face. The cloudy, blind eye and terrible scar were intimidating. Nikolaus focused on Serapio's good eye.

Serapio liked the youngster's steady gaze. "I hear good things about you, Nikolaus. You come here if you ever need help. We have something in common, young man. I was once a slave, a *gladiator,* owned by a rich man in Rome. Take good care of him, Adas. I like him."

"Thank you, Sir. I am glad to meet both of you."

Adas reached for Fabiana. She hugged him as a mother hugs a son. "Well, I guess we better get going. I will write to you. I carry both of you in my heart." He received a good back slapping from Serapio. Nikolaus hoped someday Adas would look at him with the same camaraderie as he did at Serapio. They jumped back on their horses.

As they trotted down the street, Adas said, "For reasons I can't explain right now, I might need Serapio's help someday, and I may not be able to go to him. If I send a message to you with the word *musculus* in it, I will need you to fetch him for me. I know it will be dangerous, so be careful."

"Yes, Sir. I will do my best for you."

"I will not ask unless it is an extreme emergency."

Nikolaus was filled with pride that Adas put such trust in him. He was determined to never let the centurion down. They caught up with the other five men at the Valley Gate. They had gone about twenty miles when Andreas suggested they stay at an inn on the far side of Emmaus since the sun would be setting soon. The darkness was never safe for anyone. They turned into the courtyard of the inn. Andreas went inside to ask the innkeeper if rooms were available. He came out with the innkeeper and several boys to help with the horses. The soldiers went with them to unload the equipment from the pack horses. Adas went to sign for the rooms. After tending to the horses, Nikolaus brought Adas's knapsacks to him.

"Sir, what are your instructions?"

"Instructions? For what?"

"For tonight, Sir. Do you wish for me to stay with the horses? There are posted shackles in the stables for slaves."

"I have no use for shackles, Nikolaus. As far as I'm concerned, you are my assistant. One does not chain his assistant to a post."

"Sir, I-I'm not sure what you're saying."

"We cannot pretend you have your freedom. When we go back to the Antonia, you will still belong to Tribune Salvitto, but for the next four months, you have a choice to make. Will you be my assistant, or will you be a slave? I refuse to see you as both."

"But, Sir, what if I ran away? You would be held accountable."

"Yes, I would appreciate it, if you didn't."

Nikolaus frowned, not seeing Adas's lopsided grin. "How can you trust me so much? There are so many directions I could run."

"I trust you, Nikolaus, because I have tested you. You do more than I ask of you. You take my instruction willingly, never grudgingly. Do you remember when you found my knapsack in the stall? I didn't get five steps down the lane before you ran to return it. All of the apples were still in it."

"You left it on purpose?"

"No, but I knew how many apples I had bought. Nikolaus, I will not waste my time on someone who must be chained. You can either be a runaway slave, or you can be my assistant. I will not chase after you. However, be prepared to accept the consequences of your actions."

"Then I am terrified I will disappoint you. Do you not know how freedom sings to me like the sirens sang to Ulysses? The temptation to run is always in my heart! But like Ulysses, if I give in to temptation, it will be my death. I will be captured and crucified. So perhaps you should chain me to a post so I will be safe from temptation. Did not Ulysses accept his weakness, knowing it was impossible to resist leaping to his death at the lure of the sirens?"

Adas thought for a moment. "Ulysses told his men to tie him to the ship's mast because he wasn't strong enough to resist the sirens' song, but I believe you are. You must tie yourself to the 'mast' of my faith in you. I believe you have more strength and courage than you realize. Otherwise, you could not have survived the loss of your family. I see your intelligence, your abilities, and your willingness to work hard." Adas's voice softened. "I cannot imagine how it must feel to live twelve years of contented freedom and then lose so much. So, I cannot make this choice for you, Nikolaus. I am asking you to have faith in yourself as well. The horses will be fine without you tonight. There is a bed for you indoors." Adas turned to walk back in the inn.

"Sir! Today is my birthday. Today, I am seventeen years old."

"Then this is a fine day, Nikolaus. Tonight, we will eat a good dinner together to celebrate your coming of age."

In the evening, everyone gathered around the innkeeper's dining table. They ate bread dipped in herbed olive oil, mutton stew, and good wine. Adas announced it was Nikolaus's seventeenth birthday, the age of adulthood. They congratulated him with raised goblets. There were no other guests for the night, but the innkeeper had a large family. The children sang to them while their parents accompanied them with eight-stringed harps. The men tapped their sandaled feet on the tiled floor to keep the rhythm of the music. The melody of voices and the harps lent an air of magic to the night. Adas had forgotten how much he enjoyed music.

Nikolaus had never expected to be so happy. Too soon for him, it was time to turn in for the night. Several of the children led the escort soldiers to the rooms they would share. The innkeeper led Adas, Andreas and Nikolaus upstairs to their rooms. A whisper of night air streamed through the window lattices. Andreas and Nikolaus shared a room across the hall from Adas. Andreas insisted Nikolaus choose which bed he wanted, since it was his birthday. He tried to decline, but Andreas threatened to sleep on the floor if Nikolaus didn't take first choice.

Across the hall, Adas blew out all the lamps and welcomed the darkness. He opened the lattice panels of the window for a clear view. He sat on the window sill. The moon was nearly full, casting soft, moon shadows across the landscape.

In the tranquility of the breeze-cooled night, his thoughts turned to Dulcibella, which made him smile. He took the eilat stone from his coin pouch. Adas turned the smooth stone in the moonlight and thought of how much it reminded him of the blue pearl. The two objects looked nothing alike, but both carried the promise of hope and love. He set the eilat stone down and took the pearl from the leather pouch. He held both gems in his hand. The moonlight cast shadows of the gems on the cross branded on his palm.

Adas put the stone and the pearl back in their pouches. The dry breeze drifting in from the windows felt good. He stood mesmerized by the peacefulness of the restful darkness. Contentment soothed his heart like a gentle rain on an arid landscape. When he got in bed, he gazed at the moon. "Good night, Dulcibella."

Adas was asleep before he could think another thought. However, his sleep would not pass undisturbed. He dreamed of being on a ship in heavy seas under attack by a gigantic sea creature. It clung to the ship with huge pincher-like claws and thrashed its long twisting tail as it fought to pull the vessel under the storm waves. Faceless strangers on the ship struggled against the drenching crests of water. One of the passengers reached out to him. It was Nikolaus. Adas fought the turbulent waves and tossing deck, desperate to reach Nikolaus, but the waves washed him farther away. The monster snatched Nikolaus away. Adas lunged for him as he disappeared into the sea. A crash of thunder jerked him awake. He sat up panting but settled back on the bed, telling himself it was only a dream. There was no horrific beast or stormy sea, but there was the sound of galloping hooves. He thought he should look out the window, but he went back to sleep before the sound faded.

Chapter 22

A das woke just as the sun was painting distant clouds a blazing hot pink. He remembered his dream. He dressed quickly and walked to the room across the hall. Andreas was alone, still sleeping. Nikolaus's belongings were gone. Adas felt a sickening pang as he hurried down the stairs. He stopped at the kitchen doorway when he saw the innkeeper's wife sliding small loaves of bread into the *furnus*.

"Have you seen the young Greek this morning?" Adas asked.

"No, Sir."

Adas hurried to the stables. The buckskin gelding was gone. An avalanche of emotions crashed over him. Guilt assailed him for tempting Nikolaus beyond what he could endure. He felt sure Nikolaus had the best intentions the day before, but during the night, the call of freedom proved too powerful. Aquila once told him, "It is foolish to trust anyone. Everyone is capable of betrayal." He hated for his father to be right.

Anger overtook his distress, but he wasn't sure if he was more angry with Nikolaus or himself. Adas leaned against the side of the stall, visualizing Salvitto berating him for losing his best slave. Still, he prayed God would protect Nikolaus now that he was a fugitive.

Venustas raised her head and whinnied. She tossed her head and whinnied again. The familiar clip clop of hooves sounded. Adas spun around. Nikolaus was leading the buckskin gelding. He had his head down as he walked, but he looked up when his horse snorted and laid his ears back. A wave of staggering relief washed over Adas.

"Good morning, Centurion. I was practicing the long rope techniques you taught me. Is everything all right, Sir?"

"I-I, uh, yes, I'm fine." He grasped one of Venustas's front ankles to inspect her hoof.

"Sir, is there something wrong with Venustas?"

"I was checking to make sure the infection hasn't returned."

"Sir, it was—the other—front hoof."

"Yes, of course, what was I thinking?" He started to leave the barn.

"Sir, may I speak with you? Last night," began Nikolaus, "I couldn't sleep. I came down here with my knapsack and blanket to make a bed in the straw, but that didn't help. I wanted to see what it felt like to just—go. I saddled Inventio and led him out to the road. I jumped in the saddle just before lightning and a crash of thunder nearly scared both of us to death. He took off at a full gallop. He ran so fast. I've never felt so free. The moon came out and lit our way. It never started raining and there was no more lightning. We ran for at least three hundred paces. Then Inventio slowed down and stopped, but I hadn't pulled the reins. It was as if he knew I was making a terrible mistake. I thought of how you asked me to have faith, and how you would find a way to free me. Running would ruin everything. I think Inventio read my mind, because he walked back to the inn without even a flick of the reins. I am sorry, Centurion. I needed those shackles after all."

"No, Nikolaus. Quite the opposite. You came back, which took more courage than if you had never run at all. Even after a taste of freedom, you returned."

Nikolaus took a deep breath. "Yes, Sir, I guess I did. When Inventio stopped, he stared back at me for the longest time. Then he turned around."

"You could have taken control, but you didn't. The temptation to run was never stronger than your strength to resist."

"What do you mean, Sir?"

"I heard the thunder, too. It woke me up. I heard a galloping horse, but I went back to sleep. When I couldn't find you, and the horse was gone, I thought I had lost you. I was angry with you, but then more so with myself for tempting you. I have been studying the Way of Yeshua, and have learned God does not allow temptation to go beyond our resistance."

"When I came into the barn, you were just standing there. You kept your promise not to pursue me. It scares me to think how close I came to making the worst decision of my life."

"The key to that statement is 'how close,' but you came back. You did well, Nikolaus. Last night, you made the decision of a free man, not a slave." He patted the buckskin's neck. "So, you named your horse Inventio, as in Discovery?"

"Even if he is only on loan to me, he deserves a name."

"I think Inventio is a fine name. We'll keep it. He did help you make quite a discovery about yourself. Come on, let's eat breakfast." They walked together to the inn. Their companions were at the dining table, talking around mouthfuls of bread and stew.

Andreas looked up. "There you are! We thought you two left without us."

Adas and Nikolaus exchanged a quick glance. "Deny ourselves your excellent company? Never!" said Adas with mock severity. "Besides, we're hungry."

After breakfast, they set off for Joppa. The day was crisp. The thin morning clouds had burned off, leaving behind a clear deep blue sky. They passed through Joppa by mid-afternoon and pressed on to Apollonia, a port city. Before the twelfth hour, about supper time, they reached Apollonia. Andreas suggested they stay at the Apollonia Inn, built on a cliff overlooking the sea.

When they rode into the courtyard, two girls came out to help with the horses. The older girl was intent on her task, but the younger one smiled up at Nikolaus as he released the reins to her. He slid out of the saddle and pulled his knapsack from a saddle horn. When he stepped back, she was so close he bumped into her. Disconcerted, he tried to apologize, but the amused sparkle in her eyes made him stop. She took a deliberate step back.

"What is your name?" she asked, smiling up at him with full pink lips and even white teeth. The breeze fluffed her auburn hair as her brown eyes danced at his embarrassment.

"Nikolaus." He was aware the other men were enjoying his discomfort. He tried to step around her, but she blocked his way.

"Aren't you going to ask my name? It would be polite."

"All right. What is your name?"

"Marina. How long are you staying?"

"Just for the night."

"What a shame."

Her sister, Varinia, rolled her eyes. She gathered the reins for Andrea's and the soldiers' horses, threw an annoyed look at her younger sister, and walked toward the stables. "Sometime today would be nice, Marina!"

.   "I'll help you. Wait here. I'll be right back." He hurried over to Adas.

Adas saw that Marina was watching them. Nikolaus started to ask for instructions, but Adas interrupted. "In case I don't see you at dinner, don't get in too late. We have an early start tomorrow." Nikolaus stood dumbfounded. Adas headed for the entrance to the inn. He called over his shoulder. "You two behave yourselves."

Marina watched Adas leave. "Well, he's bossy. Is he your big brother?"

"My brother! Why would you say that?"

"That's how my sister acts. If he's not your brother, who is he? He has strange eyes." She peered closely at Nikolaus. "So do you." She touched his shoulder and faced him. Nikolaus stiffened, taken by surprise by a surge of emotions. She saw his reaction and smiled. "Ask me what I see?" She waited expectantly.

"What do you see, Marina?"

"I see a black kettle, sitting in the center of a bonfire, surrounded by green smoke held in a circle of twilight. What do you call that?"

"My mother said I have hazel eyes. What would *you* call it?"

"I would call it—worth further study. What do you see when you look at my eyes?"

Nicholas took his time. "I see the long-lashed eyes of a young deer, curious, and kind."

"Well said, Nikolaus-Hazel-Eyes." She laughed and Nikolaus smiled at the sound of it. They gathered the reins of the remaining horses and led them to the stables.

"Do you have brushes for the horses?" Nikolaus asked.

Her dark eyes twinkled with mischief. "We do, for a price."

"Really? What will it cost me?"

"If I let you use the brushes, you have to answer my questions—truthfully."

"Maybe we should ask each other questions one for one. We'll make it a game."

"Deal. I go first." Marina bit her bottom lip and considered his first question.

In the inn, Adas walked out to the terrace overlooking the Mediterranean. Clouds low on the horizon looked like a flock of pink and orange sheep. Just below the clouds, the arc of the sun shot rays of light across the sea revealing golden sprites as they dipped and bobbed over the surface of the water. Adas stood transfixed by the beauty. He thought of Dulcibella and sighed. The anticipation of holding her in his arms quickened his heart. His problems in Jerusalem faded. He smiled to think how annoyed she would get when he became lost in the sound of her voice, paying little attention to the words. Her exasperation at his inattention would end with a sigh and forgiveness.

The innkeeper approached and introduced himself as Pitio. He asked if Adas was ready to see his room. He followed Pitio inside, up the stairs and down a hallway where large windows at either end encouraged a soothing breeze. He opened the last door on the right. Adas stepped in and walked to the largest window in the room. It was a bay window with a deep ledge. He pulled the lattice open and took a deep breath of salt-spiced ocean air.

"Sir, if I might warn you, the occasional seagull may fly in."

Adas nodded, but remained silent. He listened as the sea waves stroked the shore. Coming from below the white limestone cliff, the sound seemed to have a muted echo. The breeze whispering through the window was scented with pomegranate and orange trees blossoming along the courtyard wall.

"Does this room meet with your satisfaction, Centurion?"

"It does. Thank you."

"Supper will be served soon. We have clam soup, seasoned grilled fish, fresh dill bread with olive oil, and apricot *crustulorum* with honey sauce for dessert. Should I send one of my nephews to tell you when it is ready?"

"That will be fine."

Pitio pulled the door shut. Adas sat on the window seat. From his second-story view, he could see the coastline for quite a ways. As the sun dove into the waves, a sliver of green flashed above the submerging disc. He wondered if Dulcibella saw it from her terrace in Caesarea. Sailors claimed the green flash was a promise from Neptune for brisk winds and calm seas.

Adas leaned his back against the window opening and watched the stars appear. Someone came out to the courtyard to light the torches. Adas could just make out a few figures moving about in the soft glow. A tall man walking with a right-legged limp stepped out from the patio and moved to the back wall. Adas stiffened with alarm. The man turned to inspect the upper windows across the full length of the inn. He limped back to the patio, out of sight. Adas closed the lattice and went downstairs. He found Pitio in the front courtyard.

"Did you need something, Centurion?" Pitio asked.

"Yes, I caught a glimpse of someone who might be a friend of mine. Do you have a guest, a tall man, who walks with a limp?"

Pitio hesitated. "A guest with a limp? No, there is no such guest as you describe."

Adas saw no point in arguing. He went back to his room. If Cassius was following him, he was acting on Valentius's orders, and he had paid Pitio for his silence. Hopefully, there was another explanation. He decided not to worry, but to stay alert.

A soft knock sounded at the door. A boyish voice called out. "Supper is served. Please come join us, Sir." Adas joined the others in the dining hall. It didn't surprise him that Nikolaus and Marina were not there. The dinner was more delicious than Adas and his group expected. It was served with an expensive wine and topped off with the promised apricot pastry.

Adas complimented Pitio on the dinner and excused himself. He needed to write a letter to his father explaining his absence from the wedding. He sat at the desk but words eluded him. It was hard enough to express himself to his father in person and even more difficult in writing.

Another knock and the same boy called out. "Sir, do you need your lamps re-filled?"

"Yes, come in. Tell me, did my assistant and your cousin eat supper together?"

"Yes, Sir. Marina let him have her share of apricot *crustulorum*. She must like him! Apricot is her favorite. She always tries to steal mine." He finished his task and left.

Adas gave up on writing the letter. He went back to the window seat and peered out into the dark. The light of *Lucifer*, the brightest *planeta,* gleamed in the night sky amid the Milky Way. Adas removed the leather cord from around his neck. He took the pearl from the pouch. In the low light of the lamps, the opalescent blue of the pearl appeared to glow. Adas clutched the gem in his hand and held it to his chest. Since he couldn't give it to his mother, he would give the pearl to Dulcibella. He put it back in the pouch, closed the screens, and eased into bed. He barely had time to whisper, "Until tomorrow, Dulcibella," before he fell into a deep, dreamless sleep.

Chapter 23

⸻ ∞∞∞ ⸻

Adas woke refreshed. Today he would see Dulcibella and her family. He looked forward to long discussions with Marcus Cornelius and good-natured quips with Dulcibella's mother, Iovita. Adas knew Dulcibella's two younger brothers, fifteen-year-old Marc and thirteen-year-old Vitus would be eager to show him their sparring skills. He anticipated the time-honored Roman tradition of publicly asking for Dulcibella's hand in marriage, especially the first of the three required.

Adas packed his knapsack and left the room. He knocked on the door across the hall. Nikolaus stepped back for Adas to enter.

"Good morning, Centurion. Did you sleep well, Sir?"

"Yes. Did you?"

"Yes, Sir." Nikolaus glanced at Andreas and lowered his voice. "Sir, thank you for what you did yesterday. If Marina had known I am a slave, she would not have spoken to me."

"I'm not so sure of that. I think she likes you." Nikolaus suddenly needed to re-lace his sandals. Adas suppressed a chuckle as he left and went downstairs.

Pitio greeted him. "Breakfast is ready, Sir. I was told you wanted an early start."

The others joined Adas over an ample meal. Marina and her sister brought in bowls of fruit, goat cheese, and freshly baked bread. Marina caught the young Greek's eye with a smile. Nikolaus smiled back. She lingered next to Nikolaus before she set a bowl of food on the table.

It wasn't long before they were headed north on the coastline road. Andreas and Nikolaus noticed Adas glanced over his shoulder more than usual. They stopped a few times to rest the horses, but mostly they rode at a steady pace. About the seventh hour, Adas could see the familiar sight of Caesarea Maritima in the distance. At the crossroad, they thanked their escort soldiers as they turned off for the garrison. Adas promised to commend their performance to Centurion Cornelius. Adas, Nikolaus, and Andreas continued north into town. Shops with street vendors and pedestrians slowed their progress.

At an intersection, a rider on a coal black stallion drew their attention. The horse was heavily muscled with a massive chest. The wavy, sweeping mane and arched neck gave the horse a regal appearance. Its high-stepping gait disturbed little dust.

"Do you recognize the breed?" asked Andreas. "From Friesland, northern Gaul. Isn't he magnificent?"

The rider was young and richly dressed. His dark hair and beard were neatly trimmed. His dark eyes and features spoke of sophistication. The stallion started tossing his head and chewing at the bit. Adas saw pink froth fly from the horse's mouth. When the stallion reared unprovoked, Adas suspected what was wrong. The horse sidestepped blindly, coming closer to the vendors' stands, and leaving people, including children, no way to escape.

Adas signaled for Nikolaus to help. They dropped to the ground and handed their reins to Andreas, who backed their horses out of the way. Nikolaus unfastened his belt and the two men maneuvered to flank the horse. The stallion reared again, lashing out with its front hooves, causing the rider to tumble off. Nikolaus threw his belt over its neck as Adas grabbed hold of it on the other side. Both men pulled down until Adas could jerk the bridle off. At the sound of Adas's soothing deep voice, the horse stood still.

The rider brushed himself off and apologized to the crowd. Adas found blood on the hemp bridle. Carefully, he inspected the stallion's mouth, and found a gash in the upper gum behind the teeth. A newly exposed thorn was twisted into the hemp.

"I owe you a great debt," said the rider. "Blackfire is a spirited beast, but this is unusual even for him. I had no idea there was anything wrong with this bridle. I've used it for months. Excuse my rudeness. I am Silas Silvanus."

Adas introduced himself, Nikolaus and Andreas. He pulled the thorn from the bridle's bit and gently coaxed the horse to accept it.

"How did you know the bridle was the problem?" asked Silas.

"I saw blood on his mouth when he fought the reins. He is a beautiful stallion. My friend says he is from Friesland."

"We can thank Julius Caesar for pushing the empire into Gaul giving us access to these horses. I owe the three of you a debt of gratitude. Please join me at my villa for dinner."

"Silas, thank you for your offer, but Centurion Cornelius expects us at his villa this afternoon."

"Very well, gentlemen, but you must visit me before you leave. Andreas, are you familiar with the location of my villa?"

"I am, Sir. We will be in contact."

"Then I shall look forward to hearing from you. And, again, I thank you." Silas leapt onto his horse and trotted down the street.

"Well, gentlemen, looks like we saved the day. Good job, both of you."

Nikolaus beamed at the praise. "You have taught me well, Centurion."

They mounted their horses and talked as they traveled along the rest of the main street. At the first crossroad outside the city, Adas took the road leading to the cliff path. He pressed both heels into Venustas's flanks, and she took off at a gallop. Andreas and Nikolaus exchanged grins, but held their horses back. This first reunion of Adas and Dulcibella should have some privacy.

When the road steepened, Adas slowed Venustas to a walk. The road curved back and forth up the hillside until the villa came into view. The seaside terrace on the north side of the villa had a short wall and full view of the ocean. A huge, ancient oak tree stood behind the wall. Someone was pacing just under the shade of the tree. It was a young woman with brunette hair flowing down her shoulders. She was shielding her eyes from the sun as she scanned the road. When she saw Adas, she waved before disappearing from sight.

Adas clicked his tongue. Venustas covered the last of the road in a trot. At the curve leading to the courtyard, Adas saw the front door open. Dulcibella came running down the path. Alpha and Omega, the miniature greyhounds, followed close behind. Adas slid out of the saddle and braced himself as she flew into his arms. Dulcibella threw her arms over his shoulders. She buried her face against his neck. He held her as if she would vanish if he let go.

Adas gazed into the emerald starbursts of her eyes. He felt as if his heart would burst with joy. Her face was bright with excitement. She pulled his head down and closed her eyes. They kissed as if nothing else existed beyond each other. When he raised his head, Dulcibella's expression clouded with concern as she touched the scar over his eye.

"This is new. Is this why Father has been so worried about you?" She let her hand linger against his face. He kissed the palm of her hand.

"There's no need for worry. We're together."

Hoof beats sounded as Nikolaus and Andreas appeared and dismounted. Andreas greeted Dulcibella. Adas introduced Nikolaus. Dazed by her graceful beauty, Nikolaus attempted a greeting, but could only stammer. His face reddened as he busied himself with gathering the reins of the horses. In sympathy, Dulcibella covered an amused smile with her hand.

The front door flew open and Marcus hurried down the path. Iovita, Marc, and Vitus, followed him. Hugs and hand shaking were shared all around. Marcus and Adas clapped each other on the back. Alpha and Omega started jumping on everyone. Adas snatched up both dogs, one under each arm. They happily gave him a tongue licking.

"How was the trip?" asked Marcus as he nodded a greeting at Andreas.

"It went well, Sir," said Adas. "We have also been introduced to the richest man in Caesarea. We'll tell you all about Silvanus and his unhappy stallion over dinner. Nikolaus and I make a good team."

They eventually made their way into the house. The travelers were greeted with the aroma of a feast in the making. The family gathered in the main hall, while the servants gathered in the kitchen to eat. Andreas invited Nikolaus to join the rest of the servants.

After dinner, Adas and Dulcibella walked out on the terrace to enjoy the sunset under the shade of the oak tree. Dulcibella took Adas's hand and led him to the high-backed bench he made for the family when he was stationed there. Dulcibella leaned her head against his shoulder. She turned his right hand palm up and traced the scars of the cross with her finger. "Father told me you were assigned to crucify Yeshua. I suspect the pain of this injury does not come close to the pain in your heart. I know you, Adas. You hate crucifying even the worst criminal. Everyone knows Yeshua was no criminal."

"As loathsome as it was, I obeyed orders. While he was dying, he forgave me. Then his followers forgave me. Then, beyond all understanding, his mother forgave me. She even made me forgive myself. Yet, there was a far greater miracle than even that."

"I know. Yeshua is alive!"

"Yes! How did you hear about it?"

"After Andreas was healed, he and Centurion Januarius found Yeshua to thank him. They witnessed him heal all those that asked. Andreas is living proof Yeshua was no ordinary man. Because of what Januarius and Andreas told Father, he has been studying with teachers from the temple since you went to Jerusalem. They say that Yeshua is the Messiah. Many have witnessed him alive, but he still bears the marks of crucifixion."

"Dulcie, do you know how much I love you?"

"Yes, I do. I always have." He sought her lips. It was a kiss of passion and harmony. Their love was not only a matter of the heart, but a melding of their spirits.

Adas looked to the west as the sun surrendered to the sea. It would be dark soon. "Dulcie, I have a gift for you. It was given to me, and I wish to give it to you."

Dulcibella's eyes brightened. "Your expression makes me think it is heaven itself."

Adas pulled the leather pouch from under his tunic. He opened it, and tapped the blue pearl into her palm. Dulcibella gasped with wonder.

"Where. . .how? It is beyond beautiful! Caesar would invade a country for this gem. Is it enchanted? It glows as if lit from within? Even now, in twilight."

Adas told her about Zacchaeus and Yeshua's parable about the pearl of great price.

"Adas, this pearl is the most beautiful thing I have ever seen. Your story is just as beautiful. I will keep both close to my heart. The pearl is more than a gift from the sea; it is a gift from God." She curled her legs on the bench and nestled into his arms. They watched as the ocean waves changed color with the darkening sky. Dulcibella was so still, Adas thought she had fallen asleep. As the sky changed to muted shades of indigo blue, Adas thought of something he wanted to discuss. Before he spoke, Dulcibella asked, "What is it?"

"How did you know I was going to say anything?" Her only answer was a pensive smile. "I was going to ask how you want to announce our engagement."

"I've decided to leave the details to you. Surprise me."

"No hints?"

"No hints."

"No cryptic clues?"

She laughed. "No cryptic clues."

They talked until it grew dark. The star-dusted lace of the Milky Way made a glittering curtain across the sky. Moon shadows came and went as gossamer clouds sailed past, racing each other to the horizon. Adas walked Dulcibella into the house, but came back to the terrace. He put a few blankets on a lounge chair to make a bed. He would sleep under the stars.

Adas woke early to the sound of the ocean tumbling on the beach far below the cliff. The rising sun sent sparks through a bank of clouds igniting them into a gold and red blaze. The first thing he wanted to do was find Marcus and Iovita to discuss his plan for the marriage proposal. They were on the rooftop, watching the changing colors of the ocean as the sun rose behind them. They had already spied Adas while he was asleep on the terrace. Marcus called down to him as Adas stood up and stretched. He hurried to the outdoor stairs. When he told them his plan, Iovita laughed and cried at the same time. Adas told her what he needed her to do. She happily accepted her role. Marcus said he would make sure he was nearby when the big moment arrived. They were both elated for Dulcibella and Adas, but not surprised. Their relationship had grown stronger with each passing year.

Marcus remembered the first day he met Adas when he was the assistant to the *primus veterinarius*. The garrison received news of a man threatening to kill his family. He had them trapped in their house while he stood on the roof armed with a bow. The crazed man had already injured four men. Marcus ordered his men to distract the shooter while he climbed a tree and leaped onto the roof. The man turned with an arrow already drawn and let it go. He missed. Marcus charged the man. He took a swing at Marcus and lost his balance. The man fell from the roof, breaking his neck. But the arrow hit the horse of a decurion. The horse collapsed pinning the soldier's leg in the sand. The decurion's right arm was broken so the soldiers could not grasp his hands and pull him free. Marcus approached the thrashing horse as closely as he dared in order to take aim. Killing the horse seemed to be the only way to save the soldier.

"Please, Sir," said a young soldier, "if you miss the kill spot, it will make things worse. I know what to do. I can save both of them." Marcus saw determined confidence in the young man's strange eyes. Adas saw doubt in the centurion's eyes. "Sir, I have done this before. I can save this man and his horse." Marcus lowered his bow.

Adas slowly approached, talking softly to calm the horse. Using a sash, he covered the animal's eyes. Gradually, the horse grew still. Adas grasped the injured man under the arms and pulled him away. Then he successfully removed the arrow and tended the wound. Marcus was amazed at the courage and skill of the seventeen-year-old.

The following day, Marcus invited Adas to his villa for dinner. Dulcibella asked Adas so many questions he hardly got a chance to eat, but he patiently answered. Then he began asking her questions. The rest of the family joined in the conversation. However, Dulcibella and Adas did most of the talking, mostly to each other—that was nine years ago.

When the family gathered for breakfast, Iovita announced, "Bella, did I tell you about the shipment of purple cloth Silvanus is expecting? Andreas told me the ship is in port and will be unloaded this morning. Would you like to go?"

"Can we take the carriage?" Dulcibella was pleased with the prospect of staying busy while her father and Adas were at the garrison. She also hoped there would be something suitable for a wedding *palla*, the feminine equivalent of a *toga*.

After breakfast, the men left. At the crossroads, Marcus and Andreas took the road to the garrison. Adas and Nikolaus headed for the villa of Silvanus. Silas happily agreed to help with Adas's plan. The three of them went to the wharf where Silas wasted no time rounding up the foremen of his ships. His men recruited the shoppers, merchants, and men looking for work. Even the usual groups of children playing along the boardwalk were included.

Adas and Nikolaus watched for the carriage. Silas clapped a hand on Adas's back. "Well, Sir, I know you have not asked for my marriage advice, but that won't stop me."

"I suppose I will be sorry if I don't listen."

"Yes, you will. Here's my advice. Never stop listening to her. Listen with your ears, as well as your heart and mind. Listen to her even when she is not speaking. Great meaning can be expressed with silence."

"I believe that is the best advice I've ever heard." Adas gave him a lopsided grin.

They talked of other things until Silas pointed toward the wharf. The carriage had arrived. A servant jumped from the driver's seat to help the women out. People smiled at Dulcibella as she passed by. Enjoying the anticipation of his plan, Adas watched her graceful movements as she walked down the pier to the ship. He walked along the wharf a short distance behind the two women. When Iovita steered her daughter near the right ship, she glanced back. Her eyes brightened when she spotted Adas. Everyone on the wharf looked toward Adas when he stood up on a keg of olive oil.

"Good citizens of Caesarea! Today I would like you to see an unworthy man acknowledge the most beautiful woman in Judea. She is not only beautiful in form, but in spirit and heart; she loves all mankind from the innocent child to the lonely beggar. Should I ask this amazing woman, Cornelia Minor Cornelius, for her hand in marriage?"

The crowd cheered and hands flew up in the air, waving him on. Dulcibella was amazed so many people were gathered to witness the proposal. Iovita beamed at her daughter as she backed away. She glanced over the heads of the crowd to find Marcus sitting on his horse at the far end of the wharf. He waved to her and she waved back.

Adas jumped off the keg. The crowd grew quiet. He stepped up to her and knelt down on one knee. He raised his open hand to her. "Since I first met you, I knew our lives would be forever intertwined. You have enchanted me, Little Elf. May I have your hand in marriage?"

Dulcibella blinked back tears of joy. "I have always known I would give my hand to *you* or to *no one*. Yes, I give you my hand in marriage." She placed her hand in his.

Again, the crowd cheered. Adas stood and took Dulcibella into his arms. She gazed up at him. He gently kissed her. They knew their marriage would be a union of heart, mind, and soul. For just a moment, no one else was there, only Dulcibella and Adas.

"I love you, Cornelia."

"And I love you, Clovius."

More cheering erupted from the crowd. Some of the women wiped at their eyes, and the men smiled. Husbands and wives shared contented glances, remembering when their love was new and untested.

Dulcibella laughed. "Do you remember the first time you called me Little Elf?"

"You were picking flowers up on the hill. Your mother sent me to tell you dinner was ready." Adas watched the light dance in her turquoise eyes.

"I'm afraid I was rather cross. You came up so softly you startled me. Butterflies were on the snapdragons. I thought you would scare them away. Do you remember what you said?"

"Perfectly. I said, 'They won't be frightened as long as you stay with me.' And you said. . .?"

"I said, 'Why not?' And you said. . ."

Adas used his best authoritative tone, "Because they think you're an elf. You see, butterflies are really baby elves."

"And I believed you! I really thought butterflies were elves."

"You were, barely, nine years old."

"I was heartbroken to learn butterflies are bugs. I so wanted them to be baby elves." They laughed, lost in the moment of a treasured memory. "I have waited for this day for so long. After we marry, we will never part from each other again." She lightly stroked the scar over his eye. "My gallant wolf, fearless before men, yet gentle in my arms. You have captured my heart."

"No, not captured. A man must win a woman's heart by giving her his own heart."

She placed her hand on his chest. "Then you have mine," She put her hand over her own heart, "and I have yours."

"It is as it should be. We have traded hearts." Suddenly, he remembered Mary's words. 'Keep the pearl close to your heart.' Adas laughed at the poetic fulfillment of her counsel.

He glanced over at Iovita, and nodded. She was waiting for his signal and brought him a linen pouch. Adas thanked her. "To seal our vow, I have a gift for you." He handed Dulcibella the pouch. She eagerly opened it.

She gasped with delight as the breeze unfurled the silk scarf of peacock colors. "It's beautiful! Where did you get it?"

"In Jerusalem. There were many other scarves, but only one matched the colors of your eyes." She waved it in the air for everyone to see. The people clapped and smiled before they turned back to their work.

But not everyone enjoyed their betrothing. At the back of the crowd stood a tall man who never took his eyes from the scene. His solemn expression darkened as he limped away. He found his horse and climbed into the saddle. Grimacing, he rubbed his knee. His old injury was more painful than usual. No one noticed his departure as all eyes watched the young centurion seal his proposal of marriage to the daughter of the Roman commander.

Dulcibella tied her hair back with the scarf.

"We will share a good life together, Dulcie." His eyes brightened like sunlight on native gold. A hand touched his shoulder. He released Dulcibella as she reached for her mother. Iovita hugged her daughter.

"Your father and I are so happy for both of you." The three of them walked up the pier amid congratulations and smiling nods of approval.

Marcus walked toward them. "Well done, Adas. I believe your engagement to my daughter has been approved by the entire town. Who could ask for more?"

"Certainly not me," chirped Dulcibella. "How did you manage to get so many people down here? I've never seen this many."

Adas gestured toward Silas. "I had some help from the chief employer in town." Silas grinned and bowed his head in salute.

The townspeople went back to their usual routines. For the newly betrothed couple, life had new meaning. They were bonded in the eyes of the law and God.

Chapter 24

Friends gathered at the villa to celebrate the betrothal of Adas and Dulcibella. They decided not to set a date for their wedding until Adas secured his transfer, now that the required two years in Jerusalem were nearly fulfilled. They could have married while Adas was in Caesarea, but due to protocol, being married would slow the transfer process. Instead of transferring to Caesarea in a few weeks, it could take many months.

A letter from Aquila, forwarded by Tribune Salvitto, arrived for Adas at the garrison. At the end of his shift, he rode Venustas to the beach below the villa. He sat on a log of driftwood and began to read.

Centurion Clovius Longinus
10th Legio, Jerusalem, 10th Cohors, 6th Centuria

Dear Adas,
We have set our wedding day. It will be on Janae's birthday when she turns twenty-two, the 27th of next month. She is much younger than I am, but it is not unusual for a man in his early forties to have a wife in her twenties. Marrying Janae is the right thing to do. Her young son and husband died in a tragic accident after they had been married four years. I trust you will have no problem attending. I have written directly to Tribune Salvitto to assure your attendance will not be a problem. There is not enough time for you to send a reply, so I expect your arrival around the 20th of next month to welcome Janae, who is looking forward to meeting you. She expresses her condolences to you on the loss of your mother. When you come home, I will explain everything. There are complicated circumstances.

In the meantime, I trust you are enjoying the benefits of centurion status. Also, you will be pleased to know that Janae owned several slaves, but in honor of your mother's wishes, I bought their freedom. Their new status will be effective when Janae and I wed. Two of them wish to stay as servants. It is what your mother would have wanted.

I know you don't remember, but you had a younger brother once, for a few days. His name was Martialis. Your mother nearly died giving him birth. She was devastated when Martialis died, but she took solace in you. Your mother was never able to conceive again. With Janae, I once again have the opportunity to assure my legacy. Since you are now twenty-six, and remain unmarried, my hope now is with Janae. My marriage to her will enable the Longinus clan to thrive long after I am gone.

With hope and trust,
Minor Consul Clovius Longinus

Adas slowly rolled the letter back on the scroll. He stared at it as waves of conflicting emotions washed over him. This letter wasn't just insensitive; it was a betrayal. He threw the scroll as far as he could into the sea. The thought of welcoming a woman four years his junior as his "mother" was more than he could stomach. The man was still his father and he should be honored, but Adas decided to never visit his father again. His absence would leave nothing to stop Aquila from embracing a new family. Adas was sure he had never met his father's expectations anyway. His absence would be his wedding gift to the new wife.

Adas led Venustas up the road to the stables. Nikolaus was there, brushing Inventio. The young man took one look at Adas and knew something was wrong. Adas handed the reins to Nikolaus without a word and turned to leave.

"Are you all right, Sir?"

Adas answered without stopping. "No." He took a few more steps and turned around. "Apparently, my father is planning to marry a woman on her birthday, the 27th of next month. She will be twenty-two. So, no, I am not all right. But, thank you for asking." He saw Dulcibella out on the terrace and joined her.

She patted the bench and he sat next to her. "Do you want to talk about it, Adas?"

"Talk about what?" He crossed his arms over his chest.

"When Father came home, he said you received a letter from your father. I've been out here ever since. I watched you throw the scroll into the sea. I called down to you, but you did not hear me. Do you want to talk about it?"

Adas stared at the sea, avoiding her gaze. "My father makes me so angry. I can't even think of the right words to explain it."

"What has he done to make you so angry?"

"He thinks he's always right! He treated my mother's death like an inconvenience. He interferes in my life. He humiliates me. He's written me off because I don't have any children to assure his precious legacy. And he's marrying a woman four years *younger* than I am! I'm not even sure why that makes me so angry. Wait, yes I do. It dishonors my mother's memory."

"Perhaps your father cannot bear to lose another beloved wife, so he has chosen a woman who will most likely outlive him. Give him a chance to explain. A letter cannot communicate the tone of the words, or the expressions on the face. You must talk with him in person."

"How am I ever going to understand him? When we're in the same room, he talks *at* me, not *with* me. And does he ever listen to me? No!"

"Perhaps he is trying in his own way. It is more telling what a person does, not what he says. How did he treat your mother?"

"I don't know. I guess he was good to her. She was the only one who could reason with him. He says marrying this woman *'is the right thing to do'*. How can it be right?"

"He must have good reasons. How will you know before he explains? It can be difficult to put feelings into words. And what you see as interference may be his way of trying to show his love. He did not write to you while Marsetina was alive. Did you write to him?"

"No. I don't know what to say?"

"You don't know what to say. Maybe your father doesn't either. He wrote 'it is the right thing to do' as his reason for marrying Janae, and he will explain the situation when he sees you. It sounds like there are unusual circumstances involved."

"But Dulcie, the first letter was so cold and detached."

"Adas, some people have to hide the pain until it feels safe to deal with it. They won't reveal their feelings, but they still *have* those feelings. Maybe your father is the cold manipulator you think he is, but maybe he's just a frightened, lonely man dealing with a great loss. You said your father was good to your mother. In what way?"

"He would bring things he found, like a handful of wildflowers, an unusual rock, a pretty stone, or sometimes those rocks that look like seashells. She loved things like that. Once, he gave her a rosewood jewelry box full of beautiful seashells. They were all different shapes and color patterns. I remember how delighted she was."

"Don't you see what that means, Adas?"

"No, it was just stuff he picked up."

"You are refusing to see the obvious. While he was away, he was thinking about her. He brought her these things because he knew it would please her. I believe Aquila is a good man. I know this because he helped to make you who you are. There's another reason why I know your father is a good man."

"What is it?"

"You remember the madman who was shooting people from his rooftop. He tried to kill Father, but lost his balance and fell. You saved the soldier and his injured horse. The oldest son of that family presented Father with the *Crown of the Preserver*. Your father referenced that incident when he sponsored my father's promotion."

Adas's jaw dropped in shock. "*What!* Are you telling me my father *initiated* the promotion for Marcus? I thought he was trying to get Marcus in trouble."

"No. Father was promoted from the 2nd *Cohors* to *primus pilus* centurion of the 1st *Cohors* because your father sponsored the recommendation."

"I wrote to Mother about the incident. She wrote back saying Father was 'looking into it' and might ask me for testimony. Why did I assume his motive was negative?"

"It is easy to misunderstand when you form an opinion without all the facts."

"Fine. I confess. I misjudged him."

Dulcibella rolled her eyes. "Misjudged *and* convicted! What am I going to do with you, Clovius Longinus?"

"You can kiss me, Cornelia Minor Cornelius." Adas stood and gathered her in his arms.

When their lips met, the last of his anger dissolved. He turned her to face the ocean and wrapped his arms around her waist. She leaned back against his chest. They watched the sun play hide and seek with a tattered veil of ice-crystal clouds. Gradually, a halo of gossamer pastels formed around the sun.

"It's so beautiful. What makes the clouds do that?" asked Dulcibella.

"I think it's a trick of the butterfly elves."

"They're such clever little beasties." Hand in hand, they walked into the house.

Over the following weeks, the family settled into a comfortable routine. Every day, Adas and Nikolaus worked at the garrison, but they reserved time to train with weapons and in unarmed combat. Nikolaus was a zealous student. His confidence increased as his skill improved. Gradually, proper nourishment added muscle to his willowy frame as he grew stronger. Three full meals a day and restful sleep improved his health as much as the physical training.

Nikolaus had a natural aptitude with a bow. As a belated birthday gift, Adas gave him a bow of the highest quality yew wood, strong yet flexible. Marcus gave him a leather quiver filled with arrows. Nikolaus was overwhelmed with gratitude, but worried about the gifts being confiscated, once they returned to Jerusalem. Adas promised to safeguard them in his quarters. He hoped Nikolaus would be allowed to train with Malchus who was the most skilled archer Adas knew. Together, they determined what was affecting the horses and developed a treatment. The cultural barrier between free man and slave eroded more each day. Adas crafted a wood and leather box, filled it with tools and vials for animal care, and presented it to Nikolaus. Into their third month in Caesarea, Adas decided to confide his concerns about Valentius. He found Nikolaus in the stables and suggested they go for a ride.

"Nikolaus, you know I do not see you as a slave, or even as a servant. I see you as a friend. And as a friend, there are some things I need to share. This information could put you in difficulty, but I'm afraid not knowing could put you in actual danger."

"Sir, it is an honor for me to have your confidence. But my ability to keep secrets has never been tested under *quaestitio*. The torture techniques of the *quaestionarii* are effective."

"It will not come to that, Nikolaus. Tell Valentius everything he wants to know. You can pretend to be angry with me. That will make you appear to be a willing informant."

Adas described the events of the crucifixion of Yeshua, and the attempt on his life by Lucius, Hektor, and Falto. Nikolaus was shocked, but what Valentius did to cover up the assault upset him even more. Now he understood why Lucius accused him at the soccer game.

"This is why I wanted you to meet Serapio and Fabiana. If anything happens to me, you must go to them. They will protect you. Until I can negotiate your freedom, Nikolaus, you are under your master's orders, but Serapio can still protect you. Tribune Salvitto holds Serapio in great respect. I don't know the story behind that, but Serapio has alluded to some incident involving a relative of Salvitto's. Don't forget our code word, *musculus*."

They climbed the cliff road, and were approaching the stables when Andreas came running. "Adas, Nikolaus, come with me. Something has happened. Marcus needs to see the three of us immediately."

Upstairs they found Marcus waiting for them. "Please, sit down. Something amazing has happened. I believe I have been visited by an angel from God. He told me to summon a man named Simon Peter in Joppa." Adas smiled, but didn't interrupt. "When this man arrives, he will tell us what we are to do. I have been blessed with this visit because of my wish to know God, my prayers to him, and because of my offerings in his name. So, I am asking if you will go to Joppa and find Simon Peter. He is staying with a man also named Simon, who is a tanner."

"Of course, we will go. We'll leave first thing in the morning." Nikolaus and Andreas left to begin preparations for the trip, leaving Adas and Marcus to talk.

Marcus looked relieved. "Good, it is settled. I am quite astonished by this event. I wasn't sure if I was dreaming or hallucinating, but no matter how it happened, it *did* happen. I have never experienced anything like this before."

"I have. The man who appeared at Yeshua's tomb was also a divine messenger. Maybe the same messenger who visited you. I am sure Simon Peter will come."

"You sound very confident. Have you heard of him?"

Adas told Marcus his experiences with Simon Peter. They left the office to share the news with the family. The discussion lasted through dinner.

The next morning, the household was up early, making breakfast and helping with travel preparations. Adas took his leave of the family but stopped in front of Dulcibella. With gracious formality he knelt on a knee, and extended his hand to her.

"Cornelia Minor Cornelius will you grant your hand in marriage to me?"

This being the second of three required public proposals; she laughed with delight, and placed her hand in his. "Clovius Longinus, I give you my hand in marriage. I pledge the rest of my life to you as you have pledged the rest of your life to me."

Adas stood and whispered in her ear. "I will do your father's bidding, and be back tomorrow, but my heart is saddened to be gone even a day."

The family watched with enthusiastic approval as the second proposal was sealed. Dulcibella hurried over to the terrace to watch as the three men rode down the cliff path. Although she wished Adas didn't have to leave, she looked forward to meeting the man who was preceded by an angel.

They reached the outskirts of Joppa by late afternoon. An inquiry led them to the house of Simon the tanner. Adas called out to a woman pulling weeds from her courtyard garden to enquire if Simon Peter was there. She went into the house to get him. Adas slid out of the saddle.

A man came out. "I am Simon Peter. Why have you come?"

Adas stepped out from around Venustas. "Does a friend need a reason to see you, Simon?" The big man laughed and strode out the gate. They clasped hands as Adas introduced Peter to the others.

"I am here on business," Adas said. "Centurion Claudius Cornelius, a just man, one who fears God, and has a good reputation among the Jews in Caesarea, was instructed by an angel to summon you to his home, and to hear your words. I know it is unlawful for you to enter the home of a Gentile, so we will do as you say."

"I will go with you. Come in. I must tell you the dream I had before you arrived. It was God's way of telling me that all believers are welcomed by God."

The door flew open. It was Jamin and Cleopas. "Adas! It is good to see you," exclaimed Jamin as they clasped hands. More introductions were made before the men followed Peter into the house. Their host, Simon the tanner, extended an invitation for the night. Adas asked Jamin and Cleopas if they wanted to accompany Peter. They accepted eagerly.

"There are four other devout men of Joppa I wish to invite," said Peter.

"Tell the men to plan on a few days in Caesarea," said Adas, "Cornelius will be greatly pleased to host the seven of you for as long as you can spare."

They spent the evening talking of the latest news, but Adas noticed Peter was distracted. When Adas tried to question him, he promised to tell him everything the next day.

The next morning, they awoke early and were on the road before the sun climbed over the horizon. Adas reined Venustas in to let Peter's horse catch up. "What has happened? It is obvious you are disturbed."

Peter began his story. "There was an incredible miracle on the Day of Pentecost. The Spirit came to us and many others, all Jews and Gentile converts from many nations. The number of believers is growing; the word is spreading, which has caused the Sanhedrin great concern. John and I were arrested for preaching Yeshua's message, but they couldn't find a way to punish us without causing a riot, so they let us go. Other events occurred, but mostly the Sadducees rose against us. Again, we were arrested and put in the common prison. But that night an angel of the Lord opened the prison doors and brought us out. The angel told us, '*Go, stand in the temple and speak to the people all the words of this life*.' So the Sanhedrin had us arrested again. They told us not to preach that Yeshua is alive. But then Gamaliel, a Pharisee, suggested they should leave us alone. He said that if we were of man, our movement would die on its own. But if we were of God, the council would find itself fighting against God himself."

"Did they listen to him?"

"Yes, but they beat us anyway. It was an honor for us to suffer for Yeshua. It was only a little compared to what Yeshua suffered." Peter glanced at Adas. "Listen my friend, we all crucified Yeshua. You know this."

"Yes, but it still shames me."

"You didn't do anything worse than what I did. How many times did I profess my dedication to Yeshua? Yet, when he was in his darkest hour, I denied even knowing him."

"There's more to your story, isn't there? What happened after the Sanhedrin let you go?"

"Something grievous. One of our seven, Stephen, who was chosen to see to the needs of our people, was in dispute with the Synagogue of the Freedmen. Stephen preached Yeshua is the Christ, killed by our own people, just like all our prophets. In a blind fury they rose up and stoned him to death in the street. Those who did not throw stones approved of his murder. One man, Saul of Tarsus, even held the murderers' robes. Have you witnessed a stoning?"

"Only from a distance."

"They take off their robes so they won't get splattered with blood."

"I grieve with you, Peter."

"When Stephen was about to die, he asked the Lord to forgive his murderers. Shortly thereafter, Simon invited me to come to Joppa. Persecution against the Way is intensifying. Many have dispersed across the land, fleeing from arrest. The message of Yeshua is spreading because of this persecution. For the time being, it is good to be away from Jerusalem, but I will go back soon."

"I grieve with you and for those forced to leave their homes. I find it incredible to hear how Stephen forgave the people in the very act of murdering him. How was he able to do that?" Adas tried to imagine forgiving Valentius, but just the thought made him angry.

"Forgiving frees the victim from the power of the offender," said Peter. "Stephen handed over his murderers to God. However, the hardest thing about forgiving is that resentment sometimes comes back. One may have to forgive many times."

Adas remembered how calmly Zacchaeus expressed no bitterness against the men who attacked him. Adas had regretted not catching them, yet Zacchaeus had said he left them to God. Adas urged Venustas to catch up with Nikolaus.

"Were you able to hear what Peter was telling me?" asked Adas.

"His voice carries well," Nikolaus answered. "I don't understand why the Jewish rulers are so threatened by Yeshua's followers."

"It's simple and complicated at the same time. Many men of the Sanhedrin feel they are in the right, believing Yeshua was an imposter. In truth, Yeshua, as the true

Messiah, established a new covenant with God, but the Sanhedrin rejects the premise. The Sanhedrin believes they are *defending* God, not fighting him."

Jamin joined their conversation. "Peter didn't tell you what happened in Lydda and Joppa. In Lydda, God used Peter to heal a man named Aeneas who had been paralyzed for eight years. Peter said to him *'Aeneas, Yeshua the Christ heals you. Arise and make your bed.'* And the man got up immediately. He had strength in legs which had been useless for years. Now there are many believers in Lydda."

Nikolaus was amazed. "Peter can heal people like Yeshua did?"

"God healed me through Peter," said Adas. "Don't you remember the injuries I had the night I went missing?"

"I wondered how you healed so fast. So what happened in Joppa?"

"The people of Joppa sent for Peter to heal a good woman named Tabitha. Before he could get there, she died; but he went to her house anyway. Peter put the mourners out, knelt beside Tabitha's dead body, and prayed. He said, *'Tabitha, arise.'* She opened her eyes and when she saw Peter, she sat up. Then he gave her his hand and lifted her from the bed. You should have seen how the people reacted when Tabitha walked out to them."

"God used Peter to raise a woman *from the dead*? This is truly incredible!"

"Yeshua raised people from the dead," said Adas, "but it is beyond extraordinary to see God using Peter to do the same thing."

When they approached the main street in Caesarea, people recognized Adas as the young man who asked the commander's daughter to marry him. Peter asked why so many people were pointing him out. Adas told him about the marriage proposal.

"You may wear centurion's armor over your heart," exclaimed Peter, "but it beats to the music of angels, my friend." Adas grinned at the big fisherman.

When they topped the switchback road, Dulcibella was waiting for him. Adas slid from the saddle and pulled her into his arms. "I feel I have been away forever. Was it only yesterday morning you gave me your hand for the second time?"

"Yes, it was yesterday, and yes, you've been gone too long. Welcome home, Centurion! I see you have brought friends. You must introduce me."

Adas was about to respond when Marcus, followed by his family, came striding down the pathway straight for the riders. The other men had dismounted and were standing in a group. They saw the intense focus in his purposeful gait. He went straight to Peter, knelt down on one knee and bowed his head. The men wondered at the sight of one of the highest ranking centurions in all of Judea showing such respect to a Galilean fisherman.

Peter took Marcus by the arm, and pulled him to his feet. His deep voice resonated. *"Stand up; I myself am also a man."* Marcus greeted Peter with clasped hands. Peter turned to his traveling companions to introduce each one. Marcus introduced his family, in turn. Together the group walked back up the path to the courtyard.

When they entered the villa, friends of Marcus and Iovita, along with a few soldiers from the garrison were waiting for them.

Peter entered the house and announced, *"You know how unlawful it is for a Jewish man to keep company with or go to one of another nation. But God has shown me that I should not call any man common or unclean. Therefore I came without objection as soon as I was sent for. I ask, then, for what reason have you sent for me?"*

Eager to hear how Marcus would answer, the group waited expectantly. He said, "Four days ago I was fasting until this hour; and at the ninth hour I prayed in my house, and a man stood before me in bright clothing and said, *'Cornelius your prayer has been heard, and your alms are remembered in the sight of God. Send men to Joppa and call Simon here, whose surname is Peter. He is lodging in the house of Simon, a tanner, by the sea. When he comes, he will speak to you.'* So I sent three men I trust to summon you. Now, we are all present before God, to hear all the things commanded to you by God."

Peter explained God's plan has always been to send his Son for the salvation of the world. He finished with God's instructions. *"And He commanded us to preach to the people and to testify that whoever believes in Him will receive forgiveness of sins."*

While Peter was still speaking, the *Spiritus Sanctus* fell on all those who heard the word. The men of Joppa were astonished to see the Holy Spirit poured out on Gentiles. Peter and the others heard everyone in the room speak with languages other than their own, professing the works of God, and the men of Joppa understood their words.

Peter looked around. "Should any of us keep these believers from being baptized with water? Out there is water, let us baptize in the name of the Lord."

Marcus took Iovita's hand as they led the way outside. Nikolaus walked with Adas and Dulcibella. They left the house, and walked down the cliff road to the beach. Peter baptized each of them, finishing with Adas and Dulcibella. She went first. After Adas was baptized, he and Peter waded back to the shore. Adas extended his hand to Dulcibella.

"Dulcibella, I ask you the final time, will you bless me with your hand in marriage?"

She answered so everyone could hear. "I give you my hand in marriage. We will share our lives and our love for God."

"You have done well, Adas and Dulcibella," said Peter. "I pray that God will bless your marriage. Together, you will be faithful servants for the Lord. When you face the dangers of this world, remember God's blessing this day."

Adas whispered in Dulcibella's ear. She nodded eagerly. "Dulcibella and I have a request, Peter. When I return to Caesarea, will you come with me to perform our marriage rite?"

"Of course, I shall be honored and greatly pleased." The family and friends surrounded them with congratulations.

Over the next few days, Peter and the others stayed with the Cornelius family, teaching and answering questions before they returned to Joppa.

A few weeks later, Adas and Nikolaus prepared to return to Jerusalem. Neither one could believe the four months were nearly over. Marcus insisted that Andreas and the same squad of soldiers escort them. The morning of their departure found the Cornelius household subdued. Adas was grieved to leave Dulcibella and her family. They dreaded what the few remaining weeks in Jerusalem might involve. Centurion Valentius was still a threat. Adas also worried about the complications in securing Nikolaus's freedom.

Marcus pulled Adas aside. "I sent a permanent transfer request for you to Salvitto. It will hold more weight than if you file a personal request. Let us pray you'll be back here quickly. Keep your wits about you. I know how dangerous Valentius can be as does Centurion Tacitus. Don't hesitate to confide in Tacitus if the situation worsens."

Dulcibella and Adas embraced. "I live for the day when we are together again," she said. "Remember, I will be thinking of you every time you look at the eilat stone."

"I will remember. And every time you look at the pearl, I will be thinking of you." He drew her in and kissed her before he turned away. He jumped into the saddle as Venustas tossed her head impatiently.

Dulcibella turned toward Nikolaus. "My friend, you must watch out for him. He trusts you and so do I. Once, he wrote to me that if he had a brother, he would want him to be just like you. I pray that when Adas comes back you will be at his side."

"I pray that as well, not only for me, but for him, my lady. Nothing will bring me more joy than to witness the two of you wed."

Andreas nudged his horse, and the group started forward. Dulcibella threw herself into her parents' arms. She wept, while Marcus and Iovita tried to reassure her.

"Sweet Bella," her father said tenderly, "I do not believe God would bring the two of you together only to let you be torn apart. Even after the darkest night, the sun always rises."

Chapter 25

The journey back to Jerusalem was over too quickly for Adas and Nikolaus. As they passed through the west gate of the city a foreboding settled over them. Their dread deepened when they entered the gates of the Antonia. They both dismounted in front of Salvitto's office. Adas knocked on the office door. When he entered, he opened the door wide enough for Salvitto to see Nikolaus before stepping inside.

"Reporting for duty, Sir." Adas handed him a small scroll. "From Centurion Cornelius."

Salvitto tapped the scroll on his palm with a smile. "A letter of commendation, no doubt." He waved a hand to a chair. "Sit down, Centurion. I have also received the request for transfer for you from Cornelius. You will be missed, but I will approve the transfer as soon as the full two years are completed, on the 28th. You should be back in Caesarea before the end of the month. The port city suits you. You look fit and rested. Did you cure the horses?"

"Yes, Sir. Nikolaus proved to be indispensable as an assistant and a horse trainer."

"Good to hear. From the look of him, I think someone was training him as well. Are you trying to turn him into a *gladiator*?"

"Nikolaus is an excellent sparring partner. I'd like to keep using him."

"I don't mind, as long as he gets his work done." The tribune's expression grew solemn. "The situation here has changed. Herod Antipas has been exiled to Gaul. Seems he made Emperor Gaius angry when he asked to be officially declared a king, the same title as his nephew, Herod Agrippa, who has taken his place. The followers of the Way and the Sanhedrin are locked in battle, so to speak, and King Herod wishes to please the Sanhedrin. I've never seen people who take their religion so seriously. Followers of the Way would rather die than deny their beliefs, and two already have."

"Two? I only heard of one." Adas hoped his alarm was not obvious.

"You probably heard about the one stoned to death? Herod had the other one beheaded. They say he and his brother were two of the original followers."

"Do you know the man's name?"

"I believe his name was James. Herod will be making another arrest soon, which makes more work for us. The people love these men and think they have divine power like the Nazarene. They say if the shadow of this man, Simon Peter, falls on a person, he or she is healed. If there was no evidence, the stories would stop. They're not stopping. Why don't you ask around and see what you can find out. I'm curious about these healers."

"Yes, Sir. I will."

"You probably won't have time this week. Valentius did a bit of grumbling about your absence. He might make up for lost time, literally. But let me know what you learn. Dismissed."

Outside Salvitto's office, Adas told Nikolaus what he had learned.

"Are Peter, Jamin and Cleopas in danger?" asked Nikolaus.

"No, not if they're still in Joppa. Come on. I'm going with you to the stables. I expect I'll need to have a talk with the other boys."

They walked the horses back to their stalls. Adas rounded up his stable boys. After he explained why he had taken Nikolaus, the other boys seemed to understand. They were even glad to have Nikolaus back. Adas left Nikolaus to his work. He went to the common room to check the duty wall. He was assigned night patrol, but was also on the prisoner duty rotation. If a prisoner escaped, all the guards would be executed, making it the most hated assignment. If a prisoner who was not already sentenced to death was harmed or killed, the commanding officer received the same treatment. The centurion responsible for assigning the guards had to control his men or pay the price, sometimes the ultimate price. However, if a centurion volunteered for the job he would earn a bonus. A higher ranking centurion could assign a lower ranking centurion to supervise the guards. In that way, he could earn the bonus without actually being present, but he would still be responsible for the prisoner. He had to choose his men carefully.

Adas went to his quarters to write Dulcibella a long letter. He posted the letter, and then headed for the *cafeteria*. He sat at his usual table.

Onesimus approached. "Centurion, I am glad to see you. We have fish or mutton today."

"I'm glad to see you, too, Onesimus. Mutton will be fine." Adas scanned the room. "Where is everyone? The fortress seems empty."

"It's been like this for weeks ever since a Galilean was executed, the one they called James. The patrols had already been doubled after the other man was stoned to death. I'll go get your dinner, Sir."

A voice sounded behind Adas. "Did you check the duty wall, Longinus?" demanded Valentius without preamble. "You're set for street patrol tonight."

Adas stood up and came to attention. "Yes, Sir."

"Did you enjoy your vacation in Caesarea?"

"Tribune Salvitto has my performance evaluation from Centurion Cornelius, Sir. His report would best answer your question."

"I'm sure Cornelius would never find fault with his future son-in-law. Especially since his daughter is past the age of marriage. He wouldn't want to scare you off. I'm sure the union will benefit your career, however." Valentius stalked out of the *cafeteria*.

Adas stared after him. Just as he had suspected, it must have been Cassius Quintus who followed them to Caesarea and witnessed the first proposal to Dulcibella. Somehow, Cassius had been recruited to report to Valentius.

After dinner, Adas walked to Serapio's shop, leaving Venustas to rest. A hearty laugh greeted him when he appeared before the open door of the shop.

"Fabiana, look who's at our door step!" Fabiana rushed into the room to give Adas a welcoming hug. Serapio gave Adas his usual back-slapping greeting. "It is good to see you. Come in here and sit down and tell us all about your adventures. Nebetka will be disappointed he missed you. He is making deliveries this afternoon."

"We got your letters," said Fabiana, "Apio insisted on reading them out loud to us over and over. Nebetka and I have them memorized. We're so happy for you and Dulcibella. And it sounds like Nikolaus proved to be an able assistant."

"I got your letters, too. Sounds like you managed, somehow, without me. However, I can't manage without you two. Salvitto has approved my transfer, but for the next few weeks, Valentius is still a threat. I might need your help."

Serapio and Fabiana exchanged concerned looks. "Of course," said Serapio. "You know we will always help you. You are a son to us, Adas."

"I know and it gives me comfort. I am fine for now, so take those 'sour wine' expressions off your faces."

Fabiana rested a hand on his arm. "We have always prayed for your safety, Adas. These are dangerous times."

Adas thanked them and headed back to the fortress. The gloom which had engulfed him when he first returned to the Antonia was beginning to lift. The nearness and assurance of help from good friends, along with the anticipation of returning to Caesarea, was comforting. The last thing he needed to arrange was securing Nikolaus's freedom. Once he accomplished this, Valentius would permanently be left in the past.

When Adas got back, he went to the stables to find Nikolaus. He was cleaning stalls. "Nikolaus, I have permission from Tribune Salvitto to keep you as my sparring partner. You'll be able to keep up your lessons in self-defense and. . . Are you all right?"

Nikolaus hesitated. "Y-yes, Sir, I'm fine." He continued to work.

Adas clasped a hand on the young man's shoulder. Nikolaus winced. He pushed Nikolaus's tunic aside and saw a dark, bruise. A quick inspection revealed the other shoulder was also bruised. "Who did this to you, Nikolaus?"

"It was an accident."

"These injuries don't look accidental."

"Sir, really, I'm fine." He avoided Adas's intense gaze.

"Nikolaus, did the other boys do this?"

Nikolaus dropped his shovel and knelt down to re-lace his sandal. "Sir, maybe it wasn't an accident, but I couldn't see who it was."

"I'm sure you don't want to get anyone in trouble, but you know you can come to me for help." Adas knew he wouldn't get any more information from him. He headed back to his quarters. The sun was setting and he would have to report for night patrol.

About a week later, after a Saturday morning lesson, Nikolaus asked to speak to Adas. "Sir, I have heard stories about a certain legionary."

"What is it?"

"I was working on a horse's hooves and two soldiers stopped to talk about Legionary Octavean. They said he went into opium withdrawal while he was in the pit. It was so disgusting, the guards threatened to beat him to death if something wasn't done. They had to isolate him in an interrogation room. They also discussed a wager on Octavean and you, Sir. They didn't actually say what the bet was about, but apparently many men are taking part in it."

"Did you see the men?"

"Yes, Sir. One of them was the Greek who takes bets at the soccer games. They didn't refer to you by name."

"Then how do you know they meant me?"

"They used your nickname, Sir. They call you *Lupus Legatus*."

"Yes, the Wolf Commander, I've heard it once or twice. Good job, but be careful. Opium addiction explains much about Octavean. Don't mention this to anyone else."

A few days later, since Adas would not be on duty until sundown, he went to see Serapio. Adas told him what Nikolaus overheard about the soldiers' wager and Octavean's addiction.

"Opium makes surgeries possible, but it is addictive." Serapio ran his hand down the side of his face. "Opium would have helped with this injury, but none was available."

"Have you had any meetings with the Way?"

"I met with Malchus a few times. He said Caiaphas was becoming secretive around him, sending him on errands during high-level meetings."

They discussed how this situation could affect the followers of the Way. Fabiana came in from visiting with Dorrian's wife. She invited Adas to stay for lunch. He spent most of the day helping Serapio with a few projects. He left in the late afternoon.

Hoping to rest before duty, Adas headed for his quarters. He was almost to his door when Cassius came out of his quarters. The decurion called out to him and limped in his direction. Since Adas had been back for over a week, he assumed Cassius was avoiding him for obvious reasons, but he waited for him to catch up.

"I heard you were back. How was Caesarea?" Cassius looked genuinely pleased.

Adas paused, trying to read Cassius's expression. "It was good. How were things here?"

"I don't know. I just got back today from Hebron."

"You did? How long were you gone?"

"We left not too long after you. Why?"

"Just curious. Didn't know you were assigned a mission. What was it?"

"A zealot led a rebellion against a corrupt mayor, but Rome wants him in office. Things got messy. We took care of it. So, have you heard?"

"Heard what?" Adas listened with growing unease. If Cassius had just returned from a long assignment, he couldn't be the source of Valentius's information.

"They arrested the Galilean. He's in Holding under heavy guard. Salvitto had to offer a double bonus since this man escaped from the common prison. He didn't need to worry. I heard Valentius practically ran to Salvitto's office to claim the bonus. I hate to be the messenger of bad news, but Valentius put you in charge."

Adas let Cassius ramble on while he tried not to panic. He quit listening until he realized Cassius had gone silent and was staring at him.

"What? Sorry, I was thinking about the change of assignment. I expected to go on patrol tonight." Adas left Cassius staring after him. Peter must have left Joppa. He knew there was no chance the new prisoner could be anyone else.

He headed for the common room. One glance at the duty wall confirmed what Cassius told him. His dismay increased when he saw Valentius had selected the legionaries, rather than let Adas chose his own men. Equally unnerving, four squads were listed, an excessive number for a nonviolent prisoner. Adas saw Octavean, Hektor, and Falto were on the list along with twelve others who were not in his *centuria*. It was allowed, but highly unusual, and very concerning. As Adas weighed possibilities, the slave in charge of the duty wall entered. Adas asked who had been assigned temporary duty out of town.

"Two *centuriae* were sent to Ituraea to repair some roads. Another *centuria* was called out to Jericho, to rebuild a collapsed section of wall. There was a wildfire in Bethany that Decurion Corvus handled."

"No one else?"

"No, Sir." The slave began to whitewash the old assignments. Adas turned to leave. "Sir, I forgot. There was another decurion and his men sent to Hebron. It was an uprising. They were gone nearly as long as you were."

"Decurion Quintus?"

"Yes, he's the one. He just got back today, Sir."

Adas thanked him and left the common room. His stomach twisted with alarm. Valentius must have forced information about Dulcibella from Nikolaus, hence his injuries. Adas could not confront Valentius without putting the young man in more jeopardy. Worst of all, Nikolaus had not warned him. What had Valentius threatened that guaranteed his silence?

Chapter 26

———∽∾∽———

Adas hurried to Prisoner Holding, a limestone building across from the stables. He approached the pair of guards standing outside the main door. When they saw him, they snapped to attention. The centurion gestured at the door, and they opened it. He walked down the hall, passing doors which opened to interrogation rooms. The pair of guards outside the main room at the end of the hall jumped to attention, but did not open the door.

"I didn't come here to stand outside. Open it," Adas demanded.

The two guards exchanged anxious glances. "Sir, this prisoner is a sorcerer. He vanished from the prison while guards were standing outside the locked doors."

"Unlock the door, now!" They obeyed. As soon as Adas stepped inside, they slammed the door shut and relocked it.

The incarceration room consisted of stone walls, a dirt floor, and a ceiling of heavy, reinforced wood planks. The walls were equipped with sets of chains with shackles. In the center of the room was a long table and benches which could seat up to a dozen people. The table and benches were bolted to the floor to prevent their use as a barricade. There was no inside lock on the door for the same reason. If a prisoner succeeded in neutralizing his guards and secured the door, he could then commit suicide rather than be crucified. The door and surrounding stonework would have to be destroyed to gain access to remove the dead bodies.

Most of the guards were playing board games while a few tossed dice in a corner of the room. Peter sat on the floor, sound asleep with his back against the wall and shackles around his wrists. Adas shook his head in disbelief. Only Peter could be this relaxed while incarcerated with nervous guards. When Adas entered, one of the soldiers called the others to attention. He gestured for them to go back to their activities. Adas jostled Peter awake.

"Simon, I am very sorry to see you in here. I grieve with you for James. The Way must be discouraged."

"It is true we grieve for his loss, but we will see him and Stephen again. They are with God now. As for me, I go where the Lord allows me."

"I would unlock your chains, but only cohort centurions have keys."

"These chains are a blessing since I am counted worthy to bear them in Yeshua's name. Do not worry. What God wills cannot be altered. The difficulty lies in our short lives and God's great patience. A thousand years for us is but a day for God. Take heart, my friend. Even the viper posed to strike can be snatched away by the hawk."

"True, anything can happen. I'll be on duty tonight so we'll have plenty of time to talk."

"Good. I'll be here all night."

"Perhaps not, my friend. You might walk out before I do."

Peter chuckled softly. Adas approached the *principales* and reminded him to keep the prisoner safe. When he signaled at the door, one of the guards opened it quickly, but Adas was barely through before the soldier slammed it shut.

"This prisoner is not a sorcerer," Adas said, "but he is divinely protected. Remember that." The guards acknowledged his command.

Shift change would occur at sunset. Adas had time for a brief rest and dinner before he went on duty. He left his quarters early to be on duty well before shift change, but an aide intercepted him. The tribune wanted to see him.

Upon entering the office, Salvitto gestured for Adas to sit. "You need to be extra watchful of this prisoner, Longinus. He escaped once before, but fortunately, it was under the Sanhedrin's guards. Someone on the inside must have been sympathetic." Adas thought about Caiaphas's suspicion toward Malchus.

"Centurion? Did you hear me?"

"Yes, Sir! Sorry, Sir. I will be extra watchful."

"As you know, Centurion Valentius has the lead on this assignment."

The eagerness of Valentius to be involved with Peter's incarceration made Adas uneasy. Salvitto continued to discuss the prisoner and other issues. Finally, he dismissed Adas, but the meeting had taken up precious time. Adas went to find Onesimus who would be easier to locate than Nikolaus.

"I need you to deliver a message for me, Onesimus. Tell Nikolaus a *musculus* is nesting in Venustas's stall. Tell him to take care of this first thing in the morning. Can you do that?" Onesimus nodded eagerly. Adas left the *cafeteria* and headed back to Holding. Someone called to him from behind. Startled, he spun around. He had not heard the man approach.

"Centurion Longinus," said Demitre as he bowed his head. "My master wishes to speak with you about your prisoner."

"Tell your master Tribune Salvitto has already warned me. My immediate duty is to report on time." He left Demitre staring after him.

As the centurion approached, the guards outside the main door jumped to attention. At their feet lay several wineskins. Adas eyed them suspiciously. "That wine better be watered down."

The legionaries looked confused. "Sir, Demitre said the wine was a gift from you."

"Since when do I send another man's slave to do my bidding?"

"Yes, Sir! Sorry, Sir," the two men responded in unison.

"Now get inside. The sun has set."

The guards opened the door for Adas and followed him inside. They locked the door which had a pin tumbler lock fitted with steel springs, a Roman improvement on the Egyptian lock. It could only be unlocked with a slotted skeleton key from the outside, but no key was needed from the inside. Following protocol, the guards would remain in the hallway, along with the two guards manning the detention room door at the end of the hall. One of the soldiers took an ember from the firebox and lighted the two torches near the main door. Adas walked down the hall. The two guards manning the detention room door already stood at attention. The two torches next to that door were already lighted. Several empty wineskins lay at their feet.

"You already drank all of it?" Adas demanded. Their enthusiastic nods turned into confusion at his anger.

"Sir, Demitre said the wine was from you," exclaimed one of the men.

"No, it was not. You just came on duty. Why would you drink it so quickly?"

"Sir, Demitre told us to report an hour early by your order," said the other soldier.

Adas was stunned. It was not uncommon for centurions to give their men diluted wine or to have them report early. However, for Valentius to act without Adas's prior knowledge was unusual, but not disallowed. A higher ranked officer did not require the approval of a lesser ranked officer. Adas considered that he might be overreacting. Perhaps Valentius was only demonstrating how effortlessly he could manipulate the soldiers.

Adas gestured at the door. They pulled the slide lock and opened it. By the light of the torches, Adas saw empty wineskins scattered around the floor. Hektor sat at the table with several sheets of papyrus and an ink pot. He had his back to the door, and was engrossed in estimating his profits. The wineskin by his elbow was empty. Falto was asleep in a corner. Lucius was leaning against the wall, staring listlessly at the floor. Lit by torchlight, his face looked haggard and pale. When he looked up, his eyes were as dull as tarnished iron. He coughed and wiped at his mouth with the back of his hand.

Someone signaled, and the men came to attention. Hektor hurriedly pulled the empty wineskin over the papyrus. Adas snatched the wineskin away. It was a wager tally divided into two columns, one marked with the sketch of a wolf, the other with a sketch of a lion. Adas drew his sword and brought it down, slicing the sheets in half. He left the sword embedded in the table. He crushed the papyrus into wads and threw them across the room. Grabbing Hektor by a shoulder strap of his leather armor, Adas lifted him from the bench.

"If I ever catch you taking bets on me again, I'll split *you* in two. Is that clear?" His golden eyes looked more wolfish than ever under black scowling eyebrows. Adas whispered in Greek, "If I ever see you pick up another rock, I will take your hand. Do you hear me?"

Hektor's face turned ashen. "Yes, Sir! Understood, Sir!"

Adas pushed the man down on the bench. He had to grab hold of the table to keep his balance. Adas grasped his sword with one hand and pried it from the table. He pointed it around the room. "How dare you neglect your duty!" He picked up a wineskin and threw it across the room. "Did any of you consider the effect this wine would have on you?" They lowered their heads in shame. "So, a slave brought it to you; told you to report early?"

"Yes, Sir!" responded the men in unison.

"Since when do soldiers take orders from slaves? You should have checked with me. You better hope you don't fall asleep. You will be painfully awakened."

Lucius placed a full wineskin on the table. "Demitre left this wine for you, Sir. He said Valentius wanted to reward the men on your behalf."

Adas threw Lucius a withering look as he slid his sword back in its scabbard. He sat on the bench in front of Peter. In Hebrew, he asked, "Did you drink any of this wine?"

"I was surprised the slave offered it to me. But Adas, a man can drink twice as much without missing a step. Even if you did not supply it, why are you so concerned? It's just watered-down wine like normal."

"It could be nothing more than a spiteful prank, but it concerns me that Valentius wanted these soldiers to have plenty of time to drink it before I got here. He even tried to delay me, but Salvitto already had." A shadow fell across them. Adas stood up quickly, dropping his hand to his dagger.

It was Lucius. "Sir, it is most important I speak with you."

They moved to a corner of the room. It was obvious Lucius was not fully recovered from his ordeal in the pit. The thinness of his face aged him, emphasizing the scar. Adas put his back to the wall to keep an eye on the other men.

Lucius also scanned the room. "There is a greater problem than the wine. I suspect Valentius plans to smuggle the prisoner out of here to get all of us executed."

"Do you have proof?" Adas didn't bother to feign surprise.

"See those men playing Twelve Lines and those three, talking? Valentius had them thrown in the pit for delaying the crucifixion of the Nazarene. Valentius was fined two weeks wages for abuse of authority. Blandus told me Valentius ordered the eight men to reimburse him. They threatened to report him. Now they're here. Blandus is the one talking to Hilarius."

"Those are the men who paraded Yeshua around after they beat him."

"Yes, but Blandus blamed a tribune from Rome for suggesting it. Blandus and his men took up the suggestion while the tribune watched. Blandus said this tribune looked like Death, but wore fine clothes and gold jewelry. He sounds like that silk merchant who accused you of murder. One of those men in the hall, Laelius, told me Valentius owes the four of them a great deal of money. They were planning to submit a formal complaint, which they can't do if they're dead. Valentius also assigned them to observe the arrest of the Nazarene. If it had occurred during daylight, there would have been a riot. Yet, Valentius required them to go unarmed. The tribune was there as well, the one that Blandus told me about. They both described him having a raspy voice, just like that silk merchant. I can still hear him hissing in my ear, telling me what a pampered. . .," Lucius clamped his mouth shut.

"The merchant was talking about me, wasn't he?"

Lucius nodded, avoiding the centurion's eye. Adas felt a shiver run up his spine. The emaciated stranger seemed to appear when Yeshua was at his greatest suffering. Adas shook his apprehension off, thinking it had to be a coincidence.

Lucius continued, "Valentius has been trying to get those four men killed for some time."

"You tried to kill me. Were you under Valentius's orders or did you act on your own?"

"I deserve the maximum punishment for assaulting you, but I hit you with my fist when I could have killed you. Falto was going to knife you, but I stopped him. Hektor hit you with a rock, but he could have thrown his dagger, instead. I was tempted to cut your throat, but couldn't go through with that either. Since Valentius no longer has a hold over me, he's afraid I will testify to his cover-up of my assault on you. If Salvitto offered me immunity, I would. Valentius would be dishonorably discharged without a pension. I'm a threat, and here I am in Holding with you, who he detests with a passion."

"After being his spy for two years, you bring accusations against him?"

"I was his spy. It is for that very reason I accuse Valentius. I know how he thinks. I know how he uses others to accomplish his schemes."

"So why are Hektor and Falto in here?" asked Adas.

"Valentius hates the Weasel, but so does everyone. As for Hektor, Valentius owes on his gambling debts. Hektor is afraid to refuse him credit, but not afraid to complain about it—loudly."

"Why didn't you kill me when you had the chance?"

"I never planned to do you harm, Centurion, but something the silk merchant said made me angry. The impulse to kill you was almost overpowering. I can't even remember what he said, but I remembered what *you* said. Your own words stopped me."

"What do you mean?"

"At Golgotha, when I taunted the Nazarene, you said I was not a coward, and I shouldn't pretend to be one. That's what stopped me, at least partly. Also, Valentius ordered me to only spy on you. He said he wanted you for himself. Sir, I swear to you, I don't know why. I am not afraid to die. I deserve execution for many reasons. But Valentius *will not* have the satisfaction of being my executioner!" A few of the men looked over at them.

"Keep your voice down. What was his hold on you? Opium?"

"So you know?"

Adas snorted. "I think the whole garrison knows."

"I guess they do. The pit was bad enough, but withdrawal was agony. I was living the same day of misery over and over. I had already been sick for some time. Now it's gotten worse. It's hard to breathe. Sometimes I cough blood."

"Sounds like you have consumption." Adas studied the men. They were quiet, but awake. Perhaps Lucius's suspicions were just paranoia. "How did you get started on the opium?"

"Demitre, who else? After the soldiers broke my arm."

"I questioned the men who attacked you, but they swore Valentius told them it was a test for your promotion to *beneficiary*. That you were expecting it."

"That's a lie. I had no warning. While I was healing, I was addicted before I knew what happened. I was turning over half my pay to that slimy little toad. I complained to Valentius. He just laughed in my face. 'Who do you think Demitre gives the money to?' he said. So I became a spy—and an *opio addicta*."

Adas scanned the room. "I don't see any ill effect with the men, but precaution won't hurt." Adas told a soldier to summon a centurion. The man called to have the guard unlock the door, but there was no response. Adas peered through the small barred opening. The torches in the hall had gone out. He held a torch to the opening. The guards were sprawled on the floor.

"*Wake up!*" Adas shouted. "*Legionaries!*" The soldiers didn't move.

"Centurion, what's wrong with them?" asked one of the men.

"They drank themselves into oblivion. I personally give you permission to kick them into the pit when they wake up."

A few of the men chuckled and went back to their activities. They were not worried. If they couldn't get out, neither could the prisoner.

"They're not just drunk are they?' Lucius asked. "Demitre put his sleeping potion in the wine. The men in here will be next."

"You didn't drink any of it, did you?"

Lucius shook his head. "I know you only drink water when you're on duty, Centurion. Valentius must not know that, which explains why Demitre left a wineskin for you."

Adas knew there was no way out. Aggravated, he thumped his fist on the door.

"Now what?" Lucius asked.

"We wait for Valentius and overpower him. He will not be expecting a defense."

"Centurion, there is another way. Valentius is in charge of this assignment so he is responsible for the prisoner's safety. He assumed all of us would pass out before we knew anything was wrong. But if, somehow, the prisoner ends up. . ."

"No! You're thinking what is done to the prisoner will be done to the lead commander."

"Why not? Valentius would suffer the humiliating death he has planned for us. Herod might punish us since he'll be cheated out of making sport with this Galilean, but Valentius would be dead. We can trap him in his own scheme. I will enjoy watching Valentius die." His smile withered when he saw the centurion's rage.

"I will *not* let you kill this man. No prisoner has ever suffered in my custody, and it is not going to happen tonight."

"Protecting this useless zealot plays into Valentius's trap!"

"You want Valentius? Then stand with me so we can take him together. But we are not harming this prisoner. He is more important than all sixteen of us put together."

"He's just a useless fisherman. What is this man to you, Centurion? How can one man's life be more valuable than the lives of sixteen? You think you're better than everyone else, treating slaves like pets, giving drugged wine to crucified criminals, burying the thief's carcass. You even demanded we show respect to one lousy Nazarene. Now you want to sacrifice us all?"

"*Yes*, if that's what it takes."

Lucius backed away. Determined to get Valentius under the executioner's blade, he knew what he had to do. He would need to wait until the other soldiers passed out. Lucius collapsed into a corner as if he accepted defeat. Adas crossed the room and sat on the floor next to Peter.

Peter pointed his chin at the door. "What's wrong with the soldiers out there?"

"They're unconscious. We're trapped. The situation is worse than an ugly prank."

"Are you in danger?"

"Yes. We all are. Remember how I met Malchus, Jamin, and Cleopas?"

"They intervened when your own men attacked you. Jamin said your commanding officer covered up the assault."

"All true. Those men are in this room."

"That's unfortunate. The angry one in the corner—is he one of them?"

"Yes, but he's had a change of heart about me."

"That's good."

"Not really."

"Why not?" Peter stifled a yawn.

"He's decided to go after you."

"I see," Peter yawned again. The wine was taking effect.

"I will protect you, Simon."

"I believe you will. You and God."

The men had stopped their games and grown quiet. One by one, they passed out until only Peter, Adas, and Lucius were awake. One of the torches sputtered. Adas checked the oil pot. Each shift was required to refill it before going off duty, but it was empty. With the distractions, Adas had forgotten to inspect it. He decided to burn one torch at a time to conserve them. Adas reached for a torch when he heard a sword sliding from its scabbard. He spun around to find Lucius standing over Hektor with a sword in his hand.

"Centurion, I will not forfeit my life or my chance to see Valentius executed. Herod is going to kill this prisoner anyway."

"Lucius, Valentius *will* be executed when we capture him in the act of treason."

"Can you guarantee success? We can't secure the doors against him. Apparently, we'll also have to fight in the dark. We can't just capture him because he could say he was only checking on us. If the prisoner is dead, it won't matter what he does. He'll be executed." A thick cough gurgled in his chest. He wiped the back of his hand across his mouth.

"Lucius, think. If you kill me you'll still be executed."

"This isn't my sword. It belongs to Hektor. In the morning, they will find blood on *Hektor's* sword and blood on *your* sword. You'll both be dead. Your friend will be dead, too, accidently killed while you two fought. The men will testify you were angry about the wager and threatened him. I will claim that Hektor attacked you and I was unable to help you. If you manage to wound me now, I will say that Hektor did it. When Valentius shows up, I'll slip out the door and be waiting for him with the watchtower guards. We'll catch him dragging the body out, trying to make it look like the prisoner escaped. It will be my word against—no one. The end result will be the crucifixion of Valentius for treason. And I will be commended for killing Hektor after he killed you. I'll be promoted to a *principales* and a raise in pay."

Peter's chains rattled as he tried to move out of the way. "Adas, trust in God," He struggled to stay conscious, but the sleeping potion was too strong.

Adas drew his sword. He knew nothing would change Lucius's mind. The legionary swung his sword as Adas blocked the blow. He glanced behind to see if he had room to maneuver. Adas countered, and Lucius blocked it easily. Adas hoped to wear him down. Back and forth they slashed and blocked, trying not to trip over unconscious soldiers. The clattering of metal against metal echoed off the stone walls. Sparks danced along the blades as they clashed. A torch went out, leaving only three burning.

Adas struggled to stay between Lucius and Peter. Lucius tried to force Adas back, but the legionary was beginning to tire. He grew pale as sweat ran down his face. There was a wheezing sound as Lucius panted for air. Adas pressed forward, forcing Lucius to stumble, but he regained his footing. He turned sideways and blocked Adas's sword. The centurion's sword slid down the blade of Hektor's sword, cutting Lucius's hand. The sword slipped in his bloody hand before he realized he was injured. Adas pushed his advantage, backing Lucius further away from Peter.

Lucius stepped back and lowered his sword. His chest heaved as he struggled for air. "You win, Centurion. I can't go on. What have I got to lose now? I'm dead, no matter what happens." He leaned against the wall, but his wary expression belied his words.

"Then drop the sword!"

Lucius tossed it aside. It clattered to the stone floor. He looked at the gash running across his hand. Lucius put his hand behind his back and pressed it against the wall as if to apply pressure to the wound.

"Sit! Shackle one of your wrists," Adas ordered. Lucius didn't move. Adas pressed the point of his sword on Lucius's chest. He pulled Lucius's dagger from its sheath and threw it across the floor. "Let me see your hands!"

Lucius sagged against the wall as the fire went out of his eyes. He started to drop to the floor. Adas stepped back. Suddenly there was a blur of motion as Lucius lashed out with a dagger, but missed. Adas raised his sword. Before Lucius could recover from the downward swing of his arm, Adas was already bringing his sword down to deflect the dagger further. The motion twisted Lucius's body, pinning him against the wall. He was defenseless. Adas hit him with his fist so hard he felt the energy of the blow reverberate up his arm. Lucius's head snapped back, he hit the rock wall, and collapsed. A dagger fell from his hand, and hit the floor. It was Hektor's dagger.

Panting from the fight, Adas shook out his left hand. It was then he saw a dark stain spreading down the front of his tunic. He gasped when pain erupted across his chest. Lucius had not missed, after all. A laceration crossed the entire width of his chest, just below the collar bones. Adas could pass out. Lucius was sprawled on the floor, but could regain consciousness any time. Adas dropped his sword. He clamped shackles around the legionary's wrists. He slumped to the floor, trying to keep a clear head. He cut through his tunic with his dagger and pulled the garment off. He rolled the cloth up to make a long, wide bandage, and used his belt to secure it. He fastened the belt as tightly as he could as pain surged through his chest. Nausea and vertigo hit him as the room swam around him. He waited until the dizziness passed. Another torch went out, leaving only two burning. He picked up his dagger, and stepped over to Peter. He had to be ready. Valentius would be coming.

Another torch went out, leaving only one burning. The single torch created more shadows than light. Adas whispered, "Yeshua, help me." The pain of the laceration began to subside. Adas saw the room go dark as the last torch went out, but he was not afraid. He knew Peter would be safe somehow. As Adas lay in the dark, a soft light began to glow. It had to be Valentius creeping down the hall with a torch. As a cohort centurion, he would have a key to the outer door. Adas grasped his dagger more tightly. The light filled the room even though the door was still closed. It was not torchlight. The light came from the figure of a man dressed in a tunic, golden chest armor, and *caligae*, with a sword strapped to his back. Adas could see the sword's handle above his right shoulder. He knew the man was an angel of God. Enthralled by the masculine beauty of the angel's face, Adas realized this was not the same angel who appeared at Yeshua's tomb. The angel called out to Peter, but he didn't respond. The angel jabbed him in the side, startling him awake. Adas watched in fascination.

"Arise quickly!" the angel said. The shackles clicked open, and fell from Peter's wrists. The angel handed him shoes and a cloak. *"Gird yourself and tie on your sandals. Put on your garment and follow me."*

While Peter dressed, Adas heard the iron bolt slide on the other side of the door, and it swung open. But he could see by the angel's light that the soldiers were still sprawled on the floor. No one else was there. Peter and the angel walked out of the room leaving the door wide open. As they approached the outer door, it swung open, making a dull thud as it hit the outside stone wall. They stepped around the unconscious soldiers and walked out. Adas lay still, feeling no fear. Simon Peter was safe. Adas sighed with relief and fell asleep.

The angel escorted Peter out of the building and across the quad. The iron gates to the fortress opened before them. There were no guards visible in the towers. No alarm was sounded. Peter realized he was not dreaming when he found himself out in the street, alone. He thought of the consequences for Adas and whispered a prayer. He headed for the home of Mary, mother of John Mark. When he knocked on the door, Rhoda opened it, but was so shocked to see Peter, she slammed the door shut. She told the others Peter was standing at the door, but they refused to believe her. He kept calling out to them. Finally, they opened the door and he told them how he was released by the angel of the Lord. He asked them to tell the rest of the brethren about his deliverance. Then he left them full of joy and wonder.

Chapter 27

A   t sunrise, the blasting of the ram's horn awakened the occupants of the Antonia. Nikolaus and Onesimus rushed to the windows with the other slaves. Shouts were coming from the detention building. Tribune Salvitto was striding across the quad, gesturing and calling to legionaries as they streamed from the barracks. Onesimus remembered his task.

"Nikolaus, Centurion Longinus told me to give you a message this morning. He said there's a mouse in his horse's stall that he wants you to take care of."

"*What?*" Nikolaus snapped. "Tell me his exact words."

"He said, 'Tell Nikolaus there is a *musculus* nesting in Venustas's stall and to see to it first thing this morning.' I'm sure that's what he said."

Nikolaus stiffened with fear. He would have to bring Serapio to the garrison. It would not be easy with the entire legion on high alert. Centurion Longinus walked around the corner of the *cafeteria* escorted by a legionary and Tribune Salvitto. Nikolaus could see that Adas was injured, yet he walked without assistance.

The door to the slave quarters swung open. Nikolaus hurried out in time to see legionaries being escorted from Holding to the Pit House. *Optio* Victorius led Legionary Octavean out last. The side of his face was bruised. His right hand and forearm were stained red. The Lion and the Wolf had crossed swords.

Nikolaus went behind the torch station near the west gate. Soldiers were milling around as centurions barked orders. The gates were shut, but Nikolaus knew supply wagons made deliveries early every morning. Within minutes, tower guards shouted for the gates to be opened. Outside sat a large wagon loaded with sacks of flour. As the wagon moved inside, Nikolaus sprinted to the back of the wagon. He dashed out the gate, ducked behind the wall, and casually crossed the street. Within minutes he was banging on Serapio's shop door.

The door flew open. "What is the meaning. . ." Nikolaus's agitation was obvious. Serapio pulled him in, slamming the door behind him. "Nikolaus, what's wrong?"

"Centurion Longinus has been injured. They were guarding Simon Peter. The whole fortress is on alert. I think Peter has escaped! Centurion Longinus will be put to death!"

Serapio refused to panic. "Nikolaus, we have to get you back. Come on." He snatched up a chair, and they went to the stable. Serapio hitched his donkey to the delivery cart, tossed in the chair, and covered it with a tarp. "Get under. No one will care what I bring *into* the garrison." Serapio flipped the reins to nudge the donkey into a quick pace. They were stopped at the gates to the Antonio.

"What business do you have here?" demanded the guard.

"I have a chair to deliver to Centurion Longinus."

"I doubt he will need a chair much longer."

"It is still his chair. I am here to deliver it. I will speak with Tribune Salvi. . ."

"No need. Be quick about it."

Serapio drove the cart across the quad. He turned behind the corner of the stables for Nikolaus to climb out. "Let me get my *veterinarius* kit." He came back with the wooden box Adas had given him. They hurried to the officers' quarters. Two legionaries were standing outside Adas's door.

Serapio stepped down from the wagon. "I have a chair for Centurion Longinus and . . ."

A guard raised his hand. "Are you Regulus Novius Serapio?"

"I am. I'm here to . . ."

"What's in the box?" Nikolaus opened the box. The soldier glanced at the contents. "Go ahead. Tribune Salvitto has cleared you."

Adas was lying on the bed. His belt and rolled up tunic lay on the floor. A blanket covered his legs. He seemed to be asleep with his face turned away from the door with his hand thrown across his eyes.

"Adas? Are you awake?" Serapio asked as he sat in the chair.

Adas turned his head. "You two here to break me out?"

"Not with the shape you're in. What happened?"

"There was a situation. Octavean and I sharply disagreed on how to solve it."

Serapio grunted. "Sharply, yes. I can see that." He found a towel and the water pitcher to clean the wound. Nikolaus poured water into a kettle and hung it over the fireplace.

"Nikolaus, thank you for getting Serapio."

"Sir, do you want me to stitch the wound?"

"Might as well. You could use the practice."

"Adas!" Serapio's sharp tone spoke volumes. "This is *not* over yet."

Adas turned to face Serapio. His scarred face showed no fear. "How did you get in here so easily? Did you promise them a furniture discount?"

A corner of Serapio's mouth curved. "No need to waste my profit. You know Tribune Salvitto and I go way back. What happened in Holding?" Adas told them about the attack.

"So Valentius dragged Peter out while you were unconscious? He's as good as dead."

"No. Peter left before anyone showed up."

"What do you mean, Peter *left*? Who let him out?"

"An angel of God, but not the same angel I saw at Yeshua's tomb. Their features were very different. This angel had a sword. He told Peter to get dressed, and his shackles opened and fell off his wrists. The doors unlocked themselves. Then they just walked out. Herod will be furious, but Valentius has succeeded."

"Perhaps not. God works in unexpected ways. God knows you protected Peter."

"And what if protecting Peter is my final purpose. God let Stephen and James die. Why should I expect to have a longer life than they had?"

"Do you know the mind of God? What God plans for one is not the same as for another."

"You think I'm feeling sorry for myself?"

"Yes. If you give up faith, you're not worth saving."

"You grouchy old bear. You always could crack the whip."

"Did it sting? Because if it didn't I can come up with something else."

"I know you don't want me to die. I don't either. But if I am to die, I accept it."

Serapio went back to cleaning Adas's wound. Nikolaus took the needle and strands of horsehair from the hot water. He set them aside to dry. Serapio filled a mug with water and helped Adas sit up. He gulped the water and lay back down. Serapio asked Nikolaus to get vinegar or honey from the *cafeteria*. Nikolaus slipped out.

"Serapio, I'm sure Herod will move quickly to save face. If he was away, there would be time to present proof against Valentius. But since he is in town. . . Serapio, I need you to take Venustas and my possessions. See to my last testament with Salvitto. Offer my weapons to Salvitto in exchange for Nicholas. Do everything you can to free him." Anguish filled his heart. "Take Venustas to Dulcibella."

Serapio mumbled something about getting more water. He walked outside, giving Adas a moment of privacy. While he was gone, Adas remembered Simon Peter's blessing on his and Dulcibella's marriage. If he could hold on to that promise, fear would lose its hold on him. When Serapio came back, Adas had recovered some composure. "You're right, Serapio. There is hope."

Running footsteps and voices sounded outside the door. Nikolaus came in. He set a jar of honey on the bedside table. "Cook said honey is better for warding off infection than olive oil or vinegar."

Nikolaus took a pair of *forficulae* from his kit and set them on the bed. Serapio picked up the *forficulae* and put his thumb in one circular handle and his fingers in the other. He clipped the air watching the two blades slice together. "How clever. Who invented this?"

Relieved at the distraction, Adas said, "I'm sure you would have many uses for scissors. I should get you a pair for your birthday. When *is* your birthday?"

"I don't remember."

"You ol' liar."

"Sir, the horse hairs are dry enough now," said Nikolaus. He sat down by Adas's side. "This is the longest wound I've ever stitched." His face was pinched with anxiety.

Serapio handed Adas his belt. "You're going to want this between your teeth."

"I survived having a cross branded in my hand. Believe me! That hurt much more than this will. Just do your best, Nikolaus. I trust you."

Nikolaus flinched. "You should not trust me."

"I know what happened. Valentius forced you to tell him about Dulcibella."

"I have betrayed you twice. The first time was when I ran away and then after I swore allegiance to you in my heart I told Valentius everything."

"Nikolaus, you can't expect to be perfect. None of us are. Besides, you did return on your own, and you followed my instructions with Valentius. But why didn't you warn me?"

"I was afraid. If you had acted differently around Valentius he would have . . . I-I was too ashamed to tell you."

"I hold nothing against you, Nikolaus."

"Why not? Why do you forgive me?"

"Because Yeshua forgave me. I have no right to *not* forgive *anyone*."

Serapio nodded approval. Nikolaus breathed a sigh of relief. He threaded the needle with horsehair. During the stitching, Serapio kept up a steady stream of useless conversation to distract Adas. He closed his eyes and listened to the sound of Serapio's deep, resonant voice. Nikolaus worked quickly. With the stitching done, he anointed the laceration with honey and covered it with a linen bandage. He secured the bandage with long strips of linen.

Voices sounded outside. Tribune Salvitto walked in carrying Adas's knapsack and weapons. He set them on the table as he nodded a greeting to Serapio. "Centurion, I have to take you to the palace. Herod wants to interrogate all of those on duty last night. I can give you a few hours, but we'll need to be there before the sixth hour. Have you gotten everything you need?"

"Yes, Sir. Nikolaus did a fine job tending to me. Thank you, Sir."

"I have spoken with Octavean. He admitted he tried to kill the prisoner. He said you fought him off. Since he is facing execution, he said there's no reason to lie. He told me his suspicions about Valentius, but I don't have proof he smuggled the prisoner out. Not yet."

"There's a wineskin full of the tainted wine, if Valentius has not disposed of it."

Salvitto opened the door to talk to the guards. One of them trotted off. Salvitto came back inside. "If the wineskin is gone, is there any other proof?" Adas shook his head. "Nikolaus, you stay with Centurion Longinus. Get whatever he needs. Serapio, as I've told you, my friend, the soldiers know you are always welcome here." He walked out and shut the door.

"Take my weapons, Serapio, and the copper mirror, and my coin pouch. The eilat stone belongs to Dulcibella. Tell her. . .tell her I love her."

Serapio raised his chin defiantly. "It will not be necessary. You will tell her, your-self. As for the stone, I will keep it safe until I can give it back to you."

"I don't understand," said Nikolaus with angry frustration. "Why would God take Peter out when you were guarding him? Why didn't the angel come for Peter when he was first arrested?"

"I don't know," said Adas. "If only we could see the future and be sure of the outcome."

"I, too, share your fear, Nikolaus," said Serapio. "But I have seen Death brush past me and others many times. As long as there is life, there is hope."

Chapter 28

⸻❦⸻

The legionaries were held in the pit, but would be taken to the palace for interrogation. Lucius saw Falto staring at him. "What do you want?"

Falto moved closer. "I need to tell you something. When they broke your arm, it wasn't an accident. I heard them planning it."

"Your warning is a bit late, Weasel."

"I'm sorry. I was more afraid of Valentius than of you. I have lived my whole life in fear, but I fear death most of all. What if Hades is a real place, a place of eternal torment."

"We'll find out soon enough, won't we?" Lucius moved to the other side of the pit.

Within the hour, they were escorted to the palace. Herod vented his anger on them, shouting that half the legion was forced to hunt for Simon Peter because of their incompetence. He questioned the legionaries together. The interrogation was grueling. They had little to contribute until Lucius asked to speak. He told Herod everything he knew. Herod began to form a plan. He needed someone to take the blame for this botched attempt to put Simon Peter on trial, especially since he was newly appointed in his uncle's place. The soldiers were dismissed. Herod ordered his guards to bring Centurion Longinus to him. The king shot questions at Adas, many which seemed unrelated to the situation. Exhausted and light-headed, he struggled to understand Herod's line of questioning, especially information about his father. Adas was finally dismissed. Centurion Valentius was presented. Herod questioned him at length, but with little satisfaction. Frustrated, the king was about to abandon his plan.

"Your Excellency, are you having the men executed?" Valentius asked.

"I am."

"Beheading?"

"At least you keep *your* head, but you forfeit that hefty bonus Salvitto offered."

"The bonus means nothing to me if you are displeased, Your Excellency. Perhaps I can redeem myself. May I suggest making a public example of these men to please the Sanhedrin? Their executions could be a sporting event, a competition for my elite team of *sagittarii*. I could make the arrangements today. The executions could take place tomorrow, at your pleasure."

"You don't think taking their lives is punishment enough? Didn't you personally select these men? Yet, you want to publicly shame them?"

"I selected them because they were the best men for the job. They betrayed both of us. A tournament, offering a reward to the winner, would demonstrate your superiority over your uncle, Herod Antipas, who was weak and indecisive."

A slow smile spread across the King's face. "Your suggestion has possibilities. You would make all the arrangements?"

"Yes, Your Excellency. May I suggest a year's wages for the prize? If there is more than one winner, they will share it equally. I would disperse the prize in any manner you see fit."

"Four squads were on duty. Sixteen men. How long will this contest last? I have no time to waste. Convince me that it will be worth my precious time."

"It will be a competition of skill, Your Excellency. The *sagittarius* who uses the *fewest* arrows to kill his 'target,' from twenty paces, wins. If a prisoner is no longer able to stand, the distance requirement will be eliminated, but any arrows shot at close range will count as three. The contest will progress quickly, yet news of it will define your demand for justice. The Sanhedrin will be indebted to you for your superior response to the prisoner's escape. They will remember that your uncle couldn't even force the Nazarene to answer a question."

Herod rubbed his beard as he evaluated his options. "Agreed. The contest will occur tomorrow at the seventh hour in the Theater of Herod the Great. Attendance is mandatory. You, Tribune Salvitto, and High Priest Caiaphas will sit with me in the portico. Invite Caiaphas to bring a few attendants. The Sanhedrin also 'misplaced' the blasphemer, Peter. But this contest will prove my commitment to God. Make the arrangements."

Trying to keep his expression neutral, Valentius bowed and left the room. Herod called for Chuza, his business manager. "Chuza, I want you and Blastus to search my archives. Find anything you can on Felix Pomponius Valentius and Adas Clovius Longinus, including *Minor Consul* Aquila Clovius Longinus. Look for a previous connection between Longinus and Valentius." Chuza left to round up his scribes.

Every passing hour that Peter could not be found, intensified the sting of embarrassment for Herod. A simple fisherman was making a fool of him. This was one reason the king agreed to Valentius's contest, but he had stronger motives. The *sagittarii* contest was the perfect way to unmask a traitor in front of High Priest Caiaphas and the Sanhedrin.

Within hours, Chuza and his scribes found something useful. The proof was circumstantial, but Herod knew skillfully presented speculation would be just as convicting. Herod was certain that after tomorrow, his position with the Sanhedrin and Emperor Gaius would be secure.

As for Valentius, he was ecstatic over Herod's approval and rushed back to the Antonia. He found Demitre in his office. Barely able to restrain himself, Valentius exclaimed, "Finally, all my plans have been approved. I will have my revenge. My debts will be paid. We will be free from this place, free to go wherever we wish. Tomorrow will be a glorious day!" Valentius filled two cups with wine.

Demitre settled in a chair and drank deeply. He propped one leg over an armrest, dangling his sandaled foot in the air. "I take it you remembered everything I told you. Did you appeal to Herod's vanity and hatred of his uncle? Did you say something about the Nazarene?"

"Of course! Just like we practiced. He approved the contest, didn't he?"

"Julie would be so proud of you." Demitre raised his cup. "To Julia, my sweet sister, your adoring wife. May she rest in blessed peace."

"You should be proud of me, too. You would have been impressed with how cleverly I manipulated Herod. There was one problem. I had to alter the contest rules from our original plan. I told him the man using the *fewest* arrows, wins."

"Why did you do that? More arrows will introduce the poison properly."

"I'll simply tell the men to disavow Herod's rules and obey mine. They will do as I instruct, especially when I promise bonuses. Besides, the poison is only for Longinus."

"So tell me, how did you get the Galilean out without anyone seeing you?"

"I didn't. Somebody beat me to it. When I got there, he was gone. The soldiers were passed out like dead rats. Longinus and Octavean were wounded. Apparently, Longinus shackled Octavean to the wall like a dog."

"That must have pleased you. How fortunate the two of them fought. Let's hope a few soldiers were still conscious to witness the start of the fight. No one will question their deaths. You used their own weapons to finish them off? Yes?"

The grin faded from Valentius's face. "Didn't you see Longinus and Octavean escorted out of Holding? They'll be executed with the others."

"*What!* Why didn't you kill them? They will jeopardize our plans."

"No, they won't. I changed my mind about killing them."

"They could ruin everything! You had a perfect way to silence them for good."

"No! I want them to suffer like I have! I want to see them humiliated before the entire legion, especially that fraud Longinus. He discredits the title of centurion. This supreme dishonor will devastate *Consul* Longinus. My timing is perfect. Tomorrow, the *Consul* is to wed his young bride. I will cherish the pain he will know when he learns his son died on the same day."

"Who cares? You should focus on our plan to steal the pensions of sixteen dead soldiers and the prize money. You left Octavean shackled, didn't you? An outside intruder would not have keys."

In the excitement, Valentius had forgotten that only cohort centurions had keys. "Of course I left him shackled," he lied. In reality, Valentius didn't want to leave proof that the Wolf had defeated the Lion single handedly, something no individual combatant had ever done.

"Did Herod agree to a year's wages for the prize? Are you sure we can trust the *dispensator* to forge passable pension claims? Not even one document can fail inspection."

"Yes, yes, yes, to all your petty questions! He is quite competent. He releases the forgeries to me, collects his bribe, and disappears as planned. Before the Antonia's pension nullification documents get to Rome, we claim the gold in Caesarea. Both of us will be long gone and forgotten before anyone in Rome realizes the gold is missing."

"I still think we should eliminate the *dispensator*. Why waste money on a bribe? I can make it look like he died of natural causes."

"I suppose it would be safer. The man is getting old. Do what you must, Demitre. However, try not to kill *this* man in front of witnesses, *this time!*"

Demitre's black eyes flared with resentment. He had been forced to disguise himself as a slave since his mid-thirties because of the murder he committed to protect his sister, Julia. He was weary of his performance, but once he got his share of the money, it would be over.

"I can't wait until tomorrow," exclaimed Valentius. "My revenge will be so perfect even the gods will be jealous."

Demitre thought, "The gods don't even know who you are." Yet, he arranged his face into a proper smile and held up his cup for more wine.

"We should celebrate our victory," suggested Valentius. "Get some of my opium. I'll even share, just this once."

While Valentius and Demitre were celebrating, Adas lay in his bed, completely drained. Several times he nearly passed out during Herod's interrogation.

There was a knock and Nikolaus came in. "Sir, may I bring you something to eat."

"Get food for both of us, and ale. I don't want wine."

"Sir, you should know. There will be a contest tomorrow, for the *sagittarii*."

Seeing the despair on the young man's face, Adas knew what that meant. "I take it that my men and I are to be the targets. Go get food, Nikolaus, lots of it. I need my strength back."

Learning his execution would be entertainment for five thousand men spurred Adas to action. He moved to the table to write to Dulcibella. If she had to get this terrible news, it would come from him. Nikolaus came in with a tray, but sat and stared at the food.

"Nikolaus, where were you this afternoon?"

"I prepared Venustas to go with Serapio. Sir, do you want me to take your letter to the tribune? He has written letters to Centurion Cornelius and your father. He said to tell you."

"Maybe later. Were you questioned this afternoon?"

Nikolaus's eyes went wide with alarm. "Yes, Sir, I didn't want to worry you."

"Were you questioned by King Herod, himself?"

"He asked me questions about your habits, where you went when you are off duty. Things like that. He asked if I had witnessed any confrontations between you and Valentius."

"Was that all?"

Nikolaus defiantly looked Adas in the eye. "Yes, Sir."

Adas knew he was lying, but he let it go. He handed Dulcibella's letter to him. "Go ahead and take it. When you get back, help me eat this food."

Nikolaus left with the letter and returned quickly. When they finished eating, Nikolaus picked up the tray. "Sir, is there anything else you need?"

"I can't think of anything."

"*I can!* I wish I could get you out of here! I want you to go back to Dulcibella. And I want to get revenge on Valentius. He's responsible for all this misery, and probably this disgusting contest. Why has God allowed him to succeed? I don't understand any of this."

"Nikolaus, I was tempted to give up hope. But I believe I was with Peter for a reason other than the schemes of Felix Valentius. God could have protected Peter in a hundred different ways, but he chose me. If it is my time to die, then I accept it. But if God wishes me to live, I will."

He gestured for Nikolaus to sit down. "Why don't we just talk? Tell me about your family and your childhood. Tell me about your sister, Dionysia. You've never been just someone who saddles my horse, Nikolaus. We're friends." Adas realized he would never have met Nikolaus if his father had not orchestrated his transfer to the Antonia.

Chapter 29

After being questioned by Herod, the prisoners were taken back to the Pit House. Lucius was leaning against the wall when one of the sentries called his name. "Get up here, Octavean, you have a visitor." The ladder was lowered. The guard grasped his wrist to help him over the rim. "They're letting you have more time than usual," said the guard as he opened the door to an interrogation room. Lucius walked in. The door slammed shut.

Someone in a cloak was seated on one of two chairs. The person seemed too slight to be a man. The face was obscured by a head scarf. Exhausted from standing all day, Lucius gratefully sat down to face the seated figure.

A small hand pulled the scarf away. "Hello, son," said Sevina.

"*Mother?* What are you doing here?"

"I was forced to leave Rome, Lucius. Despite tending their children, your sisters' husbands have no use for me anymore. They threw me out. I had no place to go but here to my sister. I heard the terrible news about you. I've been trying to find the courage to talk with you and. . ." she sniffed and dabbed at her eyes with a sleeve.

Sevina was a stunning beauty when she was young, but in forty-nine years, she had not aged well. Despite his shock at seeing her, he wondered if his father would have been so eager to marry her now.

"This isn't right! They say you were drugged with tainted wine. The Roman Army has betrayed you once again."

"I didn't drink the wine." Recovered from shock at seeing her, he knelt to hug her.

She threw her arms around his neck, but quickly pulled away. "There is something you should know. If I had your father's courage, I would have come sooner."

"Why are we talking about him now? It was twenty-three years ago."

"You don't know the whole truth."

"The truth is obvious, Mother. I killed my own father."

"Yes, but you don't really know why Rufino was there. *Praefectus* Junio came to your father to convince him to participate in a test. The *praefectus* said you were smarter and stronger than any recruit he had ever trained. He said you were the son who would make any father proud. He told Rufino you could qualify for the Praetorian Guard."

"I know. He wanted to train me for the emperor's elite."

"Yes, but he had one final test before he could officially start your training. It was crucial for Rufino to participate. Of course, Rufino didn't need to be convinced. He always put you first—before me, your sisters, even before himself. Sadly, we could have used your signing bonus, but he gave it to Junio to buy the best weapons for you."

"Junio was supposed to pay for my weapons?"

Sevina cursed under her breath. "Of course, he didn't. Why am I even surprised? How ironic! He asked Rufino to pose as a thief, yet Junio was the real thief."

"What do you mean 'pose' as a thief? He was innocent?"

"Junio swore he would stop you if you made the wrong decision, but when you did, it was too late."

"The *wrong* decision? I obeyed his order. How was that wrong?"

"He told you to kill your own father, or he would kill both of you. The *praefectus*, as your training officer, had to also train your heart and mind, not just your body. If you were going to protect the emperor, you must be willing to die for him even if he did terrible things. You had to demonstrate there was someone you would be willing to die *for* or *with*. Junio knew you loved Rufino more than anyone. If you defended your father, at any cost, you would pass the test. Despite how much Junio bragged on you, he underestimated you. When he came to tell me you had killed Rufino, he said you acted too quickly for him to even grab hold of the spear. He said you didn't even hesitate. You failed, Lucius."

"I was supposed to *disobey* the order? That was the test?" The taunting guilt he always tried so hard to silence was screaming in his head.

"Yes. Junio lied to test you, but he overplayed the test when he slashed your face. He expected an eleven-year-old to make a man's decision in an instant. Junio said you 'should have thought it out.' His words. How can a child think after being slashed with a dagger? Even as Junio pretended to beg me for forgiveness, he blamed you."

"I still don't understand. I was trained to obey *every* order without hesitation. This doesn't make sense."

"This was also your father's fault. His pride in you overtook his common sense. I told him you were too young for such a test. Rufino was not guilty of theft, but he was guilty of false pride. He bragged about you as if he had no other family. His selfish love for you killed him just as effectively as your spear. He left me a widow. He left our daughters fatherless. I was so angry with him and Junio; I couldn't even reach out to you. But you paid the greatest price."

"No, not me. Father did. So did Junio."

"The *praefectus*?" She pulled back in surprise. "When? How?"

"I have never told anyone this. After I left the training camp, I was sent with a *cohors* to repulse an attack of Scythians. Junio was there. We had just won a skirmish. I went past a few more hills than the others to collect the weapons of the dead, as ordered. Junio was collecting amulets off the dead soldiers, both ours and the Scythians. We were alone except for the dead. He was so intent on ransacking the bodies; he didn't hear me until it was too late. He spun around, but had no weapon in his hand. I put the point of my sword to his throat. He begged for mercy. I slashed his face with my dagger. I said, 'Looks like I caught a thief.' Then I killed him. I laughed in his face as he died."

The gleam in Sevina's eyes belied her well-practiced sympathy. "So you carry the guilt of his murder as well."

"What guilt? He deserved it."

"That is true. The man was a cheating womanizer." She shot an uneasy glance at Lucius. When he said nothing, she relaxed. But Lucius heard what she said. Something still did not make sense, but he couldn't quite grasp it. It was as if he was looking at his clothes chest, but couldn't remember what was in it.

"Did Junio take any of the blame for father's death?"

"Take responsibility? Hardly! He didn't even have the decency to come in the house. He only said you failed. I was so distraught, I begged for details. He said you moved so quickly he couldn't stop you, and then. . ." she shrugged her shoulders, ". . .he was gone, as if Rufino's death was nothing."

"The simpering coward said nothing else?"

"Not a word. He couldn't turn tail fast enough."

"Then how did you know he slashed my face? You've never seen this scar before now."

Sevina coughed, stalling to give herself time to think. "I—I forgot. He did tell me about that. No, he didn't *tell* me. He *bragged* about it. I just forgot. You can't expect me to remember every little thing. You're not the only one who was traumatized."

"Then, I find it odd he wanted your forgiveness, but confessed to assaulting me, a mere child. When people beg for forgiveness, they rarely add more sins to the list."

Sevina had fallen for his trap. She quickly thought of a distraction. "The Roman army is your enemy, Lucius. You dedicated your whole life to Rome, and this is how they repay you. Rome has taken so much from both of us. Now you are unjustly sentenced to die."

"Do not think my death sentence is unjust. No matter how you feel about Junio, I did murder him. He was unarmed. I have baited men for the sheer pleasure of beating them. I watch for their weaknesses to use against them. I pick fights to cause others pain. There is an evil within me I choose not to control. I have nurtured it like an old friend. It makes me feel good."

"Surely, you exaggerate. You followed orders. You did what was necessary to survive. How is that wrong? It's what we all must do?"

"Survive? For what? To live another day just to make the same mistakes? One of those mistakes got me thrown in the pit. I deserved worse, but Centurion Longinus intervened. I was an *opio addicta*. I thought I was going to die without the opium, but the pit did for me what I could not do for myself. Those forty days freed me from the addiction." He coughed deep in his chest. Sevina leaned away and turned her head. "Yes, I'm sick—probably dying anyway. But don't blame Father for volunteering for my test. I'm sure he did what he thought was right. It is good to know he never dishonored our family. Not too long ago, my squad was ordered to crucify three men. I saw something I've not told anyone. I picked up a spear, and suddenly, right in front of me, there was Father."

"Rufino's ghost! Surely not! You must have hallucinated."

"Maybe. Maybe not. I don't even care how it happened. I was going to use the spear to make sure the Nazarene was dead, but Father blocked my way. He looked as if I could touch him. Can you touch a ghost?"

"He cursed you, didn't he?"

"I am sentenced to death by law, not by a curse. Father spoke to me. Over and over, he said, 'Not your fault. Not your fault.' He looked the same as the day he died. He even had the same expression as when—just before—I killed him." Lucius frowned. There was always a blank spot in his memory of that day. He could never remember the moment he thrust the spear into his father's chest. "The look on Father's face has always haunted me. He wasn't afraid. He was calm. I couldn't understand. How could an innocent man about to be executed by *his own son*, look at me with. . .with such. . .what? What was it? What was he thinking?"

The horrendous day was submerged deeply into his subconscious. He had to struggle to visualize it. For decades he had pushed the memory as far from conscious thought as possible. He tried to concentrate, but could only glimpse fragments of the event.

"I don't know why it matters, but it does. I can't figure it out. The expression on his face is forever sealed in my memory as if it were sculpted in stone. Yet, my heart refuses to comprehend it." Closing his eyes in concentration, Lucius pictured his father standing before him. Without warning, a memory burst through the darkness. "I remember his eyes. He looked so sad, like he'd suffered a great loss. It was as if he felt sorry for me. For me! Not himself! Why? Did he know Junio had lied to him? That I might be forced to kill him? If so, why would he agree to participate? There was something else in his sadness. Ah, that's it. The very last look in his eyes was—the same as that crucified Nazarene. It was *forgiveness*. A father's forgiveness for his son. He knew he was about to die!"

Sevina's expression hardened. "What does it matter now? We have to think of the future. My future, at least. What will happen to me? You have sent me part of your pay every month of every year. It was my only income since I have no husband. Now, I won't even have that. Surely, you want to take this last chance to right your wrong. You could do a wonderful thing for me. Do you think Tribune Salvitto will grant me your pension claim? It's not too late."

"Mother, I am being executed tomorrow. When a soldier is executed, his pension is forfeit. Surely, you know this."

"Yes, Lucius, I do, but you're still alive. Can't you try? What harm could it do to ask? If Rufino truly did forgive you, then he would want me to have it, too."

Realizations clicked into place. Lucius understood. "Who told you about my execution?"

"I-I heard it from a neighbor. She told me."

"But how would this neighbor know that I, personally, am to be executed? No one in Jerusalem knows my name. You just moved here from Rome. You didn't come to the Antonia to see me. You came to file your new address with the *dispensator*. You didn't want my wages to go to my sisters. The *dispensator* told you about my execution, not some neighbor. You're not here to tell me about Junio! Was any of it true?"

"Yes, Lucius! It's all true! I swear!"

"You said you tried to talk Father out of participating in the test. If you thought it was such a bad idea, why didn't you warn me?"

"I didn't want to interfere."

"Liar! I can see it in your eyes. You're hiding something."

"I came here to tell you the truth! Instead of thanking me, you accuse me. Instead of begging for *my* forgiveness, you shout in my face. You're as selfish as he was. Rufino loved you more than anyone, and you killed him! Now you leave me with nothing!"

"Do you think I *want* to be executed?"

"No! But you did choose to kill your father. It wasn't because Junio ordered you to do it. You didn't even do it to save yourself! You murdered Rufino so Junio could take his place!"

"*Have you lost your mind?* I hated Junio. He made me fight for everything, even for food or a decent night's sleep. If one of the other boys tried to befriend me, he would make us fight nearly to the death. He belittled Father in front of the other boys. I would get so angry I wanted to choke him. He didn't need to bait me with his lies. I was already eager to please all my trainers. Why would he say those things?"

"How should I know?" She looked away, avoiding his eye.

"Father was an imposing man. Other men feared his disfavor. Why did Junio belittle him? If I didn't know better, I would say it was jealousy."

"Junio just wanted to motivate you. You said it made you angry, so you fought harder."

An uncomfortable silence fell over them. For the first time in decades, Lucius wanted to know the truth. He knew it was hidden in his own mind if he could be strong enough to face it. He thought about Junio's meeting with Sevina. Something wasn't adding up.

"Junio told you he didn't have time to grab the spear from me?"

"Yes, you moved too quickly."

"That doesn't sound right. I did hesitate. I remember arguing with Father. I remember they brought me out. Father was tied to a post. Junio made me stand in front of him with the point of my spear, right here." Lucius placed his fingertips just below his sternum. "When he told me Father was caught stealing, I knew he was lying. I begged Father to tell me what happened, but he wouldn't answer. I kept pleading with him, but he wouldn't speak. Then with no warning, Junio slashed my face. He kept waving his dagger in my face. My blood was on it. I couldn't look away, but I never let go of the spear." He swallowed hard, trying to remember every detail of that catastrophic day.

The unspeakable secret began to claw its way out of his memory. "I was desperate to look at Father, but I couldn't see around the dagger." Lucius closed his eyes again, and struggled to remember.

His eyes shot open as color drained from his face. The truth had always been right in front of him. "I know what happened. The spear pulled me forward. I was holding so tightly. It pulled me. I nearly lost my footing. I looked around the dagger just in time to see Junio's hand. It was coming *off of the spear!* It was deep in Father's chest, but I never saw how it got there. *Junio killed him!*"

Lucius lowered his head into his hands. His eyes watered with tears of relief. "I did not kill my father. It wasn't me. It was Junio. The other soldiers grabbed me. They took me in the common room and surrounded me. They clapped me on the back as if I had single-handedly slaughtered a horde of barbarians. Junio came in, strutting around, cheering the others on. Then he congratulated me in front of all the men. He said, 'Today, you have proven yourself. You are truly one of us.' And I—believed him. No, I *decided* to believe him. The training officers, the legionaries, they finally accepted me. I felt like I had a family again, something I could belong to. For months, Junio lavished special treatment on me. I was given minor positions of authority, but to an eleven-year-old, it felt like the keys to the kingdom. Then everything began to fall apart. I knew it was all a lie, but I was trapped. How does a boy find the courage to stand up to grown men and reject their approval? I could not. Instead, I buried the truth, but it was never gone. Never gone!" He brought his fist to his chest. "Always there! Twisting and squirming like a living thing, a venomous thing. It made me love the violence of war."

"You see there! There's the proof! Junio lied to Rufino to get his cooperation and he lied to me. He intended to kill Rufino, all along. He praised you in front of the others so you wouldn't accuse him. He killed your father because he wanted a son of his own. He wanted you!"

Decades of bitter self-condemnation dissolved with a single moment of truth. So many years had been wasted on self-hate. A vicious anger consumed his entire being. He leaped to his feet. With clenched teeth, he raised his fist. Before his rational mind could catch up with his raging heart, he slammed his fist into the wooden door.

"Nooo!" The sound of cracking bone was muffled by his scream.

The guard on the other side jumped back, slapping a hand to his dagger. The other guards stared at the door, wide-eyed. They knew a woman was with Lucius, but they did not see to her welfare. No one wanted to unlock the door.

Sevina sprang to her feet, knocking her chair aside. She pressed herself against the wall. Panting, Lucius cradled his broken hand to his chest and dropped to the floor. When he made no attempt to move, she sat next to him.

"Lucius, you should have left the past in its grave."

"Like you did, Mother? Did you know what Junio really planned to do?"

"Of course not! How wicked do you think I am?"

"Then why, just now, did you show no surprise? I just told you how Junio murdered your husband. You never so much as blinked. Even in my anger I saw your face. Even as I ruined this hand, I knew what was in your heart. Your eyes were cold with calculation."

"I—I did actually suspect Junio. What you said confirmed my suspicions. I didn't tell you because I wanted to protect you. You should thank me, not accuse me! But you avenged your father when you killed Junio. I'm proud of you for that."

He coughed, deep in his chest. He wiped at his mouth. "Yes, I did kill Junio, but it didn't make me feel better?"

"Well, it should have. Didn't killing Junio honor your father? Junio was a lying cheat. The man used you. He used all of us!"

Lucius looked at his shattered hand. He wanted to laugh. The army would have to retire him now, if they weren't going to kill him. "What did you mean by that, Mother?"

"What? About your pension?"

"No, about how Junio used all of us. He did use me. He used Father. But how did he use you? You accused me of wanting Father out of the way. I think *you* wanted Father out of the way. *You* wanted Junio to take his place. Did you know Junio was planning to kill Father?"

Sevina blanched. Her tongue flicked out to wet her lips. "No, of course not! I—I am trying to help you understand. I know you're very confused about all this. You were just a child. Can't you see I'm just trying to help?"

"Are you? Am I confused? Or am I just now seeing things clearly for the first time? You say Junio wanted me for a son. Junio did want someone, but it wasn't me. He wanted you! You two were lovers! Did you plan my father's murder together? You knew Junio killed my father and you let me take the blame. Are you even capable of comprehending the guilt I have carried all my life? It ruined me!"

Sevina tried to pound on the door, but Lucius blocked her way. She backed away as her face creased with resentment. "What was I supposed to do? Your father was obsessed with you! Don't you understand? No! Of course not! Every spare coin went to you. How was I supposed to deal with that? *You* could have helped us."

"I don't remember you and my sisters suffering. I'm sorry if I was too young to understand. But how could I have helped? As you keep pointing out, I was a child."

"So what! Child or not, you had eyes, didn't you? And it wasn't me who ruined your life. I didn't know what Junio was going to do. I don't think he planned to kill Rufino; it just happened. Afterwards, what could I do about it? I hadn't done anything wrong."

"Is adultery wrong, Mother? You knew Father was murdered. What about your silence?"

"*My* silence? What about *yours*? You said you 'decided' to believe you had killed Rufino! You reveled in their approval and praise. Don't blame me for your self-deception. The only thing I ever wanted from your father was food on the table, and a roof over my head. He couldn't even manage that because of you. He *gave* everything to you; *did* everything for you. When your training officers came to him for money, he couldn't push it at them fast enough. Your sisters and I barely made ends meet with the paltry amount left for us. And now you've got yourself under a death sentence so, once again, you leave me destitute! You and your father always put me in second place. I gave him children, and in return, he stole my youth."

"And you stole his *life* when you conspired with Junio, that sniveling jackal! You stole my life when your secrets left my heart to rot! Can anyone be more depraved than a mother who sacrifices her own child? And I was a child; not a grown man capable of standing up to Junio's manipulation. I was eleven years old! How could I be expected to have the understanding or courage of a grown man?"

Her lip trembled as she frantically tried to think of a defense. Lucius stepped closer, looming over her. "Tell me, was Junio worth it? Did he give you comfort? Or did he discover you were too vile even for him?" Sevina slapped him across the face as hard as she could. He didn't even bother to retaliate.

"You come to me the day before my death. You trap *yourself* in a web of lies. You openly admit to knowing what that spineless maggot did, and you dare to beg for my *pension!*"

"Why shouldn't I? I need that money! Besides, everyone I've ever known has taken from me. You owe me! Why shouldn't I get what I legally deserve?"

Emotionally drained, Lucius knew it was futile to expect his mother to regret her treachery. He wondered if she were even capable of regret. He would die the next day, leaving nothing behind, no property, and no family of his own. All of his adult life had been fueled with hate, but his anger was spent. He closed his eyes and tried to slow his breathing. Yeshua's words came to him. *'Forgive them, Father for they know not what they do.'*

The most unexpected release filled his heart. It was as if someone pulled him to a sunlit shore from the depths of a cold, dark lake. Knowing he was not to blame for his father's death liberated him. After condemning himself for over twenty years, Lucius was free of the suffocating guilt that had molded him into a violent man. What was done could not be changed, but he still had the present. Lucius decided his final hours would not be wasted on the past. He didn't want to hate anymore, not Junio, not Valentius, not Longinus, not even Sevina.

"Mother, if I could leave my pension to you, I would. I do not wish to keep it from you. I certainly can't take it with me. I doubt my sisters need it more than you. No matter what you did, you are still my mother. I am sorry I will no longer be able to provide for you."

"Yes, I'm sure you're sorry. Sorry you can't give it to your father! If *he* were alive you'd figure out a way. Because of you, I will be penniless *and* homeless. I can't stay here in Jerusalem much longer. My sister's useless pig of a husband hates me. But after tomorrow, it won't be your concern, will it? So don't pretend you care about me. Don't try to make me feel sorry for you. We're both better off dead." She pounded on the door. The guard let them out.

Lucius headed for the pit, but a soldier gestured for him to approach. "Here, I'm sure he wants you to have it back." He pulled a flyswatter from his belt.

"What are you talking about?" Lucius frowned at the flyswatter.

"Longinus, he's the one who tossed it in there." The soldier tilted his head toward the pit. "You were the only prisoner, so I figured he made it for you."

Lucius took the flyswatter. He stared at it, unmoving. He looked across the pit at his mother standing in the open doorway. She was asking a soldier to point the direction to Salvitto's office. The forgiveness evident in the small gift of a flyswatter, and his innocence in his father's murder, caused Lucius to call out to his mother.

"Wait! There *is* something I can give you. Something I need to say."

"Keep your curses! Nothing you say can hurt me!" She rushed out the door.

Seeing the expression on Lucius's face made the guard curious. "What were you going to say?"

"I was going to give her what I've never given to anyone—my forgiveness."

Lucius climbed down the ladder. The other prisoners left him alone. The Lion was clearly in no mood for conversation.

In Tribune Salvitto's office, Sevina introduced herself. Salvitto invited her to sit. "I have seen my son, Lucius. He told me he cannot grant his pension to me." She waited, but he didn't correct her. "Is there nothing I can have to remember him by?"

"Yes, you can take his possessions. I am sorry the law requires the life of your son. A soldier will escort you home."

"Thank you. I appreciate that. The streets can be dangerous. Besides, I cannot carry a heavy load."

"I doubt it will be heavy." Salvitto looked at her with sympathy.

She made no attempt to hide her displeasure. "I see. Then I'll take what there is." Irritation crossed her face as she got up to leave.

Chapter 30

S unlight edged the darkness away to end a fitful night for Adas. His blanket was in a twisted mess. He was numb with sorrow. It was the day of his execution. The temptation to sink into despair was powerful. He thought about Dulcibella, her family, Serapio, Fabiana, his father, and Nikolaus. His death would affect them in the worst way. Resolved to deny Valentius the satisfaction of seeing him defeated, Adas accepted his situation. He also prayed for Peter's safety, knowing that even if the fisherman turned himself in, the executions would still continue, but their deaths would be in vain.

Adas looked at Nikolaus asleep on his blanket in front of the door. The guards had removed the bolt, but Nikolaus was making sure no one came in uninvited. He hoped Serapio would find a way to free the young man. He replayed the memories of Dulcibella placing her small hand in his work-scarred hand when she accepted his invitations of marriage. He remembered the joy in her eyes when she held the blue pearl up to the sunlight. The pearl's message of hope gave him comfort. Adas knew all was not lost somehow. If only he could hold on to this assurance, he would face the day with courage.

Adas drank from the cup on the bedside table before he lay back on the bed. He thought of what he should say if Herod allowed him to speak at his execution. He would proclaim to the entire 10th *Legio* how Simon Peter escaped. Adas did not tell Herod who had freed Peter for fear the king would execute him in private.

In Valentinus's office, Demitre finished mixing wine with opium for the condemned soldiers. The opium would subdue the men and desensitize them to pain, which would aid the accuracy of the *sagittarii*. Most importantly, it would allow the executioner to use a maximum number of arrows on Adas. Demitre treated the arrows reserved only for Adas with the root of *belladonna,* a highly poisonous plant. The *medicus* had tested the centurion's tolerance of the poison after he cauterized his hand. Adas would act terrified before the entire legion when he hallucinated, destroying any possibility of favorable support.

Demitre cautioned Valentius. "Use both edges of the dagger, but sparingly. Make two cuts, but no more than three inches long. This is important. If the poison builds up too quickly, it will stop his heart. You want him to receive very small amounts, gradually, to maximize the hallucinations. With every arrow, a tiny amount of poison goes to work. You want the arrows to kill him, not the poison. Even though the poison would kill him eventually if the arrows didn't."

Valentius waved Demitre off impatiently. "I'm not an idiot! You haven't forgotten my experience with *belladonna*, have you?" Demitre did not respond. Valentius left to give instructions to his *sagittarii* and to announce who he had selected to execute Longinus.

At Valentius's suggestion, the *sagittarius* named Porcius started a wager on who would be selected to execute Centurion Longinus. Valentius knew no one would bet on Porcius. To legitimize the wager, Porcius bet heavily on other men. Valentius would then select Porcius as the winner and they would split the proceeds.

Valentius waved the sixteen men in closer. "You are my best *sagittarii*, but this competition will challenge your skills. Forget Herod's rules. You will do precisely as I say. You must use *as many* arrows as possible to kill your target. Aim for non-lethal areas. When the target can no longer stand, move up as close as you want, but then each arrow will count as three. The sooner you drop your target without killing him, the higher your count will go. If there is more than one winner, you will split the prize evenly. Herod will announce the winner according to his rules, but I will dispense the prize according to my rules. If *all* of you follow my instructions, without complaint, each of you will be promoted in rank and pay."

Despite this promise, the men were uneasy. Roman punishment was usually cruel and degrading, so they didn't question the morality of such a contest. However, to ignore the rules Herod had specifically approved was another matter. Valentius expected their hesitation.

"The prize will be a full year's wages. Are we in agreement?" A year's pay for one day's work promptly removed their reluctance.

"I know you've been waiting to hear who will be selected to execute Longinus." With a flourish, Valentius pointed at his favorite *sagittarius*. "Porcius, you are the most skilled. I honor you with the task of dispatching the centurion."

"Thank you for this unexpected reward, Sir. May I request the use of my favorite bow?"

"Granted. You shall have it, Porcius."

During this exchange, the soldiers watched a man named Thracius to see his reaction. Most of them had bet on him since he was actually the most skilled of the *sagittarii*. However, Thracius refused to grovel for the centurion's praise, and if praised, showed no appreciation. Valentius resented his autonomy. As usual, Thracius remained unperturbed.

Thracius was suspicious of the contradictory instructions and decided to defy Valentius. He saw the prize and promotions as bribes to entice their cooperation. Also, Herod would surely retaliate if he found out that Valentius had circumvented the rules. Thracius would obey the lawful order to execute a soldier, but he would not deny the dignity of the man.

Porcius approached Thracius. "You expected to be chosen, didn't you? I'm going to win the prize money, too. So much for your long hours of practice." Thracius did not respond.

Two *sagittarii* overheard. One said, "Apparently, Porcius, the Pigman needs his favorite bow. There must be enchanted skill in that bow since there's none in the man."

The other man scoffed, "Maybe there is. Let's find out. How good would Pigman be without it? An 'adjustment' to his bow would tell us." The two men had bet on Thracius. A little revenge might compensate their loss. They smiled in anticipation.

The ladder dropped into the pit. The soldiers climbed up. They were ordered to remove their belts, tunics and, *caligae*. Being barefoot deleted their status as soldiers and equated them with the lowest of the impoverished. Each man was given a pair of ankle-length, red-dyed *bracae*, pants usually worn by women for horseback riding. Considered effeminate garments, this was a graphic insult to the men. After the prisoners changed their clothing, their wrists were bound in front and tethered to a lead rope. Lucius was the last man. It was then they learned of the contest. The prisoners grumbled in dismay.

"Lucius, I need to speak with you," said a man who had slipped into the Pit House. "I am Thracius, one of the *sagittarii*. Tell the others they must stay on their feet as long as possible." He whispered the details in Lucius's ear. As the prisoners were led from the Antonia, each one repeated Thracius's warning to the man in front of him.

Herod's Theater was a large, open-air showcase built of limestone. It had three half-moon tiers with multiple rows of stair-stepped seating. There was a raised platform in the center of the lowest tier, called the portico, which was reserved for dignitaries. There was a large central stage built of wood planks supported by six-foot, wooden posts with trap doors for actors and props to either appear or disappear. A thirty-foot backdrop, the only straight-line construction in the complex, had towers at either end which connected to the tiers. There was a pit between the front of the stage and the portico. Twenty slaves with kettle drums stood in the pit with their overseer.

When the convicted legionaries arrived at the theater, every row of seating was packed to capacity. Seated at the portico was King Herod, his aide Blastus who was holding a number of documents, High Priest Caiaphas, the chief priests, and a few temple guards. Tribune Salvitto and the ten *cohors* centurions, including Valentius, were present.

The condemned legionaries were led to the back of the stage facing the spectators. Their wrists were unbound and retied to ropes attached to iron rings staked every five feet in a line parallel to the audience. Only the last spot remained empty. When Adas was led in, Valentius wanted all eyes on him.

Much to Valentius's surprise, the effort to disgrace the men with the red-colored *bracae* backfired. When the condemned men appeared, an angry buzz erupted. Hecklers called for Valentius to be forced to wear *bracae*, among other suggestions. Despite the success of Valentius's plans, one detail had slipped out of his control. *Optio* Victorius overheard Octavean telling Salvitto about the drugged wine delivered by Demitre. News of the betrayal spread quickly among the soldiers, even as they sat in the theater.

Outside Adas's quarters, a slave presented a garment and a rope to the guard. They protested when they saw the *bracae*, but one of them knocked on the door and handed the garment to Nikolaus.

Nikolaus shook out the rust-colored item. "These are for women!"

"Valentius is symbolically disavowing my status. Perhaps he doesn't understand there is more to being a centurion than the clothes."

There was a knock and Serapio entered. His face was lined with grief, but his voice was calm. "The tribune gave me permission to walk with you, Adas. Nikolaus, I will stay with you." Serapio frowned at the *bracae*. "I heard Peter quote from a Psalm once, '*The wicked plots against the just. . .to slay those who are of upright conduct. Their sword shall enter their own heart, and their bows shall be broken.*' Perhaps that will happen today."

There was another knock and the door opened. "Sir!" said a guard. "We have orders to escort you to the Theater of Herod the Great."

"What are your names?" Adas asked.

The first legionary answered. "I am Zaphnath, an Egyptian, and this is Otho."

In Egyptian, Adas said, "I am sure you were told to bring me bound. Where is the rope? I will not have you punished on my account."

"Sir, it is gone. You saved my brother's life. Paaneah was bleeding to death. His own centurion gave him up for dead. You did not. You spoke in our tongue which calmed him. Your surgery saved his life. Paaneah is the only family I have left." Zaphnath raised his head defiantly. "I *will not* drag you through the streets like a runaway slave! You are the Wolf."

"You honor me. Otho, do you agree to this?" Otho nodded emphatically.

"Sir, he is mute," explained Zaphnath. "A Scythian cut out his tongue."

By trusting him to remain in their custody, the guards were risking their lives. Adas would not belittle their courage by refusing their offer. He walked down the lane with Nikolaus and Serapio on either side. Zaphnath and Otho followed behind them.

Not wanting to make their farewell more painful when they reached the theater, Serapio steered Nikolaus toward the tiers. With grim acceptance, Serapio nodded once at Adas. Nikolaus looked back when Serapio pulled him away.

When the overseer saw Adas, he signaled to the slaves. They beat their drums in a steady rhythm. The soldiers of the 10th *Legio* saw Adas walking unrestrained. They understood the significance of the guards' trust and the honorable presentation. They stamped their feet and began a low chant. "*Macte! Macte! Macte!*" Their chant of, "*Bravo!*" overpowered the beating of the drums. Adas raised his right hand in recognition of their respect. He walked up the steps of the stage to the last space. Lucius stood next to him.

Valentius vaulted out of his seat. "I ordered them to bring him bound and tethered! I will see them flogged for their disobedience!"

"No, you will not," declared Salvitto. "Longinus is a centurion, which gives him the right to present with honor. The legionaries have the right to risk their lives by trusting his honor." Valentius curled a lip and stiffly took his seat. "Centurion, if you are unaware of this law, perhaps you need to be tutored—in the pit." Valentius apologized.

When Adas took his place in line, the drums stopped. A hush fell over the men. A whistle sounded. Every soldier simultaneously stood to attention. Five thousand men raised their right fists to their chests and chanted in unison. "*Salve Lupus Legatus!*" The booming roar of their salute, "Hail the Wolf Commander!" thundered across the city.

Adas was overwhelmed at their show of respect. He knelt on one knee and lowered his head. He raised his right fist to his chest. He came to his feet, threw his hands into the air and shouted, "*Antonia militis! Semper fortis! Semper honorabile! Semper fidelis!* Soldiers of the Antonia! Always brave! Always honorable! Always loyal!"

Zaphnath and Otho faced Adas. Zaphnath said, "Centurion, we are ordered to tie you to the rings. We beg your forgiveness."

"There is nothing to forgive. Obey your orders."

The escort guards picked up the hemp ropes to tie Adas's wrists. Otho jerked his hand from the rope and found blood on his finger. He looked at the rope more closely. Small thorns were woven into the hemp. Otho looked at Adas apologetically.

"Otho, obey your orders."

Rebellion blazed in the man's eyes as he pulled his dagger from his belt. He pressed the rope to the stage floor and scraped it with the blade, pulling some of the thorns out. Zaphnath did the same. Again, Valentius started from his chair to protest.

"*Sit!*" Salvitto snapped. Valentius sat down. The men guessed what the guards were doing and shouted encouragement, but they grew quiet after the soldiers tied Adas to the rings.

King Herod turned to Valentius. "Well, Felix, did you enjoy their salute to the centurion? I certainly did. I am surprised, however, to see these *Roman* soldiers clothed like prisoners-of-war, in pants, no less." Valentius did not miss Herod's insult. A prestigious man like Herod would only call a slave by his *praenomen* in public.

A slave carrying a pitcher and a cup stepped up on the stage. He stopped at each man and gave him a full cup to drink. The slave reached Lucius, but he shook his head to refuse. The slave whispered something. When he held the cup up again, Lucius drank it. The slave stepped over to Adas and poured the last cup.

"What happens if I don't drink it?"

"Nikolaus will be beaten."

"I see. What did you tell Octavean?"

"His mother would be arrested. That is what I was told to say."

"By Valentius?"

"No, Demitre." The slave held the cup and Adas drank it.

Valentius addressed Herod. "Should I remove the centurion's bandage after I explain the rules of the contest? The men might think it hides a shield."

"I suspect they *hope* the bandage hides a shield. But go. Present my rules of play."

This was Valentius's moment of glory and he savored it. Valentius swaggered to the stage and bellowed, "King Herod has decreed the *sagittarius* who kills his 'target' with the fewest arrows, wins! If a prisoner is unable to stand, the distance requirement is waived, but each arrow will then count as three. Soldiers of the Antonia, do you approve?" He waited for the men to cheer, but there was only silence. Taken aback, Valentius tried to hide his embarrassment. He turned to strut in front of the condemned until he stood in front of Adas. "So, Longinus, I understand your father is getting married today on his bride's birthday, no less. It's such a shame you won't be there." Valentius grinned at his reaction.

Adas's stomach twisted. Nikolaus had followed orders a bit too well.

"Your precious pet betrayed you. He gave you up, with barely a slap." Valentius took on a taunting pout. "Demitre was so disappointed. He had hoped to use a little coercion."

Hoping to harm Nikolaus ignited his anger. "Is the wedding today? I had forgotten. I wonder if my father will notice I'm not there."

Valentius's satisfied sneer faded. He angrily thrust his dagger under Adas's bandage and ripped the linen. He rotated the dagger to use the other edge. He slid the weapon under the shoulder bandaging. With clenched teeth, Adas silently endured the pain. Again, Valentius ripped the linen. He threw it down and eyed the centurion triumphantly.

"Now that is quite a sight! Octavean got you *good!* Wish I could have been there."

"So do I. I would have shackled you to the wall with him! *That* would have been quite a sight. The mighty lion chained with his cringing mongrel!"

"You dare to insult *me*?" Valentius stepped behind Adas and pressed the dagger against his right shoulder blade. The men saw Adas react as Valentius sliced downward across his back. The soldiers leaped to their feet, shouting accusations of cowardice at Valentius.

The pain dropped Adas to a knee. The image of Yeshua on the cross sprang into his mind. He had inflicted much worse pain on Yeshua. Adas struggled to his feet and raised his head. The men cheered his courage.

Valentius stepped in front of Adas. "What is this? You accept my torment like a beaten animal. You're worse than Falto, the little weasel." He set the flat of his dagger against Adas's hip to clean it on the *bracae*. He grinned with satisfaction despite the jeers from the soldiers. His mocking expression changed to calculation. "Tell me. Does it still hurt?"

Adas blinked in surprise. The pain was fading. "You've drugged us again, haven't you?" He looked at the cuts on his chest. "You wanted to see if it has taken effect."

"You were the last one to drink it. I had to be sure it's working. How clever of you to figure it out. But I also wanted to give you an extra treat." He waved his dagger in the air. "There's poison on this. Soon you'll be seeing monsters, *again*. Demitre tested it on you after he cauterized your hand. You don't even remember drinking it, do you? He watched as you slept. You cried out like a terrified child. And soon you'll be screaming in front of all these men. Won't that be entertaining? I think it will. I saw the monsters once. It was horrifying. You're going to wish Octavean killed you when he had the chance."

Chapter 31

———— ⊙⊚⊙ ————

The soldiers erupted with anger when Valentius raised the dagger again. "*Canis Ignavus! Canis Ignavus!*" The soldiers chanted as they pumped their fists in the air. "*Cowardly Dog!*" They repeated over and over.

"Valentius, that's enough!" Tribune Salvitto shouted. "Get over here!" Valentius sheathed his dagger, and gave Adas a last look of hatred before he stalked off the stage.

Despite the severity of his injuries, the pain subsided quickly, and an odd sensation took its place. The sunlight seemed to brighten, hurting his eyes. His vision blurred, but then corrected itself. His mouth began to feel dry. His heart rate quickened.

Lucius looked over at him. "Centurion, I was a fool for not trusting you. If I had helped, we wouldn't be here, and Valentius would be missing his head by now."

"Don't call me centurion. Titles are meaningless now. And this is not your fault."

"Oh, but it is!"

Several slaves stepped onto the stage to place bows with bundles of arrows in front of each prisoner. The men's angry reaction to the arrows pleased Valentius. The bundles were tied with white string, except the one for Adas was black. The arrows had single, tear-drop-shaped, copper blades instead of the bronze, three-bladed, barbed arrowheads usually used for killing. Since the copper blades caused little damage, it would require many arrows to kill. No barbs made these arrows well suited for target practice, which further dehumanized the prisoners.

The king rose to his feet to face the soldiers. The construction of the theater enabled sound to carry to the top tiers from the portico or the stage. Valentius squirmed in his chair until Herod gestured for him to stand and face the audience. Herod addressed the five thousand as if he were the central actor in a play.

"Felix, tell me! Who do you think released Simon Peter?"

"It is obvious isn't it, Your Excellency? Longinus is a known sympathizer of the Way. He even carved a cross into his hand after he crucified the Nazarene. Then he begged my slave to burn his hand with the cauterizing rod, declaring he deserved to suffer. His misguided guilt proves his disloyalty to Rome since he was ordered to execute a lawfully convicted criminal."

"I'd like to see this cross for myself." Herod ordered Adas's escort guards to bring him. "Show me this cross on your hand, Centurion." Adas raised his hand. "Why did you mark yourself with the symbol of shame?"

"Your Excellency, I bear this cross because I *am* ashamed. I put this mark as a reminder to never execute an Innocent, again."

"Yeshua was convicted of blasphemy."

"It is only blasphemy if his claim is false. Yeshua was innocent!" The soldiers grumbled among themselves, not liking his answer.

"You have been deceived! Yeshua was a fraud. Tell me, how badly do you want to live, Centurion Longinus? I will spare your life if you renounce Yeshua as a liar and a blasphemer!"

The men cheered at the offer. Valentius turned ashen. High Priest Caiaphas frowned.

"My life is not worth supporting such a monumental lie! You would spare my life so I could live in cowardice! I will only swear to the truth. Yeshua is the Truth! He is and always has been *the Son of God!*" The spectators groaned. Valentius sighed with relief.

"I give you one other option, Centurion." Herod noted how quickly Valentius stiffened. "I will allow your guilt be passed to a slave. The slave will die in your place and you will live. Choose a slave and I will grant it."

Nikolaus started to stand up. Serapio clapped a hand on his shoulder. "No, Nikolaus. Didn't you hear what he just said? He will not live in cowardice."

"King Herod, you offer too late," Adas answered. "Yeshua has already taken my place. He died to pay the penalty for the sin of all humanity—including yours."

"You reject my mercy!" the king gestured angrily. "Go to your death then!"

When Adas turned his back, the men saw the laceration Valentius had inflicted. They grumbled in protest. Herod pointed a finger at Valentius. "You—take that arrogant smirk from your face. You will get your wish because the centurion will die today. Even though his loyalty is misguided, compared to him, you are nothing more than a sniveling hyena. What did Longinus say before you slashed him? I saw your anger. Whatever he said must have cut *you* deeper."

Desperate to save face, Valentius exclaimed, "Your Excellency, by his own admission, Longinus is a sympathizer. It is clear he released Simon Peter!"

"Really? Wouldn't it be smarter to arrange an escape so he would *not* get executed?"

"Your Excellency, Longinus refused your pardon. He would willingly sacrifice his life to save a follower of The Way. Being in Holding would guarantee he could help him escape."

Herod snorted. "How? Do you think the other fifteen men would happily hold the door open so *they* could be executed? If your accusation were true, Longinus would not have reprimanded them for drinking the wine. In fact, *he* would have supplied the wine. When they fought, Longinus would have killed Octavean to eliminate a witness. Furthermore, the prisoner's shackles were found unlocked, not broken. All the keys have been accounted for, even yours, Felix. Must I remind you how no one assigned to guard duty has keys? No one *inside* Holding could free the prisoner without keys. The guards at the doors were unconscious, and they stay *inside* the outer door at night. Meaning, someone would need a cohort centurion's key to enter the outer door. Yet when the morning shift came on duty, the doors were standing wide open. Longinus and his men were still there, *unconscious*. Apparently, they were *that* eager to be executed. No, Longinus did not free the prisoner. It had to be someone with a shackle key and a door key, like yours. By the way, did you thank Longinus for saving your life when he stopped Octavean from killing the prisoner?"

Valentius nervously licked his lips. "But Your Excellency, he didn't fight Octavean to save anyone's life. Octavean challenged him because Longinus falsely accused him of assault. I have a letter of confession written by Longinus."

"Ah, so they hate each other?"

"They do, King Herod. They disregarded their duty so they could settle the score."

"You swore to me that you personally selected these men. Did you not tell me they were the 'best soldiers for the job?' I believe those were your words. If they hated each other, why did you assign them together to guard my most valuable prisoner? Perhaps you were *hoping* they would fight. Tell me, where did this alleged assault occur?"

Valentius remembered too late he had sent Adas to guard Yeshua's tomb without authorization. "Your Excellency. . .I. . .perhaps I. . ."

"Can't think of the right answer? Did it happen at Yeshua's tomb? Did Longinus make the accusation because it was true? In fact, three legionaries assaulted him, not just Octavean. The same three legionaries are up on the stage. All three are about to die, conveniently for you, since you covered up their crime. Why would you do that? Did you conceal the crime because you assigned them to guard the Nazarene's tomb without orders?" Herod waved a dismissive hand. "Don't bother to answer. Octavean had many interesting things to tell me. He said you got him addicted to opium so you could force him to spy on Longinus. You encouraged the legionary's insubordination against Longinus." Herod gestured at Lucius. "He confessed attacking Longinus. Furthermore, he said he confessed it to you!"

"He's lying! None of it's true!"

"It is *precisely* true! You've been abusing my soldiers, Felix—assigning imaginary orders, instigating insubordination, extorting money, ignoring protocol, and who knows what else. I want this apology Centurion Longinus wrote, since it smacks of *your* guilt."

"It-it's gone missing, Your Excellency. My slave destroyed some old documents and it may have been mixed in."

"*Who released the prisoner, Felix?*" Herod pointed a finger in Valentius's face. "Longinus did not! Let me present a scenario. A centurion has a problem with certain soldiers and wants to get rid of them. Wouldn't it be clever to have me do the dirty work? This centurion assigns all these soldiers to guard a high profile prisoner. When the guards are drugged, he takes the prisoner. He kills the prisoner, and disposes of the body, which would explain why we can't find him. Then the pesky soldiers get executed." Herod gestured at the condemned men. "All the problems gone."

The king held up a finger. "Let's examine possible motives. I imagine owing a lot of money to some of them would be a good reason to kill them. Or perhaps the scheming centurion was fined when he threw eight of them in the pit even though they performed their duties, a bit creatively, yes, but within bounds. Perhaps the centurion demanded these same soldiers reimburse him to cover his fine. This is what they get for refusing. However, this doesn't explain why you assigned Longinus to guard my prisoner. I found no evidence of conflict, monetary, or otherwise." Herod tapped his lips with his forefinger, a favorite gesture. "Do you have a son?"

Taken aback by the abrupt question, Valentius sputtered, "N-no, I-I do not."

"*Did* you have a son?"

Valentius sensed a trap. Herod must not know what happened to Aurelius. Fortunately, his son had legally changed his name.

"No, my wife never conceived. We had no children."

"What was your wife's name?"

"Her name?" Valentius gulped. Salvitto had that information. "Her name was Julia Darcinus Julius, Your Excellency."

Herod snapped his fingers at Blastus. "Now how can a man forget his own son, Felix?" The aide handed a document to the king. "My very competent manager found a birth decree of a male child named Aurelius Pomponius Julius. Normally, Blastus would not have given it a second glance, but the parents' names caught his eye. His mother is Julia Darcinus Julius *Valentius* and the name of the father is Felix Pomponius *Valentius*. It's interesting that your son took his mother's clan name. I wonder why?"

"Your Excellency, there are many men with the same name as mine, married to a woman with the same name as my Julia."

Herod snapped his fingers at Blastus. The man handed him another document. "Here is a transfer for Centurion Aurelius Pomponius Julius, from Rome, to the Antonia, dated two years ago. It has your seal, Felix. Is there another cohort centurion named Felix Pomponius Valentius here at The Antonia?"

"No."

The king studied the paper. "Here's an interesting notation. It says you instigated this transfer, but he tried to cancel it! Why would you want this particular centurion at the Antonia so badly if he were not your son? Why did he try to avoid coming here?"

"Your Excellency, you know it is not proper for centurions of the same family to serve at the same fortress. I would never go against regulations."

"So, now you admit that Aurelius was in fact your son? You lied to me."

"Your Excellency, it was a complicated situation. I was being too literal. Yes, he was my son. I did not mean to mislead you."

"You *absolutely* meant to mislead me. But, let's move on. Centurion Julius only had to reveal he was your son to nullify the transfer, yet he did not. I think he didn't want to dirty his reputation by claiming a scandalized, demoted soldier as his father. You were court-martialed and demoted. Is that why he had his name legally changed?"

Fear wrenched Valentius. He felt for a vial of opium in his coin pouch. None was there. He wiped at his watering eyes and sweaty brow.

"Oh my, Felix, are you feeling ill?"

"I'm fine, Your Excellency. If Aurelius was assigned to the Antonia, why isn't he here?" He hoped the question would distract from his lying.

Herod snapped his fingers and received another document. "It's amusing you should ask since Aurelius *is* here, in a manner of speaking. This is a request by Centurion Julius to remain in Rome, *instead* of coming here. Right under 'Request denied' is the stamp of your seal ring. You knew your son didn't want to come here, but you forced him. He had to comply or face execution. Did I mention he traveled in a *navis* belonging to my fleet? *The Scarlet Jade*."

Blastus handed him the next document. "And here's a document describing how the voyage ended. This is a copy of the original order to cremate the remains of Centurion Julius. Cause of death is listed as drowning when a storm sunk *The Scarlet Jade*. Apparently, his body washed ashore, and was retrieved by the surviving crew. You must have your son's ashes since this copy was signed with your seal ring. You set the tragic death of your own son in motion by forcing him to come here. He was fated to die, no matter what he did. A week after you got the news. . .oh, I'm being insensitive. I am so sorry for your loss." Herod pursed his lips in mock sympathy. "A week earlier you found a letter on Tribune Salvitto's desk. Do you remember?"

"No, Your Excellency, I don't remember."

"Well, then, let me refresh your excessively flawed memory because Tribune Salvitto came in his office and found you reading it."

Blastus gave Herod the letter. "Here it is dated a little over two years ago, from *Consul* Clovius Longinus requesting that his newly titled son, Centurion Clovius Longinus, be placed at the Antonia. The centurion position was available because of the death of your son. What a shock it must have been for you to have your son *replaced* by this underage, undeserving centurion, by request of this arrogant politician! Now tell me, Felix, didn't you burn with bitterness to see *Consul* Longinus's son here, very much alive, while your son's ashes sit in an urn? How monumentally unfair! Aurelius has been here all along. Longinus replaced a ghost."

Valentius's face turned gray.

"If your son couldn't live, then Longinus's son shouldn't live either! Am I close?" Herod knew this was a weak motive, but he wanted to see Valentius's reaction. To his surprise, Valentius squared his shoulders. Anger crossed his face so undeniably it erased all traces of fear.

"How did *Consul* Longinus know the Antonia needed a centurion unless he . . .? His lips compressed into a thin line.

"By the gods! Do you think Longinus *created* the vacancy? That he had your son killed? You risked taking responsibility for Simon Peter to get these men executed, especially Longinus. This contest is about revenge. You think the *consul* had your son murdered."

"No, Your Excellency! That's ridiculous! I never thought such a thing. I only wonder how *Consul* Longinus knew there was a vacancy so quickly after Aurelius's death. And I do not personally have anything against Centurion Longinus or the others! Yet, you think I had something to do with Simon Peter's escape. In truth, there is no proof I was ever in Holding. I couldn't release him if I was never there."

Herod flashed a wicked smile. "Thank you for reminding me of that fact. After Longinus bested Octavean, he shackled him to the wall. Octavean told me he was, indeed, shackled. So how is it possible the morning shift found Octavean *not shackled?* No one on duty in Holding has shackle keys. The shackles of both Octavean and Simon Peter were not broken. They were unlocked! An outside intruder, caring only about the prisoner, would have left Octavean shackled. He would not want to set the mighty Lion free. Only someone with a vested interest in *appearances* would have unshackled Octavean."

"It wasn't me! Why would I unlock Octavean's chains?"

"I don't care why! But it proves *you* were in there. No other intruder would have even glanced at Octavean. Whatever your reason, you were the only one at the Antonia with keys *and* sixteen motives."

"I'm not the one who lost the prisoner!"

"I agree. You're not the one who lost him. But you are the one who found him *and killed him.* Where did you bury his body?"

Valentius gulped for air as he stared wide-eyed at his accuser.

King Herod addressed Adas. "Centurion Longinus, tell me, do you think Felix freed the prisoner from Holding?"

Adas felt a palpable tension descend over the theater. If he said 'yes' it would strengthen the case against Valentius, but it would be a lie. Adas declared in front of Nikolaus an angel released Peter, and Nikolaus was questioned by Herod. Had he told the truth as willingly as he had when Valentius interrogated him? Adas knew the only power he had left was the truth.

"I believe he intended to do so, but—*No!* I do not." The men standing with him groaned with disappointment as did the soldiers in the stands. Lucius threw him a disgruntled glare.

The king gestured at Adas. "That is the sound of truth! I already knew what his answer should be. He did *not* lie to me, even though it would have been to his advantage. I wanted to test Centurion Longinus. He has passed the test. It appears Longinus has saved you once again, Felix. Someone overheard him saying that a stranger took Simon Peter from Holding."

Valentius went slack with relief. "Thank you, Your Excellency. You are most gracious to acknowledge my innocence."

"No, you did not release the prisoner." Herod scanned the men, making sure he had their full attention. "*But your keys did!* Who did you bribe to smuggle the prisoner out of a locked room with sixteen guards? Past the guard towers! Out of the fortress gates! *Who was he?* Was Longinus asleep when you crept into Holding to make sure the prisoner was gone? Is that when you unshackled Octavean? Again, I ask you, where did your accomplice bury Simon Peter's body? Did you do it yourself? Did you dump it in the crematory, knowing the temple guards would not step foot in such an abomination. I have soldiers looking there now." Valentius was paralyzed with confusion.

The king rose to his feet and addressed the soldiers. "Centurion Longinus actually saw a man, who he did not recognize, take the prisoner out. Yet, he was too injured to stop him. Still, he could have claimed it was Valentius, but he did not. Because Centurion Longinus spoke the truth, I will reward his honesty by reinstating the pensions of the condemned. The heir you name today will receive your retirement claim, in full. The claim letters will be distributed by Tribune Salvitto." Valentius's jaw dropped in shock. He had just lost access to the pensions.

"*Primus dispensator!* Go write down the heirs for each of them."

A man holding a tablet, accompanied by an assistant *dispensator,* stepped down from the first tier. It was the same assistant *dispensator* Demitre planned to murder once they had the forged pension claims. The two men went to Adas first. The chief accountant requested, "Centurion, Sir, state your heir, the relationship of your heir, and the address of your heir."

"Regulus Novius Serapio. He is my. . .guardian." The chief accountant nodded approval and his assistant wrote it down. They already knew Serapio's address.

The men went to Lucius. He responded, "Sevina Major Sevinus Octavean. My mother."

The head accountant again nodded approval. "It is good of you to provide for your mother. Our mothers rarely get the reward they deserve."

"No, they don't. And neither will mine. I leave my pension to her, in spite of what she deserves. Use the new address she filed with you." The assistant frowned and started to say something, but the head accountant had already moved to the next man.

Lucius looked at Adas. "Thank you. My mother desperately needs this money, but I do this more for me, than for her. Centurion, if only I had listened to you."

"Don't call me centurion, Lucius, and again, this is not your fault. Valentius did not release Simon Peter. A man similar to the one at Yeshua's tomb walked him out. I saw it happen. I think they are angels of God."

"I don't care how he got out. If I had stood with you, the worst that could have happened would be to die with honor. Instead, as I have before, I played into the hand of my enemy."

Adas thought of Nikolaus. He was troubled Nikolaus didn't tell him everything Herod asked him, but there must have been a good reason. Adas deeply regretted he would not be able to tell Nikolaus he understood.

Tribune Salvitto addressed Herod. "Your Excellency, as you have undeniably proven, these men were unwitting pawns. Surely that is sufficient reason to spare their lives."

"On the contrary, it makes their guilt worse than ever. Were they forced to drink the wine? *No!* They did so willingly, and quickly. They didn't wait until Longinus came on duty, but rather took the word of a slave. Did they perform their sworn duties efficiently? Again, *No!* They knew Peter had escaped from the common prison. They knew I wanted him to answer for his blasphemy. Did any of them show responsibility? No, they are guilty of disregarding their duty."

Salvitto persisted. "Longinus and Octavean did not drink the wine."

"Yet they chose to fight each other. They might as well have been drunk like the rest because they were incapacitated by their injuries. End result—escaped prisoner!"

"It is true they fought, but Longinus did so to defend the prisoner's life."

"Did Longinus kill Octavean? No." Herod sneered with disgust. "Unprovoked, Octavean attacked him, yet Longinus spared his life."

"There was no point in killing Octavean since. . ."

"But there was a point—the point of the legionary's dagger! What if Octavean had killed Longinus, and *then* Simon Peter? With no witnesses, Octavean could have claimed any justification. The results? Only Valentius would be executed, and Jerusalem would riot, thinking I ordered the Galilean's murder while in my custody. Do you think Emperor Gaius would be pleased with me? And you would have to contain the riot. Would *you* be pleased?

Salvitto looked away in defeat. "No, Your Excellency."

Herod gestured at the four squads. "Every one of them deserves to die for the public humiliation they have caused me—and to uphold Roman law."

Salvitto brushed caution aside. "I submit to Roman law, but making their executions a contest makes a mockery of the law. Giving a prize to an executioner is. . ."

"Ah, yes, the prize!" Herod turned toward Valentius. "Felix, I have decided to take your suggestion. The prize will, indeed, equal a year's salary. In fact, I have decided it will be the full year's salary of a *cohors* centurion. I will have the gold delivered to you today."

"A *cohors* centurion earns forty times as much as a legionary! That is very generous of you, Your Excellency." Valentius smiled. All was not lost, after all.

"I am going to enjoy this contest, so very, very much," declared Herod. He had not missed the glint of greed in the centurion's eyes.

Chapter 32

As Adas struggled to endure, euphoria from the opium swept over him. It numbed his senses, but his other symptoms weren't caused by the opium. His heart was racing, he had stopped sweating, and his mouth was almost too dry to swallow. He shook his head to clear his vision, but it didn't help.

The slaves beat their drums. The *sagittarii* entered the stage and formed a line in front of the prisoners. The legion chanted. "*Nullus Honor! No Honor!*" The *sagittarii* did not expect the hostility. The first *sagittarius* sounded a command. Each man strung his bow. Leaving the weapons on the stage, they exited to reform a line in the pit between the stage and the portico. Only the first man remained on the stage. King Herod stood to give the command for the contest to begin.

Adas called to him. "Your Excellency, do I have the right to speak?" The king waved a hand for him to proceed. He was curious at what the centurion would say.

"Roman law states that any soldier guarding a prisoner who escapes must be put to death. I submit, King Herod, I alone should bear this responsibility. The men had no reason to refuse the wine given to them by the slave, Demitre. However, I was not there to caution them. Knowing we held a high-priority prisoner, I should have been there much earlier."

Salvitto bowed his head in guilt. Summoning Adas to his office had delayed him long enough for the men to drink the wine, making the tribune an unintentional co-conspirator.

Adas continued, "I should have acted on my suspicions sooner, especially after Octavean shared his concerns. I take full responsibility. Therefore, only I should pay the consequences."

The condemned soldiers looked at Adas with unexpected hope. A murmur rose from the men in the stands. Serapio glanced over at Nikolaus, who had remained quiet up to now. Hearing Adas condemn himself was too much. Nikolaus lowered his head to his hands.

Herod studied the centurion. "You suggest I break precedence with Roman law?"

"Your Excellency, there are mitigating circumstances. You asked me if I believe Valentius smuggled the prisoner out and I said, 'No' which is true. Simon Peter did not escape. God *released* him from the Antonia just as God *released* him from the common prison!"

"Are you saying God freed the prisoner, a known blasphemer?"

"Who could materialize inside a locked room? Who could open shackles and locked doors without a touch? An angel of God did those things. I saw it happen. If you kill these men, who had no power to act—sober or drunk—you expect the impossible. Roman law states a man may stand in for a convicted offender. I accept my death. I offer myself in exchange for theirs. Let these men live to serve you as you command."

Lucius stared at Adas in amazement. He knew Herod would never let them go, but that was not the point. The fact that Adas offered to take his place meant everything. Just as his father had sacrificed himself for his needs, Adas was making the same offer. Rufino had offered himself out of love for his own son, but the centurion made this offer for men who had sought to kill him. Lucius burned with regret. A coughing fit seized him, but gradually subsided.

A low rumble rose from the five thousand soldiers as the king shouted, "I commend the courage of Centurion Longinus! He truly honors the title. But *you* expect the impossible, Longinus, not me. A convicted criminal can be pardoned if an *innocent* man takes his place. By your own admission you are equally guilty." Herod clapped his hands together. "Enough of this! Proceed with the executions!" He sat down amid a groan of frustration from the spectators. Adas bowed his head.

Valentius signaled for the *sagittarii* to begin. The first man stepped to the marked line twenty paces from the first prisoner, Laelius, who had observed the arrest of Yeshua. The *sagittarius* pulled the bowstring. The slaves beat the drums in unison. The man took aim and let go. The drummers stopped. The first arrow hit Laelius in the side. He staggered back as much as the ropes allowed. He gazed at the arrow with a blank expression.

King Herod frowned. "What is the matter with him? Does he not feel the arrow?" He narrowed his eyes at Valentius. "What was in that drink the slave gave them?"

"Only watered down wine, Your Excellency! Giving drink before an execution is a small gesture of mercy, is it not? If anyone tampered with the wine it was without my knowledge."

"Are you suggesting that someone did, indeed, tamper with it? You seem to be eager to share your wine, Felix. Why is that?"

"I haven't done anything that is not allowed, Your Excellency."

"Perhaps. Perhaps not. We shall see."

After many more arrows, Laelius lay dead on the stage. Herod's *medicus* checked for life. The *medicus* drew his hand across his throat. The *sagittarius* left the stage taking his bow and the remaining arrows. A slave held up a large slate with XIII written in chalk. The last two arrows had counted as six.

Hektor was next. He eyed his executioner as the man came up the steps and faced him. Hektor called out, "*Sagittarius,* let's make a wager just between the two of us. I bet you will *lose* this contest. Since money is a useless option, I call on the Furies. Eternal torment is our wager. If you lose, the Furies will torment you for eternity! If you win, the Furies can have me."

Before the man could respond, a soldier cried out, "He accepts!" The other men roared with laughter. The soldier was trapped. If he refused to accept the bet, his fellow soldiers would endlessly ridicule his cowardice. If he accepted, his fate could be in the clawed hands of the red-eyed, snake-haired creatures of revenge.

The *sagittarius* did his best, but Hektor stayed on his feet. Ever the gambler, he determined the odds of where the arrows would land, how long the man took aim. Hektor leaned to the right. He counted the seconds before the tenth arrow was released. At a precise moment, he shifted. It was a lethal hit. When the *medicus* declared him dead, the *sagittarius* knew he had lost the bet. The Furies would find him in this world and in Hades. He turned to face Valentius. Silent anticipation settled over the men. The *sagittarius* set his bow down, and called to Valentius. He slapped a hand over his upper arm and raised his fist. The soldiers exploded with laughter.

The king chuckled. "My, my, such vile disrespect aimed at you, Felix."

Valentius bit back his anger. He would see the man punished for his insolence.

The next executioner took his place in front of the third prisoner. Lucius turned his attention to Adas. "Why were you willing to die for us? I've tried to kill you twice. I was going to murder you and Hektor to save myself. Why would you stand in for me?"

"Because Yeshua stood in for me. I will go to him when I die. Yeshua stood in for you as well. For everyone. It's not too late for you to go to him today."

"You are talking about the Son of the Hebrew God. What are we to God?"

"We are *everything* to God, Lucius. We are his creation. We killed Yeshua. You saw him die, yet Sunday morning I saw him very much alive with his wounds completely healed!" Adas told Lucius stories about Yeshua. He listened to distract himself from the approach of death.

The man next to Hektor, Hilarius, lay dead on the stage, pierced with more arrows than Laelius or Hektor. The slave held up the slate with XIV chalked on it. It was obvious the *sagittarii* were ignoring Herod's rules. Every time a *sagittarius* pulled back his bow, the drums would sound, but the men began to chant to overpower the monotonous beat.

Lucius focused on Adas. "How can I know what you say is true? You said you saw the Nazarene alive, but I didn't. How can I believe without proof?"

"The same way all generations will believe. They will believe without seeing what we have seen. There is proof in everything God has created. I think, in time, continuing discoveries will reveal the magnificence of God's creation. But there are still many things I can tell you now." The drums sounded. The men died one by one. As they fell, Adas told Lucius about Zacchaeus, and how Peter came to meet Cornelius. He described miracles Yeshua had done.

Falto died when the last of many arrows brought him down. Valentius squirmed in frustration at the man's unprecedented courage. The slave held up the slate with IX chalked on it. Falto stayed on his feet until the last arrow. Throughout the ordeal, the legionary never took his eyes from his executioner. For once in his life, Falto stood his ground.

Lucius pulled his attention back to Adas. "You say God cares about us. How do you know? What has God ever done for me?"

"Even a thousand years would not be enough time to answer that question. But most importantly, Yeshua forgave us while we were in the very act of crucifying him. You said we did nothing wrong, but we did. We executed an innocent man. Still, he forgave us. Why would he do that if he didn't care about us?"

"Why are you telling me these things? Why do *you* care?"

"Because I know the truth and I am compelled to share it. If you refuse to believe and there *is* no God, then nothing is lost. But if God exists and you refuse to believe, then *you* will be lost for all eternity. This is your last chance to find peace, Lucius. You can end your suffering today, forever. The world, at some point, did not exist, and then it did—from nothing. There was nothing to give birth to the first living things. Life had to be created. The first man and woman had to come to life without parents. Someone had to create them. If God is the creator of all things, then God cannot consist of anything which must be created. Therefore the Creator is an eternal spirit of unlimited intelligence and ability."

"If God is the greatest entity, why would he care about humanity? Why care about me?"

"If you go to him today, you can ask *him*, yourself. The world he made for us is an amazing place filled with life, beauty, order, and renewal. If God did not love us, would he provide us with the bounty of nature? Would he have given his Son for our benefit? But to be with him for eternity, we must acknowledge him, believe in him. Right now, God only wants your belief, Lucius. There's no time for anything else."

"Even if I were to live, I'd have nothing to offer, in return. All I have ever known is violence. I have been a soldier since I was eight years old. I only know how to fight."

"Then fight for your soul, Lucius, because you do have something to offer—your belief."

"How can I trust something I can't even see?"

"You *can* see God. All of nature is the evidence of God."

As they talked, more men died. Finally, only one soldier remained standing next to Lucius. It was Blandus. One by one, the arrows flew.

"Lucius, do you remember the young thief? When he believed, Yeshua said, '*I say to you, today you will be with Me in Paradise.*' I think the thief was already there before he died. He felt no pain when you broke his legs. Even after you broke his legs, he looked serene. You and I know his reaction was impossible."

A fourth arrow hit Blandus. Lucius looked away. "It is too late for me. When I heard them insulting Yeshua, I joined in. I have taunted many men as they died. You said it was shameful to ridicule a defenseless man. I have done that more times than I can count. I don't deserve a second chance."

"Neither did Demas. He admitted he deserved execution. Lucius, he only had time to believe. Like you, Demas ridiculed Yeshua as soon as they were on the crosses. While they were dying Yeshua talked with him. Demas began to understand with, literally, less than an hour to live. Yet, Yeshua's promise to him was fulfilled. We saw it happen."

Two more arrows found their mark. Blandus staggered and fell to a knee, but he struggled to his feet as the men shouted praise and encouragement.

Valentius grew irritated at the tenacity of the condemned men. "Why do they keep getting up?"

"Why do you care?" the king demanded "You want them to cower before their executioners. The strength in others intimidates you, doesn't it?" Valentius looked away.

Lucius continued, "But, Centurion, how can we know the thief didn't believe in vain? I would believe if he told me, himself. "

"He did tell you! You saw his joy. When you broke his legs, it was obvious he was not in pain. If Yeshua was a mere mortal, he would have no power to grant such a thing!" His tone softened. "And don't call me centurion."

The final arrow for Blandus hit the artery in his upper leg. The *medicus* checked for a pulse. The slave wrote XI on the slate.

"I let a terrible lie rule my life," Lucius said, "a lie I could have revealed. When it was too late, I began to believe the lie. Until yesterday, I was convinced that deception was the truth. I was weak and foolish, eager for approval from all the wrong people. I betrayed my father, his memory, and myself. If I say I believe in Yeshua, how do I know I'm not lying to myself again?"

"This lie you convinced yourself to believe, how did it make you feel?"

"Angry. Bitter. It made me take pleasure in violence."

"What do you feel when you think of Yeshua?"

Lucius lowered his head. Moments passed in silence. He slowly raised his head. "The same way I felt yesterday when the truth freed me from my father's death. Even before he died, he forgave me. He knew exactly what was going to happen, and why, and *still* he offered himself. The look in his eyes told me everything. No one else has ever looked at me like that—until Yeshua, when I picked up the spear. Then my father was there in front of the cross. That's why I dropped the spear."

Adas remembered the fugue that overtook Lucius. "You know the truth, Lucius. God knows what's in your heart and mind. If your belief is there, he knows it."

The *medicus* confirmed Blandus was dead. The *sagittarius* collected his unused arrows and left the stage. Only the Lion and the Wolf remained. A hush fell over the soldiers. Valentius had hoped they would spend their final hour in misery. Instead they were calmly talking.

Lucius ignored the silence. "You say it is not too late. I have lived a lifetime of hate and violence. Yet in my final hour, I can be spared from Hades? How is that fair to people who have lived good lives?"

"I have no idea. Now is really not the best time to debate that issue. Since Demas admitted he was on the cross for good reason, why was *he* spared from Hades? So you have a few minutes left. What of it? As long as you're alive, Yeshua will accept you. Once you're dead, the offer expires for eternity."

The next *sagittarius* took his place on the stage. It was Thracius. Lucius locked eyes with him and nodded once, silently thanking him for the warning about the contest rules. Thracius nodded in return, but conflict strained his expression.

Lucius grasped the rope binding his unbroken hand. He pulled until the hemp creaked from the tension. Age-weakened fibers began to snap apart. He felt the rope give way. Lucius closed his eyes and whispered. When he opened his eyes, they gleamed with determination. He pulled with all his strength. More fibers broke. He let up on the tension and yanked the rope as hard as he could. It broke apart. For just a moment, there was silence. Then the soldiers roared with approval.

Lucius lunged toward the portico until the rope binding his broken hand stopped him. He pointed at Valentius. "*You* don't take my life, Valentius! I murdered my training officer, so I deserve to die. Justice is served today, but not by you!" Lucius threw his free arm out in a gesture of invitation. "Shoot your arrows, *Sagittarius*! I surrender my life to you!" Lucius made no attempt to untie his other wrist.

The soldiers cheered, "*Macte, Leo! Macte, Leo!*"

Thracius chose an arrow, yet he hesitated. Standing below the stage, the other *sagittarii* watched. Porcius moved stealthily down the line of men to stand below Thracius. Just as he drew his bow to release the first arrow, Porcius forced a cough. Distracted, Thracius jerked the bow slightly. The first arrow hit Lucius in the leg, but only superficially. He stared at the arrow, and a slow smile curved his lips. He grasped the shaft, easily pulling it free.

Lucius pointed the arrow at Valentius. "You see this arrow, Valentius? My blood is on it. My death will make it venomous. The blood we have both shed cries out with condemnation. Therefore, I hold no grudge against you. My execution is justified." He clamped the arrow between his teeth and snapped it in two. He pointed the broken pieces at Valentius. "You are this arrow, broken and bloodied!" He tossed the pieces into the crowd.

Valentius watched in horror as several men snatched hold of the fragments. A roar surged across the city. Thousands of fists beat the air as the men shouted. They knew what the curse of a broken arrow meant. If the pieces were caught before they hit the ground, the cursed man would die within the year. In the minds of the superstitious, Leo had sealed the fate of Cerberus.

The soldiers chanted as they stamped their feet. *"Leo De Sagitta Frangere! Lion Of The Broken Arrow!"*

Lucius stepped toward Thracius as far as the rope allowed. "Will you give me a warrior's death?" Thracius nodded. Lucius gratefully returned the gesture. The *sagittarius* drew his bow and took aim. The arrow flew past Lucius, barely missing his neck. The men grew quiet, anxious to see what this *sagittarius* would do. Again, he took aim and released. The third arrow hit Lucius in the ribs. He barely staggered.

The soldiers in the stands rose up. They roared, drowning out the beat of the drums. Thracius knelt down, taking his time to select the next arrow, allowing Lucius a last few moments of vindication.

Adas shouted over the roar, "Lucius! Call on Yeshua! Believe in him. He has already forgiven you. *It's not too late!"*

A raking cough seized him. "I don't deserve to be saved."

"None of us do! But you must *accept* Yeshua's offer!"

"You don't understand. I have done unspeakable things. God cannot possibly forgive me." At the taste of iron, he wiped at his mouth. His hand came away bloody.

"As a friend once told me, it is arrogant to think your crimes are too great for God's forgiveness! Of all the evil *ever* pardoned, is there any worse than murdering God's own Son? Yet, Yeshua forgave us. You can believe like the thief believed. The *only* thing Demas had time to do was to believe! God knows your heart, Lucius. Call on him!" The drums beat, the men roared. Thracius fumbled with his arrows, pretending to find the straightest one.

Lucius looked back at Adas. "Yeshua looked at me as my father did. How is that possible unless what you say is true? No mere human would look with compassion on the men torturing him. No mortal man could decide to die by sheer will, or live again after being dead for days. Yeshua did. Yeshua—*is God!"*

Thracius raised the bow and aimed. Valentius shouted at Adas, drawing his attention. The arrow flew from the bow. It hit Lucius below the collar bone, severing the artery. The fatal shot dropped him to his knees, yet he raised his head. His eyes went wide, gleaming like quicksilver. Thracius watched as an unexplainable look of astonishment illuminated Lucius's face.

Valentius shouted, "His death is on you, Longinus!"

Adas struggled against his ropes, but they held.

Lucius stretched out his free hand. *"Adas! He's here."*

Lucius Equitius Octavean collapsed. The men rose up as one. Bedlam erupted. Adas tore his eyes from Valentius as Lucius drew his last breath.

Thracius rushed forward and knelt by his side. "Octavean, who did you see?" He shook Lucius by the shoulder. *"Tell me!* Who was it?" But there was no answer.

Chapter 33

The men of the 10th *Legio* heckled Porcius as he stepped to the stage. He nervously eyed the soldiers, surprised at their hostility. Valentius glared at the boisterous soldiers and wished that Herod would silence them. This was the highpoint of his grand scheme. He had been dreaming of this moment for decades. Valentius believed that the murder of Aurelius was the worst injustice done by the Longinus family, but it was not the first.

Porcius smirked at Thracius as he left the stage. He spotted his favorite bow and smiled. Valentius had kept his word. Porcius faced the centurion and nocked an arrow on the bowstring. Focusing on the least vulnerable extremities, he selected his mark. He started to raise his bow.

"Stop!" shouted King Herod. "Lower your bow!" A hopeful buzz sprang up from the soldiers. Serapio and Nikolaus stiffened as they listened intently. The king addressed Caiaphas. "Joseph, would it please you if a temple guard executed the centurion?"

Caiaphas's eyes brightened. "Your Excellency is most gracious."

Herod pointed at the man standing behind Caiaphas. "You will be the final archer."

Valentius gawked in panic. "*What!* The contest is for my *sagittarii*! We agreed."

"And we agreed on the fewest arrows to win. Apparently, you forfeited that agreement Felix?" Herod again pointed at the temple guard. "What is your name?"

"Malchus, Your Excellency."

"Take your place on stage, Malchus." The king gestured at Porcius. "You! Get off!" In disbelief, Porcius started to protest. Herod shouted, "Get off or you can take the centurion's place!" Porcius dropped his bow and ran.

The soldiers made snorting noises. They chanted "Pig Man" and stamped their feet. "*Por-Cus He-Mo! Por-Cus He-Mo!*" Porcius disappeared under the stage.

"And you!" The king pointed at the overseer. "Stop that infernal noise! Centurion Longinus, I give you one last chance to save yourself. Do you believe Yeshua was from God?"

"No, Your Excellency, he was not from God." A pleased smile curled Herod's lips, but Adas wasn't finished. "No, not *was*—he *is* from God. *Yeshua is the Son of God!* And he *is* alive! I saw him alive after I split his heart in two! *Iesus, est Felius Dei! Via, Veritas, Vita! The Way, The Truth, The Life.*"

"You blaspheme God! Then I send you to God's judgment."

A familiar voice sounded in Adas's mind. *"I am with you."*

Adas answered, "Your will be done, Lord."

"What is the winning count?" Herod asked.

"Three," Salvitto answered, not even trying to conceal his revulsion.

"Three arrows, yes, for Octavean." He signaled for Malchus to step forward. "Remember; use the fewest arrows to kill. It seems the others were unexplainably determined to lose. Go, Malchus. Do God's will for us."

Malchus started to refuse, but a voice spoke in his mind. *"I will guide you."*

Malchus made his way to the stage. He picked up the bow and selected an arrow. "Centurion Longinus," he called out. "I do not stand here by human command, but to indeed do the will of God. However, for inflicting the pain you will suffer, I ask for your forgiveness."

"I grant it willingly!" shouted Adas. "God's will be done!"

Malchus nocked an arrow on the bow. He pulled the string back and set his bent thumb against his cheekbone. A loud crack sounded. The top end of the bow snapped off. The bow flew out of Malchus's hand as the string of the bow popped back, cutting his right eyebrow. The arrow arced over the stage to hit the back wall. Two of the *sagittarii* glanced at each other, annoyed and disappointed, but not surprised.

Grumbling rose from the stands. Malchus touched his eyebrow. His fingertips came away bloody. He tried to see out of his eye, but couldn't blink the blood away. A slave handed Malchus another bow. He nocked an arrow on the string, pulled, and released. The arrow flew past Adas, but the thin blade notched his shoulder close to his neck, forcing the arrow to ricochet into the air like a flat stone thrown over a pond. It hit the back wall, splintering the wooden shaft. Adas was surprised to see blood flowing down the center of his chest since he felt no pain.

Malchus selected a third arrow. Sweat dripped down his forehead, stinging his eyes. When he wiped his brow, he noticed an odd shine on the arrowhead. Malchus fingered the copper. It was sticky. He touched a few more blades. They were all sticky. He frowned, but nocked the arrow onto the bowstring. All the while, Malchus prayed for God to intervene. He tried to aim, but his vision was too obscured by blood. Trusting God to guide the arrow, he closed his right eye. He pulled the string back and released.

The arrow sang through the air. Adas staggered back, but the ropes held him. He felt his leg fold under him. He went down on a knee. Valentius jumped to his feet, a manic grin distorting his face. The arrow hit Adas squarely in the heart.

Adas's amber eyes sparked with tenacity as he grasped the ropes. The thorns bit into his hands, but the sting only increased his determination. He raised his eyes, and saw the most bewildering sight. Standing atop the highest wall was a young woman. Flowing back from her perfect face were long tresses of wind-teased flames. A swirling gown of liquescent gold clung to her from head to toe. She held a violin on her shoulder. The most extraordinary music Adas had ever heard surrounded him. Time stood still. Everyone in the theater stood in suspended motion as if they had been instantly frozen. They could not hear the angels's voices flowing from the strings of the instrument. The young woman danced as she played. Her bare feet seemed to prance upon empty space as she twirled with the cadence of her song. Then the instrument melted away, and a snow-white dove sprang from her hands. The beautiful dancer leaped into the air. She flung her arms wide and they blossomed into wings of flaming feathers. Adas watched in fascination as she plummeted from the wall and soared directly at him. Her fiery hair twisted in the wind as she flew over his head and out of sight. The bird hovered in front of him.

"*Nullo desperatio*," trilled the white dove. "Despair not."

Adas watched as the bird shimmered into rays of light and vanished. He felt no pain, no anger, not even fear. He leaned on the leg fixed solidly in front of him. His heart thundered in his chest as he prayed for one last burst of strength. Slowly, Adas struggled to stand as the five thousand men of the 10th *Legio* leaped to their feet as if they had suddenly come back to life. The triumphant smirk melted from Valentius's face.

The men roared as one, "*Absolvere! Absolvere! Absolvere!*" over and over as they pumped their fists in the air. Their demand for absolution was too much for Valentius. He cursed them, but his efforts were futile. The roar of the men drowned him out.

Adas's vision blurred. He felt himself falling as his knees buckled beneath him, but he never hit the ground. He was floating. Dulcibella smiled at him as she reached out with her hand. She spoke softly, "I love you, Adas. I always will." Then someone else was with him. His heart beat one more time and he died.

When Adas collapsed a groan of disappointment rose from the stands. The *medicus* ran across the stage and pressed his fingers against Adas's neck. He shook his head at Herod as he pulled his hand across his throat. The king nodded with approval.

Malchus stared in horror. He dropped the bow and ran to Adas. He knelt down and looked into golden eyes, sightless and dead. Malchus gently closed them. He hung his head, devastated that he had killed his friend. Caiaphas frowned at his servant's odd reaction, considering he had just won a great deal of money. In the stands, Nikolaus threw his arms over his head and rocked back and forth in despair. Serapio began making his way down the steps. Nikolaus followed, his face etched with misery.

Tribune Salvitto hurried up the steps of the stage. He knelt beside Adas's body. He, too, pressed his fingers on Adas's neck. There was no pulse, no visible sign of breathing. Herod sighed with satisfaction. He felt vindicated before the 10th *Legio* and the Sanhedrin.

Valentius's shock turned to fury. He ran down the portico steps and took the stage steps by twos. He stood over the body of Adas, hands clenched into fists, veins pressed out in his neck and forehead. He looked at the men as they shouted and pumped their fists in the air.

"Animus Herous! Heart of a Hero!" they roared.

For all his scheming, the only thing Valentius had accomplished was seeing Adas die as an honored champion, instead of ridiculed as a failure. There was nothing he could do to change this last triumphant remembrance of Centurion Clovius Longinus.

Livid with frustration, Valentius dropped to his knees, raised his fist, and slammed it down on Adas's chest. There was a crunching sound, but Adas did not react. Malchus tried to push Valentius away, but the centurion pulled his dagger and raised it in both hands. Someone seized Valentius by the neck of his tunic, and threw him on his back. Recklessly, he cursed his attacker, but choked on his profanity when he saw Tribune Salvitto standing over him.

Salvitto's voice shook. "You've done enough evil, Valentius! *I should kill you myself!*" Valentius dropped his dagger and backed away. Salvitto grabbed the weapon and threw it against the back wall.

Seeing what Valentius had done, the men shouted with rage. *"Valentius Igvania! Valentius Igvania!"* They defined the man with a single word, *cowardice.*

King Herod left the portico and stepped onto the stage with Blastus trailing behind. He raised his hands and shouted, *"Silentium!"* His voice roared across the theater. The men slowly took their seats. "Using only two arrows, the archer has won! The winner is awarded the annual salary of a centurion! Yet, it is not the salary *equal* to a centurion's! It will be the *actual* salary of a *specific* centurion. The prize is the salary of Centurion Pomponius Valentius for an entire year!"

Valentius rounded on Herod. *"What?* You can't do that!"

The king burst into laughter. "Of course, I can do *exactly* that! After all, this contest was *your* idea. Did you expect me to supply the prize out of my budget?"

"But I retire in two days!"

"Fine, the prize money will be deducted from your pension." He whispered to Blastus, "Confiscate his entire pension. He won't need it." Blastus acknowledged the order.

Herod clapped his hands for attention. "Now, we shall reward the winning archer!" He nodded at Blastus who hurried back to the portico. He dragged a leather knapsack out from under the king's chair and carried it to the stage. "You!" The king pointed at Valentius. "You will award the gold to the winner."

"*Now!* You said the gold would be delivered tomorrow!"

"I did say that. I lied. I wanted to see your reaction. Your wonderful expression of greed confirmed everything I suspected. I think opium has made you stupid."

"How did you know about the opium?" Valentius stared in shock.

Herod waved a nonchalant hand at the soldiers. "Who doesn't?" He jabbed a finger at the prize money. "Pick it up!"

Valentius retrieved the heavy knapsack. He unceremoniously dropped it near Malchus. The soldiers cheered to see Valentius, literally, pay for his betrayal, and to see his *sagittarii* gain no profit. Valentius hurried off the stage and ran from the theater.

The king addressed Blastus, "Tell Tribune Salvitto to prepare a charge of high treason against Valentius. Send it to me as soon as possible."

Herod turned his attention to the spectators. He raised his arms in gesture, encouraging the soldiers' display of approval. As he had hoped, this day was a triple triumph for him. He had appeased the soldiers by punishing Valentius, pleased the Sanhedrin with the executions, and upheld Roman law. However, his victory celebration was short lived. Soldiers on the top tier of the stands began pointing toward the west. They were shouting something. Gradually, the rest of the men began to notice.

"*Tempestas!*" the soldiers shouted. "*Tempestas!*" A fearsome rolling brown cloud was approaching Jerusalem. A towering wall of blowing sand, a *sharav*, was the most dreaded of Judean desert storms. This *sharav* stretched across the entire western horizon. Herod wasted no time signaling his entourage. Caiaphas and the chief priests followed suit. Malchus did not look up as they passed, missing the suspicious frown of Caiaphas.

The men rushed from the stands. Only camels with their double eyelids and flexible nostrils could tolerate a storm of this magnitude. But Serapio and Nikolaus headed for the stage, fighting their way through the retreating soldiers. Tribune Salvitto knelt next to Malchus, who remained by Adas's side. Once on the stage, Nikolaus ran to Adas and fell to his knees. He shoved Malchus back.

"Get away from him! How could you?" Nikolaus cried. "He told me how you protected him from Octavean, how you took him to safety! How could you kill him now?" Malchus didn't try to defend himself. He had been so sure God would spare the life of his friend.

Salvitto tried to explain, "Nikolaus listen to me! He saved him from torture. You saw how many arrows it took to bring them down. Valentius will answer for this travesty! I know what he meant to you. Stay with him when they take the bodies to the crematory. Then report directly to my office when you get back. Nikolaus, these men will be avenged, despite what Herod allowed here today. I promise you!" Salvitto left the stage, his head hung in misery.

Nikolaus unfastened his belt and pulled his tunic off. He folded it into a pillow which he carefully placed under Adas's head. Serapio sat next to Nikolaus, too grief-stricken to speak. Malchus shook his head in despair, unable to leave. Nikolaus pressed his hand on Adas's chest and smeared blood on Malchus's tunic. "Here's his blood, since you were paid so well for it!"

Malchus said nothing. While the three of them sat in huddled despair, Nikolaus wept uncontrollably. As his tears ran, he leaned over Adas, shielding his face from the sun.

Nikolaus swore, "I don't care what happens to me! I will kill Valentius!"

"No! I will take care of Valentius!" declared Serapio.

"If anyone has the right to kill him, it is me," declared Malchus. "I was so sure there would be a miracle when Yeshua spoke to me. I-I couldn't even see to aim. I just trusted God."

Nikolaus ignored both of them. "I will kill Valentius! What else can I do?"

"You can. . .stop getting. . .me wet," someone said.

Gasping, Nikolaus fell back on his elbow. Malchus and Serapio gaped in disbelief. *"Adas! Are you alive?"* Serapio exclaimed.

Adas blinked at the three men. "Maybe—are you alive?"

Serapio and Nikolaus hugged and slapped each other's backs.

Malchus choked back a wave of relief. "Yes! Yes! We're all alive!"

"We thought you were dead!" cried Serapio. "Everyone did."

"I was dead, for a little while. She told me to stay with her until it was safe. Did you hear the music? Did you see the girl with fire hair? The dove spoke to me." The three men were puzzled, but said nothing. "Opium, there was opium in the wine, lots of it. It tasted awful. Where did everyone go?"

"There's a *sharav* heading for us!" Serapio explained. "We've got to get you out of here somehow! For now, the opium is a blessing."

"Valentius said I would see monsters. What does that mean?" Serapio exchanged a fearful look with Malchus. Adas tried to move, but the attempt sent a radiating pain from the center of his chest. He coughed in reaction to the sensation, which made it worse. He looked to find the source of the pain. "There's an arrow in my chest." He tried to touch it, but the ropes restrained him. "Can I go back to the rainbow place? Just want to. . ."

Then his face filled with terror. His eyes darted from one face to the other. The monsters were making their appearance. Adas slipped into semi-consciousness, aware of sounds and sensations, but unable to react. Serapio found a rapid pulse in his neck and frowned with renewed fear. Quickly, he inspected the arrow wound. The blade was embedded in two ribs and pressed against the right side of the sternum danger-ously close to the heart. They realized the blood flow from the neck wound masked the lack of bleeding from the chest wound. To the distant observer, it appeared Adas had been shot in the heart. No one would question his death.

Serapio grasped the arrow with his powerful hands. "I've got to break this off."

"Can't you just pull it out?" demanded Nikolaus.

"No! If I jerk it out, it will cause even more damage. I can remove it properly if we can get him to my house. When I was a *gladiator*, I often patched up the others." Serapio gripped the arrow as close to the wound as he could. "Hold him down in case he wakes up. This is going to hurt." Malchus and Nikolaus pressed Adas's arms down. Serapio exerted pressure on the arrow. There was a loud snap as the wooden shaft broke, leaving about three inches of the arrow protruding from the wound. Adas cried out and began to struggle.

"What's wrong with him?" exclaimed Nikolaus. Frowning, Serapio shook his head.

A rumbling sound from the entrance signaled the approach of a wagon. It was the cremator sent to dispose of the bodies. If Adas called out in his delirium, all would be lost. Serapio was about to take drastic measures, but Adas grew still. The three men breathed a collective sigh of relief when Serapio found a pulse. Adas had passed out.

Serapio spoke hurriedly. "I have a plan, but you two will need to pay attention and be creative." He called out to the cremator, "*Ohe*, if you take the wagon under the stage, we'll pass the bodies through a trapdoor. He'll open it." He gestured at Nikolaus.

The cremator shouted, "I'm supposed to collect the arrows for the armory."

Serapio waved him off. "We'll get the arrows." The wagon disappeared under the stage. Serapio said to Nikolaus, "When we lower Adas, distract him."

"How will we get him away from the cremator?"

"Malchus and I will get my cart. We'll find you on the road. Be looking for us. For now, keep the man distracted." Nikolaus hurried off the stage and unfastened a trap door.

Malchus pulled arrows from the bodies while Serapio cut the ropes. A brown blur appeared over the top of the theater walls. They didn't have much time before the storm would engulf them. When the trapdoor opened, Serapio handed his dagger to Nikolaus. "You'll need it to cut sections of cloth from the *bracae* to cover Adas's face and wounds, and your face."

Malchus gave the arrows to the cremator. When they handed down the first body, the man started counting. "That's one."

When Serapio and Malchus reached Lucius's body, Serapio studied the man's scarred face. "Whatever demons tormented you in life, I pray you are free of them now. You faced your death with courage." He gently closed Lucius's eyes, and carefully lowered him into the wagon.

Just before Serapio and Malchus lifted Adas, Nikolaus walked over to the horses to explain the tribune's instructions to the cremator, forcing the man to keep his back to the wagon. Occasionally, he glanced over his shoulder in an attempt to keep count of the bodies. Nikolaus reminded him to cover the horses' and his own eyes for protection. The cremator pulled linen scarves from under the wagon seat just as the men lowered Adas into the wagon.

"That's sixteen," Serapio said.

The cremator climbed on the wagon seat. Nikolaus got in the back with Adas. Malchus handed Nikolaus his tunic through the trapdoor. "You'll need this for protection. And here, take my robe to cover his wounds."

"Malchus, I'm sorry what I said about the prize money."

"It's all right. Adas and I will need it since we're both out of a job." Nikolaus frowned. It was true; Adas would have to leave Jerusalem.

The wagon moved from under the stage and headed for an exit. Malchus grabbed the knapsack containing the gold. He and Serapio bolted for Malchus' horse. Outside the theater walls, they could see the approaching *sharav*. It was a boiling, brown, tsunami of sand.

Nikolaus covered Adas's chest and head with Malchus' robe. He tied it down with strips of cloth from the other men's *bracae*. He used his own body to shield Adas from the fiercest impact of the storm as the hot stinging winds strafed them. Nikolaus was unaware of a threat far greater than the injuries he could see. Demitre's poison had already stopped Adas's heart once. Even now, the poison coursed through his veins, trapping him inside a nightmare world.

Chapter 34

The wall of churning sand hit Serapio and Malchus just as they reached the shop. They jumped from the horse, and Serapio pushed the front door open.

"Get in!" he shouted to Malchus over the roar of the wind. "Tell Ana what happened! I'll take the horse around back." Malchus rushed in the door. Serapio ducked his head, covered the horse's eyes, and led it to the stable. He harnessed his donkey to the delivery cart as Malchus, Fabiana, and Nebetka hurried into the stable.

"Nebetka, take care of Malchus' horse," said Serapio. "Ana, take the knapsack and hide it in a safe place." Fabiana's eyes were red and swollen, but her expression was one of hope.

"Hurry, Apio!" Fabiana pleaded as Serapio wrapped linen around the donkey's eyes. Fabiana handed Serapio and Malchus head scarfs, which they tied around their faces, leaving slits to see through. Fabiana and Nebetka held the double doors open as Serapio and Malchus coaxed the donkey into the street. The two men jogged as best they could through the stinging sand while they held on to the donkey's halter. They passed through a city gate and on to the road leading to the crematory pits.

Nikolaus strained to spot Serapio's cart, but the wall of blowing sand obscured anything beyond a few paces. Trying to see through tiny holes in his makeshift mask made it even more challenging. To make matters worse, Adas became agitated. In desperation, Nikolaus cut the rope from one of the dead men's wrists. He crossed Adas's wrists and tied them together, trying to avoid the cuts and abrasions. He tied the rope around Adas's waist to prevent him from dislodging the arrowhead. Desperate to subdue him, Nikolaus pulled a corpse over Adas's legs. If the cremator saw Adas move, all would be lost. Fortunately, he heard nothing suspicious, due to the howling wind. Nikolaus prayed the man would not turn around. Keeping a dead man restrained, and his injuries protected would be unexplainable.

Nikolaus feared he may have to get Adas out of the wagon on his own when a vague image of two men and a donkey materialized out of the swirling sand. Nikolaus released the bolts securing the tailgate, holding it tightly against the wind. Serapio and

Malchus led the donkey as closely behind the wagon as they could. Nikolaus jumped down to take hold of the donkey's halter. Serapio and Malchus kept pace, carefully lifted Adas out, and placed him in the cart. Serapio pointed at Adas's bonds.

"I couldn't keep him still," Nikolaus yelled in Serapio's ear. He nodded. Nikolaus trotted after the wagon and hoisted himself up. Malchus helped him pull the tailgate up. Relieved that Adas was safe, Nikolaus watched the two men and the cart disappear into the gusting sand.

Adas tried to sit up, but Serapio pushed him down. Malchus restrained Adas with the cart straps. His struggles were becoming more violent. The more he struggled, the more the pain across his back and chest intensified, but the poison prevented him from understanding the cause.

The debris-filled air swirled around them as Serapio led the donkey, and Malchus pushed at the back of the cart. When they reached the shop, Serapio banged on the stable door. Nebetka opened it quickly. Safely inside the stable, they untied the robe from Adas's face. He was flushed, but not sweating despite the heat and trauma. He lifted Adas by the arms while Malchus held his legs. Adas's struggles made it difficult to carry him. They went to Nebetka's room and laid him on the bed his brother, Dorrian, once used.

A pot of boiling water with metal tools protruding from it hung over the fire. Fabiana had set out several pitchers of water, a basin, wool towels, a jar of honey, and several jars of vinegar. Linen-covered, wooden frames were secured in the windows to hold the sand out, but they couldn't mask the sound of the screaming wind or the caustic smell of dirt.

Adas was a mess. Sand was caked on his stomach and back despite Nikolaus's efforts. When they cut the ropes, Adas tried to jerk free. Serapio tried to re-tie the ropes to the top bedframe corners. Adas cried out. His breathing became labored.

Baffled by his combative behavior; Fabiana's voice shook with fear. "What is wrong with him? Why is it so hard for him to breathe?"

"I don't know. Opium wouldn't do this. Nebetka, get the straps from the cart. The leather will be less abrasive." The young man ran from the room.

Nebetka returned and helped Serapio tie the straps to Adas's wrists, avoiding the rope lacerations as best they could. Fabiana cut the ropes away. They tied the straps to the sides of the bedframe. Malchus held Adas's legs down as they secured his ankles. Adas fought to free himself, but with his arms repositioned, his breathing relaxed.

Fabiana removed the robe from Adas's chest. She hesitated at the sight of the injuries, but her face hardened with resolve. She took a towel dampened with vinegar and began cleaning the wounds. She dampened another towel, handed it to Malchus, and gestured at his split eyebrow. He thanked her and gingerly pressed the cloth to his eye.

Serapio frowned with deep concern. "Valentius must have poisoned him with something. His difficulty in breathing is because the arrow broke his ribs or his sternum or both."

Malchus grimaced. "It's the sternum and it wasn't from the arrow, or at least not completely. When Valentius hit him with his fist I heard a cracking sound."

"Yes, I can see bruising and swelling over the sternum. The impact of the arrow would have weakened the bone. Every time he breathes, the broken sternum rubs together."

"Valentius was going to stab him, but Salvitto stopped him."

"Apio, do you see this?" Fabiana pointed. "It's a rash and is spreading up his neck."

"No! It can't be!" Serapio gently checked Adas's eyes. His pupils were dilated. "Oh dear God in heaven, he's been poisoned with *belladonna*!"

"*Belladonna*!" cried Fabiana. "Could it kill him?"

"Yes, even in very small amounts if it's not diluted. It causes a rash, delirium, hallucinations, confusion, and then death. *Belladonna* effects the body quickly, but takes many hours to kill. This is why Valentius said he'd see monsters. Malchus, were the. . ."

"I know what you're going to ask. Yes, the arrows were sticky. They must have been smeared with *belladonna* root. I think they were intended only for Adas because his arrows were tied with black string."

Serapio sank into a chair. His face was drawn with despair. "I can remove the arrow and stitch the wound, but the poison will kill him before the sun rises."

"Adas will die," Malchus proclaimed. "But *not* today! I will get Simon Peter. He has the healing touch of Yeshua."

"You know where he is?" asked Fabiana.

"Yes. He's in my quarters. The soldiers have looked in every house in Jerusalem except for the high priest's estate. I will be back quickly!"

"If you're not back in half an hour, I will go ahead with the surgery."

Malchus understood. Serapio left the room with him. He returned with a *horas vitrum* to measure the hour and a tray of medical instruments. He turned the hour glass upside down on the bedside table, and the sand began to flow. "Ana, did you put both the *confibulae* and the *forceps* in the boiling water?" She nodded. Serapio tested the *confibulae* to be sure it would spread the bone apart smoothly. "I pray he can withstand the pain. Maybe the opium already in his system will last."

"They have to come," said Fabiana. "I cannot bear to lose another son."

"Neither can I." A quarter of the sand had trickled through the hourglass.

"These cuts on his chest and back," Fabiana said, "who did this to him?"

"Valentius, when he removed the bandages. The men taunted him for cowardice. I believe they would have attacked him if it were not for the storm."

Nebetka leaned forward in his chair. "So we have to wait?" Serapio nodded. Fabiana wet another towel, and gently wiped Adas's face and neck. She tried to dampen his lips with water, but there was no reaction. She poured water over the cuts on his wrists and hands, washing away bits of hemp and sand.

Restlessly, Serapio began to pace. The shrill wind was unnerving. The dusty air irritated their throats. "We should remove Nikolaus's stitching in a few days. That young man would make a good *medicus*. He has a steady hand and a good eye." He sat down and studied Adas's face. "Our son could use a shave, don't you think? Or maybe he should grow a beard like a Judean, since he can talk like one. It would give him a good disguise, if it wasn't for his eyes. He has eyes like his mother, but his father's features and build. I remember being surprised that a bureaucrat could look so athletic. Adas mentioned that he and his mother went to soccer games to watch his father compete. Aquila is taller than Adas, and has pale blue eyes like the people of Gaul. Did Adas ever talk about his father with you, Ana?" She shook her head. "Yes, I think the boy could use a shave. However, beard or not, it won't help. His eyes will give him away."

"He doesn't need a shave," murmured Fabiana. "He's still just as handsome." She sat on the side of the bed, dipped a towel in water and again wiped his face and neck. "Apio, he looks so much like, you know. . .the son we lost. The first time you brought this waif home, I thought I was seeing a ghost. I was so angry at first, but then. . ." She sighed.

Serapio's stern expression softened. "I know. I thought the same thing the first time I saw him. I've never told him."

"Perhaps you should. In fact, I have an idea." She told Serapio her plan.

"Are you sure?"

"Yes, I'm sure. We can't bring him back, but the memory of him will have new meaning. Besides, Adas looks like you when you were his age."

"Ana, your memory is failing. I was never handsome." He put his arm around her waist.

"You have always been handsome to me," whispered Fabiana.

"I would have given up a long time ago, if not for you." He glanced at the hourglass. "Ana, I am worried! Malchus has been gone too long; something is wrong. The longer the arrow sits in his chest the quicker the opium wears off. I am loath to do this with my limited skills, but we cannot wait any longer."

"Apio, no! God will save him! Give Malchus more time."

"I believe with all my heart that God *will* save Adas, but what if God wants to work through me? God worked through Malchus to make everyone believe Adas was dead. If only God would speak to me now, I would know what to do!"

"Just a little more time," she begged. "If you do this without more opium, it will be no different than torturing him. Please, Apio! Wait just a little longer!"

The rash was spreading to Adas's arms and stomach. The flushed look of his skin was beginning to pale. "Ana, look at him. I can't stitch his back until I get the arrow out, and he's losing blood. How can I sit here and do nothing?"

Nebetka looked at the hourglass. "Father, half of the sand has emptied into the bottom. What do you need me to do?"

"We need your help, Ana. I need you to be strong, for Adas."

She bit her lip anxiously. "All right. I will assist you." She moved to the side of the bed and spoke softly. "We're here, Adas. You're not alone."

"Even restrained, you'll have to hold his legs down, Nebetka. He's as strong as a bull. We can't let him thrash around."

Adas groaned. His breathing was ragged. He balled his hands into fists and pulled so hard on the straps, they could hear the wooden bedframe creak. Nebetka sat near the end of the bed and wrapped his arms around Adas's lower legs. Fabiana cleaned the area around the protruding arrow. She rolled a small towel, dampened it with water, and pressed it between Adas's teeth. Serapio picked up a retractor clamp. He whispered a desperate prayer.

Chapter 35

———— ⌀⌀⌀ ————

Serapio gently inserted the bone spreader on either side of the arrowhead. Fabiana steeled herself to watch. Nebetka looked away. Serapio slowly cranked the retractor clamp open. A guttural cry sounded in Adas's throat as he clamped his teeth down on the gag. He tried to jerk his arms free. Tears began to seep from the corners of his eyes. Fresh blood pooled in the gaping wound. Serapio inserted a hollow reed. Holding the reed steady while keeping a ready pinch on the upper end, he sucked air up inside the reed, pulling the excess blood with it. After a few more suctions, he could see how deeply the blade penetrated the ribs. Using the *forceps*, Serapio grasped the arrowhead and gently pulled. He heard a scraping sound as the broken bone of the sternum rubbed together. Adas tried to cry out. Serapio immediately released the arrowhead. He frowned in frustration.

Fabiana wiped the sweat from Serapio's face. "Nebetka, you're going to have to hold him down at the shoulders," said Serapio. "I have to use another *forceps* to prevent the sternum from moving when I pull the arrow out." Fabiana handed him a second bone *forceps*. Nebetka pressed down on Adas's upper arms. Fabiana wrapped her arms around his knees. Serapio grasped the arrowhead again with one *forceps* and held the sternum down with the other. He whispered another quick prayer and tentatively pulled. The arrowhead didn't move. It had jammed tighter every time Adas had been moved. Serapio tried again. Nothing happened. He pressed down harder on the sternum as he pulled on the arrowhead. Suddenly, it came loose. Adas's eyes shot open. They looked more like the eyes of an owl at night than a wolf. Despite Nebetka's efforts to hold him down, Adas struggled to free himself. As gently as possible, Serapio released the tension on the bone spreader and removed it. Nebetka let go. Adas moaned, but no longer pulled on the leather restraints. Fabiana pressed a fresh cloth over the wound.

She blinked back tears when she saw the dread on Serapio's face. He picked up the jar of vinegar, knowing the worst was about to happen. In desperation, Serapio prayed aloud, "Dear God, help us!"

The back door slammed shut. They heard men's voices and footsteps rushing up the stairs. Malchus burst in the room followed by Simon Peter. Serapio, Fabiana, and Nebetka nearly collapsed with relief at the sight of the two men.

"Thank, God!" exclaimed Serapio. "We feared for you as much as for Adas!"

Peter saw the bloody arrowhead on the mattress. He sat on the edge of the bed, placed his hand on Adas's arm, and whispered under his breath. In a few moments, Adas relaxed. Peter's eyes drooped with sadness.

"He has suffered much on my account. Malchus told me about the *belladonna*. His injuries are not nearly as dangerous as the poison. Unbind him and remove the gag. He will be still now. Then, please, wait downstairs."

They did as Peter instructed. Serapio picked up the arrowhead. Fabiana gently moved Adas's arms to his sides. They closed the door as Peter turned solemn eyes on Adas. He moved a chair next to the bed and sat down.

Serapio and the others sat downstairs hoping and praying. Outside, the wind gradually subsided. The shadows grew longer. The sky would darken soon. The stuffy air began to cool. Nebetka sat on the floor and leaned his head against Fabiana's knee. She rested her hand on his head and occasionally ruffled his hair. Time passed. It seemed as if they had waited forever. Then the bedroom door opened. Peter stepped out on the upstairs landing.

"You can come up now." He looked exhausted, but he was smiling.

Serapio bounded up the stairs. He found Adas sitting cross-legged on the bed. Instead of a gaping wound over his heart, a new scar had taken its place. Serapio cried out with astonishment. Adas beamed at them as they gathered in the room. A healthy coloring had returned to his face.

Serapio stood at the foot of the bed. His face glowed with relief. "Oh, praise God, praise God!" His heart filled with gratitude.

Fabiana hugged Adas. She couldn't say a word, but tears of gratitude flowed freely. Malchus stood next to Serapio, happily grinning. Peter sat down on the other bed. Fabiana took Adas's face in her hands and kissed his forehead. She gasped as her eyes went wide with awe.

"Apio, look! All his wounds are healed!" Serapio gently pushed Adas forward. There was a new scar across his back.

"Even the bruises are gone. Lean forward again!" Serapio pressed his ear to Adas's back and listened. "Breathe deeply. Ah, your sternum was broken, but not anymore! Your pupils are normal. The rash is gone. Your injuries are healed. The poison is gone! And to think, only a few hours ago there was no rational reason for hope."

Serapio bowed his head. The others joined him as he thanked God for providing everything needed to save the life of his young friend. Serapio faced Peter. "I thank you, too, Peter. We know Herod has half the army looking for you." Serapio's voice was husky with emotion. "But you still came despite the risk."

"We had difficulty leaving Caiaphas' estate, but the *sharav* helped," said Malchus.

"I never thought a sandstorm could be such a blessing," Serapio declared.

Adas looked at the bed sheepishly. "Fabiana, it appears I owe you a new *culcita*," The mattress was stained with blood and dirt.

Fabiana chuckled. "This old thing? I was going to throw it out, anyway."

"Peter, what will you do now?" asked Serapio. "They're still hunting for you."

"I am not foolish enough to test God's protection now that the *sharav* is gone. I'll stay here tonight. Tomorrow, we'll see."

Fabiana selected a tiny hooked blade and a pair of tweezers from Serapio's medical instruments. She gestured for Adas to lie down. "Those stitches need to come out. Be still and behave yourself," she said with feigned severity.

"Yes, Mother," said Adas as he grinned at her.

She playfully cuffed his arm. "That's right! That's what you say when I speak to you, young man." Fabiana arched an eyebrow at him, but she couldn't keep from smiling. The others laughed, relieved to see Adas himself again. With practiced skill, she removed the stitches.

Adas talked as she worked, telling them about the events leading up to the angel leading Peter out of Holding. He described trying to convince Lucius to join forces with him against Valentius and their discussion during the executions.

"Lucius called out something just before he died," said Adas, "but I didn't hear what he said. The men were shouting so loudly and Lucius had broken a rope so he was standing well ahead of me." Adas looked at the others anxiously. "We must pray for Dulcibella and her family. They will probably get the letters tomorrow. I pray God will comfort them until I can get there. I also pray for your safety since you are in danger as long as I'm here. You have already risked your lives for me. I still have no idea why Valentius hates me so much, but he would take matters into his own hands if he knew you helped me."

"Valentius has been planning an attack on you for some time, Adas," said Malchus. "Tomorrow, after you're rested, we will talk. Could you hear what Herod said?"

"Not much. He was facing the soldiers, so, just a word now and then."

Fabiana took the last stitch out. Adas sat up. She hugged him again. "I am so grateful to see life in those golden eyes of yours. Tonight, we celebrate. Let us enjoy some good food and get a well-deserved night's rest."

The horrors of the day were receding for the others, but not for Adas. "Peter, when we were upstairs, you said there was a reason God let the other soldiers die. Why not me?"

"Malchus told me Herod offered you a pardon if you would renounce Yeshua. Instead, you glorified Yeshua's name. God chose you for this purpose. Herod also offered to let a slave die in your place. Again, you refused. Malchus also told me you asked Herod to execute only you and let the others go free. Yeshua told us, *'Greater love has no one than this, than to lay down one's life for his friends.'* From what I have been told, all sixteen of you participated in some way with Yeshua's final hours. Yet, you were willing to die in their place. Yeshua also told us, *'For whoever desires to save his life will lose it, but whoever loses his life for My sake will save it.'* God did not take their lives. The evil of Valentius did so. You might ask why God allows evil to exist. It is because he created us with the ability to make choices. As long as a person has free will, bad choices can be made."

"I understand," said Adas. "But what of the innocent people they harm? I'm worried about Nikolaus. Even if they arrest Valentius, Demitre could get to him. Will God protect him?"

"Tonight, Nikolaus will be safe under Salvitto's protection," Serapio assured him. "Tomorrow I will go see the tribune. If anyone can convince him to let Nikolaus go, it is me. He owes me a great debt, and I am not above reminding him of it when it comes to our young friend."

"Serapio, I'm holding you to that." Adas slapped at the *bracae.* Puffs of dust billowed from the pants. "I'd also like to get my own clothes back."

"I have your clothes trunk here. I will gladly get you a clean tunic. Besides, you look ridiculous."

"Thanks for not mentioning that earlier," exclaimed Adas with a grin. Serapio left the room chuckling. He came back with Adas's *caligae*, belt, and clean garments. Fabiana left washcloths and water for him. They went downstairs while Adas cleaned up. When he joined them, he threw the *bracae* into the cookfire.

Fabiana and Nebetka brought out bread, olive oil, smoked mutton, wine, cheese, and fruit. Peter asked a blessing. "Now we celebrate the beautiful thing God has done for us today! Let us rejoice for the life restored!" It was the first food Adas had eaten all day. While they ate, they discussed the details of the day's events.

"You should have seen Valentius's face when Herod put me in as the last archer. He insisted the contest was for his *sagittarii.* Herod quickly set him straight. Valentius went into a panic when he realized I won. I can understand being annoyed, but not panicked."

"It makes sense if he was planning to keep the prize money for himself," Adas suggested. "But why the *belladonna?*"

"He must have wanted you hallucinating and terrified for the soldiers," said Serapio. "The last thing Valentius wanted was for you to die a hero."

Malchus added, "Herod exposed Valentius's conspiracy. Surely, he has been arrested."

"If Herod knows Valentius is to blame, why execute the guards?" asked Fabiana.

"That's what Salvitto asked," Malchus said, "but Herod had to obey Roman law. He also faulted the men for drinking the wine when they knew they would get drunk. He faulted Octavean and Adas for fighting."

"Poor Nikolaus. I hope he'll be safe," said Fabiana.

"I have lived in Jerusalem all my life," said Malchus. "I have seen few *sharav* which stretched across the entire horizon and three times taller than the towers. The storm was part of God's miracle today. I believed God would save you, Adas, but the miracle was not what I expected. It was better. Yet, when you died, I lost faith."

"We all did," said Serapio.

"When you came to," Malchus continued, "you said something about a girl and a bird. Obviously, the poison was working on you, but what did you see?"

"She looked like an angel. She made the most enchanting music I've ever heard. She moved as gracefully as a hummingbird dancing with the wind. Everyone froze as if they were statues, and then she flew right over my head. She had flames for hair and fiery wings. A white bird spoke to me. It said, 'Do not despair.' It was beautiful."

"When you opened your eyes you said, 'She said to stay until it was safe.' Was it Dulcibella?" asked Serapio.

"No, it was my nanny, Misha. She called me *Tigris Catulus*. It was her nickname for me. Misha made up stories about my mother being a tiger who was turned into a human, and I was her cub." Sadness clouded his face.

"We are sorry," Fabiana said softly. "We know you grieve for your mother."

"I do. And for Misha. I still miss her. She taught me Hebrew and Greek and tolerated my dogs. I taught them tricks to make her laugh. I was just a kid when she died. My mother grieved as much as I did. They were very close."

"What happened when you saw Misha?" asked Malchus.

"I kept asking her where we were, but she wouldn't answer. She seemed to be waiting for something. These words came into my mind. *You have lifted me up, and have not let my foes rejoice over me. O Lord my God, I cried out to You, and You healed me. You brought my soul up from the grave.*"

Peter nodded. "That is a favorite Psalm to sing."

Adas frowned. "Perhaps Misha used to sing it to me. After that, she touched my chest right over my heart. I immediately felt an intense pain. There was also a cracking sound. Then I was back in the theater on the stage."

"Valentius hit you. He was so angry," Malchus said. "That must have re-started your heart. After all of Valentius's efforts to take your life, he actually saved it. A poisoned arrow killed you, the *medicus* declared you dead, and then Valentius revived you. Unbelievable!"

"And you saved Valentius when you protected Peter," observed Serapio. "You saved each other. How strange! The difference is *you* never tried to kill *him*."

"That's not entirely true. I did try to kill him. I had my dagger, but the door bolt jammed and I couldn't get out of my quarters. Serapio, remember when I bought the new chair? I smashed the other one against the door because I was so frustrated. I can't remember ever being that out of control."

Fabiana patted Adas's arm. "We thank God for that jammed door bolt."

Without explanation, Serapio went upstairs. He came back holding Marsetina's mirror and the coin pouch containing Dulcibella's eilat stone. "Adas, as I promised, I have kept these treasures for you until I could give them back."

Adas took them gratefully. He clasped the eilat stone. "I'll be with you soon." Then he looked into his mother's mirror. "*Ohe,* I guess I could use a shave." Everyone laughed.

Fabiana whispered in Serapio's ear. He turned to Adas. "Since Centurion Longinus is no more, Ana and I would like to make a proposal. However, I need to confess something first. Years ago when I stopped those thugs from attacking you, I was going to leave you there and be on my way. I changed my mind for a selfish reason." Serapio hesitated.

"What was it?"

"You told me your name."

Adas remembered how his father accused Serapio of staging the attack to extort a reward. "You mean Longinus?"

"No. Your *praenomen*—Adas."

"I don't understand."

"Your name was almost identical to our son's name. It was Adan. How could I meet a boy who looked so much like the son we lost, called by a name so similar? If Adan were alive, he would be twenty-four. I was very angry about his death. He was healthy one day. The next day he was dead. Adas, haven't you ever wondered why we took you in? We didn't expect to love you like a son, but it happened."

"I grieve with you. No parents should ever outlive their child. I wish I could have known him. What was Adan like?"

Fabiana gazed off sadly. "Adan Novius Serapio was in love with life. He made us laugh. He made us cry. Adan could be perfectly clear, yet a complete mystery. I miss him terribly. We still have his birth decree, but we never registered his death. So officially, he's still alive. You look so much like him, except for your eyes, of course. Apio and I would be honored if you would take his name. Think it over and. . ."

"I don't need to think it over. It is a beautiful gift. From now on, I will be Adan Novius Serapio, son of Regulus and Fabiana Serapio. I am not a soldier. I am a furniture maker. I am twenty-four years old. I get to live the last two years over again. How much better can this get?" They laughed and Fabiana came to her feet. Adan gathered her in his arms. He whispered in her ear. "I love you, Mother."

She took his face in both of her hands. "And I love you, Adan." Serapio lumbered to his feet to pull Adan into a back-slapping hug.

Eventually they settled back down to finish their supper. But there were more things which needed to be discussed before they could rest for the night.

"Serapio, I know you're going to try to free Nikolaus," said Adan. "But it will require going back to the Antonia. Valentius will be there. Promise me you won't kill him on sight?"

"That will be a very difficult promise to keep. But for the sake of Nikolaus, I will behave myself—unless provoked."

"There's one more thing. Since Centurion Longinus is dead, you owe me a story. You said you would not tell me what happened to your eye unless . . ."

"Ah, I did promise. I will keep my word, but not today. Today has seen enough grief. Tomorrow, I will tell you."

"Tomorrow, we'll also tell you about Valentius." said Malchus. "But in short, the vendetta is about the death of his estranged son. You replaced him at the Antonia." Adan was amazed that a coincidence could cause such hatred.

Fabiana clapped her hands. "We all need our rest. We should call it a night."

Adan yawned with fatigue. "You're right. I feel like I could sleep for a week. I'm going to sleep on the roof. I want to see the stars tonight."

"Mind if I join you?" asked Nebetka.

"I welcome your company. I wish Nikolaus was with us as well. I pray he is not in danger."

Unfortunately, Nikolaus was in danger. He had to distract the cremator from discovering one of the bodies was missing. He was immensely relieved that Adas was safe, but the reality of his situation subdued his joy. To shield himself from the shrieking sand, he curled up behind the tailgate. He tried to ignore his clawing thirst as he thought about his future. Adas would have to leave Judea, and Nikolaus would be alone once again. Memories of the wonderful months of companionship in Caesarea made him more depressed than ever. He almost wished the time with Adas hadn't happened. At least then, he would not grieve for the loss of it.

Nikolaus needed to devise a strategy to "replace" Adas at the crematory. He chose one of the men who resembled the centurion's build and hair color. Fortunately, the cremator only caught a glimpse as Adas was lowered into the wagon. Nikolaus grimaced as he maneuvered the body close to the tailgate.

The wagon changed direction as they passed through the gates of the crematory. The pits were surrounded with high walls. They were an abomination to the Hebrews, but the Romans insisted on their use. The driver headed toward the crematory pit set aside for the destitute, criminals, and unwanted babies. It was a terrible place, and smelled of burnt flesh and decomposition. Normally, the open pit revealed charred wood, ash, and human bones, but the sandstorm obscured the gruesome sight.

The cremator stopped, got down from the wagon, and coaxed the horses to turn around. He backed them up until the rear of the wagon hovered near the rim of the pit. He chocked the wheels with rocks. This moment was critical. Nikolaus prayed the cremator had not seen the broken arrow shaft in Adas's chest. Quickly, he thought of a lie to cover the inconsistency.

The cremator grabbed Nikolaus's arm as he climbed down from the wagon,. The man shouted over the roaring winds, "Where's the centurion?"

"He's right here. I must pray for him. Tribune Salvitto gave me instructions."

"Hurry! He won't know if you obeyed or not."

Nikolaus knelt by the dead man. In Greek, he asked for forgiveness for using the man to take Adas's place. They pushed the body into the pit. One by one, the dead men disappeared into the swirling sand obscuring the pit. Hoping to distract the cremator from correctly counting the bodies, Nikolaus made useless comments as they worked. In spite of his stoic façade, Nikolaus grieved for the dead men. This was a pathetic way to leave the world no matter what evil they had done.

The cremator took a torch from the wagon and lighted it with embers kept in a metal box. Nikolaus moved the rocks away from the wheels. The cremator threw the torch in the pit. Nikolaus urged the horses forward to put some distance between the wagon and the pit. The oil-soaked wood readily caught fire. Twisting tentacles of flame lashed at the rebellious wind as if nature was locked in a civil war.

Satisfied that the fire would not go out, the cremator climbed up on the wagon, as did Nikolaus. "*Ohe*, I forgot to count. Why do they want me to count? They're corpses. How far can they run?" He laughed at his own joke, but choked on the blowing dust.

The biting sand engulfed them, but Nikolaus didn't care. There was too much that could go wrong in the days to come. Worst of all, he had no idea how long he would have to wait to find out if Adas had survived.

Chapter 36

———⌘———

Adan couldn't fall asleep despite his exhaustion and the safety of Serapio's roof. He was worried about Nikolaus. He thought about the cascade of emotions he experienced throughout his "execution." Facing Malchus as he drew his bow was the single most defining moment of his life. Knowing his death could be mere seconds away made him realize how badly he wanted to live. Yet when he surrendered his life with the words, "Your will be done," an indescribable peace came over him. He was truly free for the first time in his life.

The events reformed in his mind as if he, once again, stood on the stage. He remembered how it felt when the arrow hit. He looked down at the shaft with detached surprise as if it were happening to someone else. He heard the slicing thud it made on impact. He felt the pressure and the odd absence of pain. His senses were frantically trying to understand the sudden violence done to him. When his body submitted to reality, pain exploded in his chest. The scene around him blurred. Dulcibella was there, and she reached out to him. Her turquoise eyes sparkled with love. Adas tried to take her hand, but she dissolved into mist. He felt himself collapsing, but he never hit the ground. He was suspended in space. He could lift his hands. The ropes were gone. The stage, the theater filled with men, the sky—everything—was gone.

"*Tigris Catulus*," called a voice. He saw a middle-aged woman take shape as she walked toward him. She was dressed in a flowing white gown. Her silver-streaked hair hung down in a braid over her shoulder. Again, she called to him, "Tiger Cub, can you see me?"

"*Misha*, is that you?" His childhood nanny stood before him. "What is this place?"

Misha was the only one who called him the tiger cub. Whenever he was bullied by older children, Misha told him to be strong like his mother. "She is the tiger who defends her cub at all costs. She is strength. Not even a lion can defeat a tiger. Do not be afraid, my little *Catulus*, we will protect you until you can defend yourself. She has the eyes of the tiger, but you have the eyes of the wolf. You will stand on your own when you are a man."

Misha extended her hand. "You must stay here until it is safe."

"But where is—here? Are we in heaven?" Adas looked around. Misha didn't answer, but continued to gaze at him. He had forgotten how much she looked like his mother. "What is this place?" he asked again.

"Does it matter? Is there somewhere else you wish to be?"

Adas shook his head. Colors began to swirl around him. The elegance of their patterns twirled and twisted in ever changing designs until they became tiny rainbows. He touched the rainbows causing them to disperse like a reflection on the surface of wind-blown water.

"I have missed you, little Cub. But it is not your time yet. Go now. It is safe." She placed her hand over his heart.

A violent pressure hit Adas's chest with a cracking sound. Instantly, he was in the theater again, flat on his back. He felt pain, but he couldn't remember why. He wanted to sit up, but he couldn't move or even open his eyes. He heard loud voices and angry voices and sad voices. There was the sound of running feet. He felt water dripping on his face, and he wondered how it could be raining. Then, he heard Nikolaus pleading, "What else can I do?"

Adas heard a voice respond. To his surprise, he realized it was his own. There was a flurry of movement, and he knew several people were near him. He opened his eyes to find faces staring at him with unreadable expressions. The features of Serapio, Nikolaus, and Malchus came into focus. To his amazement, there was an arrow in his chest. He wanted to touch the arrow to see if it was real, but something held his wrists.

Then he remembered. Malchus had shot him. This was curious to Adas because they were friends, and friends generally did not shoot each other. He wondered why he felt neither fear nor anger. He wanted to go back to Misha and the rainbows. Things began to change as he pondered this inconsistent situation. His friends transformed into *daemons* with melting eyes of black tar. He became lost in a jumble of twisted images and eerie sounds.

He was aware of motion, smells and sounds. There was a persistent roar like a raging fire but no smoke. The air tasted and smelled like dirt, making it hard to breathe. There was sharp, radiating pain in his chest and across his back. His wrists and hands felt burned. His skin was sticky and irritated. He tried to discover the cause of the pain, but something held his wrists. He was being carried. He heard voices. Then he thought he might be safe again, as he was with Misha. There was a sensation of something cool moving over his face and neck. The smell of dirt and iron began to fade.

A terrible burst of pain erupted in his chest. He thought a spike was being driven through his heart. The pain eased. A warm, soothing pressure settled over his heart and he knew he was safe. A light began to glow all around him. He embraced the warmth of the light, and the pain ebbed away. He heard a voice calling to him. It was a deep voice that was comforting and commanding at the same time. In his mind, he reached for the source of the voice.

A familiar face was watching him when Adas opened his eyes. It was Simon Peter, sitting on a chair next to the bed. Adas was free from the *daemon* world. He was lying on a bed in a room which looked like it belonged in Serapio's house.

"Where am I?" He tried to swallow. "Is there water?" His mouth was unbearably dry.

Peter poured him a cup. Adas gulped it down, spilling some in his impatience. After several cups, he asked again, "Where am I? How did I get here?"

"You're in Serapio's house. He and Malchus brought you here. You're safe now."

"I was on a stage. I think I was dead."

"You were dead."

"Did I die here, again?"

"No, but you almost did. God has healed you. Here, turn around." He washed the dirt and blood from Adas's back, revealing a new scar.

"Oh no! Dulcie will think I'm dead! The letters—they'll get the letters! Even if I left for Caesarea today, I couldn't get there before the letters. The whole family will think I'm dead!"

"They will have a few terrible days, but God will watch over Marcus and his family. I believe you will be with Dulcibella soon. God has blessed your betrothal to her."

"Yes, I remembered the blessing when you baptized us. It gave me hope at my worst moments." Adas sat up and leaned his back against the wall. "This morning, I couldn't help but think if I had refused to crucify Yeshua, I would have been expelled from the army, but I would not have killed God's Son. I would not have been guarding you, and I would not have been sentenced to death."

"That is true. What else would be different?"

"Ah, I would not have seen Yeshua alive and healed. I would not have met you and the others, not Jamin, or Malchus, or even Yeshua's mother. I would not have learned the Way."

"You're leaving something out."

Adas tilted his head. "What?"

"You would not have declared God's power before thousands of men."

"Yes, that was exhilarating. In that moment, I didn't think about death. Yet, death was there. I am sorry about the other men. I tried to save them."

"I know. Malchus told me. You have been blessed, Adas. Do not think it's strange that you alone were spared. God's plan was to give you the opportunity to glorify Yeshua, *and* spare your life. We will talk of this in more detail when you have rested. For now, remember God always has a plan. There is a reason for what he allows to happen. In the short term, events may seem like madness, but it appears this way because of our short lives. The will of God directs thousands upon thousands of years, and life carries on."

"I was trapped in a horrible nightmare place. I knew it wasn't real, but it felt real. Valentius, Octavean, and Herod were there. I was being crucified. A man was holding a hammer and a spike. He was about to impale my hand when he turned to look at me. *It was me!* He had my face! Was I in some kind of Hell?"

"No, you were poisoned with *belladonna*."

"Yes, I forgot. It was on Valentius's dagger and the arrows tied with black string. Valentius said I would be seeing monsters. He was right. I did."

"When the Lord returned," said Peter, "he was healed, but hundreds of marks remained on his body revealing the scourging and crucifixion he endured. God could have removed all traces of your injuries, but as with Yeshua, he has left evidence of your ordeal. The memories caused by the poison may also remain like the scars."

"This is the second time Valentius poisoned me with *belladonna*. He bragged about how Demitre watched while I hallucinated. Will I forget those terrifying images? They are so clear."

"I don't know. Hopefully, in time, they will fade."

"What will happen to Valentius?"

"He has chosen a path of destruction," said Peter. "Only God can change someone's heart, but a person must first want to change. Yeshua did not hinder those who would not listen. Not even miracles could convince them. Yet Truth always finds a way for those who seek."

Adan finally felt relaxed having let his memories of the execution run their course. He thought of Dulcibella and her family. He prayed that God would watch over them.

Chapter 37

———— ∞ ————

Felix Pomponius Valentius was in shock. He was facing disaster instead of celebrating his greatest victory. Valentius needed a defense and he knew exactly who he would sacrifice to do it. He raced from the theater back to the Antonia. He burst into his office and found Demitre sitting with his feet propped on the desk enjoying a cup of wine. Valentius crossed the room and slapped Demitre's feet to the floor.

"What's wrong, Felix?" Demitre set his wine cup down.

"Get out of my chair!" He gestured angrily at the windows. "Why aren't they covered? The worst sandstorm I've ever seen is coming!" Without waiting for Demitre to obey, he snatched the covers from a cabinet and jammed them in the windows.

"A storm? You're upset about a storm?"

"No, you idiot! Our plan is in ruins!"

"What are you talking about?"

"No pensions. No prize money. I'm talking about that, *Alexander!*"

Demitre's black eyes hardened. "You were never to speak that name."

Valentius ignored him. "Everything went wrong. Herod reinstated their pensions. He ordered a temple guard to kill Longinus. The guard won outright. He already has the gold!" Valentius kicked a chair across the room. "Herod took the prize money *from my pension!* Our plan fell apart because the entire legion knows about the wine. You said Longinus and his men would never suspect they were drugged. They would just go to sleep. This is all your fault!"

"You were supposed to kill Longinus and Octavean. But no! You wanted to see them humiliated. Did your foolish pride profit from *that*?" Demitre eyed him suspiciously. "If they know about the wine, why haven't you been arrested?"

"You think I'm making this up? That I hid the money to cut you out? They will be arresting someone soon enough, but it won't be me. You, *Alexander Nisos*, will be arrested for the murder of General Claudio Merula Glavienus!"

Demitre threw his cup across the room, shattering it against the wall. The wine ran down the whitewashed wall leaving long, red stains. "Felix, think of the consequences! I am your brother-in-law, your only family. I covered for you when Glavienus wanted my sister arrested for adultery. He was going to have Julia fed to jackals because she refused to name *you* as her lover. Did you forget why I killed the repulsive brute?"

"No, I haven't forgotten. How could I? Seeing you play the slave year after year."

"Why don't you ever listen to me, Felix? I said we should use a less important prisoner, but no, you had to have *that* Galilean just so Longinus would be executed today, *Consul* Longinus's wedding day. You have lost your mind! Your obsession has pickled your brain. And you should have left Octavean out. Why did you hate him so much? Because he was handsome and fearless? There you are with your thick-soled *caligae* desperate to be just a bit taller. You pitiful little man. Did you really think you could keep The Lion caged?"

"Octavean was a convenient spy, until the pit made him useless."

"Why did you put him in Holding with Longinus? It was a complication."

"Can't you understand?" Valentius wildly gestured. "Longinus and Octavean thought I was nothing. Every 'Yes, Sir' and 'No, Sir' out of their mouths was a mockery. Everything they did belittled me to my face. But I got my revenge when I had them tethered like dogs before the whole legion." Valentius frowned and looked away.

Demitre's eyes narrowed. "Why are you frowning? What else happened?" A bitter laugh broke the silence. "The men turned on you. They ridiculed *you*!"

"Shut up!" He gestured in frustration. "A few catcalls are nothing. But a curse. . ." Valentius clamped his teeth shut.

"Did you say a curse? It must have been a truly powerful one to scare you so."

"Drop it, you little wretch. You love stabbing a man in the back. You're a vulture. You creep up on dead things to feed."

"If I'm a vulture, what does that make you?"

Valentius sprang to his feet, but his stomach twisted with nausea. He sank back into the chair and wiped his sweaty forehead.

"Feeling sick? You're more addicted than you know. You think you can manage without me? You'll overdose within the week!"

"*You'll overdose within the week,*" Valentius mimicked. "You've been telling me that for years. And I'm still here."

"You need a dose right now."

"I wouldn't if you had put a vial in my belt pouch."

"And have you partake with Herod watching? That would have been perfect. So, your big plan is to turn me in for killing Glavienus. He died decades ago. Who will identify me? No one will believe I am Alexander Nisos. I'm just a slave."

"Those witnesses in Rome will know you. You're a legend, Alexander. Roman children sing songs about you. The bounty on your head has doubled. It will compensate for my lost pension quite nicely."

"You cannot condemn me without condemning yourself. You're in withdrawal; not thinking straight. I'll get you some opium."

"Is that *your* big plan? Get me some opium?"

"No, my big plan was to make a lot of money," exclaimed Demitre. "You complicated matters when you insisted on poisoning Longinus with *belladonna*. It was a huge risk for me to sneak back in his quarters. I was just about to check his pupils when his eyes flew wide open. I barely got out the door in time. How would you explain me being out of the slave quarters?"

"You infected his hand!" shouted Valentius. "You wrapped the cauterized wound, oh so nicely, with a dirty bandage. You must have been irritated when you didn't get to cut off his hand."

"Not particularly. It did irritate *you*, however. But I still don't understand how he was healed the next day. It was impossible. He said the dead Nazarene healed him. Preposterous!"

"Nobody cares about that, but they will care about capturing Alexander Nisos. They'll forget all about me with you in hand."

"Do you really think Herod will forget you committed treason when you drugged the guards? You're more irrational than I thought. It's bad enough that you've ranted for two years about how Clovius Longinus had Aurelius assassinated! You've been looking for an excuse to destroy the Longinus family for decades. Every stupid decision you've made, you blamed them. Aurelius drowned in a storm! There was no conspiracy, Felix."

"Yes there was! Why are you so resistant to accepting Aurelius's murder? Did you have something to do with it?"

"Have you completely gone mad? If either one of us is to blame, it would be you! *You* got my nephew killed, not Longinus!"

"*Not true!* I'm the victim here. It was a conspiracy against me. I read Longinus's letter. He could not have known there was an open positon for a centurion unless he created it. An assassin on that ship killed Aurelius and used a convenient storm to cover it up. The *Scarlet Jade* sank in shallow water. Nearly everyone made it to shore. You know Aurelius could swim like a shark. He couldn't have drowned. How many times do I have to explain this to you?"

"You can explain it a thousand times, but it won't make it true."

"You used Aurelius against me. You're the one who told him to change his name."

"No, Felix, he changed his name after Julia told him who I really am. That was *when*, but not *why* he changed his name. He wanted to be a soldier, just like you, but he feared the shame of your court-martial and the stain of your guilt. But you didn't improve matters when he confronted you in the kitchen after Julia died, and you pushed him against the *furnus*. The scar on his neck was a constant reminder of his anger. He swore he would never forgive you."

"What had I done that needed forgiveness? Did he forget how I took his punishment on my own back? I bled for him. I bear the scars he deserved."

"And you never let him forget it was his guilt that put them there," grumbled Demitre. "It gave you leverage over him. Still, I had to convince you to take his place when I found out the whip was treated with *belladonna*."

"Not true! I was prepared to do it willingly. I knew the injured boy's family went to the emperor and demanded that Aurelius be flogged, despite the *Lex Valeria* decree of no cruel punishment for a Roman citizen. What a joke! I didn't see you offer to take his punishment."

"It wasn't for me to do. It was your responsibility."

"You think flogging is a slap in the face? It was ten lashes. The poison made it that much worse. The hallucinations were maddening. I could have died." The two men fell silent, lost in bitter memories.

Aurelius had done a terrible thing. Even though he was only eight years old at the time, he knew it was wrong. The young boy was forced to watch his father be publicly scourged, in his place. His father's effort only added to his already devastating guilt. Each day it took for Felix to heal was another day deeper into shame for Aurelius. Demitre did everything he could for Felix, but he was powerless against the remorse which left the boy's soul as scarred as his father's back. Demitre's grief over the death of Aurelius went deeper than any pain he had ever known, even worse than the death of his beloved sister.

Demitre broke the silence. "Are you forgetting the letter Aurelius sent after you first demanded his transfer? He was willing to come here, but not as the lowest ranked centurion in the legion. He wanted to earn the title of cohort centurion to equal your rank. The three of us could have been together as we were in Tiberius when Julia was alive. Have you ever considered Aurelius changed his *nomen* to Julius so you two could serve at the same fortress? He could have canceled your transfer request by revealing his true name, but he did not."

"Then why did he fight me on coming here?"

"I just told you! You wanted him here on *your* terms. He wanted to come, but only on *his* terms. The two of you were like spoiled children."

"There's nothing to gain by arguing about this now. At least I had my Julia's love for a time. She was the only bright light in my life. We couldn't wait for Glavienus to die. Your poison was taking too long."

"No, what you did wasn't because you grew impatient. You wanted to humiliate Glavienus. You wanted to take what belonged to him in his own house."

"It wasn't like that. Julia and I were so young then, impulsive and desperate for each other. There was no," Valentius struggled for the right words, "no conspiracy! It just happened. Yes, I took her from Glavienus. But you took his life."

"And you took Aurelius's life, you selfish monster! After Julia died, he was the only bright light *in my life!* He was the only one who didn't want anything from me except my companionship. Your obsessive need to control him is what got him killed."

Valentius's face went red. "That's a lie!"

"Is it? It eats you alive when a man refuses to be intimidated. Why else would you go after Octavean and Longinus? You're a bully, Felix. Grief has not consumed you these last two years. It's your obsessive need to dominate everyone. Death snatched Aurelius from your control. It gnaws at you like termites in a dead tree. You took his punishment to force his gratitude. Or should I say servitude?"

Shaken by Demitre's cruel accusations, Valentius slumped further in the chair.

"I see the truth in your eyes, Felix, even if you're not man enough to admit it. You know your motives were tainted. I have news for you. After what Julia told him, Aurelius hated the sight of you! He hated you even more than I do!"

Valentius froze. This day was to be his greatest victory. Instead, it was a cascade of failures. He never imagined the death of Longinus and the others would fail to soothe his inner turmoil. But far worse than failure, Demitre's bitter words were daggers in his heart. The accusation that Aurelius hated him sparked a wildfire of rage in his soul. What little reason he still possessed was reduced to ashes.

Valentius grabbed Demitre, threw the door open, and tossed him into the strafing sand. Demitre put his hands up to shield his face. He choked on dust as he gasped for air. Valentius ducked behind him and twisted Demitre's arms behind his back to use him as a shield. Demitre could not protect his face. He was defenseless against Valentius's greater strength. Demitre was forced to keep his eyes tightly shut or risk permanent blindness. Desperate to get indoors, he did not resist as Valentius pushed him toward the pit house.

Half a dozen guards stood around the pit. They were discussing the executions and Valentius's betrayal. There were no prisoners in the pit, but they had to be on duty. The sound of someone kicking on the door interrupted their conversation. A soldier pulled one of the double doors open as the two men burst inside. Valentius had an arm lock on Demitre. They were shouting at each other. The guards were shocked when Valentius's slave cursed him instead of begging for mercy. Valentius stomped past them, ignoring their astonishment. He marched Demitre up to the rim of the pit and shoved him in. The guards heard a very short scream. Valentius turned on his heel without bothering to look over the edge. The guards approached the edge of the pit. What they saw was not entirely unexpected.

Valentius went to the accounting office. The attendant was asleep at his desk thinking no one would brave the storm. The centurion pounded on the counter with his fist.

"Get my deposit box! Now! I should have you beaten for sleeping at your post!" The attendant knocked his chair over in his haste to jump to his feet. He retrieved the box. Valentius unlocked it and removed a scroll. He deliberately left the door open on his way out. The wind slammed the heavy wooden door against the wall.

Valentius entered the slave quarters and went straight to Demitre's corner. Only Demitre had a framed bed. Ignoring the stares of the slaves, he pulled the mattress away, popped a false panel, and removed the vials of opium. He dropped them inside his tunic.

Back in his office, he set the vials on his desk in neat little rows. He poured a full cup of wine and emptied an entire vial in it. Demitre had never let him have more than half a vial at a time. He gulped the mixture and grinned with anticipation. Over and over he counted the vials. He rearranged the rows and counted again. He stuffed his coin pouch full of vials.

Valentius unrolled the scroll. It was an insurance policy in case Demitre ever turned his murderous talents on him. Salvitto would find the scroll when he enacted Valentius's last will and testament. The document revealed that the slave known as Demitre was Alexander Nisos, the murderer of General Claudio Merula Glavienus. Valentius read the document over. He added details about Demitre's plan to steal the executed soldiers' pensions and the prize money. Out of spite, Valentius added the name of the *dispensator* who was going to forge the pension claims. He named the soldiers Demitre had poisoned. It didn't matter he implicated himself. The scroll would not be read until his death.

The surging euphoria of the opium overtook him. He decided the day was not a complete loss. *Consul* Longinus would learn his son had joined Aurelius in death. The double-crosser was in the pit and would be arrested for murder. The charges against Valentius died with the sixteen accusers in his opium fantasy. He no longer cared about his reduced pension now that he would collect the bounty on Alexander Nisos. He sighed and yawned. It had been an exhausting day. He put his head down on his arms. He fell asleep leaving the scroll unrolled.

As Valentius slept, Nikolaus returned to the garrison with the cremator. On the way back to the Antonia, he thought of how Valentius had taken away his only friend. He decided to confront the centurion. Valentius would kill him, or he would kill Valentius, and be executed. Either way, he would be done with his miserable life.

Nikolaus went to Valentius's office after helping the cremator with the horses. He entered quietly. He saw the centurion was asleep at his desk. His belt hung on the back of his chair with his dagger in its sheath. Nikolaus reached for the dagger, but the scroll caught his attention. After reading the first few lines, Nikolaus snatched up the scroll. He crept out and ran straight to Tribune Salvitto's office.

Chapter 38

———⊱⊰———

Valentius awoke with a start. Someone was shaking him. The legionary standing over him stepped aside, revealing Tribune Salvitto, somber-faced and silent. His crossed arms and rigid stance did not bode well for Valentius.

"Come with me," Salvitto ordered as he turned on his heel. The three men crossed the quad and entered the pit house. The pit guards joined the legionary standing behind Valentius. The tribune walked to the edge of the pit and pointed. "What is the meaning of this, Valentius?"

"Sir, do you mean my slave. The pit will do him some good."

Salvitto pointed again, "Look!"

Valentius peered over the side. Demitre was lying on the ground. His head was skewed at an unnatural angle. Valentius shrugged his shoulders. "*Ohe!* I guess it didn't do him much good, after all."

The tribune nodded at the guards. They grabbed Valentius by the arms, scooped his feet out from under him, and dangled him inside the pit. Valentius flailed, demanding to be lifted out. When the tribune nodded again, the guards let go. Valentius hit the ground on his hands and knees before he rolled across the grimy stone floor.

He came to his feet shouting. "He's my property! So what if he's dead!"

"Felix Pomponius Valentius, I am arresting you for the murder of Alexander Nisos, for harboring a known fugitive, and complicity in multiple murders. You are also charged with encouraging insubordination against a ranking officer and obstruction of justice for assault on a ranking officer. Most importantly, you are charged with treason against Rome."

"What is all this! What are you talking about?"

Salvitto pulled two scrolls from his belt. He put one under his arm. "Recognize this? It was interesting reading. We also found one of your wineskins in Holding. When the wine evaporated, we found an unknown powder in the residue. We tested it on a slave. I don't need to tell you the result. Unfortunately, this evidence did not save sixteen lives today, but it will bring an end to your life. King Herod will see to it!" He handed the scroll to one of the men. He unrolled the other one.

Valentius remembered Herod's threat. "No, I appeal to the emperor!"

"I was hoping you would say that. Did you know the emperor's father, Germanicus, and General Glavienus were close friends? But there's another matter, Felix. When I caught you reading my correspondence from *Consul* Longinus, I interrupted your invasion of my privacy. You missed the last part. *'Forgive me, Tribune Salvitto, for I am under a great deal of pressure to give an answer to Emperor Tiberius. I have submitted requests to all of the Roman bases near Caesarea and I will accept the first approval I receive.'* I just happened to send the first approval. Longinus had no idea if there was an opening at the Antonia. In addition, the entitlement of centurion was initiated by Emperor Tiberius, himself, not *Consul* Longinus. Guards, leave the dead body in there. Put any other prisoners in Holding. Take his clothing. Put him in *bracae*. Give him nothing but water and barley bread."

"I'm a cohort centurion!" Valentius bellowed. "You can't do this to me!"

"I already have," Salvitto declared as he walked away.

Valentius continued to shout at the guards. Since he was a centurion, they could not retaliate, but their tolerance was wearing thin. Finally, they submitted an unusual request to *Primus Pilus* Centurion Tacitus. Seeing no need to bother the tribune with it, he approved the request enthusiastically. The guards left the Pithouse and locked the double doors behind them.

Felix was alone with the body of Demitre. There were no conversations to overhear. There was no one to get him water or bread. The stench burned his nostrils. His eyes were fixed on the sprawled body of Demitre, lying on his chest, arms reaching as if pleading for help. His head was skewed to the side with his chin jutting forward. His eyes and gaping mouth were in shadow, making his skin appear to be stretched over an empty skull.

Felix shivered and stood up. He had seen plenty of death throughout his life. He rarely gave it a thought, but the black-socketed stare of Demitre's corpse was making him anxious. He advanced on the body and kicked it back against the wall. It was still staring at him. He grabbed the feet to rotate the body toward the wall. He wiped his hands on the *bracae* and rushed to the far side of the pit. Keeping his back to the wall, eyes tightly closed, Felix slid down to the filthy stone floor. He tried keeping his eyes shut, but the fear of something crawling on him forced his eyes open. The sight of the corpse made him squeeze them shut again. Over and over he opened and closed his eyes.

Darkness loomed across the sky, but no one came to light the torches. He would be in inky blackness with the mice and roaches that lived in the gaps between the stones. He had always feared the dark even as an adult. The slick feel of the stone floor on his bare feet heightened his anxiety. When Salvitto ordered his clothes removed, Felix had hidden his opium stash in the gaps in the wall. When the darkness had chased away the last remnants of sunlight, Felix found a vial and swallowed the entire contents. He found a second vial and swallowed it as well. The euphoria came much more quickly than usual. He slumped to the floor as fear faded from his mind.

Something dropped on him, jerking him out of his lethargy. It squealed as it ran across his shoulder and up his neck. Felix cried out as he swatted at the rat and staggered to his feet. Swaying, he reached out to steady himself. A light through the barred opening above the double doors appeared. He hoped it was someone coming to light the torches, but the light vanished. Frustrated, he kicked at the air, which threw him off balance, and he fell. The light appeared again, only brighter. Felix gasped as a cyclops glared at him through the barred windows. Its single bright eye was fixed on him with cold detachment as if he were nothing more than an insect. A cloud passed in front of the eye.

"It's the full moon, you idiot," said Demitre, in his most patronizing voice.

Felix clapped his hands over his ears. He shot a look around the pit expecting to see Demitre step into the moonlight with his most condescending air of superiority. Nothing happened. He stared at the edge of the moon shadow. He was terrified he would see a hand reach out, but he was unable to look away. He did not intend to kill Demitre but neither did he regret it. He realized the double catastrophe as he recovered from his initial shock of being tossed in the pit. Not only was he under arrest, he could no longer claim the bounty on Nisos.

Felix could feel familiar symptoms start to mount. He wiped his watering eyes and runny nose with the back of his hand. The incessant yawning was beginning, a classic sign he needed his next dose. Could he be imagining the symptoms?

"Did I just take a dose?" he asked the darkness.

"No, Felix," answered Julia. "Can't you remember? But you don't seem to remember things very well, especially promises!" She pointed an accusing finger at the corpse of her brother. "You promised to protect him, not kill him! He protected us!"

"Julia, it was an accident!" He tried to take hold of her, but his arms closed on empty air. He knew Julia would come back if he could find his opium. He reached into the crevice where he had hidden the vials. A sharp pain made him snatch his hand away. A rat squealed before it burrowed deeper into the wall. Felix jammed his hand in the crevice to feel for the vials. The rat bit at his fingers repeatedly until he got a hold of the vermin and jerked it out. He flung the rat across the pit and heard it hit the opposite wall. It squeaked and fell to the floor. Felix tried to feel for the vials again, but they weren't there. Scraping his fingers on crumbling mortar, he searched every crevice. He felt tiny feet scurry over his hands. Black shiny things ran up his arms. He shook the roaches off and kept searching.

Finally, he felt the familiar ceramic shapes. He dug a vial from the crevice. It slipped from his fingers and shattered on the stone floor. In the moonlight he could see the milky liquid puddled among the shards. Felix dropped to all-fours and licked the bitter substance from the fouled stones. As the opium digested, it surged through his nervous system. The euphoria hit him with a violent rush he had never experienced. The opiate's seductive magic convinced him everything would be fine. Salvitto would release him, and Herod would give the prize back to him. He grinned in anticipation.

Felix fell asleep, but something awakened him. He thought he heard a scratching sound like talons clawing on rocks. He sat up to look around. The corpse was further from the wall with a hand outstretched. He told himself he was dreaming and fell back asleep.

Demitre shook him awake. "Good evening, Felix, mind if we chat?" Demitre faced him, sitting cross-legged a foot above the ground.

"You're not real!"

Demitre brayed with laughter. "So true! I am a product," he jabbed Valentius in the forehead, "of your twisted little drug-poisoned mind. I'm impressed you could figure that out all by yourself. I usually have to explain things to you."

"I'm not stupid! You just treat me like I am."

"You always made it so easy and fun," Demitre smirked. "I've tricked you so many times, I've lost count. Outsmarting you is like stealing from a dead man."

"How ironic you would say that since you're a dead man! So you think you've tricked *me*? You think you're smarter than me? Let's talk about your mother, Callista. Remember when you told me she committed adultery with her husband's slave, his business manager, and you were the result? Amusing isn't it? Your father was a slave. Callista tried to turn Julia against me, so I told her what I knew. She denied it until I told her I learned it from you. She was furious *and* terrified. She was convinced you would tell others. She devised a plan to secure my loyalty and your silence. Callista's scheme would get rid of General Glavienus for me, get rid of you for her, and make us both rich. And you fell for it!"

"You're insane!" screamed the Demitre hallucination. "There was no scheme. Glavienus was going to name Julia as an adulterer and have her executed. I had to protect my little sister. How could you and Callista know Glavienus would accuse Julia in my presence?"

"Glavienus didn't know you were Julia's half-brother. We knew he wouldn't hesitate to accuse her in your presence, since you were his attending *medicus*. Callista made sure you were there when the judges and prosecutors arrived. Who do you think left the dagger on the table? Glavienus would attempt to make his accusation, and you would kill him. I would 'accidently' kill you when you resisted arrest. The emperor pledged a reward for you, alive or dead. Callista and I would split it."

"But you spared my life. Was it because we were once good friends? Can we ever be friends again?" Demitre extended a hand.

"It's true; I couldn't take your life. You sacrificed yourself to save the woman I loved. Please, Alexander, can you ever forgive me?" Felix reached to take his offered hand.

The hallucination snatched his hand back. "No! Never! You couldn't kill me because you're weak, not because I was your friend. You're pathetic and stupid!"

"Me! You think I'm the stupid one? You stabbed Glavienus in front of *eight witnesses*! We had to flee from Rome because of you. I spared your life because I'm smart. Keeping you alive gave me leverage over Callista. And who has been my slave *for decades?*"

The hallucination screamed. "You endangered Julia's life so I would kill her husband! Killing him with poison wasn't good enough? It was Callista who told Glavienus about Julia's adultery and you allowed it! What if I had not killed the brute? What then, let Julia die?"

"Dear, dear, Demitre, you're not so smart after all. I was hidden behind the screened passage, with my bow in hand. In case you didn't kill him, I would. Glavienus couldn't see me, but I could see him. My sweet Julia was never in danger."

"No! No! No! I played the slave for nothing!" The hallucination began to melt into the stone floor. Shrieking and twisting, Demitre disappeared.

"I made a fool of you, Alexander! I am the clever one, not you!" He danced a little jig.

Someone coughed. Valentius spun around. He was face to face with Julia. Her face was drawn with sadness. "You and Mother did this terrible deed? How could you? I loved you. I trusted you. All this time I thought you were protecting my dear brother. He gave up everything to save my life when he became Demitre. And now you're bragging about humiliating him!" She slashed at him with her fingernails. Valentius tried to defend himself.

The struggle jolted him awake from his nightmare. He heard a noise. It was a low scraping sound followed by a loud slap. He didn't want to look, but he couldn't keep from it. He cringed when he saw that Demitre's body was now in the middle of the pit in full light of the moon. The hand which was outstretched before was back beside the body. The other hand rested beside the oddly angled head. Demitre's mouth was wide open. There was a dark flash of motion on the stone floor. A roach ran up Demitre's arm and on to his neck. It hesitated as it crawled across his face before it disappeared into his mouth. Felix gagged. He squeezed his eyes shut but quickly opened them. He knew the corpse couldn't move if he kept his eyes on it.

"Do you really think that will work?" asked Aurelius. Felix stumbled back against the wall and collapsed to the floor. Aurelius was sitting on an invisible chair. "So, Father, you killed Longinus to prove your love for me? How touching. Since I failed to join you at the Antonia, why don't you join me?" Aurelius leaped at Valentius with a dagger. Felix shrieked. He flailed his hands to ward off the attack.

Something pushed him over and Felix woke, again. A long wooden rod disappeared over the rim of the pit. Panting, Felix peered into the darkness, trying to find Aurelius. There was only the rock walls and floor. Demitre's body was gone. He tried to think where he last saw it. His hand touched something cold and fleshy. A terrifying chill surged through him as he slowly turned his head. Demitre was slumped against the wall with sprawled legs. His head lay flat on his chest at an impossible angle. His demonic eyes glowed with reflected moonlight. Felix knew this was no hallucination. Demitre's corpse had dragged itself across the floor. Slowly his dead hands rose and danced in the air. His knees lifted and his feet danced over the stone floor. Demitre's head began to rise from his chest, but the sightless eyes stayed fixed on Felix. The mouth flopped open and a voice sounded, "I'm waiting for you, Felix. Waiting for you to die!"

A terrified scream shattered the night.

Chapter 39

⸻⸻⸻

Adan was running through a ruined city being chased by a demonic creature. He raced into a blind alley only to be stopped by a wall of blackened limestone. The creature slowed, gloating in its victory, and sprang at Adan with bared teeth and claws. He screamed and jerked wide awake, yet he could still hear a scream. It came from the Antonia. He wondered if someone was being murdered. When silence once again joined the darkness, Adan went back to sleep. The morning dawned as the sun peeked through curtains of wispy clouds. Adan threw back the blanket and sat up. The memories of the previous day flooded his mind as he gazed out over the city. He whispered a prayer of gratitude for being alive.

The brown sky was clear again. It was hard to believe how different this peaceful morning was compared to yesterday's misery. The aroma of food drifting from the windows beckoned him. He lowered the ladder, climbed down, and went in the house, leaving Nebetka as he slept. Serapio, Fabiana, and Malchus were eating breakfast. They smiled at Adan around mouthfuls of bread dipped in olive oil.

"Ah, there he is!" exclaimed Fabiana. "Did you rest well, son? Come give me a hug."

Serapio pulled up a chair. "You look rested. You must have slept well."

"I did, mostly, but I can't believe I'm having a nice chat over breakfast. Yesterday was, well, thankfully, it was *yesterday*."

Malchus twisted the head off a fried locust and popped it in his mouth. Fabiana got Adan some figs, but he was eyeing the bowl of locusts. He made good use of both.

"Where's Peter?" asked Adan.

"He's still asleep," said Serapio. "Listen, I know you're in a hurry to get to Caesarea, but we need to make preparations. You'll be on your way early tomorrow. I promise."

"I can't bear to think about what those letters will do to Dulcibella and her family," murmured Adan. "I'm not just worried about Dulcibella. I know Marcus. His sense of justice runs deep. He will not tolerate this news without sharpening his sword. Marcus might even blame himself. He recommended leniency for Valentius at his court-martial."

"I understand," said Serapio, "but God will comfort Marcus. We will have you on the road tomorrow." He tore some bread from a loaf and offered it to Adan. "When I get back with Nikolaus, we will plan how to get the four of you out of the city." Adan looked at him questioningly.

"I didn't say anything yesterday," said Malchus, "for obvious reasons, but it seems the high priest has decided to 'dramatically' end my employment. Caiaphas thinks I helped Peter escape from the common prison. My reaction after shooting you confirmed his suspicions. However, if my presence complicates things, I'll find another way."

"No. I'm glad you will be coming with us."

"So you don't mind traveling with the man who shot you with poisoned arrows?"

"If you had not, I would have stayed dead. Just promise not to use me for target practice again and I will be most pleased."

Malchus laughed. "I promise. I don't need to practice anyway."

"Ah, I feel so much safer."

"Ana, what are you thinking?" asked Serapio abruptly. Fabiana was staring off into space, biting her lower lip.

"What?"

"I know you, Ana. You're plotting something."

"I have been thinking about their escape. I have an idea, but you're not going to like it."

"I already don't like it."

Fabiana slapped his knee. "You're impossible! You haven't even heard my idea, and you've already made up your mind. Adan will listen because he's not an ol' goat like you." Serapio chuckled and Fabiana continued, "You know how they say the best place to hide is in plain sight? So I was thinking. . ."

"Now we're in trouble," Serapio muttered.

Fabiana ignored him. "If the three of you were dressed in women's robes and head scarves, you could walk past every guard in the. . ."

"Dress these men in women's clothes!" exclaimed Serapio. "How can you even think of such a thing? We only need to cause a distraction at the gate."

"You should do that as well. Keep the guards occupied while they walk past. Outside the city, they change clothes, you turn the horses over to them, and off they go. Your reaction tells me it would work. You think a man would never wear woman's clothing because it is illegal and *you* would never do such a thing. I'm hoping the soldiers think like you."

"I think it would work," said Adan.

"Ridiculous! I'll think of a plan that doesn't involve women's clothes. For now, I'm off to see Tribune Salvitto." Serapio headed for the door. "Adan, before I go, there is something you should know. When Herod offered to allow a slave take your place, Nikolaus started to get up. I stopped him."

"I'm glad to know that, more than you realize."

"Adan, I think now would be a good time for me to tell you about Valentius," said Malchus. He described Herod's presentation of evidence. Adan sat in contemplation. His life had drastically changed because of another man's delusions. He was grateful he was alive, but he and Dulcibella would have to leave family, friends, the beloved home in Caesarea, and his career. Worst of all, he had risked his life to defend Simon Peter, and now he and Dulcibella would suffer for it. She would grieve for the loss of her family. He wasn't sure he should even contact his father. Adan was surprised that it saddened him to think he would never see him again.

"The prize money will be useful to us," said Malchus, "since we will need to start new lives someplace else."

As Adan considered these things, Serapio approached the Antonia. He carried Adan's armor and weapons to offer in exchange for Nikolaus. When he reached the fortress, Serapio started to explain his errand, but the guards waved him in on sight. He went straight to Salvitto's office.

Salvitto waved a hand toward a chair. "Serapio, it is good to see you. I am sorry it is under these circumstances. My condolences to you and your wife. I know you were fond of Longinus. I was, too. If there was anything I could have. . ." He nervously rubbed his chin. "Did you ever tell him what happened to your eye?"

"No, I never did. Listen Theo, there was nothing you could do."

"Yesterday? No, but over the last two years Valentius abused his authority. Tacitus warned me enough times. He belabored his grievances so often, I stopped paying much attention. Valentius never seemed to cross the line, but he did step on it enough times. This tragedy could have been averted if I had not called Longinus to my office before his shift. He would have intercepted that drugged wine. I am responsible for much of this tragedy."

"It is tempting to second guess when things go badly." Serapio touched the scar on his face. "Has Valentius been charged?"

"Yes. It's a complicated story. How much time do you have?"

Serapio settled back in his chair. "I'm in no hurry."

"I have known Valentius for a long time. He can be spiteful and obsessive but, he has never been clever. The more I thought about the whole scheme, I realized someone else had to be involved. Valentius is simply not that smart. Then a document came to me yesterday in Valentius's handwriting. His slave, Demitre, is actually Alexander Nisos."

Serapio's jaw dropped. "You cannot be serious! *The* Alexander Nisos, the one who murdered General Glavienus in front of witnesses?"

"Yes, and the widowed wife of Glavienus married Felix Valentius. Valentius and Nisos were brothers-in-law. To think all these years Nisos was right here in plain sight. No one could imagine the wealthy Alexander Nisos would impersonate a slave. No one looked twice at him."

"Yes, in plain sight." He thought of Fabiana's plan. "Do you have Nisos in custody?"

"You could say that. He's in the pit. Valentius literally threw him in. He landed head first; broke his neck. Valentius claimed it was accidental, but I think he killed Demitre to cover up their conspiracy. He told the guards the corpse crawled around the pit all night and even talked to him. Honestly, I think a few legionaries put on a 'puppet show' for him. I suspect Tacitus knows something about it. Anyway, he has a month or more in the pit. Then he goes to Rome. He appealed to Emperor Gaius. You know, Serapio, I've just thought of a letter addressed to me about two years ago. There was another scroll inside the scroll. It had instructions for the second letter to be delivered after Valentius's death—to Demitre."

"A letter for Demitre *after* Valentius was dead?"

"Sadly, I can't remember the name of the centurion who sent it, so I don't know where it's filed. It'll probably show up when a *dispensator* is looking for an inheritance testament. Since Demitre was really Nisos, it could be very interesting reading." Salvitto shuffled a stack of papyrus on his desk. "Let me give you the pension claim for Longinus."

"What?" Serapio's eyebrows shot up.

"Adas named you as his heir to his pension. You can present your claim to the accounting office any time after today. Herod is having the gold transported here tomorrow morning."

Serapio remembered to look sad in spite of the temptation to burst out laughing. Adan would get every *aureus* of his pension. "Honestly, Theo, I had no idea he left this to me. What I'm here about is Nikolaus. Adas made me promise to buy his freedom. I have brought his weapons and armor to trade for the young man, but now I have his pension. Would you consider naming your price?"

"I'm sorry, Serapio. Nikolaus belongs to the emperor, so he is not mine to sell. He does the work of two men, and unlike most slaves, he's dependable. He is much too valuable. Longinus spoke to me before about buying Nikolaus. I have to tell you the same thing I told him. I am accountable for the emperor's property."

Serapio was too shocked to argue. He had not considered that Salvitto might reject his offer. Salvitto pursed his lips in thought at the bitter disappointment on Serapio's face.

"However, I do feel partially responsible for yesterday. Ironically, I summoned Longinus to relay a warning. He could have told Herod how I delayed him, but he didn't. I should have admitted it. It may not have done any good, but it would have been the honest thing to do." Defiance brightened Salvitto's eyes. "All right, yes, I will sell Nikolaus to honor Longinus, as well as you. I will buy two slaves to take Nikolaus's place and pay for them myself. That should appease the emperor's bookkeepers."

Serapio thanked him profusely, but had one more request. "Would you consider selling me the buckskin that Nikolaus trained? I could also use another horse, gear included."

Salvitto made a face. "You want the Akhal-Teke? Gladly! It is only good for looking handsome. Nikolaus must have a magic spell for renegade horses. He's the only one who can ride it without getting thrown. For the other, take an old pack horse. Would two hundred *denarii* be an agreeable price?"

"It is most generous of you. I can rest easy knowing Adas's last wish is fulfilled. I simply can't believe he is gone. I keep expecting to see him walk through my doorway. *Gratias.*" He handed the claim letter back to Salvitto, but the tribune hesitated as if he had changed his mind.

"Did I tell you there is a substantial bounty on Nisos? Nikolaus brought Valentius's scroll to me. When he is freed, he will be eligible to collect the bounty."

"You could claim the bounty for yourself, Theo."

"I don't need it. Nikolaus does."

"This is very generous of you, Theo. It is truly an honor being your friend."

"It is the least I can do to honor Longinus and it is far less than what you did." He deducted two hundred *denarii* from the pension claim document. He gave Serapio the document and the contract for Nikolaus. "I just sold another slave of my own to a close friend named Philemon. I think he bought a chair from you once."

"He did. Seemed like a good man."

"He is. He needed a kitchen slave. Onesimus didn't belong here. The same goes for Nikolaus. His intelligence was wasted on cleaning stalls."

Serapio shook Salvitto's hand. "Bless you, my friend." He left, put the documents in his knapsack, and went to find Nikolaus. Walking up and down the rows of stalls, Serapio called out for the young man.

"*Serapio!*" Nikolaus hurried out of a stall. "Is he alive?" he whispered urgently.

"He is. Something else has happened." Serapio explained. Nikolaus clapped his hands over his mouth. His life had dramatically changed with one sentence.

"You must save your joy until we are gone. Choose an old pack horse for me. I'll saddle it. Then gear up Inventio. He's yours now."

Nikolaus thought he must be dreaming, but Serapio looked too real to be imaginary. He found a horse and equipment for Serapio. As he ran to Inventio's stall, he whistled as he always did. The gelding raised his head, ears forward. Nikolaus wrapped his arms around the horse's neck. The horse lowered his head to Nikolaus's side.

"Come on, Inventio, let's get out of here!" Serapio was waiting for him in the arena. At the gate, he showed the purchase documents for Nikolaus and the horses. The guard waved them on. Nikolaus did not give the Antonia another glance as they hurried to the shop.

"Now listen to me, Nikolaus. His name is Adan Novius Serapio. You must call him Adan. He is my youngest son, the fourth child of six. He has two brothers and three sisters. He is a furniture maker and he is twenty-four years old."

Nikolaus nodded eagerly. "I will not forget. I promise."

"You go inside. I'll take care of the horses. Ana is expecting you."

Fabiana met him with a hug and pointed upstairs. "Go to him."

Nikolaus bounded up the stairs. When he entered the room, his expression sobered. Adan was lying on his side, revealing the new scar across his back. Nikolaus wondered how it was already healed. He prayed aloud, "Father God, please help him forgive my betrayal."

"I suspect you had no other choice," said Adan as he sat up.

"You really are alive, Sir! And your wounds are healed!" Nikolaus frowned in hesitation. "Serapio said to address you as—Adan. "

"It would be appreciated." Adan pulled his tunic on.

"Sir, I couldn't tell you at the time, but I betrayed you."

"Don't call me sir. It's Adan."

"Sir, did you hear what I said?"

"Yes, and I knew it then."

"They made horrible threats against both of us."

"Valentius and Herod?"

"At first it was Valentius and Demitre. When we got back, Demitre took me to Valentius's office. You told me to pretend to be angry with you, but I couldn't do it. Valentius put a dagger to my throat. He said he would kill me if I didn't tell him everything that happened in Caesarea. I said, 'Go ahead. I don't care.' That made him angry. He threw his dagger down and was going to hit me, but Demitre stopped him as if he was the master."

"Then what?"

"Demitre said, 'If you don't tell us, we will kill Longinus. If you tell him anything about this, we'll know. We'll kill him and his horse.' They said they would make me watch. I told them everything. I betrayed you and Dulcibella. I was afraid not to because I didn't know what they already knew."

"Nikolaus, you were willing to give up your own life to protect me, twice, in fact. Serapio told me what you did in the theater yesterday."

"It was an easy decision. I want you to return to Dulcibella. I made a promise to her." Nikolaus looked away. "It was difficult when Herod interrogated me. I didn't know what to say so I answered truthfully. He threatened to have me sold to the copper mines if I told you what he asked. I should have told you anyway."

"I don't think so. Everything happened as it should. Remember, Herod reinstated the men's pensions because I also answered truthfully. What did you tell him about Peter?"

"I said you saw a stranger take Peter out. He asked how you could see that it was a stranger because he knew the torches had burned out. I said the man had a torch. He asked about the shackles. I said the man unlocked them. I just didn't mention he did it *without* keys. He asked if the intruder unlocked only Peter's shackles. I said yes. When Herod accused Valentius in the theater, I understood the question. I told him the truth, just not all of the truth."

"You handled it well, Nikolaus. The angel *was* a stranger, and *he* was his own torch. The angel did free Peter, but not Octavean. That's how Herod knew Valentius had been in there. Your honesty cleared the way for the soldiers' pensions to go to their families. Everything turned out for the best. However, this drama is not over yet."

Serapio appeared in the doorway. "No, it's not. Now, the emperor will be interested in Valentius *and* his slave. Demitre is none other than Alexander Nisos."

"The man that killed General Glavienus in front of witnesses?" Adan exclaimed.

"The exact same."

"That explains their odd relationship."

"Sir, now that I'm here, what do you need me to do?" asked Nikolaus.

"I need you to stop calling me Sir. Call me Adan."

"But, Sir, it doesn't feel right for a slave to call his master by his *praenomen*."

Adan shot a look at Serapio. "Didn't you tell him?"

"I thought I would leave that to you."

"Tell me what, Sir? Uh. . .I mean. . ." Nikolaus rolled his eyes in frustration.

Adan relished what he was about to say. "Why don't you sit down, Nikolaus? As soon as we get to a *publicanus* we will register your slave document as null and void. You are once again Nikolaus Kokinos, a free citizen. Now you can find your sister. Malchus says he will share the prize money with you so you will be able to travel."

"Nikolaus will not need any of the prize money," declared Serapio. "There is a bounty on Nisos's head. Salvitto said Nikolaus is eligible to claim it in Rome after Demitre's identity is confirmed." Serapio beamed at the young man. "You're free to go wherever you want."

"Sir, please don't send me away!" cried Nikolaus. "My sister has her own life. I want to see her, yes, but I cannot stay with her. Please let me work for you."

Adan and Serapio were speechless. This was not the reaction they were expecting. Serapio left the room to let them talk.

"Listen to me, Nikolaus. It is your choice to stay or go. I would never send you away, but neither will you be my servant. If you stay, it will be as my friend."

Nikolaus sighed with relief. "To hear you call me friend has been my hope for some time. Sir. . .I'm sorry. This is too much to take in. I keep thinking this is a dream and I will wake up in the slave quarters. Sir, uh, A-Adan, why have you been so kind to me?"

"I have felt the absence of a brother all my life. Be a brother to me, Nikolaus, and I will be a brother to you."

"I would like that very much. I can think of no greater honor." Nikolaus's eyes fell on Adan's seal ring. "I remember my father's signature ring. It had the letters NK, for Nicandros Kokinos, carved in a ruby set in gold. Kokinos, as you know, is the Greek word for red. Father had many ruby articles of jewelry. They're all gone now, of course. But when Dionysia and I were forced to sell Father's ring, I felt I had reviled his good name. The first thing I'll do is commission a signature ring like my father's."

A grin crossed Adan's face, but he tried to keep his voice casual. "Yes, you will need a ring now that you're a free man. You might find the perfect ring just waiting for you somewhere. Come on, we have escape plans to discuss." They went down stairs to join the others.

Adan pulled Serapio aside. "How did you convince Salvitto to sell Nikolaus?"

"How long were you going to keep your pension a secret? I used two hundred *denarii* of it to pay for Nikolaus and the horses."

"*Ohe,* I forgot about my pension. But what horses?"

"Inventio, of course, and an old horse for Peter. You didn't think they were going to walk all the way across Judea, did you?"

"You have thought of everything, Serapio. I'll give Nikolaus some money from my pension until he can claim the Nisos bounty, but could you keep the rest here, for now?"

"Of course. Now we need to discuss the escape plan. First, I have to apologize to Fabiana. Her idea is excellent, after all. Here's what we do, Nikolaus and I take the cart and the horses. We stop at the publican's stall to register his canceled document while you three 'women' pass by. Nebetka and Nikolaus can cause a distraction at the gate. We'll meet you outside the city. You change clothes, get your horses, and off you go, just like Fabiana suggested. What do you think?"

Adan slowly nodded. "It should work." Malchus overheard and agreed.

Malchus addressed Nikolaus. "You will provide a perfect distraction at the tax station. You've become a free citizen again. Bring as much attention on yourself as you can."

"That will be the easiest job I've ever done."

"What should we do at the gate," asked Nebetka.

"Be creative," said Serapio and Adan in unison.

They began their preparations by sewing hems on the inside of their garments to hold a few coins. Fabiana had enough robes and head scarves to cover their faces. It was a common sight to see only the eyes and hands of a woman if the desert sun or wind was especially punishing. Fabiana suggested they wear shiny, copper bracelets and carry Hannah's baskets on their heads to draw attention from their faces. Every hour clawed at Adan's heart, knowing Dulcibella would learn of his execution. As a distraction, Adan reminded Serapio he owed him a story. The former *gladiator* kept his word.

"It was my last fight in the arena. The manager matched me with a free opponent rather than a *gladiator*. Free opponents usually volunteered to settle a wager or prove their manhood. We fought, or rather; I fought while he tried to defend himself. The spectators were jeering, demanding he make an attack. Finally, exhausted and injured, he dropped his shield, and ran at me. Instinctively, I raised my sword. He ran on it. He was dead before he hit the ground. The crowd barely cheered; they were so bored. Then the manager announced it was my last fight. They gave me a standing ovation. I dropped my shield and weapon to wave them on. I was a free man again. Then some of the crowd started pointing." Serapio hung his head. Adan noticed Fabiana and Nebetka had left the room.

"I heard something and spun around. A young girl with my opponent's sword raised over her head was right behind me. She screamed, '*You killed my father!*' and brought the sword down. I couldn't move fast enough to get out of the way. You can see the result. She threw herself over her father's body and sobbed. I suppose Emperor Tiberius was amused to see a *gladiator* win fight after fight, only to be cut down by a little girl. He started laughing. You can't let the emperor laugh alone, so the spectators joined in. I had every right to kill her on the spot, but I couldn't do it. Somehow I got her out of the arena. She ran. I had celebrated the death of a man who, apparently, did not intend to survive. I have killed many men for my bread. Now, I live with their ghosts."

"You were a slave, Serapio. You didn't have a choice," said Adan.

"I always had a choice. I didn't have to sell myself to the arena to pay my debts. I willingly lived by the sword because I was too proud to live by the plow. The first time I killed a man in the arena, the remorse was overwhelming. Every time I killed a man, I killed a piece of my heart until there was no remorse left, only the need to survive another day. The other *gladitoris* became faceless *machinae* with moving parts that bled. It took Adan's death to bring life back into my heart and my soul. The men I killed weren't just figures behind armor, anymore. They became someone's son, father, husband, brother. They became human. I know Peter can heal me, but for the same reason you carved a cross in your hand, I keep this ruined eye as a reminder to never take another innocent life."

Serapio rubbed his hand along his beard. "The man I killed in my last fight was Theo Salvitto's brother. Theo was there, trying to talk him out of fighting. The little girl who took half my sight was his niece, Drusia. Theo and his wife took Drusia and her mother into their home. You were fortunate to have a commanding officer with a good heart, Adan. Not many do."

"I grieve with you, Serapio."

"I appreciate that. Perhaps one day I will not feel the need for this reminder. Then I will ask for God's healing touch through Peter." Serapio fell silent.

Adan suggested they get some rest. He and Nikolaus climbed on to the roof.

Nebetka was waiting for them. "He told you what happened?"

"Yes, it is sad and terrible," said Adan.

"I was there. It was awful. Did he tell you the crowd screamed for him to kill Drusia?"

"He left that part out."

"He would. He's not one to praise himself. Father was in terrible pain, but the fight manager refused to give him opium. He was angry because Father didn't kill Drusia. Plus, it was his last fight, so the manager was done with him. But losing his eye was nothing compared to losing his son. He and Mother were devastated. Serapio changed; he became tormented with every win in the arena. It was then he made arrangements to adopt me and Dorrian. When the three of us left the arena for the last time—it was the best day of my life."

"I know *exactly* how you felt," exclaimed Nikolaus. "Nothing feels as wonderful as to be a person again—instead of property. Having lost my freedom, I will never take it for granted."

"It's when you have lost something," said Nebetka, "that you truly appreciate how valuable it is. I will forever be grateful to Serapio and Fabiana."

"I'm glad I know why Salvitto honors Serapio so highly," said Nikolaus. "It says much about the honor of both men. Who could know that Serapio's compassion for Drusia would help free me?"

"Serapio told me Salvitto refused to sell you, at first," said Nebetka. "He said you were too valuable. Salvitto changed his mind, not just because of the debt he owes Father, but because he felt responsible for delaying you, Adan, before your shift. His guilt tipped the scales."

"Nikolaus, I asked him about buying your contract when we got back from Caesarea. He adamantly refused."

"Remember how angry I was with God?" asked Nikolaus. "I couldn't understand why he released Peter while you were in charge. I thought it was terribly unfair."

"Yes, and here we are, both of us, alive and free."

Nebetka smiled as he gazed up at the star-sequined darkness. "Yes, life can be so unpredictable and dangerous. Then something magnificent happens at the most unforeseeable moment, in the most bewildering way."

Chapter 40

⊙⊙⊙

The late afternoon sky over Caesarea was hazy with humidity. The clouds were thin and elongated as if stretched by unseen hands. The Cornelius family had finished dinner when a courier delivered two scrolls to the villa. Marcus opened the letter addressed to him from Tribune Salvitto, as Dulcibella smiled with delight at the wolf head stamped in the sealing wax of the second letter. Marcus read the first few lines. His face turned ashen.

He dropped the letter on the table as he turned horrified eyes on his daughter. He was barely able to speak. "A prisoner escaped. Adas has been. . ."

"*Adas has been what?*" Iovita demanded.

Dulcibella ripped open her letter with trembling hands, but could only read a few lines. She dropped the scroll. Her sobs came in wrenching anguish. Vitus and Marc stared at their sister in horrified silence.

Marcus scanned the letter, but was too angry to speak. He strode from the room and rushed up the stairs to his office. He grabbed papyrus and a pen. He wrote orders putting his *optio* in charge for an unspecified time. As Marcus pressed his signature ring into the wax, a voice filled the room.

"*Patientia.*"

Marcus looked up. "What?" There was only silence.

He stared at the papyrus as a battle raged in his heart. He had defended Valentius at his court-martial. His testimony probably saved the man's life. Adas might still be alive if he had said nothing. Spurred by guilt, he was desperate to take action. How could he be patient as the voice had commanded? Against his strongest desire, Marcus put his trust in the message. Despite his frustration, he put the papyrus away. He looked up to find Dulcibella standing in the doorway. Her face was drawn with despair as she stood trembling. Marcus went to his daughter as she fell into his arms.

"It was Simon Peter. He was the prisoner," she sobbed. "Adas wrote how he fought to protect Simon, and an angel took him out of Holding. I know God had to save

Simon, but why let Adas die? Just one more day and he would have left the Antonia for good. I thought God blessed our betrothal." She shook uncontrollably as she wept.

Marcus held her as tears flowed down his own face. Iovita slipped into the room and joined her husband as they encircled Dulcibella. A muffled cry came from Vitus and Marc at the doorway. They joined the protective circle around their sister.

"Bella, I don't know how it can be possible, but perhaps Adas is not dead." Marcus murmured. "When Salvitto wrote this letter, Adas was still alive." Yet, his words sounded empty even to himself.

The rest of the evening passed in a blur of misery. Family and servants moved about as if in a trance. The next day passed under a colorless haze of wretchedness. Dulcibella could not be consoled. She dragged herself to the terrace and sat under the oak tree, staring out over the ocean. Yet, even in the depths of misery, hope would touch her heart every time she gazed at the blue pearl and marveled at its perfect beauty. The pearl's mysterious glow reminded her that Adas was safe with God. No harm could ever touch him again, but neither could she. That acknowledgment brought her agony back. The third day, Dulcibella decided she would never give her heart to another man. She prayed to God to release her from this world of misery. She leaned against the balustrade and dazed down on the beach below.

In Jerusalem, the morning after Nikolaus left the Antonia, Adan woke as the stars relinquished their dominion to the sun. His hand was clenched around something in his palm. He had slept all night clutching the eilat stone. Nebetka and Nikolaus had already gone into the house. Adan hurried down the ladder to join the others at breakfast. After greetings and hugs, Adan filled his plate. Fabiana had made sweet wine cakes, one of Adan's favorites. She had also baked extra bread for their journey.

Serapio gave final instructions to Nikolaus and Nebetka. They packed the three men's clothes in a knapsack that Nikolaus would keep with him. Fabiana demonstrated how they should walk. They could not afford to attract the attention of even one observant soldier. It was unlawful for a man to wear women's clothing, but that was the least of their problems. Adan would have to be particularly careful about keeping his eyes lowered. Fabiana instructed the men to hold the baskets on their heads with both hands to hide the breadth of their shoulders. She slipped polished copper bracelets on Adan's wrists to hide the scars. She looked at him with a mix of bittersweet emotions.

"Don't worry, Fabiana. You will see me again." He held her hand gently in both of his. "I understand your fear; we all share it. But there is a peaceful anticipation in my heart. Please don't worry."

She took his face in her hands. "I will trust in God and your resourcefulness." She forced a smile. "Now, let me see the three of you convince me you're women." The three men gave each other doubtful looks. "Come on!" Fabiana clapped her hands. "You need to take small steps and swish a little from the hips. No striding along as if you're marching in a parade."

They took turns demonstrating their best attempts. Fabiana shook her head. "No, no, no, you're not a herd of water buffalo slogging through the mud." She bit her lower lip in thought. "I know. Think cheetahs. You know how they move with a stealthy 'slink,' like this," Fabiana moved across the room in a fluid motion. Serapio stood in the doorway watching.

Adan tried to mimic Fabiana's gracefulness. "How was that?" Peter and Malchus looked at each other and burst out laughing. Adan threw his hands in the air. "Why is this so hard?"

Serapio cleared his throat. All eyes turned to him as he moved across the room in a perfect imitation of Fabiana's gait. The three men gawked at him. "How did you do that?" exclaimed Adan. "You're built like a bear! Bears lumber. They don't walk."

"It's easy when I pretend I'm walking on wet clay. I have to plant my feet carefully. You must move into the step, not stomp."

"Seriously? Wet clay!" Adan strode to the doorway and turned to face them. He closed his eyes. He imagined a muddy street and tried again.

Fabiana clapped her hands. "You've got it! Just take your time. Place your feet carefully." She beamed at Serapio as he gave her a wink.

"If a *gladiator* can do this, then I guess a fisherman can, too," declared Peter as he took a turn. Then Malchus tried. After a little more practice they had their walk perfected.

"You will write to us. Yes?" Fabiana asked. Adan promised he would. "Now go before you make me cry. I love you, Adan. We already miss you!"

Adan hugged her. "I love you, too." He started to turn away, but whispered in her ear.

She whispered back. "The 7th of August—why do you ask?"

"I have a birthday gift in mind."

She hugged him one last time. "God be with you."

The men wrapped the scarves around their heads and across their faces, revealing only their eyes. The bright sun blazed over the city, making the extra skin protection reasonable. Fabiana eyed the three of them carefully. She nodded her approval.

"Remember, walk like a cheetah. She has grace in her strength." She unnecessarily adjusted Adan's robe. Adan set his basket down. He hugged her one last time before he walked out the door. Serapio and Nikolaus waited in the delivery cart. Nebetka was on foot.

The three "women" concentrated on relaxing their pace and avoiding contact with other pedestrians. Twice as many soldiers were on patrol ever since Peter escaped, and Malchus was wanted for questioning. They would be expecting the fugitives to hide in a wagon. Serapio and Nikolaus knew they would be under close scrutiny, which was to their advantage. As they wove their way along the busy streets, Serapio talked loudly with Nikolaus, gesturing and laughing, drawing as much attention as they could. They saw the soldiers watching them closely, but ignoring the three "women" as they causally ambled down the street. That scenario could abruptly change if a scarf slipped or a verbal confrontation erupted.

The number of soldiers manning the west gate was significantly increased. Serapio pulled up at the publican's stall. By the time the "women" were nearing Serapio, he was in an animated narration of how Nikolaus, now that he was free, planned to journey to Herculaneum. In case any soldier asked why Serapio was alone when he returned, this information would back up his story. When Nikolaus saw a keen-eyed soldier looking at his knapsack, he opened it willingly to show there was nothing to be taxed. The soldier frowned when he saw centurion *caligae*.

Nikolaus proudly declared, "They were my brother's *caligae* before he was stricken with leprosy. My master let me keep them because my brother was in his *cohort*."

The soldier jerked his hand out of the knapsack and moved away. Serapio joked with the publican, who was smiling by the time he paid the registration fee. The publican stamped the slavery document with his seal ring, officially declaring the contract void.

As expected, the soldiers scrutinized the underside of the cart. "What are you going to do with these horses?" asked one of the men. "The gray one is a handsome beast. If it is for sale, I might know someone who . . ."

Another soldier roughly elbowed him. "What's the matter with you? Don't you recognize that horse? It belonged to Centurion Longinus." He pointed at Serapio. "I know you. The centurion gave the horse to you the day before he died." Serapio nodded sadly. "You must have been a very good friend to Centurion Longinus. He will be greatly missed."

"Yes, he was like a son to me. I know Valentius is in the pit. What of the *sagittarii*?"

"They are disavowed, except for Thracius. They admit that Valentius ordered them to ignore Herod's contest rules and promised them promotions. We want Valentius crucified. *Optio* Victorius would drive in the nails himself."

Across the street, the three "women" drew even with the cart. A man accidently bumped into Malchus and muttered an apology. Malchus stared straight ahead as he continued walking. One of the soldiers was watching the "women" with a curious eye. He started to glance away, but refocused his attention when Malchus did not acknowledge the apology. Nikolaus and Nebetka saw the legionary stiffen. Nebetka tried to get closer. Nikolaus nudged Serapio and pointed his chin at the soldier.

Serapio called out, "Legionary, I see you carry a hilted sword. Does it interfere with your agility? I, myself, was a *gladiator*. I preferred a small hilt; just enough to keep my hand from slipping." The soldier ignored Serapio. He began to walk toward the "women." Nebetka tried to intercept, but pedestrians slowed his progress.

When the soldier drew closer, someone shouted from a shop door. "Stop him! Stop that thief!" A child with a loaf of bread under his arm sped past the soldier. The man dove after him, but the fleet-footed boy zigzagged through the crowd. The "women" continued on their way. The soldier trotted back to the taxing station sporting an angry scowl.

"Looks like he got away," observed Serapio. Still ignoring him, the soldier spotted the trio. In an instant, sunlight reflected off Adan's copper bracelets. The soldier looked away, but too late. The intensified light blinded him. He blinked and wiped at his eyes. By the time his sight recovered, the three women were lost in the crowd. Serapio's business with the publican was completed. The soldier stalked over to the next cart in line. He barked at Serapio to move out of the way.

"What was he looking at? Could you tell?" asked Serapio.

"No, but something caught his eye."

Serapio laughed. "Sunlight on copper caught his eye. Bless my Ana. Those bracelets were her idea. I have unfairly dismissed her cleverness at times. And speaking of clever, that was a nice touch about Adan's *caligae*. Nobody wants to touch a leper's clothes."

Back at the publican's station, the curious legionary turned to another soldier. "Did you see those women walking on the other side of the street?"

"Which ones?"

"The three carrying baskets. I spotted them way down the street. Not once did they speak to each other. A man bumped into one of them, but she just ignored him. They didn't even comment to each other."

"Why do you care about women who can hold their tongues?"

He shrugged. "I don't know. It was unusual, that's all."

The soldiers were questioning every man who approached the gate. Nebetka watched for the three "women" and Serapio to draw near. Then he jumped in front of the cart. "*Ohe!* Where do you think you're going?"

Nikolaus shouted back. "I don't answer to you! Get out of the way!" The shouting continued back and forth until everyone was staring, including the soldiers. Nikolaus egged Nebetka on with taunts. Serapio bellowed at the two of them. Several soldiers came over to break up the "fight." The trio ambled through the gate unnoticed. Nebetka ducked into the crowd. The soldiers waved Serapio though after another inspection.

Safely out of the city Adan looked back and spotted Serapio and Nikolaus. He smiled knowing Nikolaus was officially free. They headed for a grove of ficus trees. Nikolaus hurried to them with his knapsack. The trio changed clothes and joined Serapio at the cart. They saddled the horses. Serapio talked softly to Venustas as if she could understand every word. Sadness etched his face as he "instructed" the horse to get her master to Caesarea safely. Adan smiled to hear the big, gnarled *gladiator* talking to Venustas, but then he remembered they may be parting for the last time. Promises to send letters were repeated.

"Tell Fabiana how well her plan worked," said Adan.

"I will, but she'll be insufferable now. I will hear, 'I told you' for the next three weeks. *Ohe*, who am I kidding? I will hear about this day for the rest of my life." Serapio stalled their parting with suggestions and observations. He clamped his huge hand on the back of Adan's neck to pull him into a hug. He tried to keep a stoic expression as he told the others farewell. The four men waved to Serapio as they headed down the road. He waved back, watching them until they disappeared from sight.

As much as Adan hated leaving Serapio, Fabiana, and Nebetka, he grew more encouraged with every step closer to Dulcibella. When they arrived at Simon's house in Joppa, Adan didn't realize how tired he was until Nikolaus had to wake him to eat supper. Nikolaus insisted on hauling pallets and blankets up on the roof while the others visited downstairs. Simon didn't need to light any oil lamps for his guests. Soon after the sun bedded down in the sea, Adan and the other travelers bedded down on the roof.

As exhausted as Adan was, he slept restlessly, waking often from hauntingly vivid nightmares. In one particularly terrifying dream, the silk merchant who accused Adan of murder lured Dulcibella to a cliff overlooking the ocean. The emaciated figure whispered in her ear as he coaxed her to the edge. Far below the cliff frothy waves crashed over jagged boulders. Dulcibella stared down at the rocks as if hypnotized by the luring sound of the thundering waves. Adan was watching from a rocky pinnacle out in the water. He shouted to Dulcibella to not give up hope. He dove into the water to swim to her, but he could make no progress. As he struggled, the silk merchant pushed Dulcibella off the cliff. Adan could only watch helplessly as she plummeted into the rock-strewn waves.

Adan jerked awake, panting and covered in sweat. He pressed his hand to his heart as he tried to calm down. He told himself it was only lingering effects of the *belladonna*. He prayed for God to protect Dulcibella and again fell asleep.

Chapter 41

A dan woke not knowing where he was or how he got there. Reality pushed through the mental fog. He felt a pang of fear in the pit of his stomach when he remembered his nightmare. What if by delaying his departure to secure Nikolaus's freedom, Dulcibella had come to harm. Adan tried to dismiss the notion. He surveyed the land around Simon's rooftop. There was a full view from the sea to distant craggy mesas low on the horizon. He took in the sea-scented air and pictured Dulcibella rushing into his open arms.

Peter and the others were still asleep. Adan slung his belt over his shoulder. Quietly, he climbed down the ladder and entered Simon's house. He found his knapsack and pulled the copper mirror out. His reflection was startling. The five day shadow of beard intensified the wolfish look of his eyes. There was a mirror on the wall in the main room. Adan pulled his tunic off and turned his back to the mirror. He looked in the copper mirror. For the first time, he saw the full length of the scar. His jaw tightened in anger. The reality of his situation was depressing. His euphoria at surviving the execution had long since vanished. Earning the respect of his men and accepting the most dangerous assignments without complaint was all for nothing. His career was over.

His freedom to associate with his friends, even with his father, was gone. Having to renounce his family name was causing more grief than he had anticipated. Pretending to have no connection to Marsetina or Aquila left him unanchored. He realized he was proud of the respect his father earned from other men and the way he conducted his duties as the *minor consul*. Adan had taken many qualities of his lifestyle for granted. That lifestyle was now gone.

He wondered how long Dulcibella would be content living away from her family, possibly never seeing any of them again. Would resentment eventually tarnish their love? Bitterness stirred in his heart. Valentius had failed to take his life, but had succeeded in taking the foundation and familiarity of his life.

Staring into the mirror, Adan estimated at least sixty stitches would have been required to mend Valentius's handiwork. "How could Stephen forgive his murderers?" he asked aloud. He tossed Marsetina's mirror on a chair. He put his tunic on and fastened his belt.

Someone cleared his throat. Adan spun around to find Peter. "I heard what you said about Stephen. You have suffered because you defended me, but more importantly, you refused to denounce Yeshua even in the face of death. God turned the evil of Valentius into an opportunity for you to proclaim that Yeshua is alive. When we suffer because of these opportunities, it is far less than what Yeshua suffered. If you harbor resentment against Valentius, you will cancel the good you did when you opposed his evil. If you let God deal with Valentius, your good deeds will stand. You need to forgive him."

"I hear you. I understand what you're saying, but I can't let it go. I want to see Valentius suffer. Just the thought of forgiving him sickens me."

"Forgiveness can be elusive. Even if you forgive someone, the resentment can return. However, you will not find peace until you do. Valentius will forever torture you until *you* release his hold on your memory. He will assault your thoughts and dreams. His darkness will damage your relationships with the people closest to you. Neither justice, nor his suffering, nor even his death, will dispel his power over you. Adan, you are giving him permission to ruin the rest of your life. He still controls you and only forgiveness will dispel that control."

"Even if I forgive him for the evil done to me, fifteen men lost their lives to his greed. Do I declare him blameless for that?"

"No, Adan, you do not have the authority to declare anyone blameless. Your forgiveness does not erase his transgressions. Only God can absolve sin. Everyone is accountable for his own misdeeds until he asks God for forgiveness. Yet even when we ask God for forgiveness, he only forgives those who have forgiven all others. If you do not forgive Valentius, neither will you be forgiven. I heard Yeshua say many times, '*And when you stand praying, forgive if you have anything against anyone, so that your Father who is in heaven may also forgive you.*' You cannot hold others in debt and expect your debts to be canceled."

"What if Valentius delights in my suffering. Never feels remorse. Do I still forgive him?"

"It doesn't matter if he feels remorse or not. You can only control yourself. And when you forgive others, it frees your heart from despair. Forgiving others is the kindest thing you can do for *yourself*. Let God deal with Valentius."

"I'm not ready to do that."

"Adan, did you ask Yeshua to forgive you when you crucified him?"

"Yeshua is the Son of God. I don't have his strength, or his heart." He turned away.

Peter knew there was nothing he could say to convince him. He hoped with time, Adan would understand. "So, are we prepared to finish our journey?"

Adan was relieved to change the subject. "We are. I'll be very glad to be on our way." Sounds came from the kitchen. Peter went to greet the early riser.

Adan went outside to clear his head until Nikolaus told him breakfast was ready. They ate eagerly, enjoying the sharp flavor of bread baked in sea air. Before they left, Adan expressed his gratitude to Simon by purchasing a new leather belt. Simon beamed with pleasure when Adan selected the one of highest quality.

Farewells were said, blessings exchanged, and they were on their way to Caesarea. If there were no difficulties, they would arrive sometime around late afternoon. Venustas, sensing her master's eagerness, kept taking the lead. Since they could not avoid Apollonia they wrapped shawls over their heads and put some distance between each other. A single man passing through town would be less memorable than four together.

They passed without attracting attention, or so Adan thought. The owner of the Apollonian Inn was sitting outside under the shade of a tree enjoying the ocean breeze. He saw a dapple-gray Arabian he recognized from Caesarea. A gust of wind revealed the rider's face. The observer was shocked at what he saw. If his guests from Jerusalem were telling the truth, the rider of this horse was dead. Limping as he walked to the stable, he saddled his horse.

Once through Apollonia, Adan and the others regrouped. From then on, it was a clear road to Caesarea. Adan found a path branching off from the road. It went around a small hill to a grassy area under a group of oak trees. They stopped to rest the horses out of sight from the road.

Caesarea came into view about four hours later. The villa of Marcus Cornelius was a mile and a half north of Caesarea. When Adan saw the cliff road, he urged Venustas into a trot.

Dulcibella stood at the balustrade and stared listlessly at the sea. Her eyes were red and swollen as she watched the waves dash themselves against the shoreline. Her beloved home had become a dungeon. She pictured the face of the only man she had ever loved. She thought of the mischievous sparkle in his eyes when he teased her. She visualized his good-natured, lopsided grin. The touch of his hand and the reassurance in his voice always calmed her when she was troubled. The thought of the children they would not have clutched at her heart. Fresh tears filled her eyes. How could Simon Peter be so wrong when he promised God would bless their marriage? Why would God send an angel to release Peter when Adas was in charge?

The rhythmic sound of the churning waves was hypnotic. Dulcibella thought how she could be with Adas if she only slipped the bonds of this world. It would be so easy to simply let go of life. The breeze ruffled her hair as she stood looking down the cliff. She placed her hands on the balustrade, thinking how pleasant it would be to feel no pain, or grief, or fear.

Leaning further over the balustrade, she felt the slight tug of the pouch around her neck. She took the pearl out and looked at it. Its soft blue color seemed to glow with more intensity than usual. A new thought came to her as she held the pearl up to the sunlight. It symbolized a promise of not only eternal life, but a better life now. As she embraced the hope of the pearl, her despair lightened. She prayed that her grief would fade with time.

A gentle voice whispered in her thoughts, "*Exspectare.*"

"Expect what?" she said aloud. There was only silence. She put the pearl back in its pouch. Her parents were not only grief stricken, but also deeply concerned about her. She turned from the balustrade to go to them.

At the base of the cliff road, Adan couldn't hold back any longer. He pressed his heels against Venustas's flank. She raced back and forth up the switchbacks as swift as the wind.

"*Dulcibella!*" He cried out as hooves thundered up the road. "*Dulcie!*"

She heard her name and ran back to the balustrade. Her heart leaped at the sight of Venustas. She saw a cloak fly as the rider tore it away. Dulcibella gasped and ran to the house. She burst into the kitchen where Marcus and Iovita were sitting at the table in miserable silence. She grabbed her father by the shoulder and shook him.

"*It's Adas! He's alive!*" She ran through the house and out the main door. Marcus and Iovita stared at each other. Dulcibella ran through the courtyard to the end of the path just as Venustas cleared the curve. Adan vaulted from the saddle. Dulcibella launched herself into his arms. He staggered back, clutching her to his chest. She threw her arms over his shoulders as she buried her face in his neck. Trembling and sobbing, she clung to him. Adan embraced her with all his strength as tears of joy ran down their faces. He wove his fingers in her hair and tilted her head back. Feverishly he kissed her until her knees gave way. She felt his powerful arms tighten and she gasped. Their tears mingled as their hearts raced. Adan gently wiped the tears from her face. Tenderly this time, he kissed her lips and then held her head against his chest. She could hear his heart thundering.

"Will you still be here when I open my eyes?"

"Yes, I will still be here."

She took his face in her hands. "What happened to you?"

"That's not important now. We're together. Nothing else matters."

The sound of a low cough made Adan look up. Marcus clasped Iovita to him as she swayed. The shock of elation overawed their senses. Marc and Vitus joined them as the family surrounded Adan with hugs and exclamations of joy.

"I am so sorry I have caused you pain." Adan looked from one to the other.

"You're alive! That's all that matters," declared Marcus.

"You must understand that all of Jerusalem thinks I am dead. My name is Adan Novius Serapio. My life depends on you remembering that."

Marcus saw the fresh scars on Adan's wrists. His voice shook with anger. "I swear, Valentius will answer to my sword!"

"Sir, Valentius is already in custody," said Adan. "Nothing more needs to be done."

Horses appeared, and Nikolaus, Peter, and Malchus slid from their saddles. Andreas, who had been watching the joyful reunion, clasped hands with the men. Dulcibella greeted Nikolaus with a grateful smile. His face brightened as he returned the greeting with a nod.

Marcus wiped at his eyes. "It seems the sun really has risen after our darkest night."

"Praise God for this miracle!" cried Iovita.

"But why do they think you're dead, Adas—Adan?" asked Marcus. "Obviously, your execution was canceled."

"No, I was 'executed' before the entire 10th *Legio*. They saw me die, but God used them," he gestured at his friends, "to save me. Serapio and his family helped, too, as did Salvitto." The family expressed their gratitude, but Marcus feared deadly secrets would haunt the family for the rest of their lives. "The situation is complicated. Malchus and Nikolaus can tell you details even I don't know. But you must remember I am the son of Regulus and Fabiana Serapio, a furniture maker. Herod must never know I am alive."

Running feet sounded from the front entrance. The servants ran to welcome the return of Dulcibella's betrothed. Cook nearly passed out when she saw Adan.

Dulcibella turned to Nikolaus. "I hoped you would be at his side when he came home again, and here you are. Bless you, Nikolaus. I pray you will always remain his friend." Not sure what to do, he only smiled, but when Dulcibella put her arms out to him, he timidly hugged her. Adan laughed at the blush spreading over Nikolaus's face.

Nikolaus joined Andreas as he led the horses to the stables. "Congratulations, Nikolaus. Not only do you bring joy back to this family, but I suspect you are a free man now."

"I am, thanks to Adan's generosity, but better than that—Adan is alive."

Everyone welcomed Malchus and Peter as they made their way into the house. Iovita gathered up her kitchen staff to plan a celebration feast. The men gathered on the terrace.

Dulcibella led Adan upstairs to the sitting room overlooking the sea. She soaked in every detail of his face, still in joyful disbelief. "Tell me it only *looked* like you were executed. It was a trick? Yes? How could you travel so quickly if you were severely injured?"

"Simon Peter prayed for me, Dulcie. God healed me. There was no trick. I really was dead for a few minutes, but then my heart started to beat again."

She led him to a couch in front of the window facing the sea. Adan gave her a brief summary of the events. Dulcibella swore eternal gratitude to those that helped preserve his life. She curled her legs up on the couch and nestled in his arms.

"Dulcie?"

"Yes, my love?"

"I thought I had lost you. Then I would remember Peter's blessing."

"I was insane with grief, yet sometimes I felt a touch of hope."

"When I faced Malchus, I wanted so badly to live, but then I surrendered to God's will. I was at peace. I still can't believe I am holding you in my arms."

She looked out the window at the sparkling Mediterranean. It was beautiful to her once again. When she looked back at Adan his expression had clouded.

"What's wrong?"

"Last night, I had a horrible nightmare. You were pushed off a cliff. When I woke up, I was afraid for you. Again, I held on to Peter's assurances, but nothing is better than holding on to you."

Her eyes brightened as she laughed. "I'm still in shock. I'm terrified this is really a dream. I'm going to wake up, and you'll be gone."

He kissed her. "I'm still here." He saw the leather cord around her neck. "You have kept the pearl safe."

"Yes, and I think it kept me safe today."

"What do you mean?"

Dulcibella hesitated, not sure how much she wanted to admit. "I wasn't going to say anything, but I did have a fleeting temptation to give up. I thought of how easy it would be to leave this world. Then the pearl seemed to pull on my neck, so I looked at it. A voice in my head said to 'expect with anticipation.' Then I heard you call out to me. I thought I would burst with happiness. It was the greatest joy I have ever felt."

Iovita called to them from the doorway. "Come with me. You need to hear this."

They followed her to the terrace. Andreas spoke first. "We saw Ovidis in Caesarea. Adan, he must have seen you in Apollonia because he recognized Venustas and was asking about you."

"Oh no! I thought he was gone for good!" exclaimed Dulcibella.

"Who is Ovidis?" Adan asked.

"His name is Gnaeus Flavius Ovidis," said Marcus. "He was stationed here until about a year ago. He was gone until recently. I mentioned him in a letter. He's living in Apollonia now."

"So why is he so curious about me?"

"Because he's curious about *me*," said Dulcibella. "He came here once. I told him that you and I had an understanding. He was rather angry when he left, but he made no attempt to see me again."

"Since he's been in Apollonia," Marcus added, "he seems to have an endless supply of income. Apparently his wealthy father died leaving everything to him."

"What did this man do today?" asked Adan.

Andreas explained, "I overheard him talking with one of the wine shop owners. He was asking about the identity of the man riding a gray horse. The shop owner said he hadn't seen such a horse since the centurion proposed marriage to the daughter of Cornelius. Ovidis said he hadn't either, until today. Adan, he must have been watching when you proposed on the wharf. I wasn't concerned when I heard him, of course, because I thought you were dead."

"Do you think he'll run to Herod?" asked Adan

"No," said Marcus, "but rumors will be circulated."

Nikolaus cleared his throat. "Perhaps, we can let others know that Venustas was delivered to Dulcibella by a friend, Adan Serapio. Ovidis only saw you from a distance."

Iovita declared, "Perhaps he needs to know Dulcibella *is marrying* Adan Serapio. That should end his curiosity."

"So soon after the death of her betrothed?" said Marcus. "That will look suspicious."

"What do we do?" moaned Dulcibella.

"We discuss it later," said Iovita with conviction. "This is a day of celebration. I'm not going to let some miserable busybody ruin it. Into the house everyone. Supper will be ready."

Bread was baking in the *furnus* while soup simmered in a pot. Honeyed apples were boiling, waiting to be wrapped in pastry and baked to golden brown perfection. Iovita and Marcus discussed Adan's situation with the servants. They decided his true identity would never be mentioned, even among themselves. The day Simon Peter came to the house they were blessed with the Holy Spirit, which would forever define their lives. As servants of God first, and servants of Cornelius second, they were men and women of courage and loyalty. Adan Serapio would always be safe in this household. However, Adan was not safe outside the villa, but for now, they were comforted as they gathered around the table that evening.

They sat on the terrace after dinner to enjoy the sunset. Marcus caught Peter's eye and tilted his head away from the group. The two men walked a short distance away to talk. Peter nodded as he clasped Marcus's hand. They came back to the group bearing broad smiles.

"What was that about?" Iovita asked Marcus.

"Looks like we'll be having a wedding soon."

"How soon?"

"How does tomorrow sound?"

Iovita's eyes twinkled as she laughed. "Should we tell the bride and groom?"

"Why? It would spoil the fun." He smiled at Dulcibella and Adan. "Within a single hour, so much has changed."

Iovita sighed contentedly. "Things will change just as beautifully tomorrow."

Chapter 42

When Adan awoke, he was surprised he could still hear the rhythmic music from his dream. It was the song of the cresting sea waves. He loved the wind-chiseled, white limestone cliffs with rust-red accents of sandstone. He looked to the east and saw *Lucifer,* the morning daystar. As he watched the *planeta* it was overpowered by the sun and disappeared.

Stretching his arms over his head, Adan straightened his back as he lay on the lounge chair. He liked sleeping outdoors especially on the ocean-side terrace of the Cornelius estate, the only place he truly felt at home. A seagull flew overhead calling out to any other lonesome seagulls. Momentarily suspended in a thermal rising from the beach below, the gull scanned the landscape as if enjoying the view. The wind shifted, and the gull continued its flight.

Adan pulled on the back of his chair to allow the wooden braces to catch in the frame brackets, one of Serapio's inventions. He fastened his belt over his tunic and laced up his *caligae*, making a mental note to buy a pair of sandals. Adan gazed at the shimmering sea with the sun at his back. The morning brilliance ignited billowing clouds in the west ablaze with red and gold. The brilliant colors fanned out over the ocean like a Phoenix rising from the flames of rebirth. He wondered if the fierce red clouds would grow into a storm.

The peaceful grandeur soothed Adan until thoughts of Valentius reminded him of what he had lost. He tried to think about good things. Still, the memories of those who had conspired against him overshadowed the blessings. He imagined one vengeful scenario after another, but each only increased his anxiety. His expression hardened. He wrapped himself inside his rage as if it were armor and his only defense.

Adan heard the backdoor close. Marcus crossed the terrace. "Did you sleep well?" He grabbed a chair as he walked and sat down next to Adan.

"I always do here. And you, Sir?" Adan studied Marcus's jovial expression. "You look very pleased this morning."

"As I should, considering my daughter is getting married today."

"She is? I mean, we are? Is there enough time to get everything arranged?"

"What's to arrange? Simon Peter will perform the wedding rite. Bella and Iovita will gather a few things at the shops. Cook will prepare her special recipes for the wedding feast. The servants will prepare the guest cottage." He pointed toward the cottage, hidden by trees and a hilltop rise. "I have a formal white linen tunic and a purple silk *toga* for you to wear. We have the required ten witnesses. What more do we need? *Ohe*, there is another thing. Your possessions, including a rosewood chair and your clothes chest are being transported here. Your friend, Serapio, made the arrangements. For now, concentrate on Bella and your wedding."

"Yes, Sir. I will obey your order most eagerly." His smile faded. "I only wish we did not have to leave."

Marcus looked away. "There is that. Malchus and Nikolaus told us what happened. You have been through a terrible ordeal. Bella was inconsolable. All day, she sat here under the tree staring at the sea. She wouldn't eat. She wouldn't talk. I had to carry her to her room at night. She just wouldn't move. Yesterday, when Bella flew into the kitchen claiming you were alive, I thought grief had driven her insane. I thought my heart would explode when I saw a rider jump from the saddle and embrace my daughter. Every painful, dreadful thing I have ever faced meant nothing when I saw you. Hearing my little girl laugh again is a gift beyond price."

"Marcus, your blessing on our marriage is a wonderful gift to us." They sat in silence for a while, enjoying the serenity of nature. "By the way, you know that ring I left with you for safekeeping?" Marcus nodded. "I'll need it at the wedding feast."

"I don't need to ask why. I approve, wholeheartedly. Will you present it to him?"

"I'd like it to come from you, as a father would do for a son."

"It will be my honor." Marcus stood up and offered a hand. "On your feet! There's smoke from the *furnus* and the aroma of baking bread." The two men grinned in anticipation of the simple pleasure of good food shared with loved ones.

Dulcibella was in the kitchen cutting fruit. A carefree smile graced her lips as she dropped the slices in a bowl. "What have you two been doing? You look like imps eyeing the cookie jar." Adan took hold of her shoulders and kissed the top of her ear. She laughed. "What's this? You're stopping with an ear?"

"Never try to kiss a woman's lips when she's holding a knife." He set her knife aside and turned her to face him. "There is something we should discuss. Apparently, your parents have decided to marry us off tonight. What do you have to say about that, Dulcie?"

She gave him a coy smile. "I don't know. They might be rushing things a bit. We've only been in love for years." She wrinkled her nose at him and laughed. "Tell me, when did you fall in love with me? I was just a little brat when you were a big, strong seventeen-year old."

"Fifteen-year old," he whispered and kissed her neck.

"I forgot. You're reliving two years."

"*Ohe*, Bella," exclaimed Vitus as he came in the kitchen. "We're stealing Adan for the afternoon. Marc and I are taking him clam digging after lunch. Cook wants the clams for the wedding soup. Nikolaus and Andreas are going, too. It'll be fun!" He snagged a fig from the cutting board.

"There will be no peace until my little brothers get you out on a clam dig." She shooed them from the kitchen.

Vitus went to find Marc. Adan went upstairs to get a scroll and to find Nikolaus. As he expected, Nikolaus was tending to the horses. Venustas nickered when Adan approached. She buried her muzzle in his palm for a handful of grain.

"I've been told we're going clam digging after lunch," said Adan.

"It sounds like fun." Nikolaus grinned as he brushed Inventio's sleek hide.

"Do you know how to swim?"

"Not really. All of my experiences with large bodies of water have been from the inside of a boat." He set a brush down and picked up a hoof pick. "How 'bout you?"

"Not too well, I sink like a rock." Adan watched as Nikolaus saddled Inventio. "Nikolaus, I was wondering if you'd want to go to Herculaneum and Rome with us. You can collect the bounty on Nisos in Rome. I need to see my father, and Herculaneum is not far from Rome. It's a beautiful port city with natural hot springs and streets of amazing architecture. There's a mountain called Vesuvius just northeast of the city. Smoke rises from it sometimes. It's fascinating to see. I'd like Dulcie to see Herculaneum, but more importantly, we could look for your sister. Do you want to go?"

"Yes, of course, I'd love to. It will give me time to consider what I will do when we get back. I want to establish a permanent livelihood and. . ." Nikolaus paused.

". . .and get to know a certain innkeeper's daughter. I have it on good authority she has never shared apricot pastry with anyone but you."

"After I met Marina, I tried to forget her. I was a slave. It was a fool's dream to think of her, but now I am free and with the reward money my dream is possible."

"I hope it works out, Nikolaus."

"If Marina and I are meant to be together, it will happen." Nikolaus led Inventio out of the stables. "I'm going to town. Do you need anything? Marc said I could borrow a *toga* for the ceremony tonight, but I need new tunics and a new belt." Nikolaus looked at his tattered one. "I definitely need a new belt."

"I'm going to pick up a few items at the metal shop, but there is an errand you could do if you have time."

"Sure, what is it?"

Adan pulled the scroll from under his belt. "I just finished this letter to my father." He took coins from his belt pouch. "Use a *tabellari* if he is sailing directly for Rome. They're more reliable than mailing in bulk."

Nikolaus took the scroll and postage money. Adan laced his fingers together to give him a boost into the saddle. Nikolaus hesitated.

"What? Are you going to ride Inventio or walk him to town?"

Nikolaus accepted his help and climbed in the saddle. "I'm not used to thinking of myself as a freeman."

Adan snorted. "You'll catch up with the rest of us someday." He watched as Nikolaus turned the curve to the cliff road.

"Breakfast! We're waiting for you," called Dulcibella. He followed her into the house. Peter and Malchus joined them. Dulcibella and Iovita discussed what they needed for the wedding. Marc and Vitus discussed the best places to find clams.

Adan decided he needed to introduce the subject everyone was avoiding. "I guess we need to discuss when Dulcie and I will be leaving. How are you going to explain her absence?"

Iovita waved a hand. "We'll say Bella and her husband, Adan Serapio, left to stay with her sister in Rome. Actually, Bella, you really should go see Cornelia. You haven't seen her since she and Paulus married."

"We are planning to go to Rome to see my father and Janae. We're thinking we'll go to Herculaneum first for a few weeks. I have neglected my father. I never wrote to him about my mother's death or about his marriage to Janae. But I sent a letter today. At least, he'll know I'm alive. It should get to him about a week behind Salvitto's letter."

"Your father will be so happy to see you, Adan. Everything will be all right." Dulcibella gave him an encouraging smile.

"Nikolaus is going with us. Hopefully, we will find his sister in Herculaneum. While they are visiting, Dulcie and I will enjoy the luxuries of the city. How does that sound?"

"It sounds wonderful!" chirped Dulcibella.

The rest of the morning, Iovita and the servants decorated the main hall. When Adan returned from his errand, he and Dulcibella went to find wildflowers to adorn her bridal veil. She decided on several stalks of pink snapdragons to weave into a crown to hold her veil in place. Adan carried a small pitcher of water for the flowers.

"These will look beautiful with my veil, and I will have your peacock scarf tied at my waist. The colors look beautiful with my bridal *tunica*."

Dulcibella wandered up the path to the guest cottage while Adan stopped to take in the view of the sea. She called out to him. He caught up with her, set the water pitcher down, and took her in his arms. She gazed up into his eyes.

"Remember the question I asked you this morning?" Dulcibella asked. "So tell me, before you give me that kiss you're thinking about."

A slow smile curved his lips. "Tell you what, Dulcie?"

"When did you fall in love with me?" The breeze caught a lock of her hair and swept it across her face. He coaxed it back behind her ear.

"I have always loved you Dulcie. Only the type of love has changed. When you were a child, I cared about you as a child. I loved your curiosity and your fearlessness. I was fascinated with how you saw the world. Then one day, a few years back, I realized you weren't a child anymore. That was the day I fell in love with you as a woman. That was the day I knew you and I were meant to be together. I have never let you out of my heart."

She smiled pensively as she lightly touched his face. Without warning, a terrible memory intruded into Adan's thoughts. Once again, he was on the stage facing death. Dulcibella was startled at the dramatic change in his expression.

"What is it?" She could feel his heart racing. "Adan, tell me!"

He took a deep breath. "Dulcie, when the arrow hit me. . .when I went down, the first image I saw was you. You were smiling the same way you just did. Then later there were terrible, frightful images of. . . I can't get them out of my head."

Dulcibella looked away in sorrow. "When we got the letters, I thought I would die. I kept remembering the day Peter baptized us and blessed our marriage. I tried to hold on to that moment as if my own life depended on it. Maybe it did. Now I know faith does not come easily. I know I will never take life or our love for granted. I hope our love helps you to leave the past behind. I love you, Adan."

"I love you, Dulcibella."

He lowered his head and she closed her eyes. The touch of his lips on hers was all she needed to know their love was their bond. Adan raised his head as Dulcibella slowly opened her eyes. She smiled with delight as she looked over his shoulder.

"Don't move. A butterfly just landed on the snapdragons." Very slowly she lifted her arm from Adan's shoulder. The butterfly was edged in dark gray with powdery white and gray at the base of the wings. There were black spots in a geometric pattern on the wings which were colored light gold to bronze to burnt-orange.

"Its colors match your eyes. You are a man of extremes, wolf and butterfly." She laughed at his amused expression. The butterfly fanned its wings before fluttering away.

"Now it's your turn," said Adan. "When did you first fall in love with me?"

"I heard your voice and was drawn to the sound of it. I was fascinated with your eyes."

"You were the first child who wasn't afraid of me because of my eyes. Your little brothers were, but not you. That made me curious."

"No, I noticed the color, of course, but that's not why I was intrigued. When I asked how you saved the horse after it was hit with an arrow, there was kindness in your eyes. When you told me about saving your donkey and other animals you tended, your eyes lit up with this, I don't know, joy, wonder, something special. When Father praised you or someone made you laugh, or Mother insisted you stay for dinner, there it would be—this light in your eyes. I wanted you to 'light up' when you looked at me or heard my voice. I wanted to cause that special spark of joy in your face, but love cannot be forced. I had to be patient."

Adan thought for a moment. "Now I understand. *That's* why you said it."

"Said what?"

"It was right before your sixteenth birthday. I was teaching you how to saddle your horse. You were having a hard time with the cinch. You got frustrated and wanted to ride without the saddle. I said you might fall off. You climbed up on the fence rail and jumped on your horse, anyway. When you reached around for the reins, sure enough, you started to fall. I caught you in my arms. That was the day I saw you as a woman. You looked at me and said, *'There it is!'* I never knew what you meant until now."

Dulcibella threw her head back to laugh. "I remember. Yes, it was the first time you looked at me with that sparkle. I decided, right then, I would marry you or no one." She leaned into his embrace, but suddenly his eyes burned with anger.

"Adan, what is it?"

"I don't want to leave. I want to raise our family here. Why should we have to abandon everyone we love? I protected Peter, but I feel as if God is punishing me."

"Adan, is it punishment for you to be alive? Fifteen other men are not. It is our *choice* to leave for your protection. The next place we live will be just as beautiful because we will be together. Everything was ugly and drab when I thought you were dead. The waves made an annoying clamor that set my teeth on edge. The breeze turned cold and damp. When we rushed into each other's arms, it all became beautiful again. Adan, we will make a new home."

"I don't deserve you, Dulcie. I pray you never feel you have wasted your heart on me."

She took his face in her hands and kissed him. "My heart beats inside your chest, Adan. Your heart beats inside mine. How can a heart be wasted if it nurtures life?"

"I *do* love you, Dulcibella."

"I know and I love you."

"Come on, we better get back to the house before these flowers wilt."

Adan picked up the pitcher and put the snapdragons in the water. Hand in hand they walked down the hill past the guest house and down the path to the villa. They were greeted with the most delicious aromas when they walked in the back door. Cook was preparing lobsters Peter and Malchus had caught that morning. She had Dulcibella taste her lobster sauce of pepper, cumin, rue, honey-vinegar, and oil, mixed together with a broth. It wasn't long before the lobster tails were served up in Cook's special sauce. The family enjoyed their lunch together, but Marc and Vitus would not allow Adan to sit for long.

Marc went for the spading pitchforks and to find Nikolaus and Andreas. Vitus and Adan collected a few copper pails. The five of them took off down the cliff road to the beach. Nikolaus informed Adan his letter was already on its way to Rome. Dulcibella and Iovita walked out on the terrace to watch from the balustrade. Marcus would tell them when the carriage was ready for their trip to town.

"Do you think Adan is going to be all right?" Dulcibella asked.

"What do you mean?" Iovita looked at her with concern.

"He gets distracted. Then there's this terrible anger in his eyes—anger like I've never seen in him. He won't confide in me. He's tormented, but he won't let me help him."

"You have to give him time, Bella. These things only happened a few days ago. You can't force it out of him. You would make it worse if you tried. Be patient. When he's ready, he'll talk to you."

"I can be patient, Mother, if it's a question of when, but what if he can never let it go? He won't be the same person."

"There have been times your father had to deal with awful situations. The memories would eat at him, but he would work through it. For now, Adan's emotions are raw. Just be sure when he is ready to talk, you're ready to listen. It may be the only thing he needs you to do. Always be ready to listen, Bella."

"I can do that, but I don't know for how long and that's what scares me. There's a haunted look in his eyes I have never seen." Adan and the others were halfway down the road. The sound of their familiar banter was comforting. "Mother, have you noticed how close Adan and Nikolaus have become?"

"I have always thought Adan was very lonely. I thought it was because he had no siblings, but now I think there's more to it. I see how he admires Marcus, and he always accepted my invitations to stay for dinner. I think Adan will be a wonderful father. He's even patient with Marc and Vitus. Dealing with those two can be like herding a flock of sheep over a rope bridge." Mother and daughter looked at each other and laughed.

When Adan and the others reached the beach, they took their sandals off. Adan shielded his eyes from the overhead sun and scanned the western horizon. There were dark, tangled clouds in the distance. He remembered the fiery cloud bank that morning, but he wasn't concerned. They were low and far away. He took off his belt and tunic and plunged into the surf. The others immediately followed, diving into every wave they could catch. Dulcibella and Iovita smiled to see them frolicking in the surf like a pod of dolphins.

Iovita took her daughter by the arm. "Come on, Bella. We have much to do. I'm sure the carriage is ready."

Adan paused to watch the carriage move down the cliff road. A slender arm shot into the air. Dulcibella was waving at them. Adan waved back. Marc and Vitus paused in their pursuit of tumbling waves. When the carriage moved out of sight, the boys turned around to find Adan standing in waist high water. Their eyes fell on the scars across his chest. He turned to dive into a wave. The scar across his back was obvious against his tanned skin.

Nikolaus saw their distress. "What? Are you surprised? Malchus told you what happened. Did you think he was exaggerating?"

Marc and Vitus exchanged glances. "Yes!" they exclaimed in unison.

"Well, he wasn't. It was horrible to watch."

Adan surfaced unaware of their discussion. *"Ohe,* you think we should start digging for. . ."* He frantically looked around. *"What was that?"*

"What was what?" demanded Nikolaus. "Do we need to get out of the. . .?"

Marc disappeared under the waves. Adan and Andreas immediately dived in after Marc. There was much splashing. The water turned inky black just when Andreas came up with Marc, and Adan came up with a small octopus. The octopus writhed in his hands as it twisted its tentacles around his arms.

Marc and Vitus shouted, "Don't let go! Don't let go!*"* Vitus quickly swam to Adan.

"Who are you yelling at, me or the octopus?" Adan grimaced at the squirming creature in his hands.

Marc pulled the tentacles away from Adan's arms as Vitus reached under the head and expertly grabbed the beak. They waded back to the beach. After a few failed attempts, they got the hapless creature in a pail. Marc used a flat rock to cover the top of the pail and held it down while Vitus pulled his tunic on over his wet loincloth.

"I'll be back. Cook will love me for bringing her this prize. Wait until you taste her octopus stew with red wine sauce. It's delicious!" Vitus started up the cliff road.

"Seriously?" cried Adan, "you eat that thing?"

"Come on, we better start digging," laughed Marc.

They waded out of the water. Marc pushed the tines of the spading fork in the wet sand. He upended a wedge of gritty ground. Adan and Nikolaus followed his example. They found their first clams right away. After some time, the carriage returned, but they were intent on filling their pails.

Marcus called to them from the top of the cliff. *"Did you hear me?"* he yelled and waved his arms. "Hurry, Bella is upset about something. She wants you up here, Adan!"

Chapter 43

A dan handed his pail to Nikolaus. He threw his tunic on and took off at a run. "What's wrong?" Adan demanded, when he joined them on the terrace.

"It's Ovidis," cried Dulcibella. "He was in the candle shop. He practically interrogated me. I lied about you and made things so much worse. I've ruined everything."

"Come on, Bella," urged Marcus. "Let's go in the house."

They went inside, and Dulcibella described the encounter. Nearly done with their shopping, Dulcibella went to buy beeswax candles while Iovita was across the street in a wine shop. Dulcibella and the owner agreed on a price. She turned to leave, but someone spoke to her.

"Are you buying wedding candles, Dulcibella?" said the voice. She spun around to find Ovidis. "I heard you were in mourning."

"What are you doing here? I thought you lived in Apollonia."

"You're ignoring my question. Travelers from Jerusalem told me Herod executed four squads of soldiers in a grand style. It's quite the news in Jerusalem. The centurion executed with the soldiers was your betrothed. Yet here you are, looking rather cheerful and buying wedding candles."

"Be concerned with your own business, Ovidis." She turned toward the door.

"I saw the most beautiful horse yesterday. It was a dapple-gray Arabian, very distinctive. The rider looked just like your betrothed. But that is impossible. He was executed—or was he?"

"How would you know what he looks. . .looked like?"

"I was in Caesarea when you and your centurion put on quite a show down on the pier. He does cut a handsome figure, doesn't he? Not someone who can be misidentified."

"Have some decency! Adas is dead." She backed closer to the door.

"Then who are the wedding candles for, Dulcibella? And why did the rider of the gray horse look just like your centurion? Did Herod kill the wrong man?"

"They look alike because they should. The rider is his half-brother. We are to wed tonight. His name is Novius Serapio. Now, try to remember how a gentleman *should* act." She hurried from the shop and joined her mother, who was waiting in the carriage. Ovidis watched them from the doorway as the carriage went down the street.

Dulcibella was in tears by the time she finished. "I shouldn't have lied."

"Dulcie, it'll be all right," assured Adan. "He'll forget about us in a few weeks."

"Adan is right, Bella," said Marcus. "He was just being rude. Nothing more than that. We have a wedding to celebrate tonight." Iovita agreed and led Dulcibella upstairs.

When they were out of earshot, Marcus turned to Adan. "Ovidis could be trouble."

"He sounds like it. This growing web of lies is making it increasingly dangerous if I stay much longer. What would Herod do if he knew you were harboring a fugitive?"

"Adan, we will deal with it as a family. Let's put this out of our minds for today. This is yours and Bella's wedding day. Besides, technically you're not a fugitive. Actually, I'm not sure what you are."

Marcus went to check on the preparations in the guest cottage while Adan went looking for Dulcibella. She was in her room by a window, looking out at the hills. She heard someone at the door and furtively wiped at her eyes. Adan took her in his arms.

"We should leave as soon as possible," she murmured.

"No. We'll leave when we're ready. Ovidis is not going to run us off. He's a bully and bullies are cowards who pick on people they think won't fight back. Does he know what a good right-hook you have? All you need is your sword to send Ovidis diving under the nearest rock."

Dulcibella managed a smile. "I hear you caught an octopus today. Cook makes delicious octopus stew."

Adan rolled his eyes. "Your little brothers are rascals. They were quite excited when the slimy thing latched on to me."

"They do love octopus stew." She laughed at his doubtful expression.

Running footsteps sounded and Vitus appeared at the door. "Have you looked outside lately? You better come see this!" He rushed out as they followed him to the terrace. Everyone was at the balustrade and looking out across the sea.

"Uh-oh," said Adan. "I wondered about this when I saw the sunrise this morning. The clouds have grown since we went swimming."

The western sky was filled with thick charcoal clouds. There had been an odd stillness only an hour before as if the atmosphere was holding its breath, but now, the ancient oak tree swayed with gusts of wind. The waves battered the shore. Occasionally, a white-capped wave crossed the narrow beach and slammed into the cliff, sending up frothy spray.

"I don't ever remember seeing the sky look this ominous," Dulcibella declared.

"There was a terrible storm only a year before we came here," said Marcus. "It almost wiped out Judea's coastline. In fact, I came here to supervise the reconstruction of the harbor."

Iovita took Dulcibella's arm. "Bella, we need to prepare for a wedding *and* a storm."

Dulcibella placed her hand on the grooved bark of the oak tree. "Be strong, old friend."

The fronds of palm trees lining the courtyard rustled as if they were telling secrets. The shorebirds had disappeared. The air was pungent with the scent of ozone. The boiling mass of clouds reached ever higher. There were frequent flashes of lightning even though the thunder could not reach them yet. The temperature was dropping.

Servants brought firewood into the kitchen from the stacks. Dulcibella and Iovita filled pots with water. The house was plumbed for running water from the well, but storms could overload the system. Marc and Vitus shuttered the windows and stuffed rags in the gaps around the panels. The men secured the animals in the stables. Marcus told the servants to send for their families. They would be safer at the villa.

"This is no simple thunderstorm," Peter said to Marcus.

"It may be a *procella*. Fierce ones are rare in the Mediterranean, but possible."

"You speak of hurricanes. I have heard of such storms. You wisely built this villa from limestone on a foundation of rock. I believe we will be safe in this house."

Dulcibella, her mother, and several servants went upstairs to prepare for the ceremony. Iovita expertly braided Dulcibella's hair into a complex pattern. With her thick brunette hair braided back from her face, her pixie eyes looked more enchanting than ever. Iovita fastened the necklace for Dulcibella that held her birth locket. Every Roman girl gave her birth locket to her father at her wedding. She slipped on her ankle length lavender wedding *tunica*. Her mother pinned the shoulders of the tunic with *fibulae* made of mother-of-pearl. She added a few touches of rose and iris oil. She slipped on white leather sandals. All Roman brides wore a sash around their waists, usually a white woolen cloth, but Dulcibella insisted on the peacock-colored sash.

Iovita held the sash. "Cornelia Minor Cornelius, are you ready to become a bride?" she asked with traditional formality. A flash of bright light filled the room followed by a low growl of thunder. The servants blinked in trepidation.

"Let the storm come," Dulcibella lifted her chin. "Yes, Mother, I am ready."

"Then I shall tie the knot of Hercules." Placing the peacock sash around her daughter's slim waist, she tied the complicated knot which only the husband was allowed to untie. The varying shades of turquoise in the sash blended beautifully with the lavender tunic and the colors of Dulcibella's eyes. The last items were the bridal veil and the crown of pink snapdragons. The veil covered both the front and the back of her *tunica* down to her knees. The gentle folds on either side framed her bare arms. The servants beamed at the sight of such a beautiful bride. Their beloved mistress was indeed a visual image of her name, Sweet Beauty.

Downstairs, Nikolaus and Andreas joined Adan and the brothers. They talked while Adan trimmed his beard close to the jawline and dressed. When his preparations were complete, they tried to keep him occupied while they waited for the ceremony to begin. Occasionally, he would pace the floor or rearrange the rags stuffed around the shutters. Marcus appeared in the doorway to announce it was time.

The main hall was adorned with jars of flowers. A soft light, cast by candles and oil lamps, offset the darkness of the storm-shuttered windows. The traditional red carpet made a path across the tiled floor from the bottom of the limestone stairs to the fireplace. A pedestal table stood to the side of the blazing fireplace. Three candles, two small ones, and one large one sat on the table.

Gusts of wind rattled the shutters as rainwater seeped in around the frames. Occasionally, a rag would come loose. A servant would quickly replace it. Some of the servants looked around nervously with every crash of thunder, but their anxiety eased when the house stood strong. A crash sounded as if a giant had dashed a tree against the house. Torn tree limbs pelted the outside walls. The wind wailed with a high-pitched intensity few had ever heard. The young children of the servants cried while they clung to their parents.

In the kitchen, Cook and her staff watched over the wedding feast preparations. The wedding cake was decorated with honey glaze, bits of dried fruit, and nuts. The octopus stew was ready, along with steamed clams in wine and butter cream sauce. The bread was to be served with herbed olive oil. The best wine was chilling in the well house. Everything and everyone was ready. Iovita sent a servant to announce the bride was ready.

Iovita appeared at the head of the stairs wearing a pale yellow silk *stola* pinned at the shoulders with copper *fibulae*. Over the *stola*, she wore her favorite cream-colored *palla*. It draped beautifully over her left shoulder and around her slender figure. The pastel colors complimented her dark plaited hair. Dulcibella joined her mother at the top of the stairs. Iovita and Dulcibella smiled into each other's eyes. Standing together, everyone could see mother and daughter shared a timeless elegance, not only of form, but of grace.

Dulcibella looked radiant in her lavender *tunica*. The silk veil covering her face was so sheer it could have been woven from ocean mist. Her braided brunette hair made a crown that followed the edge of her scalp. Even behind the veil, one could see the natural beauty of her elfish eyes, full pink lips, and oval face. Her eyes sparkled with the shades of the peacock sash she wore around her waist. Dulcibella's face glowed with the anticipation of her life changing forever. She beamed at Adan as he stood at the end of the crimson carpet. He looked up at her with rapture.

Adan was dressed in an ankle length white linen tunic and the purple silk *toga* lent to him by Marcus. He wore tan leather sandals which laced to his knees. His beard and mustache framed his square jaw and full lips. His ebony-black hair was brushed straight back from his temples. In the fading light, his eyes were dark discs of gold, but the flashes of lightning set his eyes ablaze like a wild predator too close to a campfire.

Iovita nodded at Andreas. He began singing Dulcibella's favorite love song. A servant girl strummed an eight-stringed harp. Iovita took Dulcibella's hand. Slowly they descended the stairs. They hesitated on the last step just as blazing tongues of lightning slashed the sky. Crashing thunder resonated through the house as if it were cracking in two. A few of the servants jumped in alarm. Alpha and Omega whimpered as they shook, their tails drooping in fear. Two servants scooped up the little dogs to comfort them. Marcus and Peter exchanged a nod of confidence. Dulcibella and Iovita stepped on to the red carpet. The bride sighed with deep contentment, knowing the next moment would forever change her life.

The ceremony began with the bride and her mother clinging to each other and the groom symbolically "wresting" his betrothed away. Adan wrapped an arm around Dulcibella's waist and took her hand. Iovita gave her daughter one last hug. Dulcibella smiled at her mother and then turned toward Adan. Iovita released her. Holding hands, Adan and Dulcibella walked the carpeted path between the two standing groups of guests. They approached Peter and Marcus as they stood before the fireplace. Dulcibella unhooked her birth locket. In a ceremonious gesture of releasing her father from his parental responsibility, she placed it in his hand. Symbolically expressing his approval of their marriage, he hooked the locket around his neck. He joined Iovita with the other guests.

Adan and Dulcibella turned their attention to Peter. Lightning filled the sky with a near constant frequency along with the responding clamor of thunder. The wind slammed into the house as if it were angry that anything would stand in the way. The violence of the rain echoed down from the vaulted ceiling, sounding as if thousands of feet marched across the roof. It seemed as if the elements of Nature were locked in combat, a civil war of atmospheric elements.

Simon Peter nodded at the groom and then the bride. "There is no union more sacred among mankind than to be joined together in matrimony. God created man and woman to be united, one to the other. The wedding vows are not to be taken lightly, but to be spoken from the heart, the mind, and the soul. Both of you repeat after me, 'We promise to cherish and protect each other whether in good fortune or in adversity, and to seek together a life hallowed by our faith in God, the Father and the Son.'"

Gazing into each other's eyes, they repeated the wedding vows. Peter selected one of the two rings from the table and turned to Adan. "Please repeat after me, 'With this ring, Dulcibella, you are made holy to me, for I love you as my own soul.'" Peter handed the ring to Adan. Adan faced his bride and repeating the vow, he slipped the ring on her left ring finger.

Peter handed the other ring to Dulcibella. She repeated the vow to Adan and slipped the ring on his left ring finger. Both rings were bronze, set with a round cabochon of eilat stone. The design consisted of two intertwined circles, never ending, always beginning.

"You may each take a small candle," instructed Peter. "As your lives were once separate, now your lives shall be one as long as you both shall live." Together, they lit the large candle with their small ones. They blew out the small candles and set them aside. Peter announced, "I now proclaim that Adan and Dulcibella are wed. You may seal your vows with a kiss." Adan carefully folded Dulcibella's veil back and took her in his arms. They looked into each other's eyes before their lips met for the first time as husband and wife.

Everyone cheered, clapped, and hugged. Nikolaus was still clapping when everyone else had stopped. Charmingly embarrassed, he ducked into the kitchen on the pretense that the staff needed help. Cook shooed him back into the main hall. Adan had specifically requested that Nikolaus be seated on his left side at the table, the place traditionally reserved for the groom's father or a brother. They gathered at the table. Heaping plates were served and wine goblets filled, while the storm shrieked overhead. Alpha and Omega recovered from their fright as soon as the first morsels hit the floor. Powerful gusts of rain slashed at the villa with talons of sand and debris. The wind screamed with fury when it failed to find a weakness. The hurricane ripped the sky apart with lightning, and thunder smashed it back together. Blessedly, the household of Cornelius was shielded from the violence of the heavens. More logs were heaped in the fireplace as it grew darker and the temperature cooled. The flickering firelight merged with the shadows in an intricate dance across the walls and ceiling.

"How will we keep Bella's marriage torch lit?" Iovita asked Marcus.

"The winds will stop for a while before they restart from the opposite direction. Fortunately, the cottage is nearby."

Iovita watched her daughter. "Ah, she is so happy."

"She is indeed," agreed Marcus. "Look at the two of them. Our blessings exceed the imagination."

"Cook is bringing the cake!" Vitus called out. She set the wedding cake in front of the bride. Laughing at something Adan whispered in her ear, Dulcibella cut the cake. Adan placed a piece on each dessert plate as they were passed to him. Nikolaus couldn't remember the last time he tasted anything so delicious. He tried to eat his share slowly to make it last longer. He grinned when Adan placed a second piece on his plate.

"You better enjoy this while you can, Nikolaus. In a few days, you go back to your training. I plan to make up for lost time."

Nikolaus laughed, "I'll be ready." He took another bite of cake. "Maybe."

With the wedding cake gone, Marcus gave Adan a questioning eye. Adan nodded. Marcus tapped his wine goblet and stood up. "This is a most joyous time, celebrating the marriage of Adan and my daughter, Dulcibella, so it is a good time to celebrate another blessing. There is someone here who has proved to be a trusted friend. Tonight, as a father would give to his son, I am privileged to present to Nikolaus Kokinos a symbol of his family's honor." Nikolaus sat wide-eyed. Adan nudged him with an elbow. Nikolaus stood up, noticeably shaken.

Marcus opened a leather pouch and tapped an object into his palm. "Nikolaus Kokinos, I present to you a signature ring, bearing a ruby carved with your initials and encased in fine gold." Everyone clapped and cheered. Nikolaus was speechless. Marcus handed him the ring. With shaking hands, Nikolaus slipped the ring on his finger, amazed at the perfect fit.

"I-I cannot describe what I am feeling. I don't have words grand enough. It's beautiful; it looks just like the one my father owned. Thank you. This ring means more to me than you know." He studied the ring with amazement. "How did you commission it so quickly?"

Adan came to his feet. "The story of this ring is almost magical considering it ends with you. My father commissioned a signature ring for me, the one I now wear." He held up his hand bearing the wolf head. "When the merchant brought it to the villa, another ring was in the same box. I asked him about it. He said he had just presented it to the buyer on his way to our villa, but the man refused it. Even though I was pleased with my ring, I was fascinated with the ruby ring. My father pointed out that the initials were all wrong for me. I said, 'For me, yes, but not for someone.' He asked if I wanted it, which really surprised me. He bought it for me. I've had this ring for nine years, waiting to find someone it would fit."

"The very first time we met, you asked for my name," said Nikolaus. "As if that wasn't unusual enough, you asked for my surname."

Adan laughed. "You must have thought I was crazy."

"I did—a little. You acted like my initials were some kind of amazing discovery."

"Then, at Serapio's," said Adan, "you described your father's ring and said that you would commission another one just like it. I was tempted to ruin your surprise right then. I felt that I should bring it with me when I left Rome. I couldn't wear it, but I didn't want to leave it behind. When I was transferred to Jerusalem, I knew it would be safer with Marcus. I think the ring was always meant for you, Nikolaus, even when it wasn't."

Everyone congratulated Nikolaus. To own a signature ring was to be a man of distinction. The signature ring represented the authority and integrity of a man. One of the servants brought out papyrus and sealing wax. Nikolaus made a test signature in the wax. Everyone gathered around to see the perfect impression.

The evening's celebration advanced along with the storm. The thunder and wind gradually lessened into silence, but the hurricane would start up again soon. The wedding torch was lighted in the fireplace. Everyone gathered behind Dulcibella and Adan for the procession to the cottage. They were surprised to see a moonlit landscape when they opened the back door. The eye of the storm twinkled with stars, but it wouldn't for long. The servants snatched up spare torches. Talking excitedly, the wedding party walked to the cottage where they made a hammock with their arms to carry Dulcibella across the threshold, as was tradition. Iovita placed the marriage candle in a bronze holder on the bedside table.

Dulcibella used her wedding torch to light the wood in the fireplace, symbolizing her acceptance of their new home. She doused the torch in the pail of water sitting on the hearth. She shook out the excess water and tossed the torch in the air. The servant girl who had played the harp caught the torch. A few elbows jostled Andreas meaningfully. He smiled shyly as he hazarded a quick glance at the girl. She bit her lower lip and blushed when their eyes met. Marcus and Iovita stepped forward to give their daughter and son-in-law their blessing. Then the guests slipped away. From under his belt, Marcus pulled the order addressed to his second-in-command written the day he learned of the executions. He set the papyrus in the fire and watched it burn. Iovita touched his arm. He placed his hand over hers. They slipped away, pulling the door shut behind them.

Adan and Dulcibella were alone. She carefully removed the wreath of snapdragons and her veil. Methodically, she unbraided her hair, letting her brunette tresses cascade around her shoulders. Adan sat down on the bed to watch the graceful movement of her fingers. She came over to him.

"Now, my love," she whispered, "will you untie the knot of Hercules?" Adan gently pulled her closer and studied the knot.

"This might take some time. I may have to clip it off," he said playfully.

"Don't you dare!" she exclaimed as she ruffled his hair and pinched his ears.

Adan laughed as he tried to rescue his ears. Giggling, Dulcibella relented. He started to work the knot loose. A complicated pattern was used to symbolize the pledge of faithfulness between husband and wife. Adan undid the final tie and triumphantly laid the sash on the bed. She pulled him to his feet. He removed the toga Marcus had lent to him.

Dulcibella placed her hand over his heart. "You have not told me what you suffered, Adan. I will see the evidence of your torture and I'm afraid."

"I am sorry, Dulcie. I should have warned you, but I just couldn't talk about it."

"Do the others know?"

"When we went swimming."

"Of course, the clam dig, I forgot." She rested her head against his chest and listened to the comforting beat of his heart.

"Dulcie," he murmured, combing his fingers through her hair as he so often did. "Put your distress aside. Think only of this night, our wedding night. I love you and you love me. It is just the two of us here. No fear, no despair. The scars you can see mean nothing compared to what I suffered when I thought I would never see you again. Your laughter is music to me. The touch of your hand is comfort. The light in your eyes shines from the beauty in your soul. Your heart is kindness. Dulcibella, when I am with you, I am alive."

"Your voice is soothing like the light of a full moon. Your touch calms my soul. Your eyes reach into my heart and I am at peace. When I am with you, there is only room in my heart for love. With you, I, too, am alive. Nothing can ever separate us from our love for each other, not even death. We will both be with God."

They kissed longingly. Lightning slashed the darkness and thunder exploded. Startled, Dulcibella pulled away. Adan snuggled her back against his chest. "Where do you think you're going, Little Elf?"

"Wherever you go, my love. Wherever, you go."

She welcomed the shelter of his embrace. The far-side of the storm had arrived. Again, lightning and thunder shattered the sky, the wind battered their home with surges of rain, but the house stood. On this tempest-tossed night, they found delight in each other's arms. As the storm gradually subsided, and the skies grew silent, Adan and Dulcibella nestled together in contented dreamless sleep.

Chapter 44

—⌘—

A few hours before the storm hit, Silas Silvanus headed for home after hiring crews to unload cargo the next morning. He saw the storm clouds in the west, but dismissed the threat. As was his custom, he urged Blackfire up a hilltop to overlook his olive orchards, vineyards, and grand villa. He enjoyed seeing the expanse of his riches. When he bought the property, Silas tore down the original villa built with Judean limestone. He built a larger, more elegant home with a central, open-roof atrium, common in Rome. To compensate for the extra cost of a much larger structure, he used clay bricks instead of limestone blocks.

Without his limestone-block barn, the family and servants would probably have died. The open-roof atrium Silas was so proud of proved to be the ruination of the villa. The rain and wind attacked the structure from the inside. The terracotta roof flew away, destabilizing the structure. The walls were toppled by the debris-filled wind. The extravagant villa was reduced to rubble.

The children trembled against their parents as the storm raged. They clapped their hands over their ears with every flash of lightning knowing explosive thunder would follow. As the storm persisted, Silas was forced to admit that he had always put his faith in his wealth. Now his family was facing calamity. Silas and his family were forced to retreat to a foul-smelling barn. Previously, he thought just entering the barn was beneath his dignity.

The storm finally moved inland. The exhausted children fell asleep just before the sun rose. Silas and Milcah, his wife, stepped out to a devastated landscape. The sky presented a beautiful day in stark contrast to the ruined countryside. It seemed as if nature offered a truce for those who could accept it, but Silas only saw destruction. His olive orchard was a thatch of upended roots. His vineyards were a chaotic tangle of greenery. It sickened him to think about his ships in the harbor and those still out to sea. With shock, Silas realized he thought of those things before he thought where his family would live since their home was in shambles.

Milcah surveyed the destruction. "We no longer have any reason to stay here. This storm has left us destitute and we have to think of our children." She called out to a servant. "Go to the Ocean View Inn and secure accommodations." She turned back to Silas. "As soon as I can book passage, I will take the children to my family in Pompeii."

"Why are you leaving? We can rebuild. We can replace the vineyards. The olive trees can be replanted." He stared at her in shock.

"Silas! Are you blind? It will take years to rebuild this estate. How can you possibly pay for it? Your ships are surely destroyed, and what of your crewmen and their families?"

"How can you abandon me like this?"

"Think! What happens when a man cannot pay his debts? Our children could be sold as slaves! Your wealth has always been first in your heart, but now you must think of us. Silas, you are a good man. You are a good father to our children. They love you. I love you. Please, let's make a fresh start in Pompeii. I still own property there with a modest villa and a vineyard. Silas, I never wanted grandeur and wealth. I wanted security, yes, but most of all I wanted a family. Come with us."

He shook his head. "No. I will make things right and then I will come for you."

The children stood at the open doors. Their weary faces steeled her resolve. "I need my dowry back. If you sell Blackfire, that will suffice. I will not take more than I contributed."

When the servant returned he advised Milcah he had reserved a room. She ordered the carriage to be readied. She asked Silas once more, "Please come with us! Don't make me choose the children over you."

"No, I will not go to your family disgraced like a street beggar. I will come for you when I have enough money."

"Then you will never come. You will never think you have enough. God has taken everything away from you, except your family. Yet, you willingly turn your back on the very thing God preserved." Milcah called to her children. "I will be at the inn until we can find passage to Pompeii. I pray that you change your mind, but I will not wait for you, Silas. I have waited for you our entire marriage, but we were always in second place. Please ask Centurion Cornelius if he can spare a few soldiers to escort us to Pompeii."

Silas nodded dejectedly. He kissed and hugged his children, bidding them farewell. They begged him to come with them, but in the end, they left with their mother. Silas saddled Blackfire and headed for the villa of Cornelius. It was slow going. The pace worsened once he reached the city streets. Soldiers and citizens worked side by side to rescue survivors and clear away debris, but he hurried past. Eventually, Silas topped the cliff road to the villa. He saw the family out on the terrace under the oak tree. It had a few broken branches but the tree still stood. He hailed them as he strode forward. At the sight of him, Iovita grabbed her husband's arm. Marcus shot a sidelong glance at Adan when he saw Silas. Adan looked over his shoulder. Silas stopped in his tracks.

"Greetings, Silas," said Adan.

"I heard. . .they said. . .the whole legion saw you die."

"It's true. I was dead. The witnesses think I'm still dead. I need it to stay that way. Call me Adan Serapio."

"I should not have come." Silas turned to leave.

"Silas, you are always welcome here," said Marcus.

Silas explained the need for an escort and Marcus promised to make arrangements.

"Thank you," said Silas, "but there is one more favor I must ask. I promised Milcah I would return her dowry. I must sell Blackfire."

Marcus didn't hesitate. "I'll pay you a fair price for the horse, Silas."

"Thank you, Marcus. I can't believe this is happening. Yesterday, everything was perfect. I have lost everything in the span of one night."

"Not everything," said Nikolaus. "You still have your life, your family, and your freedom. So you have not lost what should be most important to you."

"Nikolaus is right," Peter said. "You have a choice. Yeshua once invited you to follow him. I heard him say it. Does anything hinder you now? You are welcome to come with me."

Silas hesitated. "When I asked how I could have eternal life, I couldn't believe it when Yeshua said, *'Sell all that you have and distribute to the poor, and you will have treasure in heaven; and come, follow Me.'* Now I know why he said that to me and not others. It is not evil to be wealthy, but to love wealth above all else is wrong. Milcah was right. If Yeshua asked me to follow him now, I would, but he is dead."

"No, he's not!" they responded together.

"I saw him alive, days after I made sure he was dead," said Adan. He gestured at Peter. "So did he and many others. Yeshua truly is the Messiah, Silas."

"Malchus and I leave for Jerusalem soon," said Peter. "Come with us."

The storm had done for Silas what he couldn't do for himself. His wealth had become an addiction. It gnawed at him to have more, always more. He was never satisfied. Silas remembered his father's blessing, "Silas, I hope you remember that earthly treasure will either use you, or you will use it. May you always know the difference." Silas looked around at their expectant faces, and made his decision. "I will go, Peter, but I can't promise for how long I'll stay with you."

"That is a good start, Silas. There will be hardships and dangers, but someday you will see Yeshua again. Perhaps, he will say, *'Well done, good and faithful servant.'*"

"I will disperse what I can salvage to the families of crewmen who have died. Then I will go with you."

"You are welcome to stay here," offered Marcus. Silas shook his head.

"The old law no longer applies," said Peter. "*Elohim* is the God of both Jew and Gentile. You may enter this home without penalty."

Adan caught Marcus's eye, and they moved away from the group. "I believe God has used Ovidis and Silas to show me what I should do. I need to return to Jerusalem and face King Herod. I will ask that he proclaim my sentence fulfilled. Technically, I was executed. Will you come with me?"

"Of course. When do you want to leave?"

"Let's go after the city repairs are under way. In the meantime, I will see to the repairs here. Thank you, Marcus. Your presence will be greatly appreciated. I hope Dulcie will understand my decision." They rejoined the group. Dulcibella studied Adan's expression.

"You're going back to Jerusalem," Dulcibella stated.

"We both knew this would happen, I think. Your father is going with me."

"So will I. We will face Herod together. Actually, I'm relieved. I'm tired of being afraid. God will be with us." Refusing to give in to fearful possibilities, she ran her hand down the side of his face. "So, does this mean you're going to shave off your *pirata* beard?"

"Do you wish me to do so?"

"I do. It tickles when you kiss me."

"Then it shall be gone this very day, but let's give it a good farewell." Adan bent to kiss her but she playfully clapped her hand over her mouth and ran. He caught her in a few strides. She yelped, laughing too hard to wriggle free. Adan scooped her up. She squealed and kicked her legs even as she wrapped her arms tightly over his shoulders. "You're such a wicked pirate!" she giggled as he took the path to their house.

Marcus could hear their laughter through the kitchen windows. A grateful smile chased away his anxiety. There were few things as precious to him as the sound of his children's laughter. He went to tell Iovita the plan. He didn't expect her to be surprised, and neither did he need to ask his daughter if she planned go to Jerusalem.

A *tabellari* from the courier service returned Adan's letter a few days later. The ship had returned to port before the storm hit. The *tabellari* would have sent the letter with the next ship, but the papyrus was damaged by salt water.

"Are you going to write another letter?" Dulcibella asked.

"My father won't get Salvitto's letter for at least a month, if at all, since the storm may have affected that ship as well."

Dulcibella frowned. "Adan, the news will reach your father one way or another. He's already lost your mother. Do you want him to suffer even more?"

"Suffer? I suppose he will, even though he has a new wife to distract him."

Dulcibella's eyes clouded with sadness. "It grieves me to hear you talk like that. It's not like you to be cruel."

"I can't write to him now, Dulcie. Things have changed. We don't know what Herod will decide. Wouldn't it be worse if my father gets Salvitto's letter saying I'm dead. Then my letter saying I'm alive, and then a third letter saying now I really am dead? I shouldn't have written this letter. What if it had fallen in the wrong hands? We need to see Herod first."

After weeks of storm repairs, the day for Adan and the others to leave was drawing near. An argument erupted one morning. Marc and Vitus wanted to go with them to Jerusalem. Marcus wanted them to stay with their mother. Iovita wanted them to go with their father. Adan and Dulcibella slipped out of the kitchen and ate breakfast on the terrace.

Dulcibella chewed on toasted bread and fig jam. "Nikolaus is taking his bow, the one you gave him for his seventeenth birthday. He practices every day. Did you know that? Sometimes he's out there for hours, it seems."

The kitchen door slammed. Marc stalked across the terrace, stiff with anger. "Well, Father won. Vitus and I have to stay here. Somehow he got Mother to change her mind. Adan, could you tell them to let us go?"

"No. I don't think you should go either. Do you realize I may be put to death?"

"That can't happen!" Marc exclaimed.

"Yes it could."

The boy lowered his head dejectedly. "I didn't think of that."

"Are you and Vitus going to continue with the house repairs while I'm gone?" Marc shrugged as he intently watched a beetle scurry across the terrace. "Marc, look at me." The boy grudgingly lifted his eyes. "There's still much to do."

"Can we go for a clam-dig before you leave?"

"Sure, we might even catch another octopus."

Marc abandoned his ill humor. "I'll go find Vitus. He'll help us if I mention octopus stew." He hurried for the house.

After staying with the Cornelius family for a few more days, Peter, Malchus, and Silas prepared to leave. Before they bid farewell, Malchus pulled Adan aside.

"When you stop in Joppa, come to Simon's house. I will face Herod with you. I want to return the prize money to him when you make your case."

"It will be an honor to have you with me, but you should keep the gold."

"This money is tainted. I've thought about giving it away, but it doesn't feel right. It's like stealing money from a rich man to give to a poor man. It is a dishonorable act disguised as charity."

"But Malchus, what if Caiaphas has you arrested?"

"He might, but I'm still going with you."

Adan clapped a hand on Malchus's shoulder. "I pray for your safety. Your presence before Herod will remind him that he ordered you to do God's will. And you did. Perhaps Herod will find it difficult to argue against his own command."

Peter, Malchus, and Silas left for Jerusalem within the hour.

Chapter 45

Adan woke early. The dreaded day had arrived. He stole a look at Dulcibella as she lay on her side. He was going to slip out of bed to let her sleep, but as he sat up, she murmured, "Aren't you going to wish me a good morning?" She pulled his arm until he lay back down.

"You looked so peaceful I didn't want to wake you."

Dulcibella sat up. Adan studied her flawless complexion, the gentle curve of her neck, and shoulders. He tried not to think about what they would face the next day. She saw the sorrow in his eyes. The same fear clung to her.

"Dulcie, I know you're scared."

"I'm all right," she mumbled.

"We're taking a huge risk confronting Herod, but why should we be forced to leave here? This is our home. This is where we belong."

"It's so unfair!" she cried. "Why does Herod decide if you live or not?"

"Herod does *not* decide. God decides."

"I know, Adan, but what if God . . .you know? God allowed Stephen and James to die. They wanted to serve Yeshua, yet God allowed them to be killed."

"Where did he take them, Dulcie?"

"They're in heaven. But what of the people who loved Stephen and James? What of those left behind?"

"They grieve terribly. I agree there is nothing good in that."

"I will die without you," she whispered.

Adan took her hands in his. "Sweet Beauty, you have wisdom and the heart of a *bellatrix*. Don't let fear overtake you."

"I'm trying. But, the possibility of losing you, *again*, is terrifying. I want to run away."

Adan kissed the palms of her hands. "But you're still here. We'll face this threat together." She leaned over to kiss him.

Persistent scratching sounded at the door. Alpha and Omega were relentless when they wanted in. Adan groaned. "I think the 'children' are feeling left out."

"Come on then, let's join the others for breakfast."

They walked to the main house to find ample food on the table. After breakfast, they changed clothes. The servants prepared the pack horses. Marcus and Adan both wore the tunics and *caligae* of centurions. Marcus also wore the belt reserved for a *primus pilus* centurion. Dulcibella packed a *stola* and a *palla*, but for the journey she wore women's *bracae*, and a mid-thigh-length tunic. With the final preparations completed, the travelers made their farewells.

Iovita gave up trying not to cry. Marc and Vitus plastered stoic expressions on their faces. Marcus led the way to the cliff road. The family hurried over to the terrace to watch them ride down the switchbacks. Hands waved to the travelers as they waved back.

In Caesarea, the soldiers and townspeople had cleared away the storm debris. They were surprised that Adan stopped at the Apollonia Inn when they reached Apollonia.

"Greetings to you, Nikolaus," chirped a feminine voice. A young girl with auburn hair smiled up at him. "You do remember me, yes? I'm Marina."

Nikolaus could not help smiling at the pretty girl with the laughing eyes. They spent the evening talking together the last time they saw each other. Nikolaus remembered he had lied to Marina, letting her think he was Adan's servant. A blush crossed his cheeks, but Marina thought Nikolaus was remembering the kiss they had shared.

"Of course, I remember you, Marina. How could anyone forget you?" He dropped from the saddle. "It's good to see you." He noticed a fallen tree. "Did you have much storm damage?"

"We did! It was quite exciting! Well, the owner didn't think it was exciting."

"I thought your father was the owner. I'm sorry. I must have misunderstood."

Marina bit her lower lip. "No, you didn't misunderstand. Gnaeus Flavius Ovidis is the owner. My father is his manager."

"Ah, then, I should confess that . . ."

"No you shouldn't."

"I lied to you. At the time, I was a . . ."

She put her finger to his lips. "Shhh, I know. I knew then you were a . . .weren't free. But I also knew you did not belong to the centurion. I was confused. He treated you like a little brother, but you acted like a slave. So did he free you?"

"He did—well, Serapio helped, but Adan nullified my contract."

"Who is Adan?"

"Uh. . .well, he's. . .uh. . ." Nikolaus couldn't think of an explanation. Fortunately, a distraction covered his dilemma. Adan and Dulcibella were arguing. It ended abruptly when a man with a limp crossed the courtyard and headed toward them.

"Well, it seems I have guests," announced Ovidis. One side of his face had been badly abraded, but had healed, leaving scars. His arm was in a sling.

Dulcibella whispered, "Did you do that?" Adan rolled his eyes.

"Marina!" Ovidis called. "Will you take their horses? Give them water and grain."

"Yes, Sir!" She glanced at Nikolaus. "Want to help?" The two of them gathered the horses' reins and walked around the side of the hotel.

Ovidis approached Marcus. "Centurion Cornelius, Sir, it is good to see you again." Marcus returned the greeting. Ovidis nodded to Dulcibella. "You are more beautiful than ever, Dulcibella." She nodded stiffly. He turned to Adan. "Let me congratulate you and your wife. Did you have the ceremony in spite of the storm?"

"Yes. The imps of Nature were so eager to gaze upon Dulcibella's beauty; they attended the wedding, uninvited, of course." The others smiled and Dulcibella snickered. Adan asked, "Is lunch still available this late in the day? I remember having exceptionally good food here."

"Yes, of course. Come inside." Ovidis led the way. The others went inside, but Adan asked to speak with Ovidis alone. "I want to thank you."

"Thank me? For what?"

"For being curious about me. Using a false name seemed a good idea at the time, but it's not working. We are returning to Jerusalem to face King Herod. Your information was correct. I was executed, but as you can see, I did not—stay dead."

Ovidis's eyes went wide. "I don't understand." Adan explained the circumstances. Ovidis shook his head. "I must apologize to Dulcibella. I treated her disrespectfully. Last year when she emphatically rejected me, I suffered a bruised ego rather than a bruised heart. But many things have changed since the storm. At first I thought the inn had escaped serious damage. My manager, Pitio, his two daughters, and I were inspecting the inn when a section of the bell tower fell. Varinia, the eldest daughter, was the closest. I pushed her out of the way. Some of the bricks fell on me. Varinia, quite the nursemaid, wouldn't leave my side. I had been so distracted with business that I was blind to her charms."

Adan laughed. "Come on, you must tell Dulcibella your story." They walked together into the hotel dining room where Andreas, Dulcibella and Marcus sat waiting. Not surprisingly, no one asked what happened to Nikolaus. They ate and talked. Varinia joined them. She added a few details to the story. Ovidis swore she was exaggerating. She swore he was being modest. The listeners enjoyed their playful banter.

Marcus thought it was time they should go when Nikolaus and Marina came in. Ovidis talked a moment with Adan, gesturing at the damaged areas of the inn, while he occasionally glanced at Nikolaus. Adan and Ovidis shook hands. "I hope things go well for you, Adan."

"And you as well." The travelers headed out and left Apollonia behind. They arrived at Simon's house after a few hours.

Peter, Malchus, and Silas were overjoyed at seeing their friends. During supper, they traded news until it was time to get some sleep. After everyone was bedded down, Adan crept outside and sat on a flat boulder of sandstone. There was no moon. The star-paved Milky Way twinkled as if alive. The hypnotic melody of the ocean waves calmed his spirit. Adan gazed at the heavens, marveling at the beauty of the night. He tried to think of what he would say to Herod, but images of Valentius kept intruding until he could no longer concentrate.

"Lord God, grant me the opportunity to confront Valentius," Adan prayed aloud. "Let him see that he failed to take my life. Allow me to see him as a prisoner, as he saw me."

Adan heard the door open. A figure approached. "I couldn't sleep either." Dulcibella sat down next to him.

"I hope I'm not making a mistake, Dulcie."

"What you said is true. To hide in a lie cannot be right. Over these past weeks, the increasing need for deception tied me into knots. Every time I heard horse hooves on the road, I was terrified. As fearful as tomorrow might be, I am glad we're finally facing it."

Adan pushed off from the rock and helped Dulcibella to her feet. "Come on, Little Elf. Let's see if sleep will find us now." They went inside the house hand in hand. However, Adan and Dulcibella were not the only ones who would have a restless night.

Far from Judea, in Rome, Tribune Salvitto's letter was delivered to the villa of *Consul* Longinus. Aquila was in his atrium enjoying the solitude of a late afternoon. He sipped from a goblet of wine as he relaxed in his lounge chair. A tall, young woman with chestnut hair and almond-shaped, brown eyes sat down next to him.

"Janae, you're back. Did you find the baskets you wanted?" asked Aquila.

"Yes. They should look quite lovely around the fountain."

A servant entered the atrium and presented a letter. Aquila glanced at the wax seal. It was from Tribune Salvitto. He set his goblet down hard, nearly toppling it. Quickly, he broke the seal and unrolled the scroll. Color drained from his face. He dropped the letter and lowered his head to his hands.

"What is it?" Janae snatched the letter from the floor. After reading a few lines, she covered her mouth with a shaking hand. Her eyes filled with tears. She knew too well the devastation of losing a child.

"My son is dead," whispered Aquila. "How could this happen? According to Salvitto, Adas's commanding officer, Centurion Valentius, conspired to have him executed. This man will pay for murdering my son." Aquila glared around the room as Janae helplessly watched him. "This is my fault! If he had never left Caesarea, he would still be alive."

"You can't blame yourself for what someone else did."

"You're right, but I can blame myself for what I did. I didn't encourage him, or praise him. I thought it would spoil him. I thought my silence would make him strong.

But I'm afraid it only made him resentful. I should have given him what my father never gave me, love without conditions. It broke his mother's heart when playmates were kept away from him, but I dismissed it. I thought Adas was not interested in having friends. So I did nothing. No wonder he kept company with the *veterinarii* at the garrison. They accepted him as I should have. Children should never be forced to doubt the love of their parents."

Aquila began to pace the room. "I was so angry when he enlisted. I didn't even present him with weapons and armor, as a father should. I was so determined to keep him out of the army. My efforts probably pushed him right into it. My father was a *primus pilus* centurion. He took me with him on campaigns when I was a boy. I saw what war does to a man when he is forced to kill over and over. They say it gets easier. Some begin to enjoy it. I know my son. He has. . .*had* the compassion of his mother. War would either destroy his heart, or he would grow accustomed to it, which would destroy his soul."

Janae could only watch, helplessly. Aquila glanced at the letter. "I can't believe he's gone. I never got to explain why Marsetina didn't answer his last two letters. He must have thought she was ignoring him. She didn't want to answer until she was well. But she never got well. When I did write, I didn't have the heart to tell him his mother had died before his last letter arrived. If I had written when she first became ill, he could have come home to see her, but I kept thinking she would get better. She refused to let me send for him. I loved Marsetina dearly, but she had her pride. She didn't want him to see her sickly and weak."

Janae rose to take him in her arms. He bowed his head to her shoulder. Having lost her own son, Janae understood the depth of his despair. "I'm so sorry, my love. I will grieve with you."

Aquila took a labored breath and shuddered. They stood for a few moments until he pulled away. His face was lined with regret. His voice trembled. "It's too late to be the father I should have been."

Chapter 46

Despite the rising sun promising a beautiful day, Adan and the others were grim as they bid farewell to their friends. Nikolaus or Andreas would attempt to start a conversation, but the others were too distracted to respond. As they passed through Emmaus, Adan tried to lighten the mood by asking Dulcibella if she thought he should keep Adan as his *praenomen*. She nodded approval, but added no comment. Adan and Dulcibella reined their horses to a stop when the wall of Jerusalem came into view. Without a word, they took each other's hand. "We're going to get through this, Dulcie." She nodded and gently squeezed his hand.

The congestion of travelers increased as they approached the city. They could hear shouts from men gathered around a wagon with a broken axel. They were working to unload the wagon, which left little room for other traffic. The loose sand on either side of the road was not conducive to wagon wheels. They stopped behind the wreck to allow an oncoming company of soldiers to pass. They were escorting a prisoner. His head was bowed in an effort to avoid eye contact. The soldiers passed the wrecked wagon and drew even with Adan and the others.

Adan scrutinized the prisoner and felt a rush of elation. It was Valentius. God had granted his prayer. When Valentius rode past, Adan saw that his back was scarred, obvious signs of a past scourging. Marcus saw Adan tense as he eyed the prisoner and looked more closely. Marcus told Andreas to take the others around the wagon after the escort soldiers passed. Adan and Marcus exchanged a meaningful glance. They turned back in pursuit of the soldiers.

Adan spun Venustas abruptly in front of the escort squads. "Stop! Who is in charge here?" The prisoner jerked his head up. His eyes went wide with shock. His face drained of color as his mouth gaped open.

The lead *principales* answered, "Centurions, Sirs, I am! My name is *Optio* Naevius of the 1st *Cohors*, 1st *Centuria*."

"Where are you taking this prisoner?" demanded Adan.

"*Nooo! You're dead!*" screamed Valentius as he dug his heels into the flanks of his horse, trying to get closer. The *principales* backhanded him. He would have been knocked from the saddle except for the ropes binding his wrists.

"Shut your mouth!" Naevius shouted. "Or I will shut it for you!"

Overpowering gratification seized Adan as he watched Valentius struggle to understand the shocking truth.

"Sirs!" pleaded Naevius, "please accept my apologies for this prisoner's disrespect."

"Which centurion took responsibility for him?" demanded Adan.

"No one, Sir. King Herod declared him *persona non grata*. He is only safe from us." He gestured at his men. "Herod instructed that we are not to defend him if he is attacked. We will suffer no consequences if we have credible witnesses."

Adan grinned at the unexpected situation. God was surely granting him permission to avenge his torment and the deaths of the other fifteen men. His prayer could not have been answered more perfectly.

"*Optio* Naevius, bring your prisoner forward!" The *principales* obeyed. Adan dropped his hand to the scabbard of his sword. His expression hardened as he thought of everything he had suffered and might still suffer. He grasped the hilt of his sword.

"You were dead," Valentius growled. "They burned your corpse. What kind of sorcery is this? Or is this your trickery, Cornelius?" Naevius moved to strike the prisoner again, but Marcus held up a hand to stop him.

"*Optio* Naevius," Adan said, "Take no chances with this prisoner. Take nothing he offers. He prefers the cowardice of poison rather than the skill of a sword."

"Yes Sir! The prisoner will see justice when he is crucified in Rome." Naevius glanced at Adan's sword. "If he gets to Rome."

Adan urged Venustas closer. "I *was* dead, Felix. But you were the unintentional trickster. You used too much *belladonna*. The poisoned arrow stopped my heart. Then you struck me in the chest, breaking bone, but that forced my heart to beat again. And here I am. Now you're the prisoner." Adan's eyes sparkled with malice. "I see that you wear the *bracae* well. They fit you perfectly."

Valentius bared his teeth. "Look at your pathetic anger. You think *I* ill-used *you*. Could you really be so ignorant? You brought this on yourself!" Bewilderment tempered Adan's fury. Valentius realized his mistake. He needed Adan to be angry, not confused. A perfect way to avoid the cruel justice of Rome was only an arm's length away.

"I made you suffer, Longinus," gloated Valentius. "I set Octavean on you. Demitre infected your hand so he could torture you with the cauterizing rod. Oh, how I wish I could have watched. Then he used dirty linen to bandage the burns. The inevitable amputation would also lead to infection. It would have been a slow, agonizing death. Demitre was going to bring me your hand for a trophy. I controlled you. I manipulated you. I volunteered for every nasty, filthy assignment just so I could assign it to you.

Your humiliation and misery was my greatest treasure." *Optio* Naevius raised his fist, but again, Marcus held up a hand.

Adan pulled his sword from the scabbard. Valentius's eyes widened with hope. Marcus could see Adan's rage mounting beyond his control. He tried to urge Blackfire closer, but the horse fought the rein and sidestepped nervously.

"I did suffer, even though I did nothing wrong." Adan ground the words between his teeth. "You nearly cost me my life. You still could." Adan urged Venustas closer. The weight of the sword felt good in his hand. Valentius leaned toward him. Adan set the sword against the prisoner's neck. Elation surged in his heart to see his tormentor forced into submission. A red line appeared beneath the blade. One quick slice and Valentius would die within minutes.

Marcus again tried to move Blackfire closer. Murdering Valentius would require an investigation, complicating Adan's appeal to Herod. As before, Blackfire resisted, backing up and fighting the reins.

Valentius locked eyes with his soon-to-be executioner. Adan pressed the blade deeper, savoring the anticipated terror and pleas for mercy. Yet, Valentius did not cry out in fear. Instead, the ghost of a smile touched the corners of his lips.

Countless times Adan had fantasized a slow, humiliating death for Valentius, but reality was resisting his fantasy. The prisoner was not quaking in terror. There were no pleas for mercy. Valentius closed his eyes and waited.

Adan moved the sword away. He hesitated for only a moment before he slipped the weapon back into its scabbard. "You almost got what you wanted, Felix."

Valentius's eyes shot open. "What are you doing?"

"I know what you're afraid of, and it isn't death. You would be spared from your greatest fear if I killed you. I have to ask myself, why would I do that? That is exactly what you want."

Valentius sputtered curses, desperate to reignite Adas's anger.

"I realize now," said Adan, "that death is not what we should fear. To exist utterly alone, for eternity, should be our true fear. Perhaps Hades is a place of forgotten souls, alone in the dark, forever. No one is forced to go there. One goes there by choice. You have a choice. Yeshua, the man I crucified, died in your place. You don't have to go to the Terror."

"You think I care about your so-called Messiah?" Valentius laughed bitterly.

"You should. I am living proof that Yeshua is the Son of God. All my injuries and infections were healed by the power of God through Simon Peter, Yeshua's follower. I did a really good job of killing Yeshua, yet he lives. And now, Simon Peter, as God's servant, can heal any malady and raise people from the dead."

"What are you talking about?"

"Simon Peter, the man you assigned me to guard, is my friend, and the one who healed me. You planned to smuggle Peter out, and no doubt, murder him, but an angel of God really did release him from the Antonia. Then the last archer in the tournament, also my friend, brought Peter to me as I was dying from your poison. Again, God used Peter to heal me. What more evidence do you need? I cannot possibly be alive. Yet, here I am, proof of God's power."

"Your words mean nothing. You were a clay pot to crush whenever I pleased."

"Then why am I not a pile of shards? Why are *you* the clay pot now? Peter told me what I needed to do, but I wasn't ready." An intense feeling of release swept through Adan, like the sudden end of excruciating pain. "I have one last thing to do." His hand dropped to his sword.

Valentius's eyes flicked back and forth between the sword and Adan's face.

"I will stop you from tormenting me. I will end your interference on my thoughts. I will stop you from destroying my happiness. I do this for me, Centurion Valentius. I forgive you. I cannot be forgiven if I don't forgive you. And I really want to be forgiven. I'm not going to kill you. Revenge belongs to God—and only God."

Valentius spat on the ground. "That's what I think of your pathetic forgiveness and your worthless, invisible god! But you are right about one thing. I don't fear death because there is nothing after death. We simply cease to exist. You want to kill me, but you're afraid to do it yourself! You're a gutless coward! You seek the company of slaves. You waste your time with sick animals instead of commanding men. You married Cornelius's daughter to prop up your fraudulent title with his shield. You know what you are? I'll tell you! You're a *pathetic* excuse for a centurion, and a *disgusting* excuse for a man!"

"I'm impressed. I didn't know you could be so eloquent. Still, it's not going to work. God offers you 'pearls' of salvation, but you have trampled them underfoot. It is you who craves your death, not me, not anymore. I will neither deny Rome's justice nor corrupt my soul with your murder. You are snared in your own trap. I leave you to the laws of Rome."

"*You're a wretched little worm!*" screamed Valentius. Spittle shot from his mouth. His face reddened with fury. Intentionally avoiding eye contact, *Optio* Naevius struck Valentius with his fist. The prisoner snarled at the soldier like a feral cur.

Marcus addressed the soldiers. "Deliver this prisoner to Emperor Gaius, alive and unharmed! Mistreating him is not worth the punishment you would receive."

Adan addressed the *principales,* "*Optio* Naevius, I pray that God protects you and your men." Adan and Marcus urged their horses around the soldiers. They passed the wrecked wagon and rejoined Dulcibella and the others.

Twisting in the saddle to look back, Valentius stared uselessly after Adan. *Optio* Naevius cuffed him across the shoulder, reasserting his authority. "Move out!" shouted the *optio.*

"Adan, was that Valentius?" exclaimed Dulcibella.

"Yes, it was. I wanted to kill him. I almost did." Adan looked into her eyes and smiled.

"Your anger is gone. You forgave him, didn't you?"

"Yes. I thought my hate made me strong, but it was doing just the opposite. My hate made *him* strong. Peter was right. I was allowing Valentius to contaminate my thoughts."

"I know. It broke my heart."

"When the *optio* said Valentius was declared *persona non grata,* I thought God had given me approval to take his life. I was only fooling myself. God never approves of murder. When I put my sword to his neck, he smiled—just barely—but a smile nonetheless. I realized he *wanted* me to kill him and my anger vanished. I could tell others to forgive, but I believed my hatred was justified. I was a victim of my own pride." They watched the soldiers ride away. Valentius grew smaller and smaller until he faded from sight.

"They will shackle him," said Marcus, "to an oar of a ship for the month-long voyage. He will sleep where he sits. Then he will languish in the pit until Emperor Gaius remembers him."

They passed through the west gate into the city. The guards at the tax station came to attention at the sight of Marcus and Adan. One of the soldiers noticed Venustas, frowned and looked more closely at Adan. The soldier was one of the men from his *centuria*. The legionary paled when Adan nodded at him. They headed straight for Serapio's shop. Adan couldn't wait to see the grin on the big *gladiator's* face. At the open door of the shop, he jumped from the saddle and took a bundle out of his knapsack. Serapio had his back to the doorway as he worked at smoothing a plank of wood with a small block of sandstone.

"Hold on! I'll be right with you," he said without turning around.

"I certainly hope so since I've traveled a great distance."

Serapio spun around. "*Adan!*" He threw his arms out and grabbed Adan in his usual exuberant hug. "Fabiana! It's Adan! He's here!" Serapio looked out the door and shouted, "Come in! Come in! Fabiana! Where is that woman? Nebetka will be so upset he missed you. He's delivering a table."

Fabiana sailed down the stairs. She hugged Adan with all her strength. Serapio greeted the others with equal enthusiasm. He nodded respectfully at Marcus.

"Sir, you must be Centurion Cornelius," beamed Serapio. "It is a pleasure to finally meet you." The two men shook hands as Marcus returned the greeting. Serapio saw Dulcibella. "Who is this lovely young woman who has graced my humble shop?"

"May I present my wife, Dulcibella," said Adan proudly.

"Ahhh!" Serapio and Fabiana exclaimed in unison. "So you have married this wild wolf!" declared Serapio. "You must be as brave as you are beautiful. Have you tamed him? Has he learned to sleep indoors? Have you trained him to pick his clothes up from the floor?"

Laughing, Dulcibella shook her head. "Alas no, I am not a sorceress." Serapio bellowed with laughter as Fabiana snickered.

"Ah, and there are my friends, Nikolaus and Malchus," said Serapio, seeing the young men in the doorway. Serapio greeted them with a hug and back slaps. Andreas was introduced and welcomed. Chairs and stools were pulled forward.

Adan held the bundle out to Serapio. "I believe you had a birthday recently." Adan winked at Fabiana. She smiled as she watched her husband open the bundle.

Another roar of laughter erupted from the old *gladiator*. "Scissors! Well, now I can die a happy man. This beats anything I've ever invented." He passed the scissors around for their inspection. "Thank you, I will make good use of this clever tool." Then Serapio's expression sobered. "So, you're here to confront Herod?"

"We are. It was generous of you and Fabiana to offer your son's name to me. It was, and is an honor. But now it's time to face the truth. However, I would like to keep 'Adan' as my *praenomen,* with your approval."

Serapio and Fabiana exchanged smiles. "We approve!"

Malchus cleared his throat. "Serapio, have you had need of the prize money?"

"Absolutely not. It's all still here." He gestured at the wooden clothes chest. Malchus told him of his plan to return it. Serapio agreed he should. He turned to Adan, "In fact, we still have your pension, except for what you gave to Nikolaus. You must take it with you when you go home. And you will be going home!" They decided to confront Tribune Salvitto at the Antonia before rumors had time to reach him.

Chapter 47

The guards at the Antonia's gates saw that Adan and Marcus were centurions and came to attention. Several frowned as they stared at Adan. One of the guards placed himself in front of the group. "Sir, do my eyes deceive me? You look like Centurion Longinus, but he is dead. I saw his *exsecutio* myself."

"Your eyes do not deceive you. I am here to see Tribune Salvitto. Is he available?"

The soldier hesitantly answered, "Y-Yes, he is in the common room. Please wait in his office. I'll get him, Centurion."

"*Gratias*," said Adan as they dismounted. The deep baying of a dog sounded from across the quad. A leashed mastiff howled with excitement and ran to Adan.

"*Tigula!*" The huge dog skidded to a stop. He threw his massive paws over Adan's shoulders. "Good boy! Where's your master?" He scanned the quad as he ruffled Tigula's ears.

Tigula had pulled away from Cassius's hold. In shock, the decurion watched as a young man allowed the dog to greet him in a way Tigula reserved only for his master and a friend he once knew. Cassius stared as the man, who looked very much like that friend, went into Salvitto's office with several other people.

Salvitto was checking the duty wall in the common room. The door burst open, and an agitated soldier strode across the room. "Sir! There is someone to see you!"

Salvitto frowned at the soldier. "Is there a problem?"

"I hope not, Tribune!"

"Well, who is it?"

The soldier swallowed hard. "Sir! I'm not sure. He is in your office."

Salvitto grunted with annoyance. As he headed for his office, soldiers were gathering on the quad. The men were talking excitedly while others shook their heads. Some motioned impatiently as other soldiers approached. Salvitto frowned at the odd behavior. He wondered if it had to do with his mysterious visitor. He walked into his office to find Centurion Cornelius and Nikolaus facing the door. There were several other people, including a young woman dressed in riding clothes. Two men who looked familiar were standing behind her, and another young man was talking to her with his back to the door.

"Marcus!" Salvitto offered his hand. "It is good to see you again, my friend. This is most unexpected. What can I do for you?"

"It is good to see you as well, Theophilus," Marcus shook his hand. "I have come on an unusual mission." He stepped aside.

Salvitto watched as the young man turned around. The tribune's jaw dropped in shock. His face paled as his knees wobbled. Marcus took hold of his arm.

"*How?* I must be. . .I-I saw you die!" Then the full impact of who he was looking at hit him. His eyes watered with emotion. A rush of relief brought color back in his face. Salvitto gripped Adan by the arms. "You're alive! How is this possible? I saw the arrow in your heart. There could not have been a trick."

"Sir, I am sorry I startled you. It is very good to see you. Perhaps you should sit down while I explain. First I would like to introduce my wife." Adan took Dulcibella's hand. "This is Cornelia Minor Cornelius Longinus. She uses Dulcibella."

Distress again crossed Salvitto's features. "My dear lady, the letter I sent surely caused you great pain. Please accept my apology."

"Sir, I also sent a letter to Dulcibella," offered Adan. "Neither of us could have predicted what would happen."

Salvitto nodded in appreciation. "It is an honor to meet you." He looked at Marcus. "I offer my congratulations to your family, and you, Adas."

"Thank you, Sir. If I may, I no longer use the *praenomen* Adas, but rather, Adan."

"Adan—as in Serapio and Fabiana's Adan?"

"Yes, Sir, they gave me his name for my protection."

"The name suits you well."

Marcus gestured toward Andreas. "You remember, Andreas? He delivered my request to let me use Adan to cure our sick horses." They shook hands.

"And Malchus, you remember him?"

"Weren't you the last archer?" asked Salvitto incredulously.

"I was."

Salvitto started to say something, but shook his head instead. He greeted Nikolaus and invited them to sit. "Adan, as thrilled as I am to see you alive, why did you come back? Why jeopardize your life?"

"I am here to present myself to King Herod. I will ask him to officially declare my execution fulfilled. Can you arrange an audience?"

"Yes, I have a meeting scheduled tomorrow morning, but you are taking a huge risk. We never recaptured Simon Peter. Herod will not be pleased to see you alive."

"I know, but I don't believe God will let him take my life again. I protected Peter and God used Peter to save me from my wounds and the poison."

"What poison? This is the first I've heard about poison." Salvitto glanced at Marcus.

Adan explained about the *belladonna*. He added, "Malchus told me how you stopped Valentius from stabbing me. I am grateful."

"Tribune, if I may," said Malchus, "I am here to return the prize money. I wish to leave it on deposit in the accounting office."

"That is most honorable of you. It may not help Adan's case, but it won't hurt. I will send a message to Herod immediately. Our meeting is scheduled for the fourth hour tomorrow. You are welcome to use the guest facilities for the night."

"Thank you, Sir, but we will be staying with Serapio," said Adan. "We'll be here before the fourth hour. Thank you for letting us accompany you."

Salvitto slowly shook his head in disbelief. "I see you, but I still can't believe it. Only the hand of God could have delivered you from that arrow."

"Theophilus, do you believe in God?" Marcus asked.

"Yes, I do. I also wish to know more about Yeshua. Do you know of anyone who will talk to me about him, Marcus?"

"You're looking at him. Tonight I will tell you how Simon Peter and I met." Marcus clapped a hand on Andreas' shoulder. "You will also want to talk with this young man."

"Then will you stay the night at the Antonia as my guest, you and Andreas?" asked the tribune. "I will have the guest quarters freshened for you."

"We accept with pleasure. But first, come and join us at Serapio's for the afternoon." The tribune accepted eagerly.

Malchus opened the door. Adan walked out and stopped. The quad was crowded with soldiers, silently watching him with expressions of awe, curiosity, bewilderment, suspicion, fear, and even anger. *Optio* Victorius, Adan's former second-in-command, stepped forward.

"Centurion Longinus, it really is you! How is this possible? I saw you die." Victorius waved his hand across the crowd of men. "We all did. If you didn't look so real, I would think you were a ghost."

Adan clapped a hand on Victorius's shoulder. "I assure you, Faustus, you did see me die, but I am not a ghost. God saved me from death, not just once, but twice. Valentius poisoned his dagger and the arrows with *belladonna*." Victorius grimaced and shook his head.

An argument broke out among the centurions who had confronted Adan the day after he went missing from guarding Yeshua's tomb. The debate was led by Centurion Plinius of the 3rd *Cohors*.

Adan approached the men. Centurion Plinius turned to face him. "You must have deceived us in the theater! I have seen stage plays where an actor appears to bleed and die. If you were truly wounded unto death, show us the scars. A trick would leave no scars!"

"I assure you, Centurion Plinius, there was no deception. If I had faked my death, would I be here now? I *was* dead, but God brought me back when Valentius struck me in the chest."

Plinius sneered. "So you say. Show us proof."

Another man stepped in front of Plinius. It was Thracius. "Do you remember me, Centurion? I executed Octavean. Because he broke one of his ropes, he was close. I could plainly see his face. He saw someone before he died. I never saw a man so transformed, so utterly astonished! I wish I didn't care. I have watched many men die, and have forgotten their faces. But his last moments haunt me to this day. Who was he looking at?"

Plinius pushed Thracius aside. "Who cares about the dead Gaul?"

"I do!" declared Adan. "Thracius, I am sorry. I did not see what Octavean saw."

Thracius hung his head. "Then I will never know."

"Did you hear the last thing Octavean said?" asked Adan.

"Yes, he said *'Adas, He's here!'* His eyes were intently focused as if this 'He' was standing before him. Then Octavean reached out and seemed to grasp a hand."

"Then I do know who he was looking at," assured Adan. "Come to Serapio's shop with us. We can talk then. Will you come?"

"Yes! I'll go with you." Visibly relieved, he stepped aside.

Adan faced Plinius. He removed his belt and tunic. Victorius held the outer garment for him. Adan slowly turned to show the men his scars. At first the soldiers didn't move. Then Adan invited them to touch the scars. They pressed their fingers over his heart and across his back. Each one backed away to allow him to move on. The soldiers looked into his eyes and whispered among themselves. As Victorius walked behind, other soldiers who once served under Adan's command fell in line. Two men stepped in front of him with bowed heads. Adan smiled in recognition of Zaphnath, one of his escort guards.

Zaphnath addressed him in Egyptian, "Sir, I can see you remember me. This is my brother, Paaneah, the one whose life you saved."

Keeping his head bowed, Paaneah responded, "Centurion, I never properly thanked you. We are most pleased to see you alive and well." Adan spoke with them before moving on.

Doubtful expressions changed to amazement. Cassius came forward with Tigula. The mastiff barked excitedly while the two friends greeted each other.

"I saw you with Tigula, but I refused to believe my eyes. Tigula recognized you from across the quad." Victorius handed Adan his tunic and belt.

"Cassius, you must meet Dulcibella, my wife, and her father, Centurion Cornelius." Adan motioned for Victorius to join them.

"You have a wife?" exclaimed Cassius. "You've been busy while you were dead, my friend! I must meet the woman brave enough to marry a ghost."

They walked toward Salvitto's office as the soldiers parted to give them room. The men nearby listened as Adan introduced Dulcibella and Marcus to Cassius. They turned to those behind them, informing them of the identity of the young woman and the *primus pilus* centurion. The information spread quickly. Some of the soldiers began to disperse, but many pressed forward to speak to Adan and to meet Dulcibella. Another man approached Marcus. It was Centurion Tacitus, the highest ranking centurion in Jerusalem.

Tacitus greeted Marcus eagerly. "It is most gratifying to see you again, my friend. How long has it been since we fought together in Samaria?"

"Many years, my friend. It is good to see you."

"It's obvious why you're here," said Tacitus. "He's taking quite a risk."

"Yes, but the alternative of constant fear is worse. Let me present my daughter, Cornelia Minor. She and Adan have married." Tacitus greeted Dulcibella. He expressed hope for a favorable ruling from Herod. A number of soldiers standing nearby listened closely.

Victorius asked, "Sir, are you returning to the Antonia?"

"I don't even know if I'll still be alive after tomorrow. I'm here to ask King Herod to declare my sentence fulfilled. We go tomorrow with Tribune Salvitto at the fourth hour."

"I understand. It is most agreeable to see you again, Sir." They shook hands and Victorius hurried toward the legionaries' barracks.

Adan, Dulcibella, and the others went back to Serapio's house. When they arrived, they were greeted by many friends. Salvitto and Thracius were introduced and were soon deep in conversation. Mary of Nazareth was there with Salome and Mary of Magdala. Adan introduced Dulcibella, who was welcomed by all. He hoped to see Jamin and Cleopas, but they were away in Emmaus.

While Adan and Dulcibella spent the afternoon at Serapio's shop, soldiers discussed Adan, not only at the fortress, but also in the streets. A patrol returning to the Antonia paused in front of a courtyard wall when another patrol stopped to join them. A woman weaving a basket sat under a shade tree in the courtyard.

Hestalis called to one of the men in the other patrol. "*Ohe*, Caelo, have you heard the news about the *Lupus Legatus*?"

"No. Has the Wolf returned to haunt us?" Caelo's men laughed, but grew quiet when the other men remained stone-faced.

"Perhaps. The Wolf is alive and he's here! We all saw him. Some even spoke with him."

Caelo stared in disbelief. "It can't be Longinus! The arrow pierced his heart!"

"It is Longinus, believe me! I saw his wolf eyes and the scars from his injuries. I even touched the scars. The mastiff belonging to Quintus greeted him eagerly. That dog has always hated everyone except his master and Longinus. You can fool a man with trickery, but you can't fool a dog."

"If Longinus lives, then the rumors are true! He is a *versipellis*. That is why he has yellow eyes and the mastiff favors him. Or maybe he is a *vespertilio* and cannot die. When we sleep he will come for us to drink our blood."

"Don't be foolish, Caelo! Werewolves and vampires live in the mountains beyond Gaul, not here. We saw him die like any human. Did he transform then?"

"Maybe, after we ran from the storm! How else can he be alive?" Caelo and the others exchanged anxious frowns.

Several of the soldiers were new to the Antonia, unaware of the event's detail, but the others explained the situation. The woman in the courtyard heard every word. She threw the unfinished basket aside and crept to the wall to listen more closely.

"It was a trick," offered one of the men.

"How could there be a trick?" retorted Hestalis. "The arrow sunk deep into the Wolf's heart. He struggled to his feet, but in the end, he died. Herod's *medicus* and Tribune Salvitto confirmed it. We saw Valentius strike a violent blow to his chest, and there was no reaction. Longinus swears the Hebrew God brought him back to life. Some of the men fear revenge from this powerful God if Longinus is executed again."

Caelo frowned. "So what can we do about it?"

"I don't know, but I don't want to suffer in Hades for eternity. Do you remember what Herod told the temple guard? He ordered him to 'Do the will of *Elohim*.' Longinus died with only one arrow. It was windy. The archer was unprepared. Yet, the arrow hit with perfection. The other men were shot with many arrows before they died. Of course, none of them would have died if Longinus had let Octavean kill the prisoner. If Octavean had succeeded, Valentius would have been the only one executed."

The woman in the courtyard hurried into the house and slammed the door shut. Startled, a few of the soldiers looked toward the house, but returned their attention to Caelo and Hestalis.

Caelo nodded. "True, but Longinus took full responsibility. He offered to die alone if Herod would spare the others. However, Longinus may still die if Herod orders him to be executed again."

The woman came out of the house and slipped a dagger under the laces of her sandal. She moved to the wall to resume listening.

"Yes," agreed Hestalis, "that could bring the retribution of *Elohim* upon the entire 10th *Legio*. Both Longinus and the prisoner, Simon Peter, worship *Elohim*. I have heard Peter has been spotted, so both men are alive. Even if the Hebrew God does not protect Longinus again, he has powerful allies. *Primus Pilus* Centurion Cornelius is his father-in-law.

"He has taken a wife?" exclaimed Caelo.

"Her name is Dulcibella and she, indeed, has the face and form of sweet beauty. Her eyes and smile will melt your heart. I saw how they looked at each other. They are deeply in love."

"Then our Wolf has much to live for, yet here he is. Let us hope his ashes are not added to the fifteen dead men."

A soldier commented, "Some say the 10th *Legio* is cursed by the three Furies, because we did nothing when the men were put to death. We could not fight Roman law or Herod, but we should have punished Valentius. We wasted our chance when we ran from the *sharav*. If Longinus is spared a second time, maybe the curse will be lifted."

The soldiers believed the red-eyed, snake-haired Furies inflicted terrifying acts of revenge on the guilty, in life and even after death.

"Maybe it is not too late." declared another soldier. "We can turn our disgrace into honor. We have a chance now. I heard that he meets with Herod tomorrow morning."

Caelo shrugged. "What would you have us do? Offer up ourselves to take the sword in his place? I'll take my chances with the Furies."

"The curse of the Furies is real and eternal," said Hestalis. "You speak as a fool. We saw Octavean curse Valentius with the broken arrow. And now, Valentius will be dead within the year just as he was cursed."

"Perhaps there is a curse, perhaps not," said Caelo. "Perhaps Longinus lives, or not. We need to see this miracle for ourselves." He signaled for his men to follow.

"Longinus was at the Antonia when we left," said Hestalis. "But if he's gone, they say he is staying with the one-eyed *gladiator* at his furniture shop on the corner of Sheep Gate Street and Commerce Road."

"Be safe, Hestalis. *Gratias,* for the news." The patrols departed.

The woman hurried through the streets until she stood at the corner of a courtyard across from Serapio's *Suppelex*. Visitors came and went as she watched. Farewells were exchanged out in the street when the visitors left. The shop owner and his guests went back into the house.

A young man in the doorway called to a young woman, "Dulcie, are you coming in?"

"I'll be right there, Adan." She knelt to tie a lose lace on her sandal.

As Adan turned to go inside, he noticed a street beggar staring at him. The man quickly looked away. Even though beggars usually sat in the same place every day, this one was new.

The woman stepped out from around the corner. "Dulcibella, I must speak with you."

"Who are you? How do you know my name?"

The woman crept closer. "I have an urgent warning you must tell your husband."

"You should tell him yourself. I'll get him."

"No! You won't!" She raised a dagger above her head and rushed at Dulcibella. Seeing the weapon, Dulcibella braced herself as her father had taught her. She grasped the attacker's raised hand as she struck the woman with her fist. Thrown off balance, the assailant staggered back. Not expecting resistance, she shrieked, and raised the dagger again. Dulcibella dodged to the left, grabbed the attacker's raised arm with both hands, and forced her arm down. The woman nearly stabbed herself in the thigh. With her other hand, she pushed Dulcibella back, and yanked her arm free. Suddenly, powerful arms grasped Dulcibella around the waist. The attacker recovered her footing, raised the dagger, and rushed in again. Adan tried to pitch Dulcibella toward Marcus, who had followed him outside. The attacker slashed again. Adan lost his hold on Dulcibella, nearly dropping her. She stumbled, but Marcus grabbed her outstretched arms. Before Adan could face the assailant, she raised the dagger. Holding it high above her head, she aimed for the center of his back.

In a split second, there was a zipping sound, and a blur of motion as an arrow hit the blade, twisting it from the woman's hand. The weapon clattered to the street. The arrow impaled a palm tree a few paces away. Standing near the corner of the house, Nikolaus had already nocked another arrow on his bowstring. Adan dove for the dagger as the attacker tried to reach it first. Seeing she had lost her advantage, she ran. Salvitto and Thracius raced from the doorway. Thracius grabbed hold of her arm, while the tribune blocked her way. She tried to wriggle free, but Serapio burst from the house and helped restrain her.

"Who are you?" Adan growled.

"Her name is Sevina," said Salvitto. "She is the mother of Lucius Octavean. She came to my office the day before he was executed."

"What! Why did you try to kill my wife?"

"For Lucius! They said he and the others were executed because you defended the prisoner. His death is *your* fault. You killed my son. I kill your wife. An eye for an eye!"

"Lucius would not want this. I am sorry he died, but he did with great honor."

"Honor! Will my dead son's honor put a roof over my head and food on my table? Don't talk to me about honor or tell me what my son wanted. You couldn't possibly know."

"But, I do know. He told me once while we were guarding a tomb. He said he wanted to live in Gaul, the land of his ancestors, and see snow on the mountains. He wanted to run his horse across a frozen lake. He wanted to build a house for his wife and you. His last wish was for you to live in security. That's why he left you his pension."

"His pension! You know his pension was forfeited."

"King Herod reinstated the pensions," Salvitto exclaimed. "I personally saw to the claim letters. I sent yours months ago."

"What letter? I received no . . . Where did you send it?"

"I used the address on file, the one in Rome," answered Salvitto.

"No, not there! I went to the Antonia to change my address, but the *dispensator* told me Lucius was to be executed. I left without telling him my sister's address. My eldest daughter must have the document."

Curious bystanders began to gather. Fabiana ushered Dulcibella inside. Salvitto sent Thracius to find a patrol. The crowd began to disperse, but Adan spotted the same street beggar watching him. The man showed no inclination to leave. Thracius returned with a mounted squad.

"Take this woman to an interrogation room in Holding," Salvitto commanded. "Remember, what is done to her will be done to the four of you." He turned to Sevina. "You could have claimed your son's pension with me if you had not attacked the centurion and his wife. I would have canceled the claim sent to Rome. Your daughter cannot redeem the claim until she has proof of your death, since it is in your name."

"Then she will be claiming it soon enough," said Sevina in a softened voice. Tension eased from her face and she bowed her head.

"Take her," ordered Salvitto. The soldiers obeyed.

Marcus looked at Adan's back. "You better have Nikolaus see to that."

"See to what?" Adan turned toward Nikolaus as he joined them. "You left the stables just in time, my friend. Otherwise, I might not be standing here. You're quite the expert bowman."

"I don't know about that." Nikolaus rolled his eyes. "I was aiming for her hand."

Adan found Dulcibella upstairs. "Are you alright? I can't believe how that woman nearly killed you." Adan embraced her, and she wrapped her arms over his shoulders. He flinched at her touch.

She looked at the back of his shoulder. "You're injured!"

"It can't be too bad. It probably won't even need stitches. You're not injured, are you?" She shook her head. "You defended yourself well. That woman should be grateful that I snatched you away before you did her serious damage." Adan gave her a lopsided grin.

"Yes, I was about to finish her off."

"Next time, I'll stay out of the way so you can do your worst."

Dulcibella smiled, but thought of the seriousness of the attack. "What would have happened without Nikolaus? You could have been killed."

"Or you, without your skills and your father's training. It never occurred to me, you could be in danger. I shouldn't have brought you here."

"My place is by your side. I will not hide in fear every time we have a crisis."

"How fortunate I am to have such a brave wife."

"You certainly are." Dulcibella kissed him for good measure.

Chapter 48

⸻❧❧⸻

The dagger injury required a few stitches, after all. Nikolaus made short work of it, but it left Adan's shoulder sore. After a night of chaotic dreams, he woke up before the sun could chase away the stars. He rolled to his side and gazed at his wife.

Dulcibella whispered, "You're awake." She turned to face him.

"How do you do that? You know I'm looking at you before you open your eyes."

Her only answer was a gentle smile. "Did you get any sleep?"

"Not much. I can't shake the feeling that woman's attack was a bad omen. I hate how these doubts keep coming back. I was tempted to snatch you up last night and run."

"I know. I'm grateful for our time together, but it is not enough. I hope God agrees." She looked into his eyes and tried to smile, but her eyes filled with tears. "Adan, I've never seen anyone look at me with such hate like that woman did. If a complete stranger wanted to murder us, how will Herod feel?" She wiped at her eyes in frustration. "I'm so scared."

"Valentius looked at me the same way. His eyes always burned with animosity when he saw me. I'm not sure which was worse, to suffer his dagger, or his loathing."

"And still, it's not over. I despise this fear in my heart."

"So do I, but our fear ends today, one way or another."

"I want to get it over with, until I remember what the outcome may be."

They held each other as they watched the darkness of the night surrender to the brightening sky. When they thought the others would be awake, they climbed down the ladder and went into the house. Fabiana had prepared breakfast, but they ate very little. They dressed in formal attire. Dulcibella wore her *stola* and *palla*. Adan wore his military *tunic*, *lorica musculata*, and *caligae*, but no weapons or helmet.

Adan, Malchus and Nikolaus rode their horses, while Dulcibella sat next to Serapio on the delivery cart. When they entered the gateway of the Antonia, they could see

Salvitto, Marcus and Andreas waiting for them at the arena. Marcus and Salvitto also wore their *lorica musculata* and *caligae*. Their greeting was somber.

"The Antonia looks abandoned," Adan commented to Salvitto.

"It has been a bad morning. There was a disturbance at the Water Gate, and a mysterious illness is affecting the men. Let's hope the day improves."

They rode to the pale-gold, limestone walls of Herod's citadel, which included an area of four hundred paces by one hundred sixty paces. The main entrance was guarded by three watch towers. The palace consisted of two buildings that faced each other. A huge quadrangle, called the *Area*, separated and surrounded the wings. The three floors of the palace wings were successively smaller, forming tiered pyramids.

When King Herod addressed large assemblies, the Gentiles gathered in the *Area* and the Hebrews gathered in the *Gabbatha*. The praetorium, which overlooked the *Area*, housed the Seat of Judgment in the south wing of the second floor. Porticos that extended into the quadrangle served as the main entrances of the ground floors of both wings. On top of each portico stood a second-story balcony supported by limestone columns and a terracotta tile roof.

The palace wings were richly landscaped with almond, pomegranate, apricot, fig, and olive trees. Bronze and marble fountains stood among the trees, surrounded by native flowers. There were blue hollyhocks, white desert lilies, aloes, pink crown anemone, and yellow, pink, and white snapdragons. Bees from the palace hives hovered among the tree and flower blossoms. Birds fluttered among the trees, signaling their territory with song. Flowers edged the canals that carried water to the palace bathhouses and underfloor plumbing for heating the rooms. Slaves kept the boilers supplied with wood and monitored the water flow from the city's aqueducts. No expense or effort was spared for the comforts at Herod's Palace.

Adan's group left their horses and the cart outside the towers. Serapio, Andreas and Nikolaus stayed with the horses. Adan and the others were led across the *Area*, where Herod's guests lingered in the gardens between the bathhouses in the north wing and the guest quarters in the south wing. Their escort led them to the second floor of the south wing. Blastus, Herod's assistant, stood at the top of the steps to escort them to the anteroom outside the court. The group filed into the room, but said little to each other.

The double doors to the court swung open. Blastus gestured for Tribune Salvitto to follow him. While they waited for the business meeting to end, Marcus asked, "Adan, do you know what you're going to say?"

"No. I don't believe Herod intends to let me go, but God will have the last word."

Finally the door opened. Blastus formally announced, "You have been called to the carpet. Enter and step to the carpet. Keep your heads bowed. Wait for His Excellency to speak and speak only when he questions you." Blastus signaled for them to stop when they stepped on to the elaborately woven rug. He continued forward until he stood next to the judgment seat where Herod sat eyeing them intently. Four slaves stood behind him as they slowly waved ostrich feather fans. Two armed guards stood on either side of the judgment seat. Four more guards stood at the back with other attendants. Blastus introduced them, even though Herod already knew their names.

"Centurion Clovius Longinus, this is an interesting situation," exclaimed King Herod. "I would suspect a trick if I had not actually watched you die. Yet here you stand. Why are you here?"

"I present myself to you for judgment. I was justly sentenced to death. Even though I was in truth executed, I am uncertain of my status before the law. I appeal to you to proclaim my sentence fulfilled."

"Are you asking me to spare your life now?"

"I am. My life was already taken from me once."

"I offered you several pardons, yet you refused them. Why should I pardon you again?"

"Your Excellency, I am not asking to be pardoned from my conviction of which I am guilty. I ask you to officially proclaim my punishment legally fulfilled."

"What will my enemies say when they hear that a man I executed is still alive?"

"Your Excellency, I cannot answer for any one foolish enough to be your enemy."

A slow smile curved Herod's lips. "I see." He turned his attention to Tribune Salvitto. "Why do you stand here?"

"Your Excellency, I stand with Centurion Longinus because I inadvertently caused him to arrive at Holding later than he intended. If I had not interfered, he would have intercepted the drugged wine. I feel responsible."

"You said nothing about this at his execution. Why are you telling me now?"

"I am at fault." Salvitto bowed his head. "I have no excuse."

"You are correct to condemn yourself. So you stand here out of guilt?"

"That is one reason, Your Excellency. I am also here because I believe God wants Centurion Longinus to live. You commanded the last archer to do God's will. I believe he did. God allowed the archer to kill Longinus, but then God restored his life."

"So you believe he died at the hands of this man?" The king gestured at Malchus.

"I do. Longinus was not breathing. There was no heartbeat. Your own *medicus* tested for life and found none. Longinus was dead."

"Why is he alive now?"

"Only God can restore life to the dead, Your Excellency."

Herod shifted his eyes to Adan. "Tell me what happened."

"Your Excellency, while I was dead, I was not in this world. I was with a woman who died when I was a child. She told me to stay with her until it was safe. Then I was hit in the chest, and I was back in the theater. I was conscious, but I couldn't move or open my eyes."

"Interesting. I would accuse you of lying if I hadn't seen the arrow strike your heart. Were you in heaven?'

"I don't know, Your Excellency, but nothing in this world compares to—where I was. There was no ground or sky."

Herod addressed Salvitto. "How long have you known about Longinus?"

"Since yesterday. I informed Your Excellency immediately."

"So you have known nothing of his activity since the execution. How conveniently ignorant of you, Tribune."

Herod turned his eyes on Marcus. "Centurion Cornelius, why are you here?"

"Your Excellency, I stand with Longinus, a man I have known for nine years. He served under my command for seven years. I know him to be an honorable soldier. He confided that he wished to present himself to you. I believe your decision will be just."

"Why? Have you studied my rulings?"

"I see the results of your rulings every day, Your Excellency, and I believe you will honor God and uphold the laws of Rome."

Herod turned to Dulcibella. "Cornelia Minor, why are you here?"

"Your Excellency, I stand with my husband. If you should rule against him, I wish to be with him as long as possible."

Herod's eyes lit with amusement. "If I condemn your husband, he will be executed immediately. How can a few moments mean so much?"

"A moment with him is better than a lifetime without him."

"Well, my dear, hopefully you will enjoy that moment." He looked at Malchus. "You were the archer. Why are you here?"

"Your Excellency, I have returned the prize money to the *primus dispensator*. I have the receipt." Malchus took the rolled papyrus from his belt.

"Why do you return it? It was presented to you fairly." Herod snapped his fingers at Blastus, who retrieved the document.

"Your Excellency, I obeyed your order with the hope God would save him, which he did. Because God returned life to him, I returned the prize to you."

"You believe God brought Longinus back to life?"

"I do, Your Excellency."

"Why would God do that?"

"I do not know the mind of God, Your Excellency, but perhaps God still has need of him in this world."

"If I execute him again, you think I will be opposing God?"

"To put a man to death a second time for the same offense is unjust. God opposes injustice therefore—my answer is yes."

"How dare you tutor me on the will of God! I should have you executed in his place!"

"I take his place willingly, Your Excellency." Adan anxiously shook his head at Malchus.

The king snorted with contempt, "Spare me your theatrics." He swished a hand of dismissal at Malchus. "However, the return of the prize money pleases me. My wife can use it to redecorate her private bathhouse." He turned his attention on Marcus. "Cornelius, if you failed to execute a condemned man with the first strike, would you strike again?"

"Yes, I would strike again, quickly, because he would be mortally wounded and suffering. But if he died and life returned to him, I would not strike again. My responsibility would have already been fulfilled. I would not interfere with a miracle."

"You say that if I execute Longinus again, I will be overstepping my responsibility to the law?" Herod smiled, thinking he had trapped Marcus.

"No, Your Excellency," replied Marcus calmly. "I am saying *my* responsibility would be fulfilled. I do not have the authority to define the perimeters of *your* responsibility."

"Then tell me, Cornelius, if you executed a man who had murdered your daughter, but he came back to life, would you let *him* live? What if he had laughed in your face while he cut her throat?" Herod smirked as the centurion paled at the horrific image.

Marcus struggled to regain his composure. "If God gave life back to the murderer it would be for a reason only God knows. Therefore, I would stay my hand. It is not for me to question the actions of God. But when my daughter dies, she will be with God, safe from the evil of this world."

Herod's face clouded. "This has been the most fascinating debate. I wonder if I should execute Longinus just to see what God will do." The attendants laughed until he raised a hand for silence.

The king turned to Adan. "Longinus, how willing are you to see whether God will save you from death a second time?"

"If it pleases King Herod to put God's resolve to the test, then I submit to your decision."

"You accuse me of putting God to the test? Then I will put your life to the test. Whether you died in my grandfather's theater and came back to life is irrelevant. I sentenced you to death, but you're not dead! I have a duty to the emperor to uphold the law. If God brought you back to life to fulfill a purpose, then it has already been accomplished. Perhaps God led you here so I can return you to him. I will be doing God's will. Enough of this!" Herod gestured at the four guards. "This has been a delightful waste of time. I have reached my decision; in fact, I did yesterday. You made things easy for me, Tribune, since you brought him to me."

Salvitto and Cornelius exchanged a look of defiance. Fearing a fight would ensue, Blastus moved toward the open doorway. When something caught his eye, he hurried down the walkway to the gazebo overlooking the *Area*.

"Take him!" declared Herod. The guards shackled Adan's wrists. "Clovius Longinus, I sentence you to death."

"*Noooo!*" cried Dulcibella as she sprang toward Adan. Grief stricken, Marcus held her back knowing the guards would retaliate. Desperately disappointed, Adan bowed his head in acceptance. Dulcibella struggled to reach Adan as tears streamed down her face.

"*Your Excellency!*" cried Blastus, appearing at the open doorway. "You must come immediately!" He pointed a trembling finger toward the *Area*. "Look—*out there!*"

A thunderous roar reached their ears. "*Hail King Herod!*"

All eyes turned to the doorway. "Guards, hold your position!" Herod commanded. "Kill anyone who tries to leave!"

Herod's face was twisted with irritation as he followed Blastus. When he reached the gazebo, he stopped in his tracks. The soldiers of the 10th *Legio* stood throughout the entire *Area*. Every soldier was helmeted and held a shield. Scattered among the rows of men, the red-crested helmets of centurions were visible. Five thousand soldiers stood vigilant. Many of Herod's guests huddled at the windows of the north and south wings watching nervously. They had evacuated the *Area* as more and more grim-faced soldiers appeared.

Primus Pilus Centurion Tacitus gave a command. The men came to attention. They raised their shields and brought them down in unison, sounding a tremendous crash as metal-edged wood hit stone. Sparks danced across the rock pavement. Herod paled before five thousand resolute warriors he had not summoned.

The king called out to Tacitus, who stood directly below the gazebo. "Centurion, why do you assemble here without my command? Do you forget this offense is punishable by death?"

"We forget nothing, Your Excellency. We came to escort Centurion Longinus back to the Antonia to take his rightful place as the commander of the 10th *Cohors*, 6th *Centuria*. A traitor conspired with a murderer to have Longinus and his men executed for monetary gain. Emperor Gaius will convict the traitor and will praise King Herod for denying Valentius his last victim."

Tacitus raised his fist. The entire legion responded. "*Hail King Herod!*"

"Your Excellency," declared Blastus. "Look! The emperor's councilmen watch from the windows. They dare not enter the *Area*."

Herod considered his options as he contemplated the enormity of the situation. The 10th *Legio* expected to take Longinus with them, alive. At the very least, they would not allow the execution to be carried out. The emperor's councilmen would be witnesses, if not victims, to a possibly violent insurrection by the legion. Herod considered how he could take advantage of the situation.

"Your Excellency," cried Blastus. "The soldiers will riot when they hear the order for execution!"

"What execution?" Herod turned and re-entered the court. He sat down as he fixed his eyes on Adan. "If you leave here today what will you do?"

"Your Excellency, if Tribune Salvitto still approves my transfer, I will return to Caesarea to serve under the command of Centurion Cornelius."

Herod studied Adan as he tapped his chin with a finger, as he often did when deliberating. "One of my spies, posing as a beggar, told me a woman with a dagger attacked your wife yesterday. Before the attacker was disarmed, you were wounded, yet here you stand. Even the cat with its nine lives eventually dies. Death will catch up with you one day, but perhaps God does want you to live for now. Join me, Centurion, as I announce that your sentence was legally fulfilled. Guards, release him."

Adan and Dulcibella exchanged a look of elation. Herod walked to the balcony as Adan followed. When Adan stepped out on the balcony with King Herod, Centurion Tacitus shouted a command. The soldiers of the 10th *Legio* again came to attention. Adan was overwhelmed at the magnitude of their presence. He nodded with gratitude at Centurion Tacitus. *Optio* Faustus Victorius stood next to Tacitus. All the *decurions* led by Cassius Quintus were present as well. Adan's heart filled with thankfulness for their courage. His eyes fell on a man standing behind Tacitus. It was Centurion Plinius. Adan and Plinius exchanged nods of mutual respect. Another command sounded. The men in the middle parted, allowing a number of soldiers to walk through in single file until the first soldier stood between Centurion Tacitus and *Optio* Victorius. It was Thracius, leading fifteen *sagittarii* who had once been loyal to Valentius. He raised his hand, and the *sagittarii* knelt with bowed heads.

Adan came to attention. He brought his fist to his chest and shouted, "*Sagittarii,* arise and be counted as worthy soldiers of the 10th *Legio!*" The *sagittarii* came to their feet. Grateful for the pardon, they saluted Adan with raised fists.

Herod clapped his hands for attention. "Soldiers of the 10th *Legio*, you were summoned to hear my decision in regards to Centurion Longinus." The men silently welcomed the lie, knowing it was a pardon for their unlawful assembly. "Roman law demands the lives of soldiers who fail in their duty. Four squads were executed, including Centurion Longinus, but God brought him back to life! No man should pay twice for the commission of one violation. Let it be said, King Herod honors God *and* Rome. I give you Centurion Clovius Longinus!"

The men shouted. "*Hail King Herod!*" Herod spread his arms wide, reveling in their approval. He gestured for them to continue. He looked across at the men and women watching from the windows. They were nodding with relief to his satisfaction.

Herod faced Adan with undisguised anger. "I allowed you to keep your life today, but do not ever test me again."

Adan bowed his head, "Yes, Your Excellency. Thank you, Your Excellency."

Herod spun around, strode back into his court, and swept out of the room with his attendants. He said nothing to Cornelius or Salvitto as he brushed past them.

Marcus hugged Dulcibella. "Bella, go! Join your husband!"

Dulcibella ran down the walkway and threw herself into Adan's open arms. The soldiers cheered. Adan and Dulcibella, locked in each other's arms, kissed with joyful relief. The men erupted with renewed cheers. Adan and Dulcibella waved to them in gratitude.

Tribune Salvitto and Centurion Cornelius walked out to the balcony. They were greeted with chants of approval. Cornelius put his right fist to his heart and nodded at Centurion Tacitus, who returned the salute with a triumphant smile.

Tribune Salvitto raised his hands for their attention and announced, "*Romani, militis* of the 10th *Legio*, I thank you for your courage and loyalty. Return to the Antonia and always remember this day of honor." There was one last round of ovations before the men dispersed.

Dulcibella and Adan wanted to enjoy this magic moment as long as they could. "I will never forget the bravery these men have shown today," Dulcibella vowed.

"Neither will I. Once again, God has answered our prayers in the most unexpected way."

Chapter 49

⊸⊷⊶⊷⊸

During the week that Adan and the others stayed with Serapio, many friends came by to visit. Marcus sent a letter telling Iovita the good news and that they would come home soon. When Jamin and Cleopas returned to Jerusalem, they were overjoyed to see Adan. They had heard about the centurion who came back from the dead.

A few days before leaving Jerusalem, Marcus and Adan went to the Antonia to bid farewell to Salvitto and Tacitus. Salvitto gave Adan his official approval for transfer back to Caesarea. They also learned Sevina was found dead in the interrogation room. An empty vial was found next to her hand. Since her death was a suicide, the soldiers guarding her were not at fault. Salvitto sent the death decree at his own expense to her eldest daughter in Rome. With documentation of their mother's death, the sisters would be able to submit their brother's pension claim for reimbursement.

On the morning of their last day in Jerusalem, Adan and the others exchanged hugs and promises of return visits. Their trip to the tanner's house in Joppa was uneventful. Simon must have heard the horses' hooves because he threw open the gate and called for Peter. There was much celebrating that evening, and they talked late into the night.

Nikolaus kept taking the lead the next day. The others teased him about his haste. Adan caught up with him. "Nikolaus, when we stopped here before, Ovidis asked if I knew anyone who could help repair the storm damage. I told him you'd be interested. Our ship won't sail to Herculaneum for a month."

Nikolaus's face lit up. "It would be good to make some money of my own."

"Why do I doubt that money is your first incentive? I'll miss you, my friend. I hope this job reaps many rewards for you." Nikolaus grinned, not bothering to ask what Adan meant.

After they stopped at The Apollonia Inn for rest and refreshment, they bid farewell to Nikolaus. Everyone saw the delighted smiles he and Marina exchanged when he accepted the offer of work. They traveled the rest of the way home without incident.

When they started up the cliff road, they heard excited shouts from above. Iovita, Marc and Vitus were waving at them. The four riders turned the last curve of the pathway and slid out of the saddles. The brothers were so happy to see Adan, they tackled him. As everyone hugged, Alpha and Omega took turns jumping on everyone until Dulcibella and Adan picked them up. The dogs excitedly struggled to lick their masters' faces.

When Iovita hugged Adan, her eyes filled with tears. "Thank you for saving my daughter. Marcus wrote that you pulled Bella out of harm's way and shielded her from the attacker. I know you love her, Adan, but many men would not have reacted quickly enough."

He hugged Iovita affectionately. "Actually, Dulcie was fighting the woman off when I looked out the door. Marcus taught her well. Nikolaus shot the dagger out of the woman's hand. Our friends stopped her from escaping. You could call it a team effort."

"All our accomplishments were a team effort," said Cornelius. "Sometimes God works a miracle through us, and sometimes in spite of us, but often in a spectacular way. I never would have imagined five thousand soldiers would risk their lives by presenting themselves without a summons. However, the emperor might have been a bit annoyed if Herod executed an entire legion. There is no mystery why Herod claimed that he summoned them."

"I thought Blastus would pass out with fright," said Adan. "I actually felt sorry for him."

"It was an intimidating sight," said Marcus. "Tacitus told me how he announced his intentions, but gave no order to follow him. He said each man made his own decision. Perhaps the courage of one ignited courage in the many."

Eventually, the family went into the house. Cook announced dinner would be served soon. That evening they gathered on the terrace, exhausted, but content.

Over the following weeks, the family eased back into a comfortable routine while Adan and Dulcibella waited for Nikolaus to return from Apollonia. After Nikolaus finished the repairs at the inn, he came back to the villa with joyful, but not surprising news. He and Marina were betrothed. They would wed when Nikolaus came back from the trip with Adan and Dulcibella. Marcus completed the transfer for Adan to the fortress in Caesarea. The *cohort* centurions assigned Adan to be a cavalry training officer and the assistant to the *primus veterinarius*.

A few days later, they boarded a ship for Herculaneum. A month later, Adan and Dulcibella were enjoying the luxuries of the resort town while Nikolaus learned the whereabouts of Decimus Lentulus, the man who owned Dionysia. It didn't take long since Lentulus was well known. Adan and Dulcibella went with Nikolaus to the man's villa.

"There's something I should tell you about Dionysia," said Nikolaus nervously.

"Is something wrong?" asked Adan.

"Depends on your definition of wrong. I would have come alone if either one of you were superstitious. Dionysia—she doesn't look like me. She's, uh. Dionysia is *alba.*"

"Light-skinned?" asked Dulcibella. "Why is that a concern?"

"I mean, she's an *alba.* She has the palest of skin, the lightest blue eyes you've ever seen, and red hair. When the crew of our ship became sick, they wanted to throw her overboard because many people believe an albino is a *daemon* from the underworld. When we became sick, the captain was able to convince the crew she wasn't at fault. But we didn't have to sell ourselves to pay the *medicus* who cured us. The doctor offered to let me apprentice to pay our debt. I lied because the truth was too painful for me to admit, even to myself. The captain claimed that Dionysia owed him because he saved her life. He wanted her to marry him, but the captain was a repulsive man, to say the least. When she rejected his proposal, he falsified charges against us. We had no rights since we're not Roman citizens. I was only twelve; Dionysia was fifteen. We were found guilty and sold as slaves. The captain, as was his plan, tried to buy her. Fortunately, a man representing Lentulus outbid him. If Dionysia had married the captain, I would have accepted the apprenticeship and never been a slave. Yet, Dionysia would have suffered and I would never have met either of you, or Marina. I admit I blamed her, but I was fortunate because Tribune Salvitto bought me. Dionysia's unique beauty complicated our lives many times."

"Your whole family must have endured harsh treatment," said Adan. "Dionysia, I'm sure, suffered the most."

"You have no idea." Nikolaus instantly regretted the words. "Sorry, Adan. I know you understand." The carriage pulled to a stop.

Adan paid the driver, and they approached the front door of the villa. Dulcibella pulled the bell cord. Nikolaus introduced himself to the servant who greeted them at the door. Lentulus was expecting them and immediately summoned Dionysia. She burst into tears of joy at the sight of her brother. Dionysia, indeed, had porcelain skin and flawless features. She had crystalline, bright-blue eyes. Her red hair was highlighted with blonde, giving it a golden sheen. Her pale pink, full lips revealed even white teeth. She was a beauty.

Nikolaus hugged his sister, delighted to see her once again. After introductions, Lentulus invited Adan and Dulcibella to the atrium for refreshments while the siblings went out on the terrace. They talked excitedly about how Adan bought his freedom, and how Nikolaus wanted to do the same for Dionysia. When the siblings joined the others, Nikolaus asked Lentulus if he would sell Dionysia's slavery contract.

"You are asking to take this lovely woman away from me? Let me think." He paused and studied Dionysia. "For five hundred *denarii*, yes." The brother and sister hugged each other with delighted surprise. "However, not the children. The children stay here." Dionysia's smile faded.

"What children?" exclaimed Nikolaus.

"I never told you, Niko. I have a daughter and a son. They are his children. I cannot leave them. I *will* not leave them. Please forgive me, but I cannot go with you."

"I will pay you a thousand *denarii* for Dionysia," exclaimed Nikolaus. "Please, let the children come with me. I am their uncle."

"And I am their father! My wife can't have children, but she dotes on them, as do I. You can offer ten thousand *aureuii* for their mother, but my children stay here!"

Nikolaus took Dionysia's hands. "I am sorry, but for now you know where I am, and I know where you are. We'll see each other again. I promise."

They walked back out on the terrace, arm in arm. She reached under the neck of her tunic, and pulled out a necklace of amethyst beads and a large purple sapphire pendant engraved with the knot of Hercules. "Do you remember this?"

"Of course! It's Mother's sapphire. We had to sell it when we sold Father's ring."

"Yes, but Decimus tracked it down. He bought it back for me, at great expense. See how deep and true the color is? Purple was Mother's favorite. It must be as beautiful as the day Father gave it to her for a wedding gift. This sapphire is the only thing I have left of our parents."

"Look what I have," said Nikolaus as he held his hand out."

She gasped. "Is that Father's ring?"

"It looks just like it, doesn't it? But no, Adan gave me this ring. His father bought it years before we had to sell Father's ring. Adan kept it all this time even though he couldn't use it."

"It is wonderful to see you, Niko. I'm so relieved you are free again." Dionysia called for her children and introduced them to their uncle. With reserved politeness, they each greeted him. He hugged them and sealed their names and faces in his heart.

Adan, Dulcibella, and Nikolaus lingered in Herculaneum for another week, hoping Lentulus would change his mind, but he didn't. Nikolaus went to Dionysia one last time to bid her and the children farewell. They left Herculaneum soon after, since there was nothing more to be done. Nikolaus was gravely disappointed, but also relieved, knowing his sister was content. She loved her children and they loved her. Lentulus treated his children and their mother with affection. He had only accepted Nikolaus's offer knowing Dionysia would not leave her children behind. Lentulus wanted him to know the final decision was hers to make.

Chapter 50

The next destination for Adan, Dulcibella, and Nikolaus was Rome. Adan grew anxious as soon as they entered the city of his birth. He felt an urgency to see his father, yet dreaded the encounter. By the time their carriage arrived at the Longinus villa, he was nervously tapping his fingers. He jumped from the carriage to gather their luggage, but Nikolaus insisted he would take care of it. Dulcibella took Adan by the arm and steered him to the front door. She pulled the doorpost bell. It was taking so long, Adan was about to turn away. The door was opened by a man in his mid-forties. He took a look at Adan and blanched. He staggered back from the doorway.

"*Adas!*"

Adan grasped the man's arms. They hugged and slapped each other's backs with unmitigated joy. "Gregos! It is wonderful to see you! I have missed you terribly, my friend!"

"I must tell Sophia! What am I saying? I must tell your father! When the letter came, Aquila was inconsolable. I even feared he might do himself harm."

A frown crossed Adan's face before he turned to introduce Dulcibella and Nikolaus. Gregos greeted them warmly and called the servants to tend to their luggage. Nikolaus stayed to supervise. Gregos hurried Adan and Dulcibella into the main hall. One entire wall in the room consisted of multiple doors, all standing open to the terrace with a spectacular view of the Tiber River. A well-built man wearing a simple tunic and sandals was sitting with a young woman. Aquila turned to say something to her. Adan stopped in a doorway. He was startled to see how his father had aged. He still had his thick wavy hair, but it had grayed at the temples. The corners of his eyes were lined. He was thinner, but Adan could see the same muscular definition in his arm resting on the back of the woman's chair.

"Sir, you have visitors," declared Gregos as he stepped away, revealing Adan and Dulcibella. Aquila muttered, annoyed at the interruption of his quiet afternoon. He stood up and turned around. Absolute shock made him stagger. His eyes flared open and his jaw dropped as his face lost all color. Janae saw her husband's intense reaction. She jumped up and spun around in time for Aquila to throw a hand to her shoulder for support.

"*Adas! Is it you?*"

Adan was completely caught off guard at his father's unrestrained emotions. He stood as if he had turned to stone.

Aquila struggled to regain his composure. "Salvitto wrote a letter! He said you were to be executed." Aquila's eyes filled with tears as he stepped closer. "*By the gods, Adas*, I thought I had lost you!"

"Father, I am so sorry! I have been. . ."

Gregos cleared his throat. "Aquila, as we can see, there was a mistake, or a reprieve, and Adas couldn't contact you. There is a reasonable explanation for. . ."

"No. Salvitto wrote the truth. I was executed. I was dead for a few moments. I have neglected you, Father. I am terribly sorry!"

Frozen where he stood, Aquila was bombarded with emotion. "What did they do to you? I fear there are scars I cannot see." Color rushed back into his face. "I can't bear to imagine what you have suffered."

"I'm afraid I have made *you* suffer! Can you forgive me?" He reached for his father.

Aquila saw the scars of the symbol of shame in his son's hand. Confusion clouded his face as he hesitated. Dulcibella and Janae held their breath. Then Aquila grasped Adan's wrist and pulled him in. "Son, how can you ask me to forgive you when *it is I* who should beg *your* forgiveness?" They hugged as if they had never shared a cross word.

Aquila gripped Adan's shoulders. "I can feel you, see you, hear you, but I am terrified this is a dream. I will awaken to find you gone."

"Then I must be having the same dream," said Janae, "because I see him, too. Should I describe him so you'll believe me?" Aquila smiled at her with relief.

Adan wiped his eyes and reached for Dulcibella's hand. "Father, this is my wife, Cornelia Minor, the daughter of Marcus and Iovita Cornelius. She uses Dulcibella."

"With my greatest pleasure, I welcome you, Dulcibella. Not only has my son returned to me, he has presented me with a daughter-in-law. Today is truly blessed beyond even the greatest of hope. May I present my wife, Janae." Adan and Dulcibella greeted her with warmth. The two women smiled at each other with an instinctive bond.

"Father, I owe you an apology, actually, many apologies. I have had much time to think things over. I should have written to you, not just to Mother. After I survived the execution and was safe, I wrote you a letter. A powerful storm hit Caesarea so the letter never made it. I decided to confront Herod to ask him to acknowledge my execution. I didn't want you to get bad news twice, so I decided to wait until we could see you in person."

"My foolish pride has caused much heartache between us. I fear it hurt your mother deeply. I should have written to you as soon as she became ill. We kept thinking she would get well, but the illness worsened. I waited too long. She died before I could. . ."

"We are together now. That's what matters. There are many astonishing events I want to share with you, and people I need to tell you about. In fact, we brought one of them with us. He helped save my life. Father, his initials are NK."

"Ah, like the ring!"

"The very same. His name is Nikolaus Kokinos. You will recognize his father's name, Nicandros Kokinos, the Greek architectural engineer. I asked Marcus to present the ring to Nikolaus the day Dulcie and I were married. He's been looking forward to meeting you, Father."

"You were so fascinated with that ring. You would never have a use for it, but buying that ring seemed right." Aquila clapped a hand on his son's shoulder. "I love you, Adas. I always have even though I did not say it."

"I love you, Father. I don't think I realized how much until now."

"Tell me everything. I know how things are done so it must have taken a miracle to save you. How did you survive?"

"I will tell you the whole story tomorrow. Today, we speak only of good things. I had to use another name and I decided to keep the *praenomen* Adan. Do you approve?"

"Ah, the *praenomen* of Serapio's son. Yes, I know about his son, and I approve."

"Today, a beautiful thing has happened," said Janae. She extended her hand to Dulcibella. "Come. Let us see to your friend, Nikolaus, while our husbands get reacquainted." Dulcibella laughed as Janae smiled good-naturedly.

To celebrate Adan's homecoming and marriage to Dulcibella, the servants prepared a special feast. Over dinner, Aquila discussed building projects he knew Nicandros Kokinos had designed. Nikolaus asked Aquila about his projects in Rome. Janae and Dulcibella discussed the most interesting sites in Rome and Caesarea. Adan sat quietly, listening.

When Aquila and Nikolaus had exhausted their conversation, Adan abruptly asked, "Father, could I ask why I was given the title of centurion? I had not earned it."

Dulcibella touched Adan's arm. "Perhaps you might discuss it later."

"He has the right to know, and I wish to explain," said Aquila. "I made a mistake. I forgot I was dealing with the back-stabbing scoundrel, Tiberius. I was a fool to trust him. I oversaw building new guest quarters at the palace for him, but there was a shortage in his budget. The emperor couldn't make my final payment. He offered a favor instead, the title of centurion for you. Of course, an 'offer' from Tiberius means take it or suffer. Tiberius assured me you would remain in Caesarea to continue as a *veterinarius*. The title would give you status and increased pay. I thought, for once, I could do something to help you. Your mother was thrilled because, as a centurion, you would be allowed to take a wife. So I accepted the title on your behalf. Two days later, Tiberius sent word you would have to transfer. He gave no explanation, but I was allowed to choose your new duty station. I immediately sent out couriers to every fortress close to Caesarea. Salvitto was the first to respond with acceptance. I sent my answer to Tiberius, and it was done. When your mother found out you would be transferred to Jerusalem, she was distraught. She said you were in love with the daughter of your commanding officer." Aquila nodded at Dulcibella, "The title was already decreed. It could only be removed by court-martial. I tried to cancel the debt in exchange for letting you remain in Caesarea, but Tiberius accused me of overcharging since I was willing to forfeit the payment. If I had known what would happen to you in Jerusalem, I would have canceled it anyway."

"Possibly resulting in financial disaster," observed Adan. "Tiberius would have declared you *persona non grata*. Besides, I have benefited from my two years in Jerusalem. At the time, I thought it was the worst thing that could have happened. Being forced to leave Dulcibella and her family was traumatic. Yet, I gained more than I could have possibly imagined. I was so wrong to have assumed the worst about your motives. It never occurred to me you acted in good faith, while someone else did not."

"It was his way," said Aquila. "Tiberius loved dangling offers like a tasty red apple—with a thorn hidden inside."

"I'm curious about how Mother knew I was in love with Dulcie? I never mentioned it."

"Yes, you did. You just didn't realize it. Tina said you never wrote a letter without mentioning her. I suspect she knew you were in love even before you did."

"I deeply grieve that I will not get the chance to know her," said Dulcibella.

Nikolaus expressed his condolences as well. Aquila turned to him. "I have a question for you, Nikolaus. How did you discover the identity of Alexander Nisos? Rome talks of nothing else." They spent the rest of the evening in conversation.

The next morning, everyone shared their plans for the day. Janae and Dulcibella were going on a tour of the marketplace. Nikolaus would be at court all day to start the process of claiming the reward on Nisos. Aquila and Adan left the house to walk among the vineyards.

"Father, I can see you and Janae care for each other. But why did you marry so soon after Mother died? In your letter you promised to explain."

Aquila plucked a few dead leaves from a grapevine and dusted his hands. "I did not write to you as soon as your mother was gone. In fact, she died shortly before your last letter. I couldn't bear to put it in writing. I would stare at the paper for hours, it seemed. Before I knew it, months had gone by. That's when your last letter came. The loneliness was more than I could bear. Gregos was desperate to get me out of 'exile,' so to speak. He heard of an estate auction and dragged me to it. Janae's young son and husband had died in a carriage accident. His business partner was demanding full payment of a loan, which forced Janae to sell everything. Even as she grieved, he offered to cancel the debt if she would be his mistress. She refused. Janae was selling her slaves so I bought them in memory of my Tina and freed them. At first we only discussed business. I helped her with the final transactions on the sale of her property. She asked me to stand in for her when the debt was officially paid. I did so with pleasure. Then we began to make excuses to see each other. We talked about our grief and what we loved most about our families. Adan, we truly are fond of each other, but we both know this is a marriage of convenience. This union provides safety for Janae, and companionship for me. However, no one can take my Tina's place just as I cannot take the place of Janae's first husband. The children we might have will never replace the dear sons we have lost, but we will love them just as much."

Adan placed his hand on Aquila's shoulder. "Father, I am glad we can talk of these things now. In fact, I have never told you this, but somehow, I have always felt the loss of my brother, even though I did not remember his death. That grief has faded ever since I met Nikolaus. But Father, I completely misjudged you. Serapio and Dulcibella have been trying to help me understand for years. I have been so absorbed in myself; I didn't think how you must be grieving. I should have sailed for Rome as soon as I received your letter even though you said it wasn't necessary. I truly am glad you and Janae found each other." Adan looked down at the scars on his wrists. "And I painfully regretted missing your wedding."

Aquila snorted. "You always could joke about the most unamusing situations. But now you must tell me about that terrible day." Adan told him everything as Aquila listened with few interruptions. It was hard for Adan to rehash the details, and it was equally hard for his father to hear. They were relieved to turn to more pleasant topics.

"Tell me about your wedding," said Adan.

"It was a small, private ceremony and quite pleasant, one could even say charming. We had the ten required witnesses and a few more. I loved your mother dearly, son. I was so lost without her. To lose Marsetina, and then you within months was too much. I would not have survived without Janae. She is kind and patient. I enjoy her company. I think grief has melted away the 'armor' I once wore in your presence. Now I can act as a father should. And to see you married to a lovely young woman blesses me all the more. Adan, you have to understand, Marsetina was my whole world, but she was intense. I loved her for it, but she took all my energy at times."

"Father, there are things I have always wondered about Mother. Why did she refuse to own slaves? How did you two meet? Where did she grow up? Why did she know so many languages? I had all these questions as a child, and her silence only made me more curious and fearful at the same time."

Aquila's eyes grew sad. "The last thing I can do for her is to keep a promise. She had me swear to never tell you how we met. She was a very proud woman. What happened to her was none of her fault, but she suffered because of it."

"When I was a child, I thought you and Mother took me from a *monstrum* or a *daemon* because of my eyes and because of her silence. It didn't help that others thought the same thing."

"Tina's father had eyes the same color as yours."

"No one has ever mentioned him. You knew him?"

"No. I only saw him once. That was enough!" Aquila folded his arms across his chest.

"Was he evil?"

"Yes! How could a man do what he did—willingly?"

"But he must have cared about Mother. He gave her the mirror."

Aquila frowned. "The copper mirror?"

"Mother told me not to tell you when she gave it to me. She said you wouldn't understand why she kept it."

"She was right. I don't understand." He tilted his head in thought. "Wait, maybe I do. Since *she* gave it to you; it became *her* talisman of protection over you. Giving it to you, in essence, removed her father's connection to it. It was always passed from father to daughter, mother to son."

"Was Misha my grandmother?"

"No. Misha was not your grandmother. She was your grandmother's half-sister, Tina's aunt. Misha's mother was Hebrew and her half-sister's mother was Egyptian. Their father was Greek. I don't know much about your mother's parents. Tina cursed them when . . ." Aquila stopped himself and ran his hand across his mouth.

"Mother put a curse on her parents? They must have done something really awful." Adan thought for a moment. "Why wasn't I told that Misha was my great aunt?"

"Your mother had her superstitions. She believed you must never know you were related to Misha, even after she died. It had to do with binding the curse, I guess. I never asked."

"It's all right. I know now. Nothing can change how much I loved them both. But is there anything you can tell me?"

"I swore an oath of silence." Aquila gave him a sidelong look. "However, there are others who did not swear such an oath."

"Ah, I will keep that in mind." Adan knew exactly who he should talk to. "Father, do you still miss Mother?"

"Every single day. She was my life. I am so blessed for having known her. Come, let's see what Gregos has planned for us today."

The next day, Nikolaus asked Adan and Aquila if they would go with him to court. Aquila's presence smoothed the way with the committee on several points of law, saving time and effort for Nikolaus. The judicial committee took Tribune Salvitto's written statement and Valentius's scroll into evidence. They informed Nikolaus they would hear his oral statement after they reviewed the documents. In the meantime, Adan took Dulcibella and Nikolaus on tours of the city. Every late afternoon, Adan and his father took long walks together. They shared thoughts and observations about their experiences and memories of Marsetina. Adan described the events surrounding

Yeshua while Aquila listened with curiosity. It was a time of healing—a time of building a new relationship.

Chapter 51

The day arrived for Nikolaus to present his testimony in court. Aquila helped Nikolaus rehearse while they waited to be summoned. A man edged near to listen. Adan noticed the stranger and thought he looked familiar. He stared at Adan with an uncomfortable intensity. Adan started to ask the man if they were somehow acquainted, but he was distracted when a scribe summoned them. While Nikolaus was sworn in, Adan scanned the spectators, but did not see the inquisitive stranger. He shrugged off his unease.

When they returned to the villa, Adan thanked his father for supporting Nikolaus in court. Aquila asked Adan to follow him to his office. "I have something for you." Aquila took a small cedar box from the desk drawer. "Open it."

Adan opened the box. Inside was a *bulla*, a gold neck chain with a pouch for amulets. Every male child was given one to symbolize his place of honor in the family. Adan still wore his *bulla* on occasion.

"It was for Martialis, your little brother. I want you to have it. If he had lived, I would have put a nugget of amber in it to remind him of you."

"Thank you, Father. I know what I will do with it."

"Give it to Nikolaus?"

"Yes, he is more like a brother to me than just a friend. In fact, I have a question for you, Father. Nikolaus does not have Roman citizenship. Even though he is free now, he is vulnerable. If you were to. . ."

"Adopt him? As a son of mine, he would be protected for the rest of his life, as would his wife and children if he should marry. Have you discussed this with him?"

"Not yet. I made him a rash promise once, and it nearly didn't happen. I won't be so impulsive again. I wanted to discuss it with you first."

"Then should we present it to him together? I think there is no better way to show my appreciation for his help in saving your life. Besides, I know your mother would be wholeheartedly in favor of you having a brother. No one can replace Martialis, but no one can replace Nikolaus, either. This is a perfect time to petition the court."

"Thank you, Father. This is by far the best gift you have ever given me."

When Adan started to close the desk drawer where the *bulla* was kept, he saw a receipt for a shipment of rosewood. The delivery address was *Serapio's Suppelex*. Adan turned away quickly to hide his broad grin. He remembered Serapio had mentioned the free shipments of exotic rosewood, thinking Adan was responsible. If his father wanted to keep his gifts a secret, he would not spoil it. It pleased him to know his favorite chair was made from wood secretly donated by his own father. Adan would make sure to mention how much he liked the chair.

Aquila didn't see the grin flash across his son's face. He picked up a wooden frame holding a copy of the charges against Valentius along with the verdict and sentence. He handed it to Adan.

"You framed it?"

"Of course, I framed it. This document officially cleared your name. Ironically, the emperor found Valentius innocent of Nisos's murder."

"*What!*"

"Don't worry. He was found guilty of high treason and other charges."

Adan sighed with relief, but then remembered what a guilty verdict for treason meant, even for Roman citizens. He tried to put the image of crucifixion out of his mind.

"I was present when Valentius made his final plea," said Aquila. "He blamed Nisos for everything. The emperor said, 'Valentius, you committed treason for greed. End of story.' However, he had Valentius beheaded, not crucified. Emperor Gauis despises the nickname, Caligula. The man who coined the name was General Glavienus. Nisos killed Glavienus. Valentius protected Nisos. Therefore, the emperor was lenient. Whenever justice gets sidelined, it's because of politics or pride. Why did Valentius go after you if greed was his motive?"

"Because I was given the command originally awarded to his son, Aurelius, who drowned in a ship wreck. Valentius believed you had Aurelius murdered to make a position for me at the Antonia. His motive against me was revenge."

"Unbelievable! The man must have been insane. You had a very difficult two years."

"They were difficult, but I worked through it. At the time, I blamed you for my troubles. However, I would not have met Yeshua, his followers, and Nikolaus. What has happened was meant to be."

"I've never told you, as I should have a thousand times, but I am proud of you, son. I was a fool to think I had all the time in the world to say it. I will not make the same mistake again."

"Neither will I," agreed Adan.

"I've been thinking about Serapio. I want to thank him and the others for helping to save your life. Nikolaus told Gregos things about the executions you may not know. Your friends helped you at great risk to themselves."

"They surely did. It was the worst day of my life, but it led to amazing results."

"Being the worst is obvious, but how did anything good come of it?"

Adan described the bitterness he felt after he realized Valentius had destroyed his identity, career, and security. He described his last encounter with Valentius and how the entire legion defended him at Herod's Palace. Aquila could only shake his head in gratitude and amazement.

"You have changed," said Aquila. "You are not the hostile young man who left here nine years ago. There is a humble strength in you now. If your God is the cause of this change in you, then I want to know more."

"Then I should tell you about a treasure Dulcibella keeps close to her heart. Come on, you must see it for yourself." They found Dulcibella and Janae out on the terrace with Nikolaus. Dulcibella removed the pearl from its pouch. They stared awestruck at the blue gem. As always, it seemed to glow as if lit from within. Adan described his encounter with Zacchaeus. Dulcibella told them she and Adan would also give the pearl away some day.

"Be careful with this treasure, Adan," cautioned Aquila. "Many people would kill for it."

"We believe it is protected," said Dulcibella. "However, we do not flaunt it."

After dinner that evening, Aquila and Adan asked Nikolaus if he would consider being legally adopted into the Longinus clan. So moved with emotion, Nikolaus was speechless.

Adan grinned at him. "If you need time to think this over, we can wait."

"Think it over? I'm trying to think if I heard you correctly. I could *swear* you said—did you really say—could you say it again?" They laughed and congratulated him.

"When you lose your family," Nikolaus said, "you learn what it really means to be alone. I felt utterly abandoned without the foundation of my parents."

The following day, the family petitioned the court to have Nikolaus declared a legal son of Aquila and Janae Longinus. The judges accepted the petition. Since Aquila was the *minor consul* there was no delay on finalizing the process. The proper documents would be delivered to the villa within a few days. Nikolaus would legally become Nikolaus Kokinos Longinus.

"You know," said Adan, "there's enough space on the ruby to add an L slightly below and in between the N and the K."

Nikolaus agreed. They took the ring to the same merchant who designed it. The man had not forgotten that Aquila purchased the unwanted ring. He promised to engrave the additional letter promptly, free of charge. The jeweler delivered the ring within a few hours. Aquila insisted on formally presenting the ring to Nikolaus as he had presented Adan his signature ring. It was an honored rite of passage for the father to acknowledge that his son had matured into a man.

The following day, Adan and Dulcibella took Nikolaus to meet Dulcibella's sister, Claudia, and her husband, Paulus. Claudia and Paulus joined them often when Adan took Dulcibella and Nikolaus to see the sights of Rome. The days flew by, filled with long discussions and frequent outings. The identity of Alexander Nisos was confirmed by the end of the month, enabling Nikolaus to collect the reward. At Aquila's request, three squads of soldiers would escort Adan, Dulcibella, and Nikolaus on their return to Caesarea.

One morning, Adan found Gregos in the vineyards. "Gregos, can I talk with you?"

"I've been waiting for you to come to me. Aquila told me that you want to know more about your mother." Gregos gestured toward the gazebo, and they sat on the bench. "Let me tell you about Marsetina's father first. Your grandfather was a Parthian named Colaxais. He was a slave trader, but his 'inventory' was of an exotic caliber. He sold a beautiful woman to a Parthian warlord who claimed she developed leprosy. He accused your grandfather of deception. Colaxais offered to replace her or refund the payment, but the warlord was not appeased. Instead, he threatened to crucify Colaxais. Your grandmother, an Egyptian named Zahra, suggested an alternative."

When Gregos fell silent, Adan prompted him. "What was the alternative?"

"Marsetina's parents offered *her* as the alternative. She was fifteen years old and very beautiful. Colaxais not only kept his life, but the warlord offered him much gold if Zahra, herself, delivered Marsetina. Colaxais accepted the gold. Zahra stayed many days with the warlord until he declared that 'the delivery' was completed."

"Even a parent's love can die," murmured Adan.

"What?"

"Something Mother said to me a long time ago. Sorry. Please continue."

"Desperate to stay with her beloved niece, Misha offered to go with Marsetina. The warlord agreed to this. Zahra made no attempt to stop her. If it were not for Misha, I think Marsetina would not have survived the three years she was held captive. Livius Clovius Longinus, Aquila's father, was sent to suppress an invasion led by the same Parthian warlord."

"What! My grandfather was a centurion?"

"Your grandfather was the *primus pilus* centurion of the 4th *Legio*. He was a military judge after he retired. You were very young when he died, but I assumed you knew. Livius was born in Rome, but his ancestors lived in Gaul. He had the traits of a Gaul warrior."

"Did my grandfather defeat the warlord?"

"Yes. Aquila and I were with him. I remember every moment as if it were yesterday. Our soldiers found a woman who had escaped from the Parthian camp. She had a message from someone close to the warlord. Through an interpreter, she told Livius her niece had learned of an ambush. She said, 'Whether the warlord is defeated or not, he will know who betrayed him. Please, Centurion, do not let her life be forfeit in vain!' Livius set up his own ambush. Close to the end of the battle, your father and I went to the camp. The most ornate tent was at the center. We could hear a struggle so Aquila slipped inside. I followed. We found a young woman trying to defend herself from an attacker. When he saw us he threw a ceramic jar to the ground near her. The jar shattered, and a viper uncoiled from the shards. I will never forget the hatred on that man's face. Aquila told me to kill the snake. He faced the warrior. The man was already wounded from battle, and he underestimated your father because of his youth. Aquila backed out of the tent as the soldier went after him. While I killed the snake, I could hear them fighting. Then it was quiet. A hand reached in to pull back the opening of the tent. I braced for attack. Aquila stumbled in, wounded, and collapsed to the ground. Marsetina cradled him in her arms. How those two managed to overcome all the odds against them is amazing. First of all, there was the language barrier. Your mother didn't speak Latin, but she was fluent in Greek so I translated for them. That's why I remember so well what their first conversation was. She asked his name. He looked up into those beautiful copper eyes and told her. He then asked her name. She asked if Misha was safe. Aquila nodded yes. She said, 'You have saved me from a monster. I owe you my life.' Aquila said, 'And you saved my father and his men. It is I who owe you.' Aquila reached to touch her, but there was blood on his hand. He told me later he didn't want the dead man's blood on her; it was bad enough seeing it on his own hand. Then your father said, 'I pledge my life to you. I will never abandon you, no matter where you wish to go.' Marsetina wiped the tears from her face. She said, 'Because of you, my tears of sorrow are gone.' She nursed him while his wounds healed. From that day on, they were inseparable."

"Mother told me once that father saved her at great risk to himself and that he was the bravest man she had ever known. But that's all she would say."

"Did you know that Marsetina was not your mother's original name?" asked Gregos. Adan shook his head. "She changed it after they were married. Her birth name was Masika, but we were forbidden to say it. After he healed, Marsetina asked Aquila to escort her to her parents. He asked Livius for an escort. When they arrived, Marsetina started a bonfire outside her parents' home. When they came out, she confronted them. She had a sheet of papyrus with their names written on it. Marsetina chanted something in Egyptian and threw the papyrus into the fire. Zahra was terrified. Colaxais tried to get the papyrus out of the fire, but it was too late. That was the last time Marsetina saw her parents. Unfortunately, Livius had assumed Aquila would come back without Marsetina. Livius had decided that Aquila would join the army when he turned seventeen. Instead, Aquila returned with Marsetina as his wife. Livius and Aquila had a terrible argument."

"Only centurions are allowed to marry," said Adan. "My father married my mother despite his father's wishes. Father forfeited the approval of his father to be with my mother."

"Not only his approval. That was the last time they ever saw each other. Aquila is a strong, determined man, and he made his own way. Yet he grieved over the loss of, not just his father, but his mother as well. He never heard from either of them again. Your grandfather was a proud man—unbending and self-assured. So you see, Adan, your father gave up everything for your mother. He loved her more than he loved his own life. Aquila wanted you to have a life far from war and killing, the exact opposite of what Livius wanted for Aquila. Aquila and Marsetina were abandoned by their families, which made them bond to each other even more. In no time it seemed, Marsetina mastered Latin. It was harder for Misha."

"This explains so many things. Thank you for telling me. I am grateful you have stayed with Father all these years. So, how did you come to be with him?"

"Livius bought me when I was seventeen for Aquila's fifteenth birthday. I'll never forget when the slave trader presented me to them. Livius said, 'Take the shackles off,' and gestured at the door. 'Gregos,' he said, 'there's your escape. Either choose to be crucified as a runaway slave or live by my son's side.' He said to Aquila, 'If he runs, it will be your fault. Then you will pay me *double* what I paid for him.' I almost laughed."

"Did you ever run away?"

"No, I didn't have the courage. I'm not much good on my own. Not to mention, I was afraid of your grandfather. He was a hard man to like, but easy to admire. If you did not agree with him, you were dead wrong. However, he saw no difference between a rich or a poor man. He treated both with respect. He was as strict with himself as he was with everyone else. For anyone who opposed Livius, it was like crashing into a stone wall. It was a blessing if he took your side; a curse if he did not. Aquila freed me after he and Marsetina were married. He offered me a lifetime position as his business manager. I swore I would never abandon him. Livius gave me a choice in the beginning, but he never would have freed me. To him, freeing a slave would be like pushing a newly-hatched bird from the nest."

"How did you and Sophia meet? You two have been married. . .how long?"

"You of all people should know. We were married the day you were born." Gregos laughed at Adan's surprise. "Your mother came home from a slave auction with Sophia. The poor woman was terrified and starving. After Marsetina nursed her back to health, she asked me to take Sophia wherever she wanted to go. A few months later, we returned as husband and wife."

"Thank you, Gregos. As painful as the truth may be, it is better than not knowing. I thought my mother's silence meant she was ashamed of me, a child's paranoid imagination, I guess. My insecurity made me—resentful. I think that's why I was drawn to animals. They don't make assumptions. They have no ulterior motives. Best of all, they never lie."

"True. Horses and dogs rarely play politics. I am sorry it has taken this long for you to know the truth. Your mother is greatly missed, Adan, by all of us."

As they walked back to the villa, Gregos told Adan more stories about his grandparents and Aquila. Gregos asked Adan about his experiences in Caesarea and Jerusalem. The account of Yeshua fascinated him the most.

Chapter 52

⸺◦◦◦◦◦⸺

The family parted with promises of letters and visits the morning of their last day in Rome. The military escort went with Adan, Dulcibella, and Nikolaus to Ostia where they would board a ship the next day. The following morning, they sat outside a pier-side café as supplies were loaded on their ship. Nikolaus and Dulcibella were having a discussion about the architecture in Herculaneum and Rome. Adan recognized a man staring at him from a bench across the street. He nodded and the man nodded back, but didn't look away. Overcome with curiosity, Adan crossed the street and approached him.

The stranger was medium in height, with thinning hair, dark eyes, a strong jaw, and thick eyebrows. "May I speak with you, Centurion?" said the man as Adan drew near.

Adan sat next to him. "Do we know each other?"

"No. But you knew my father. My name is Aurelius Julius. My father was Felix Valentius. Because of me, my father tried to kill you."

Adan shook his head in disbelief. "Aurelius drowned when the *Scarlet Jade* went down."

"No, a man *identified* as Aurelius drowned. The ship sank fairly close to shore. Most everyone made it to safety, but one traveler who did not survive looked very much like me. We had a conversation the first day of the voyage. He told me he had no family, had sold his business, and decided to travel 'to the very edges of the Roman Empire,' or so he said." Aurelius looked across the street. "Your wife is quite lovely. The man sitting with her is the one who found my father's scroll?"

"How did you know about the scroll?"

"I went to Father's trial. I sat there every day, watching him. He never saw me, of course. All I could think about was how he suffocated me with demands and criticism. Treating me like an idiot child." He fell silent as a young couple walked past.

"How did you find us? Ostia is quite a ways from Rome. I assume you live there."

353

"I have contacts. They told me of a high number of soldiers assigned to escort three passengers to Caesarea. It was a simple matter of paying attention to shipping schedules."

"Did you know Demitre was Nisos?"

"He was good to me, better than my father ever was. Demitre was never in a hurry to be somewhere else. I only knew him as Demitre. In court, they made him sound like a *daemon*. Maybe he was later, but he wasn't always that way. Can a man endure the degradation of slavery without becoming tainted? Aren't we a product of how others treat us? Children who are treated kindly by their parents are kind to others. Likewise, the abused child becomes the abuser. Or so it seems. It was easy to fake my death. I'm a strong swimmer so I made it to shore first. It wasn't long before the man who looked like me washed up—dead. My first thought was, that *could* have been me. As I studied his features, I decided that it *would* be me. "

Aurelius pressed his hand to his neck. "Everything seemed so perfect, as if I had planned every detail. He must have been thrown around the deck when the waves swamped it. The side of his face and neck were scraped. The missing burn scar would not be a problem. I used his *toga* to cover this scar and it helped to confirm my new identity. He was my height and build. He had said he had no family or close friends. He would not be missed. I pulled his body behind some boulders and got his clothes off. It took some wrestling, but I got my tunic on him. I put my centurion's belt and *caligae* on him, and took his civilian clothes. It had gotten dark by then. No one saw when I dragged his body back into the waves. It wasn't long before he washed ashore again. When they pulled him out of the water, I was nowhere near. I didn't take his life. The storm did that. I just took his name. I acted on impulse. It was a singular opportunity to start a new life. The captain never spoke directly to either one of us. Both of us avoided the other passengers. The crew identified him as 'that unsociable centurion.' I was free, but I didn't consider my father's vindictive nature." Aurelius paused and frowned at Adan. "Obviously, neither did you? Why would you accept a position at the Antonia?"

"What do you mean?" asked Adan.

"My father was there! Surely you know about his court-martial."

"I've heard he was court-martialed, but how could that affect me?"

Aurelius stared at Adan incredulously. "By the gods! You don't know. Then I'll tell you. There was one judge at the court-martial who was a decorated war hero, one of the highest ranking centurions in the empire. He wanted my father to be sentenced to death by *fustuarium*. The others initially agreed with him, but then Centurion Cornelius convinced them to be lenient. This one judge refused to relent. He claimed the punishment of reduction in pay and rank was an insult to the men who lost their lives. He said, 'If you take a life, you should pay with your life.' He said there were no other considerations, despite my father's perfect record. That man was Livius Clovius Longinus—your grandfather."

Adas was stunned to silence.

"You might wonder how I know these things since only the verdict is made public. How could my father know what Longinus said in the final arguments? It's simple. Longinus told him. He said, 'You're a pathetic excuse for a centurion, and a disgusting excuse for a man.'"

Adan's eyes went wide. "The same words."

"Same words as—what?"

"Those are the exact words your father said to me."

"He *never* got past that condemnation. Father didn't just obsess over it; he ate and drank it. He wore it like a second skin. His obsession only worsened as the years went by. As for Cornelius—don't be angry because he didn't warn you. Cornelius would not have known how the judges voted individually, and Longinus is a common name."

"My father didn't know, either. He had never heard of Valentius. He and my grandfather had not communicated since my parents were married."

"I believe you. Fathers have a habit of keeping the puzzle of their lives secret, only to fixate over a single piece. I've always thought my father was ashamed of me. When I made the decision to 'die,' I honestly thought he would be relieved. That's what I told myself. Did you ever see the scars on his back?" Adan nodded. "Those scars should have been mine. When I was a kid, I left a friend out in the hills, bleeding, and unconscious. We were daring each other to look over the edge of a cliff. I got too close and slipped. Trying to get my balance, I accidently bumped my friend. He fell, hit his head, and broke a leg. I knew everyone would blame me, so I didn't tell anyone. They found him the next day. He survived, but he was never the same again. He became feeble-minded. When they announced that *Lex Valeria* would be suspended in my case, I was glad. I thought the terrible guilt would go away if I was flogged. I hated my father for taking my place. From then on, I knew he thought I was a coward to be pitied, that I was too weak to take responsibility."

"Did you ever consider your father couldn't bear to see you beaten? There's a good reason for cruel punishment to be outlawed for Roman citizens. A child might not have survived."

"Exactly! I didn't deserve to survive. I left my friend to die, and it wasn't just because I was scared. The truth is; I wanted him to die. If he had, there would have been no one to accuse me. That is the definition of a moral coward. And you're probably wondering how I could have abandoned Demitre when I faked my death. I took care of that. I wrote a letter to Tribune Salvitto with another letter inside addressed to Demitre to be delivered if he outlived my father. Demitre could have sent for me, and I would have come for him. But my father killed Demitre. My father was executed as a traitor. You were nearly executed. It all happened because I traded clothes with a dead man."

"Did you ever confront your father?"

"Yes, I bribed the jailor. I was there when they took him out of his cell. When he saw me, he was so happy. I couldn't believe it. There was no anger, no rebukes—shock, yes, staggering shock—but only for a second. He cried out, *'You're alive!'* There was this look of incredible relief in his eyes, like I've never seen. He acted like nothing else mattered. It was the greatest surprise of my life. Then he said the oddest thing. He said, 'I couldn't kill Alexander all those years ago. It would have broken your mother's heart.' I swear I don't know what he was talking about. Then he said the most unexpected thing of all. He said, 'I have always loved you, Aurelius, even when I hated myself.' Everything changed when he said that. I finally understood my father. In that moment, I realized that I should stand in for him, as he had for me. I told the attending prosecutor that I claimed the right of redemption. My father shouted, *'No!* You must live. I want you to live.' He was at peace when he died. I have made so many wrong decisions over and over. Now it's too late to make amends."

Adan thought about the second chance he and his father had been given. There would be no second chance for Felix and Aurelius. "I am grieved at your loss."

"I appreciate that. I could have handled my father differently, but I was too proud. I realize that the hate I felt for him was really hate I felt for myself. In the end, he still loved me. I just wanted you to know what really happened. I'm not asking forgiveness, but I am truly sorry."

Adan sat in silence. Thoughts, emotions, and questions tangled themselves into a bewildering web, all at once. There was so much to say, but he didn't know where to start. Aurelius stood and started to walk away.

"Wait," Adan called after him, "there is something I need to tell you."

Aurelius stopped and turned.

"I was bitter. Twice, I nearly killed your father. I'm grateful that I didn't. You said you won't ask for forgiveness. You don't need to; I forgive you anyway, just like I forgave him."

"How is that possible?" cried Aurelius. "My father and I nearly caused your death."

"Your intentions were selfish and unwise, but they were not evil. You could not predict how extreme your father's reaction would be. You should not condemn yourself for his behavior. A friend told me once, 'You can stay mired in guilt, and be useless, or you can become a better man.' No sin can defeat the power of forgiveness. The choice is yours, Aurelius. You have a second chance. Don't waste it." Adan crossed the street. Aurelius stared after him, and then walked away.

Adan joined Nikolaus and Dulcibella. She watched Aurelius leave. "Who was that? An old friend of yours?"

"No, not really," Adan took her hand as he smiled. "But, I knew his father." A crewman approached from the pier and beckoned to them. "Come on. Let's go home."

A month later, they were back in Caesarea, reunited with their family. Adan returned to the garrison in Caesarea where he eventually earned his way to the rank of *primus veterinarius.* Gnaeus Ovidis bought the candle shop in Caesarea, but not the inn, even though it was for sale. Nikolaus bought the inn. Marina and Nikolaus married shortly thereafter and moved into their new home and business, the Ocean View Inn in Caesarea.

The day Nikolaus and Marina wed, Adan presented the *bulla* to Nikolaus as a wedding gift. Inside the pouch was a crystal of ruby, a nugget of amber, and a bronze cross. Nikolaus was deeply moved at the significance of such a gift. "It is wonderful to have a brother again."

"Yes, it is," replied Adan. He gave Nikolaus a slap on the back. "Now, let's go get you married. However, I have to warn you. Iovita tied the knot of Hercules for Marina's wedding sash. She is very skilled with knots. Be patient, my friend." Nikolaus laughed as he put the *bulla* around his neck.

Epilogue

It was a bright day with feathery clouds sweeping across the blue sky like the eyelashes of angels. Dulcibella and Adan sat under the oak tree on their favorite bench. Their oldest child, Longina, led her twin brothers, Marcus and Aquila, up the cliff road with pails of clams. The children talked excitedly because Uncle Nikolaus was bringing their cousins, Adriana and Titus, to stay for a few days. Halfway up the road, the children turned at the sound of hooves.

"Uncle Niko," called Longina, "it's good to see you! Adriana! Titus! Walk with us!" The siblings slipped off their horses to join their cousins.

Nikolaus reminded the children to behave, as he always did. "Titus, I'll tell Philip you'll study with him next week."

Titus eagerly agreed. Nikolaus coaxed Inventio into a trot. Nikolaus vaulted out of the saddle at the top of the cliff, bypassed the villa, and hurried around to the terrace. He called to Adan and Dulcibella, gesturing for them to get up.

"Dulcibella put on some *bracae*. I'll saddle the horses. You have to meet the men staying with Philip. You will not believe who is with them."

Adan moved slowly. "This better be good, Niko. I was enjoying our much deserved rest, and now you are rousing us from our contentment."

"And there will be more rousing if you don't get moving. Come on!"

Refusing to accept no for an answer, Nikolaus set off for the stables to saddle Venustas. Adan saddled Blackfire while Dulcibella went into the house to change clothes. She came out as the men brought the horses around. They paused to talk with the children on their way to the back door of the kitchen.

"Gina, tell your grandmother we went with your uncle and will be back soon," said Dulcibella. "And children, we will be planning our next family reunion before supper. Gina, you and Titus will be in charge of the games." Longina and Titus exchanged excited looks. The children took off at a run for the back door to the kitchen.

"Will Mother and Father make it to the reunion?" asked Nikolaus.

"Yes, it's so exciting," said Dulcibella. "Claudia, Paulus and the kids will travel with Aquila, Janae, and their kids. I can't wait to see everybody."

As they rode, Nikolaus related how he came to learn of Phillip's guests.

"I haven't seen you look this energized since Ovidis offered you a partnership in the flour mill," said Adan. "So tell us who you're so eager for us to meet."

"You'll have to wait and see for yourselves. I don't want to spoil the surprise."

When they reached Philip's house, Nikolaus pulled the bell cord, and a young man opened the door. He was Greek, in his mid-twenties, and looked familiar to Adan. The young man welcomed them with a broad smile as he bowed his head.

"Centurion, it is a great honor to see you again. Please come in. You are most welcome in this house." Adan and Dulcibella glanced at Nikolaus questioningly.

"Adan, you remember Onesimus, your favorite *cafeteria* server at the Antonia. He was in your Saturday classes as well."

Adan's eyes lit up in recognition. He clasped the young man's hand. "It is good to see you, Onesimus."

"Sir, I remember you gave me half of your stew once, even though I'm sure you were still hungry."

"If I remember correctly you thoroughly cleaned the bowl," Adan said with a grin. "Let me introduce you to my wife. This is Dulcibella, daughter of Cornelius."

Onesimus bowed his head. She greeted him with a warm smile. "Do you live here now?"

Onesimus shook his head. "They say I may remain here as long as I wish. According to Moses, one can take in a slave who escapes to his or her gate. But God has put on my heart to return to Philemon. I will ask him to pierce my ear."

Adan frowned. "What does that mean?"

"If my master accepts me as his lifetime servant, the law of Moses directs that he should pierce my ear as a sign of my pledge."

"Then I hope Philemon will accept your pledge."

"Thank you, Sir." Onesimus steadily looked Adan in the eye, contrary to his old habit. He led them out the back door. On the terrace overlooking the sea were four men sitting around a table cluttered with scrolls and a papyrus book. The men stood when they saw their visitors. Adan and Dulcibella greeted Philip, and were delighted to see an old friend.

"*Silas?* Silas Silvanus!" Adan exclaimed, "Is it really you?"

Silas greeted the couple with enthusiasm. "Dulcibella, your smile is as heartwarming as ever. Adan it is good to see you again. I understand the noble Blackfire is still with you?"

"He's as strong and handsome as he was when he was a three-year-old. You must see him before we leave."

"Yes, I will pay my respects to the magnificent beast. Please, join us. Onesimus, could you get some more chairs and refreshment, and then join us. Let me introduce everyone. This is Paul of Tarsus and Luke, a skilled *medicus* and *scriptor*."

Paul gestured at the table. "Please forgive the clutter. We've been working on a letter to a friend, a Roman tribune. It is the second account of Yeshua that Luke has written for our tribune. Nikolaus tells me you served under him at the Antonia, Theophilus Camillus Salvitto."

"Yes, I did. How long have you known Tribune Salvitto?'

"Several years," said Luke. "Theophilus told me quite a story about how you survived an execution. I would be most interested in hearing it in your own words."

"I'm sure we can arrange a time to discuss it. It was a miraculous event."

"Speaking of that event, we have news about Malchus," said Silas.

Paul related the good news. "I met up with Malchus and his wife, Margarita, in Antioch. I stayed there about a year, preaching the Gospel. I had known Malchus since he was a temple guard serving under Caiaphas. He had to flee Jerusalem. He endured some hard times, but overcame them. For now, Malchus and Margarita are doing well as they spread the teachings of *Christianitatis* in Antioch. It was there he first met Margarita, a Jewish woman of Roman citizenship. Before they were wed, she became a believer. Now they are among a large group of believers in Antioch. We call ourselves *Christiani*."

"You remember Malchus lost his first wife and child," said Dulcibella. "We always hoped he would marry again. I find it delightful his wife has such a beautiful name, *Margarita,* the Latin word for pearl, the most precious of all gems."

"Indeed, the pearl is without equal," said Paul.

"We also have news of Simon Peter," said Luke. "He and his wife are doing well. They continue to carry the message in word and deed. Simon has a most difficult job. He carries the message of Yeshua to the Hebrews. It is hard to talk of a new covenant to those who fiercely cling to the old."

They listened to Paul describe his astonishing revelation on the road to Damascus and his journeys from city to city. "There is great concern throughout Judea. Yeshua's followers are greatly persecuted. Also, we must deal with this devastating famine foretold by Agabus, one of the prophets who came to Antioch from Jerusalem. Barnabas will go there with me when we have collected enough funds to distribute to those in need."

Dulcibella and Adan listened closely. They exchanged a meaningful look when Paul spoke of the famine. "Dulcie, are you thinking what I'm thinking?" asked Adan.

"I am. It is time for the journey to continue." Dulcibella removed the leather cord from around her neck. "Adan and I knew that someday God would reveal to us who should receive this gift. Paul, will you accept this donation?" She handed him the pouch. "You will be able to feed and clothe countless people with this treasure."

"What is it?" He opened the pouch. The pearl rolled out into his palm. "*Ah, I can't believe it—it's the blue pearl!*"

"Have you seen it before?" exclaimed Dulcibella.

Paul beamed with joy. "Yes! I once owned it! I thought it was lost."

"Tell us what happened," said Adan.

"I came by it as a boy, but I was foolish, and sold it to a wealthy landowner in Tarsus for a fraction of its value. I came upon that same man years later and learned he had sold it to a family who owns all the copper mines in Cypress. When I went on my mission to spread Yeshua's message, I went to Cypress. I learned the owner of the copper mines had died and his widow had sold the pearl."

"Do you know who bought it from her?" asked Nikolaus.

"I was told it was to a very wealthy import merchant in Jericho who sold everything he owned to buy the pearl. His name was. . ."

"Zacchaeus!" exclaimed Adan and Dulcibella in unison. Adan described the events which led to Zacchaeus giving him the pearl before he died peacefully in his home.

"Unbelievable," said Paul. He turned the pearl in the light. Its soft blue color gleamed more brightly than ever. "I find its extraordinary beauty breathtaking. I acquired it freely, but Zacchaeus was the first to give it away."

"This pearl is more than just a gem," said Adan. "It is a symbol of a promise more valuable than anything else that exists. This is why I knew I could not keep it to myself. I was going to give the pearl to my mother, but she died before I could take it to her. I gave it to Mary, Yeshua's mother, but she returned it, saying, 'This pearl is on a journey. It must continue.' She told me to keep it close to my heart. And I have. That's why Dulcibella has had it ever since."

"How did you come by it, Paul?" asked Luke.

"It is quite a story. Every Passover, my father took us by ship from Tarsus to Jerusalem. Our first stop was Caesarea. It was early in the morning. We were unloading our baggage at the pier when some fishermen came in after working all night. I watched them sort their catch. There was a cluster of oysters which had been caught in the net and had torn it. The fishermen were annoyed because they would have to mend it. They ripped the oysters away and tossed them aside. Then someone called out to me, 'You should take the oyster on top.' It was a boy about my age. The sun was rising behind him casting him in silhouette. I couldn't see his features, and he was too far away to approach. I looked at the oysters and thought, why would I want one of those? He was walking away when I glanced back. It was so odd, it made me curious. I asked the fishermen if they wanted the oysters. They laughed and said they had no use for such ugly creatures. So I took the oyster on the top of the pile as the boy had recommended. Can you even imagine, just a little, the incredible astonishment I felt when I opened that oyster? The pearl is beautiful beyond belief. So perfect and extraordinary."

"Did you ever find out who the boy was?" asked Silas.

"No, he was gone." Paul and the other men expressed their deepest gratitude to Adan and Dulcibella for their generosity.

"Adan, I'm sure you know," said Silas, "General Vitelliusa funded one of his military campaigns with only a single pearl earring from his mother. Countless people will be saved who would have starved to death if not for this gift. General Vitelliusa used a pearl for war. The blue pearl will be used for life. I might add—blue is the symbolic color of God."

Adan and Dulcibella exchanged contented smiles. The conversation turned to other matters. They talked until the sun was low in the west. They invited Paul and the others to meet the rest of the Cornelius family the next day. The four friends accepted the invitation eagerly.

When they came home, Adan and Dulcibella stood out on the terrace to watch the sun tease windswept clouds into amber and pink flames of froth. Gradually, the clouds turned a brilliant red before the sun vanished into the bobbing caps of the sea. Dulcibella leaned her back against Adan's chest. He wrapped his arms around her waist. She rested her folded arms on his, and together they watched the ocean waves at play.

"I think all this magnificence will come to an end someday," said Dulcibella. "It will be burned up in one gigantic burst of cosmic fire. And from the fire, God will make a new earth and new heavens. All his children will live with him."

"How did you get an idea like that?"

"Every time I see a blazing sunrise start the day and a blazing sunset end the day; I think the world began with fire and will end with fire."

"You could be right, Little Elf."

They held each other in quiet contentment as they watched the sky darken into a black velvet canopy adorned with the sparkle of countless, distant diamonds.

2 Peter 3: 10–13

Made in the USA
Coppell, TX
02 July 2022

79498599R00203